Journey to Aloria

Magic is Freedom
But
Love can be a Trap

By

BRANDY STOKER

Adventure Advisory

WARNING: Prepare for a Journey into the Deep End!

This tale plunges headfirst into the tumultuous currents of human (and other) experience. Consider this your essential survival guide, letting you know what dangers lurk within these pages:

- **Brutal Realities:** Expect visceral depictions of **violence**, the harsh echoes of **war**, and battle sequences that leave no doubt about their impact. Injuries are sustained, and the specter of **loss and profound grief** looms large.

- **Psychological Minefields:** Prepare for encounters with deep **emotional trauma**, the chilling grip of **mind control**, and instances of insidious **drugging**. The insidious hand of **authoritarian control** may tighten around characters and readers alike.

- **Innocence at Risk:** Be aware that precious young lives will face very real child endangerment within these pages. In the story, it is to save their lives and always with someone to protect them.

- **Complex Intimacies:** Relationships unfold with raw honesty, from tender, sensual content between consenting adults and blossoming romantic intimacy to the harrowing depiction of male sexual assault. These mature themes are handled with the gravity and seriousness they warrant.

This is a world of high stakes, raw emotions, and hard truths. Proceed with awareness and understand that some passages may be challenging. Your adventure awaits, should you dare to face it.

Reader discretion is advised. Recommended for readers 17 and over.

Disclaimer

This is a work of fiction. All incidents and dialogue, and all characters, businesses, and locations are products of the author's imagination and are not to be construed as real. Any resemblance to person or persons living or dead is entirely coincidental.

To stay informed and be eligible for giveaways and sneak peeks of upcoming novels, go to brandystoker.com.
From here, you can sign up for my newsletter.
In return, you will get bonus materials.

DEDICATION

In 2021, my life changed. To my fellow Zebras....
Life doesn't end with the diagnosis.
It did convince me that I needed to pursue my dreams.

Being neurodivergent and on the spectrum has complications
with the world, but when you find ways you can

I have some of the most supportive friends
and family, I could have asked for.
This book is dedicated to the people who have helped me
I'm pursuing my dream of becoming an author.
There are too many to list individually.

To all the readers who reached out to me to tell me how much
they appreciated the book. It is because of you that I have found
the energy and desire to keep going on my journey. It is because
of you that I feel like there are people out there to write for.
Thank you!

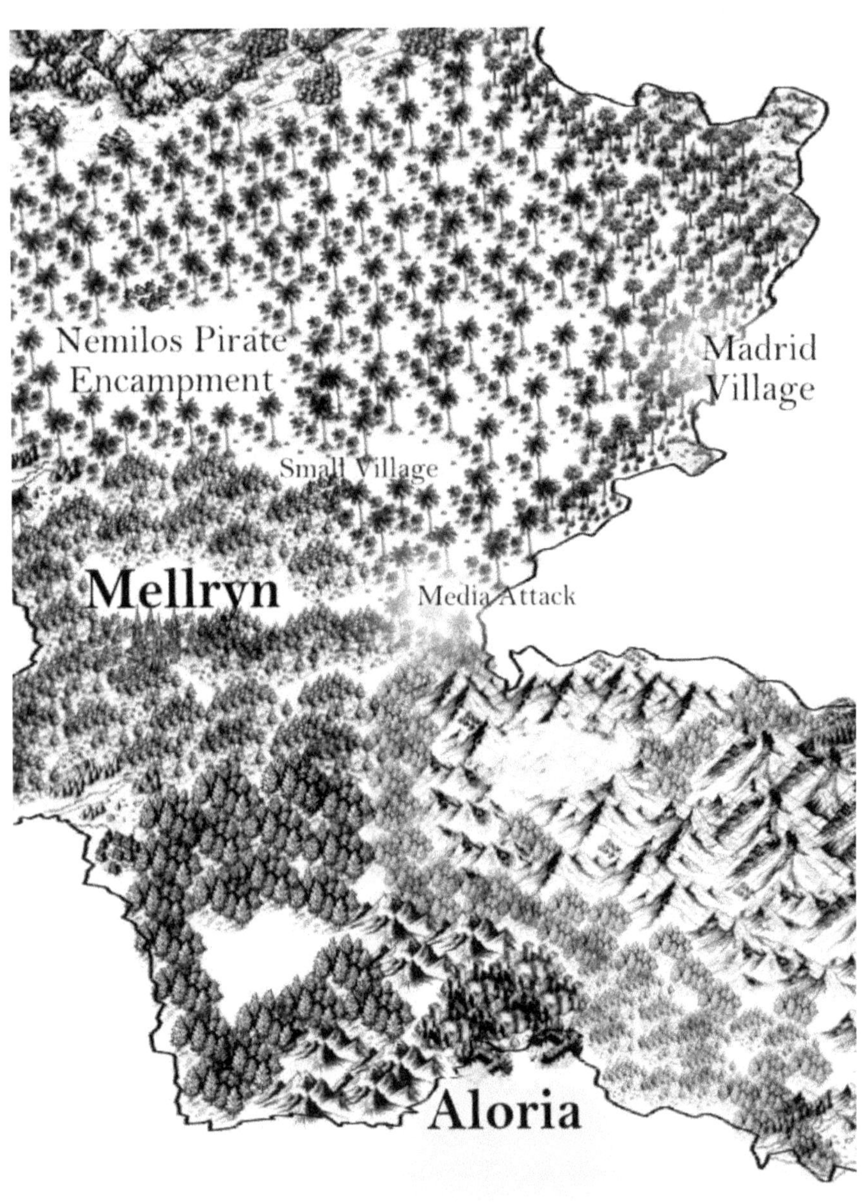

KANADA, MELLRYN, AND ALORIA

Full Map downloads are available on website

Map created by Brandy Jones

Lumara
Nemilos Pirate
Encampment
Madrid
Village
Small Village
Mellryn
Media Attack
Aloria
Draco
Mountains
Tilghan
Crossing
Sarhan
Media
Seaborn
Fellspire
Citadel
Order of
Tamris
MORDOVIA

CONTENTS

GLOSSARY

This will be a Glossary of Unusual Words

- Elven
    - Kin'ael – Cousin or Kindred Soul
    - Ael'an – Soul Love
    - Del'an sil'en nandor – My heart has found it's path back to you
    - Noor'wyn – Daughter – My Blessed Light
    - Ael'kin – Son – Kindred Soul
    - Wyn'syl – Baby
    - Del'wyn – Grandchild
    - Pir'ion – Grandfather

- Cetus – A Dragon that lives in the water and swims
- Kobold – A small, tricky spirit that is tough and persistent.

Pronunciation Guide

Name	Phonetic
Malin	May Lin
Elowen	El O Wen
Aldrick	Alde Rick
Nemilos	Nee Mil Los
Sarhan	Sar Han
Neldoreth	Nel Dor Eth
Anariel	An Ar E El
Mellryn	Mell Rin
Aloria	Al Or Ia
Madrid	Mad Rid
Khelek	Key Lick

CHAPTER 1 – MALIN

Blood streaked nearly every surface of the cramped medical bay of the Dawn's Beacon, the crimson patterns screamed panic and pain to Malin's exhausted eyes, focused on the patient bleeding out in front of her. As she slumped, her long, pale hair slipped over her shoulder, revealing the sickening crimson stain. The carnage of the night felt like it clung to her whole body like a second skin. There was no time for all the surgical scrubs or sterilization she would have used in the hospital in Media. This was the equivalent of a field hospital; it forced her healing powers to serve as the main, and often brutal, surgical instrument.

After the hours of battle and surrounded by all the blood around her, she could only imagine what the decks of the four-mast merchant ship looked like. She assumed they were dark with the stain of lifeblood and gore, soaked through the wood where the pirate attack had nearly succeeded.

Hours of saving lives left an ache in Malin's bones, but at least she had saved the most important one of all.

Her daughter, Ellie.

Just there, at the edge of her sight, lay her daughter, fragile body on the narrow cot. She was sleeping now, but she was barely healed from the pirate's blade that had driven through her; it was a memory that clawed at Malin's gut. Seeing the weapon sink in, the way Ellie's blue eyes had widened in terror... it had *almost* broken her.

It *had* shattered something deep inside.

Ellie, an eleven-year-old miniature version of herself, was her entire world. She was forced to grow up without a father, since he died before she was born. She was the fearless one who stood up to bullies, and Malin had only just discovered that she had the powers of invisibility and levitation.

Malin swallowed hard, emotions knotting tight in her chest. The memory of the battle flashed behind her eyes… Zane, or Zee as he preferred, stood with his sword clutched in trembling hands, standing over Ellie's crumpled form like a battered shield. Malin's heart twisted. At only twelve, she had seen him fight and kill at Ellie's side during the attack, standing like a man twice his years, courage burning in his every move, just like his father.

He had only met Zee a week ago, but when she married his father the night before, that made them family. She couldn't have asked for a better son. The fierce loyalty etched into every line of his small body had been unmistakable, a silent vow shouted louder than any words. He was her new stepson and Ellie's new best friend. He had saved her by protecting her with his and hadn't left Ellie's side.

He sat slumped in exhaustion, his white-knuckled grip clinging to her hand like an anchor; his curly, blonde hair was matted with blood in places, but he wouldn't let go.

He had already lost so much. His mother and the man he thought was his father had been killed only months ago; his world had been broken apart. And now, knowing that someone who had become his best friend had come so close to death, it was a wound Malin knew she couldn't heal with her magic.

She dared not look too long, as she had lives to save and focus was necessary to do so. Ellie was stable now. She was safe. And Zee, though shaken, was safe too. Although it made it hard to focus on healing the man in her hands, having her child, in a fragile condition, lay so close, years of medical training had taught her the importance of compartmentalizing.

They needed her. The crew, many of whom had been close to dying earlier. She had resolved the immediate wounds, but only to the point where they were no longer acute, so that she could attend to everyone. She tried to glance over to check on them between patients, but usually that was when triage occurred.

So many wounded were still pouring in. The sooner she healed them, the sooner she could check on Ellie and Zee, but perhaps equally important… check on Will, her new husband. She hadn't seen him yet. She hoped that only meant he was unhurt.

Her hands, shimmering with a faint golden glow, pressed against the torn side of yet another crewman, the blood still seeping hot and thick beneath her palms, a sickening warmth she forced herself to ignore. Her breath mingled with the sharp scents of brine and copper, forming a salty, metallic haze that clung to her lungs like the smoke from the attacking ship nearby. She had set it ablaze right before Ellie's attack.

With her sleeves soaked to the elbows, her entire world narrowed to the man writhing under her touch. Kneeling beside her, holding the man down was Lady Anariel, the tall, willowy elven regal, still dressed in delicately embroidered otherworldly silks that were now drenched with blood.

She had been surprised by Anariel, the way the aristocratic elf had shed all airs of command to kneel in the blood and work beside her, steady and unflinching. Not just the raw power the sorceress wielded, but the quiet empathy that infused every touch and every spell.

Malin had always been told elves were cold, detached, driven only by logic and their own ancient causes. It was a narrative fed for generations inside Media's walls. Lies, she realized now. Just more propaganda, designed to keep them isolated, afraid of the world beyond. A world she knew nothing about, but that she had joined.

She caught herself in yet another of her slips into other mental compartments, which increased in number; she was reaching exhaustion, and the spray of blood of an artery that had been nicked was the result. She clamped it with a hemostatic clamp, then tried to refocus. Even in residency at the Media hospital, she had never worked for so long without breaks. She surmised that the healing powers may have contributed to her ability to continue as long as she had. But she wouldn't stop. Couldn't. These sailors and their families were relying on her, as the ship's doctor had been killed in the attack.

When her magic faltered, she leaned instead on the skills she had spent a career mastering. Her hands were working instinctively, guided by muscle memory, honed from her years as a doctor.

At least it wouldn't go entirely to waste now that she had the power to heal.

She looked down at her feet, where blood pooled across the warped planks in thick, sluggish rivulets, glinting like crushed garnets in the flicker of a failing lantern.

Warmth surged from her palms, slow, unsteady, like a flame struggling against damp wood. Her hands trembled, not with fear, but with the hollow ache of magic stretched too thin, exhaustion rooting deep into bone. If she focused, if she forced her thoughts through the haze, she could feel the muscle knitting beneath her fingers, sinew sealing over bone like two pieces of clay being molded together. The golden light guttered, flickering weakly. A candle flailing in a storm.

"Let it flow without resistance." Anariel's voice was soft but steady, threading through the groans and rhythmic creak of the ship like a breeze across a battlefield. She was a patient teacher, and Malin welcomed her direction, as she had learned so much in the last week. "You have been going much longer than I anticipated. The more you trust it, the stronger it will become, but even that has limits."

Trust.

Malin hissed a breath through clenched teeth, the word 'trust' biting down like a phantom wound. Trust didn't seal wounds. Trust didn't suture arteries or pull people back from the brink. Control did, with precision and discipline. That was the world she knew. Even now, when her magic flickered like a dying star, threadbare and faltering, she couldn't surrender to something so shapeless, so unbound, as trust.

Lantern light threw ghostly lines across Anariel's face, framed with blood and wisps of long, dark curly hair, which softened the sharpness into something ethereal. Her violet eyes watched with unyielding calm, neither judgment nor retreat.

Malin's shoulders tensed beneath that gaze. Her magic murmured weakly in her veins, fatigued and resistant, like a limb pushed past endurance. It pulsed against her skin not with heat, but with a low, shivering complaint, strained, reluctant, near collapse.

"It is different for you," Anariel said, tilting her head as if reading Malin's soul through the rise of her breath. "Maybe it is due to your power of flames or your analytical nature. It is like it is trying to shape the healing energy within your hands. Flickering in bursts where it feels the need, rather than naturally flowing like a river."

Malin nearly laughed, a bitter, breathless sound, but it caught in her throat and fractured into silence. The crewman beneath her groaned again, his pain mirroring her own. Malin could *feel* the magic within her, a new, unsettling communication that confirmed it was alive. Months ago, this would have sounded absurd to her. As if the entire ten years she'd trained with scalpel, serum, and science had become obsolete in mere days, with this new magic that had taken residence within her. This thought, like many recent ones, was a dizzying consequence of her exhaustion.

The man's body convulsed once, then stilled.

She checked his breathing and pulse.

Good. The wound had closed. His breath deepened. Color crept back into his face. Blood covered Malin's wrists like wax, warm, thick, and clinging, but her magic… her magic had all but dimmed, flickering like a dying ember. The warmth in her hands had hollowed.

Anariel's gaze sharpened, catching the falter in Malin's light. "Enough," her voice no louder than a breath, but it threaded through Malin with the weight of command.

Malin exhaled, her shoulders sagging under the invisible yoke of spent magic. Her fingers trembled uncontrollably, and she couldn't find the gold glow. She had nothing left to give, and her exhaustion left her concerned that even her medical training would fail her. She looked around the room. Although many were still wounded, none appeared to be critically so.

"You have drained your well too low," Anariel murmured, rising with fluid grace. "Magic is not endless, even in those it favors. It must ebb so that it may rise again." She observed the line of the injured waiting. "I do not hold your level of healing, but I can help. I shall stay, but you **must** get rest."

Her hand, calm and sure, came to rest on Malin's trembling shoulder. The touch steadied nothing and everything at once.

"Go now. Rest your bones before they break. The worst is behind us. What remains can wait for slower hands and smaller miracles."

A sharp gasp escaped the crewman as Malin withdrew her hands, and he observed her handiwork. The gash was gone, and it was almost as if the wound had never occurred. The man ran his hand over the cut in disbelief, admiration, and appreciation filling his eyes.

"My family can never repay you for saving my life," he said.

Her limbs shook, feeling hollowed out as if her life had poured through her, draining into him. His words made it all seem worth it, and she smiled back at him, though the edges of her vision threatened to fray into darkness. She gritted her teeth, fighting the desperate urge to sway before forcing herself to turn from the cot.

Across the dim cabin, Ellie stirred with a soft whimper, drawing Malin's attention like a tether. Her baby lived. That fragile rise and fall, *she had made that happen.* But even that reminder wasn't enough to mend the tearing exhaustion inside her.

She forced herself forward, weaving between the battered cots to the small figure curled in the far bunk.

Zee slumped beside Ellie, his head bowed against the mattress, one hand still wrapped tightly around hers. She adjusted the pillow under his head, brushing the short blond curls from his face. The look of innocence in the sleeping face stirred the motherly love she sensed growing within her for him.

Malin's throat tightened. She sank to her knees beside them, brushing the back of her fingers lightly against Ellie's pale cheek. Cool to the touch, and no longer clammy. She gently brushed away a tangle of damp light-blonde curls from her forehead. Malin's magic, so weak moments ago, fluttered faintly against the child's skin, seeking to confirm that the concerns were gone.

Malin leaned forward and pressed a kiss to Ellie's forehead, the simple, instinctive act steadier than any magic she had left.

"She's a tough one, miss," a deep voice said behind her.

Malin turned slightly to see one of the older sailors, his arms full of bandages and splints. His face was streaked with soot and blood, but his smile was warm.

"Ms. Neldoreth…" The crewman paused, his face flushing as he caught himself. "Sorry. Ms. Hawkson." He nodded toward Zee, his voice softening. "Your young man there hasn't left her side. Not once. Not since they brought her down. At least the fighting stopped. Their ship is down, and from the rocking of the boat, it seems we are already sailing."

"I'm not surprised," she whispered, her gaze softening as it lingered on him. "He's so much like his father."

Like Will. Her new husband was fierce, reckless, and steadfast to the bone, with the same curly, dirty-blond hair and hazel eyes as Zee.

The cabin around them breathed and shifted; the world outside pressed in, heavy with threats she would have to face soon enough. But for now, for just this moment, she let herself breathe, too.

She was so glad to be away from Media, the city they had just escaped with its hate for all that is magic. This attack, on their journey to the safety of the melting pot city of Aloria, was just one of the many dangers she had been warned about before they left. She had just not expected this level of danger so soon. They had been on the water only a few days.

And there would be more wounded. More blood. More impossible choices before they would get to their final destination.

With one last touch of Ellie's cheek to feel the life, Malin closed her eyes briefly, gathering the broken pieces of herself. She stood and hobbled unbowed, every joint screaming in protest, turning toward the waiting darkness to find her room. She hoped she would find Will there. After completing a quick scrub down of her arms, face, and neck in the sink, she headed into the narrow passageway to the passenger quarters, stumbling, bone-weary, toward her cabin door. The hall was dim and swaying faintly with the ship's motion, four staterooms on each side, the captain's quarters looming larger at the far end.

Her exhaustion clawed at her, yet even now, her brain spun, making every painful step down the narrow hall, with the ship swaying faintly beneath her, feel like another fragment of her old life shattering. Her world had splintered into unrecognizable pieces in mere days.

The meticulous plans of her twenty-nine years, dedicated to science and certainty, were ash. Her father, CEO of a huge biomechanical firm, a pillar of her childhood, was now an enemy hunting them. Her mother, Chancellor of the Council of Elders, previously distant and estranged, was a stranger with terrifying secrets and powers. And she, along with Ellie, now wielded the very magic Media condemned. It was a chaotic, impossible reality, yet here she was, committed to a journey to Aloria, a place she had only just known existed. She had never left the safety of the city. Yet here she was.

Worst of all, she, Malin, the doctor who planned every variable, had, in less than a week, married a man she barely knew, driven by an inexplicable pull that defied all logic and scientific reason. She had chosen with her heart, rather than her mind. The very thought made her stomach twist, a silent argument against the profound connection that now anchored her.

She froze mid-step, startled, as the door opened to the captain's quarters, and her mother, Elowen Neldoreth, stepped into the hall. Her long, silver hair twisted on top of her head matched the elegance of the loose, delicately embroidered tunic over her tan leather pants.

"Mother?" Malin's voice cracked on the word, disbelief gutting through her exhaustion. A dozen assumptions slammed through her mind at once, none of them good.

Chapter 2 – Will

Will's muscles screamed, as the battle had been going on for hours. He was covered in blood and gore from hours of slaughter. He rammed his blade deep into the pirate's gut with a savage roar. Steel burst through bone and sinew to punch out his spine. The pirate collapsed heavily onto the deck, his death rattle barely registering amidst the ringing in Will's ears.

Will spun immediately, eyes darting, pulse thundering, hunting for the slightest twitch or shadow that might betray another enemy. But nothing stirred. Just the dead now, sprawled in grotesque tangles, their glazed eyes blind to the night. He recognized faces and felt the raw bite of regret, which he quickly buried.

Counting the dead served no purpose. Survival did.

His body hummed, tense and ready, adrenaline still burning beneath his skin, pushing through the exhaustion.

Immediately, his thoughts clawed toward something far more critical. When he had seen Ellie, so small, drenched in blood, face pale as death, then saw Malin hunched desperately over her, spilling magic like lifeblood into the wound, it nearly killed him. Nar and Zee had stood guard, vigilant but vulnerable, exposed to attack while Malin fought her own battle to keep Ellie alive.

His gut knotted tightly. He needed to see them, needed proof they still breathed. If Malin failed, if Ellie was lost...

He shoved the thought aside viciously. Useless. Dangerous.

He must focus.

The air was heavy with salt, blood, and the stench of burning flesh as he drew in a breath. He forced his shaking fingers to steady, locking his emotions behind the cocky mask he wore like armor. Unraveling now wouldn't help Malin. It wouldn't help Ellie. He needed to see them and Zee.

One step after another, Will Hawkson moved toward them, step after heavy step, his eyes scanning the shadows for any threat foolish enough to cross his path.

Will dragged in a ragged breath, the air thick with the coppery tang of blood and the sharp, briny bite of battle's end. His head spun, sharp with adrenaline, as he reached inward, gripping tight onto the lodestone magic buried at his core, a magic that allowed him to find any magic within half a mile.

It surged through him in sharp pulses, hungry, eager.

Across the ruined, creaking ship, threads of power ignited, like a constellation of flickering lights in the darkness, whispers of life among the wreckage.

But he wasn't looking for just anyone. Not here, not now.

He tightened his focus, digging deeper, desperately homing in on the one magical signature he knew as intimately as his own heartbeat.

Malin.

His magic flared as he found her glow, steady and stubborn, several decks below. Relief tasted bitter in the back of his throat because he could feel Ellie and Zee nearby, too.

Good. Alive, or at least not lost yet.

He refused to consider the alternative. That kind of thinking got men killed… or worse.

His bloodied hand clenched hard around his sword's slick hilt, knuckles white. He knew her; she'd have dragged Ellie straight to the med bay, and once there… she would be burning herself out to help others. Alive. Fighting.

Stubborn to the bitter fucking end.

His breath rattled in his chest, a painful mix of panic and bone-deep relief. Before the thought fully formed, he moved, bolting toward the nearest stairwell, driven by the brutal ache of urgency. Her presence dragged him, a pull tighter than iron shackles... or perhaps a chain he never wanted to break.

Beyond the ship's shredded rails, the enemy vessel listed sharply, slowly consumed by greedy flames that clawed up the broken masts, licking skyward in columns of black smoke. Malin's handiwork, he guessed. Her fire left a mark that was vicious and unrelenting, just like her when pushed. It was one of many facets of her that he found sexy beyond belief.

Will staggered briefly as the deck pitched beneath his bloodied boots, his sword dripping gore onto the planks below. His heart slammed a violent rhythm against his ribs, drumming urgency and pain into every bone in his battered body.

Only one command echoed clear and savage in his mind:

Find them.

Find Malin. Find Zee. Find Ellie.

He'd let the whole damn sea burn if that's what it took.

He ripped himself free from the broken bodies and splintered wood without a backward glance, the metallic taste of panic bitter on his tongue.

The med bay door loomed ahead, dented and battered, promising only fresh horror beyond. He hesitated, chest tightening. He took one sharp breath, then another, and shoved it open.

The stench slammed into him immediately, thick and caustic, a choking fog of sweat, blood, and saltwater that clung stubbornly to the low ceilings. It sank deep into his lungs, and for a moment, his breath locked in his throat.

Chaos reigned in the room, but mercifully, not death.

Makeshift beds sprawled across the floor like wreckage from another battle. Blood pooled darkly underfoot, glistening crimson in the pale light of the lantern. Bodies stirred, voices groaned in pain or barked urgent orders, but there were signs of life. Good enough for now.

At the center of it all stood Malin, bent over a bleeding patient, with Anariel by her side.

His breath caught sharply at the sight of her. She was pale, defiant, and drenched in blood that wasn't hers. Her hands pressed fiercely against a sailor's shredded side. Golden light flickered between her fingers, stubbornly holding life at bay. She swayed slightly, exhaustion etched into every tense line of her body, strands of pale hair loose and tangled around her face, but her jaw was locked tight, stubborn as steel.

Seeing her—really seeing her—ignited a fierce, possessive twist deep in his chest. This was the balm his battered soul craved: proof she was still here, still fighting, and still alive.

He wouldn't fully trust it until he could touch her, confirm she was whole, unbroken, and safe. But for now, the brutal knot in his chest loosened slightly. Malin was doing exactly what Malin always did: giving everything she had to save others, no matter what the cost. It was another thing that drew him to her.

Anariel stood beside her, an eerie oasis of composure amidst the chaos, her violet eyes sharpening like blades as they met Will's.

Instinct drove him forward, needing to reach Malin, to feel her in his arms, but Anariel's subtle shake of the head halted him.

Not yet.

Even from this distance, Will could sense the razor-thin edge Malin balanced on, one breath away from crumbling entirely. Interrupting her now could cost someone their life. He wouldn't… couldn't… risk that.

She had that look of focus that told him that she was pouring every bit of herself into her work; he worried that it could be literal. She had told him stories of how she could get at times when she was working in the medical clinic. He had hoped to see her at work one day, but he hadn't wanted it to look like this.

His fists clenched helplessly at his sides, muscles straining with the effort of remaining still, of doing nothing.

He stayed rooted to the spot, feeling like a goddamned ghost, uselessly watching the woman on the brink of breaking.

Tearing his eyes from Malin, he looked for Zee and Ellie.

He found Ellie first in the corner, pale, her skin almost blending with her pale blonde hair against the pillow. Relief slammed through him like a fist, leaving him momentarily dizzy.

Alive.

Thank the fucking stars. His new stepdaughter was still alive.

He walked to her, his brow furrowed, his fingers touching gently against her cheek, confirming what his eyes barely dared to believe.

Lying curled on the cold, blood-streaked floor beside her was Zee, his fingers desperately locked around Ellie's limp hand. Despite his height, tall for his age, Zee looked impossibly young and painfully fragile at that moment.

Will hesitated; his chest constricted painfully. At his presence, Zee's head snapped up, his wide eyes haunted, shimmering with terror and tears.

He barely managed to sit in the empty chair by the bed before Zee's lanky frame slammed into him, arms clutching fiercely around his neck, his face buried against Will's blood-stained shirt. Will's throat closed, the ache in his chest threatening to overwhelm him.

"It's alright, Zee," Will rasped softly, his voice thick with emotion as he pulled the boy close, feeling his body shudder and quake against him. "You did good. So damn good. I'm so proud of you."

Zee shook violently, sobbing silently. His grip was desperate, as though he feared Will might vanish if he let go.

Will held him tighter, whispering assurances into his hair, giving the boy the anchor he had needed so many times as a child… and never had himself.

"You were brave," Will said fiercely, each word choked by the rawness in his throat. "If she were alive to see you, your mom would be so proud."

Then he saw the small dagger clutched in Zee's hand, dark, drying blood crusting its hilt. Not his blood. Someone else's. He felt sure it was from someone who had threatened someone he loved.

Will pressed his forehead against his hair, closing his eyes against the sharp, overwhelming surge of fierce pride and aching sorrow rising in his chest. He took the dagger from Zee, assuring him it was no longer needed.

Zee not only survived.

He had been fighting and protecting.

His son. Though he had only learned he was a father recently, this boy was all he had ever hoped for.

Zee seemed to calm down, knowing they were all safe, and fell asleep, curled next to Ellie in the bed.

His family was safe, for now.

Chapter 3 – Will

He had only been sitting by the bed with Zee and Ellie for minutes. His body had only barely begun to relax when he heard heavy boots thud against the blood-slick medical bay floors, and every muscle in his frame instinctively coiled as the boots were heading straight for him.

Will turned, muscles taut, as Khelek and Nar Warden approached through the lingering haze. At a glance, no one would ever guess these tall, Elven men were twins. In this short time together, they had become some of his closest friends. He didn't have many friends that he truly called his own. The first brother, Nar, possessed a mane of fiery, unnaturally red hair that seemed to flicker like embers, paired with eyes as dark as a moonless night, a perfect complement for his command over the element of flame.

In stark contrast, Khelek, the second brother, had hair as dark as midnight, cascading like a waterfall of shadows, and his eyes shimmered with an ethereal violet hue. He had witnessed his mastery of ice when Khelek had saved them all from the flames in the West Woods outside Media.

In recent days, they had adopted more commonplace attire, with shirts that wrapped loosely around their chests, providing full views of their skin, hairless and adorned with ancient markings etched into their bodies. They said that each rune and glyph had a mystic significance, similar to many of his own, which were magical tattoos, applied for protection, speed, and both defensive and offensive purposes.

Both wore the same grim expression, battle-worn and blood-splattered, their long braids trailed dark streaks of blood. They moved with the silent precision of men who had seen too much and survived anyway. That could be one of the reasons they got along so well.

Khelek spoke first, his voice low and grave. "Captain needs you in his quarters," he said, sparing only a quick glance toward the chaos of the medical bay. "Lady Elowen is with him."

Will considered ignoring them. His place was here, within arm's reach of Zee, within sight of Malin, where he could see them breathing, healing, alive. Not in some dim corner plotting their next move.

Nar inclined his head slightly, the faintest tilt, his features unreadable. "It sounded like it might be important," Nar said, his voice pitched low, almost apologetic.

Even with Nar's input, Will clenched his jaw, every instinct screaming for him to stay. To move to Malin. To keep Zee and Ellie near, to be here where they mattered.

He glanced once, twice, at Malin, still fighting, her light guttering but holding.

His heart twisted painfully in his chest. He wanted to stay, but he knew... orders from the Captain and the Chancellor weren't likely requests. Not on a day like this.

With a low, reluctant exhale, Will briefly placed his hand on Zee's back, made a silent promise, and then rose to follow the twins.

His boots dragged against the wet planks with each step, growing heavier with each one. Blood and seawater mixed beneath his steps, turning the deck into a slick battlefield of ruin. The Dawn's Beacon groaned low in its timbers, the sound reverberating through the wounded wood like a dying breath.

The ship wasn't the only thing barely holding together.

Will pressed a hand against the wall as they climbed the narrow stairway toward the captain's quarters, his exhaustion pulling at him like an old injury. It was familiar, something he'd learned to ignore a lifetime ago.

Khelek, Nar, and Will stepped into the captain's quarters. The cramped room smelled of old paper and damp wood. The table at the center was cluttered with maps, half-spilled inkpots, and correspondence weighed down by brass fittings. Seated around it, the Captain and Elowen, his new mother-in-law, both looked up as they entered, motioning to the three empty chairs.

The family likeness was quite strong among the three ladies, each with pale blonde hair, the same blue eyes, and a great deal of strength. When he found out that his wife's mother had been giving him orders covertly for years as his senior Resistance leader, it had genuinely taken him by surprise. The stories of her cunning and strategic planning, with the almost cut-throat decisions she ordered, made her someone to be feared; and knowing how much she had given up for the safety of her daughter and granddaughter made her someone he respected.

Will scanned the scene, fighting back the urge to roll his eyes. "This had better be important," he said bluntly.

Elowen's eyes cut to him, sharp like a drawn blade.

He immediately regretted his bluntness.

One look from her, with her arched brow and thin mouth, and Will felt like a disobedient schoolboy dragged before a tribunal. No words were necessary; that look could have felled a lesser man.

He cleared his throat and sank into the nearest chair. Nar and Khelek sat in the other two open chairs. "Apologies," he muttered, scrubbing a hand through his blood-streaked hair. "It's been a long night."

The Captain grunted. Will couldn't tell if it was amusement or agreement.

The next hour blurred into a grinding slog of analysis and orders.

They dissected the pirate attack in exhaustive detail, examining what had gone wrong, what could have gone worse, and the narrow margins that had kept them alive. He had suspected the other ship catching fire was Malin's doing, but the confirmation filled him with pride. Risk assessments were hammered out, and plans spun for the next twenty-four to forty-eight hours: shoring up the wounded ship, bolstering defenses, and establishing rotations in case of another attack before they reached port.

Will sat through it all, his body in the chair, his mind half-tethered elsewhere. Every few minutes, his magic itched low and restless in his chest, a quiet pull toward Malin's signature that still glowed faintly below the decks.

The meeting dragged on, the Captain's voice a low rumble broken by sharper notes from Elowen, but the hours slipped apart in Will's head. He could have sworn he blinked and felt like he lost half the conversation.

Eventually, the discussion shifted toward Sarhan, the pirate town where they would complete the ship transfer, as well as the risks at the docks, and the fact that they were arriving nearly a day ahead of schedule because of a lucky stretch of wind.

Elowen's voice finally pulled him fully back into the room.

"What should we expect from you in Sarhan?" Her unblinking stare fixed on him. "I know you have contacts there… and enemies."

Her directness was a blade, her words sharp and deliberate. No one at the table missed their edge. Considering she could read minds, he knew she already knew the answer… she just wanted him to voice the fear that he had worried about since they left.

Will hesitated before continuing, feeling the weight tighten around his throat. "I have plenty of both in Sarhan, but what is more important is who might also be in Sarhan," he said, his voice dropping lower. "As you know, two years ago, I made some serious enemies with the Religious Order of Tamris."

Will locked eyes with Elowen. His voice was steady, but a sharp edge of accusation underlay it. "You may recall I stole something from them... the Tomes of Moresh. For the Resistance."

Elowen didn't flinch, but the sudden stillness that came over her was telling. A slight tightening around her mouth, a flicker of recognition in her eyes.

Will leaned back slightly in his chair, weary but unwilling to yield. "The Order doesn't forget," he muttered, the knot in his gut tightening like a vice. "They want the Tomes back and want me to be punished."

Elowen didn't speak. Didn't move.

So, he pushed harder, the heat rising in his chest. "I took them for the Resistance. I took them by your orders," he snapped, the anger rising fast, raw and sharp from somewhere deep.

Across the table, the Captain leaned back in his chair, his expression darkening.

Her spine straightened, her chin lifting like a banner. "I know. They're vital to the cause. That mission was not a waste, but I can see how that would cause some complications with our plan."

Will ground his palms into the battered wood between them, battling the tremor in his hands. "A year ago, they caught wind that I was running a transport. Civilians. Families. They hit the caravan."

The memory came in flashes. He could still see the blood and ash, hear the screams swallowed by fire.

"They wiped out the whole group. Just to get to me." His voice dipped lower. "That's the day I stopped transporting and moved back to Media."

Khelek and Nar exchanged an unreadable glance, their tension palpable.

He shifted in his seat as the old memory flared sharply. He could see the faces he hadn't saved, the promises he hadn't kept. "I passed the Tomes to the contact you sent. I haven't seen them since." He leaned forward slightly, his voice dropping lower. "Did they make it?"

Elowen studied him for a moment longer, then gave a slow nod.

"They're safe," she said. "They're in Kandist Valley now, with Lady Anariel's people, the Mellyrn. They're studying the magic buried in the Tomes, looking for a way to counter the suppressors."

At least some good might come from the blood that had been spilled.

A flicker of something unreadable crossed her face. He must have imagined the flicker of pride.

With a bitter taste thick on his tongue, Will leaned back in his chair, the wood creaking beneath his shifting weight. He exhaled slowly, his breath catching at the edge of something unspoken. Relief didn't come; it gave a hollow pause, like a breath too short and incomplete.

"Word's going to get out," his voice low and rough. "About me being here, about me… still breathing." He met Elowen's eyes. "And they'll come. I'll put them in danger."

A long silence, while he waited for her to accept responsibility, to provide a solution, or something that would soothe his fear that this would be the last straw for Malin and she would want as far away from him as possible. He knew she was already concerned about the dangers of the trip… and now with the pirate attack… he could only imagine she would insist on lessening the risk

"They'll come," Will said. "And they won't stop. They think it's their God's will to smite me… or something." He gave a rough shrug, but it held no humor.

"It is what they do," he spat.

He rubbed the scar along his ribs; a phantom ache flared with the memory. "That puts me in a bad place. And our family in an even worse place. I didn't care about that before, but now…"

He didn't say their names. He didn't have to. Elowen had to have known that this whole issue was an issue because she gave the order, just as much as it was his choice to follow it.

"I don't want to leave them… but I don't think I can have them with me when I'm found. Knowing this, do you still want to travel with me?" As he said the words, he feared what the answer would be.

Elowen exhaled sharply through her nose, with her fingers drumming against the table before stilling. "That is a complication, but one we can work with."

But Will saw it in her eyes. There was a faint flicker of hesitation, a quiet calculation from her.

He couldn't blame her; a man with enemies like his could sink an entire ship without firing a shot.

"There is no better transporter than you," she said. His eyes widened. He had not expected to hear that.

"There is danger, but it is because of your feelings for them that I know you will not take chances with their lives. I can't say the same for anyone else. We will do what we must to get to Aloria safely. I would feel more comfortable with Malin knowing, but that is your call. She is your wife, and she may not feel the same way I do," Elowen stated. "As you know her better than I… my guidance on what she would do is not something I can give."

Her eyes bore into him, her expression unreadable. "Is there anything else we should be aware of?"

Will hesitated, running a hand over his jaw. The stubble rasped under his fingers, another reminder of just how long it had been since he'd been running on fumes.

"Yeah," he said finally. "When I took the Tomes... I was multitasking. I was transporting someone, too. She helped me steal it."

He let the words settle, dragging in a slow breath before continuing. "I had to leave her behind. Couldn't risk bringing her into the mess. I had to head back to Media; she couldn't come with me. Safer that way. I left her in Sarhan with work as a barmaid. It was a few steps down from what she was used to in Media, but at least she was alive." His mouth twisted into something that wasn't quite a grimace. It also wasn't quite a smile.

"She has some issues. I'm pretty sure she's psychotic and she has some addictive, kinky tendencies that leaned to violence," he blushed.

"I don't know what to expect when we get to Sarhan," he admitted. "Lydia might have found another way to Aloria by now. She might still be there. Or..." He shook his head, his voice trailing off. "I just don't know. She may have thought she was more than just someone I transported."

At Elowen's raised eyebrow, he continued, "I did leave her with a job at the tavern, a fully paid-for room for two months, and enough coin to either catch the next ship or stay for several months... Technically, I did say goodbye; it could have been construed that I would see her again, though." A slight blush crossed his face as he avoided eye contact with the group.

The uncertainty coiled heavy in his gut, a knot he hadn't been able to untangle since leaving her behind. He had several exes, but she was the only one that might be problematic.

Elowen sat, rapping her fingers against the table again. The silence weighed on him, but it wasn't heavy; it grated on his nerves every time she did it though. He wondered if she was doing it on purpose.

When she finally spoke, her tone softened, taking him off guard; it almost sounded understanding. "She was your past, Will. Whatever choice she made after you left is hers. You did the best you could for her. She'll have to live with that." Elowen didn't flinch. She never did. Her eyes, calm and sharp as cut crystal, locked onto him.

The words hit harder than he expected. They felt final, almost surgical, like slicing off a limb to stop the bleeding. And maybe that's what he needed, some clean edges instead of his festering guilt. It didn't sit right.

 Nothing about Lydia ever had.

He met his contact after that to transfer the Tomes, then went back to work transporting. The next time he passed through, he checked on her, and the innkeeper, Zane, said she was gone. He had gone back to check on her….

He gave a slow nod, more out of habit than agreement. Some wounds didn't close just because someone else said so.

The Captain leaned forward. "I hate to do this, but I don't have many options. We're shorthanded," he said bluntly in his thick Sarhan accent. "First Mate's down in medical helping with his healing powers. I could use you overseeing operations until I finish with the rest of the meeting Lady Elowen has planned."

Will snorted, a low, rasping sound that scraped his throat raw. "Sure," he said. "Why not? I'm already bleeding, bruised, and half-dead. Might as well add babysitting a ship."

The Captain only grunted, used to Will's mouth.

Will jerked a stiff nod. "You'll have it," he added, in case anyone in the room doubted he'd do it.

But even as he spoke, his mind was already halfway back to the medical bay, anticipating getting back to Malin.

The Captain grunted with approval, but Elowen's sharp eyes didn't miss Will's focus drifting.

She tapped a sharp finger once against the tabletop. "Since your attention is clearly not with us," Elowen said, her voice cool but not unkind, "and since you have work to see to. Go."

Will blinked, caught between gratitude and guilt.

"I sense she'll be occupied for several more hours," Elowen added, her tone smoothing into something almost gentle – or perhaps it was just his exhaustion warping her usual bluntness. "Ellie and Zee are safe. You might as well be useful, rather than playing nursemaid."

He told himself it wasn't a dismissal, though it sure felt like one.

It was mercy, wrapped in command.

Will pushed back his chair, its legs scraping roughly against the floor, and rose to his feet. Every muscle in his body ached with a profound, marrow-deep exhaustion that no rest would fix. He dipped his head once in acknowledgment, then turned to leave without a backward glance.

He wanted to run to Malin, pick her up, and carry her to bed so he could feel the safety and security of her body beside his.

Why did it always seem that duty got in the way of what he really wanted?

He felt a hand catch his sleeve, a light but unyielding touch. He turned slightly to find Elowen standing beside him, her face seemed carved from stone.

She walked him quietly toward the door, her voice pitched low enough for only him to hear.

"You need to tell her, Will," she said. "All of it, before she starts trying to reason things out for herself." Her ice blue eyes, the same as Malin and Ellie, narrowed slightly, not unkind, but unflinching. "The way she imagines it... may not put you in the best light. She deserves to hear the truth from you. You can trust her with any Resistance secrets. Holding back secrets could mean losing her. And feel free to tell her to sleep in tomorrow. I know Malin will need the rest. Lady Anariel and I will have the children in hand. Malin needs the rest."

Will hesitated just long enough for the weight of her words to sink in. "Understood." Maybe the old battle axe wasn't as bad as she seemed.

I heard that she said in his head with a smile on her face.

Fuck. I forgot!

He reached out, placing his large, blood-scabbed hand briefly over hers. It was a simple, yet rough, gesture of gratitude; then he turned and strode away.

He wasn't all that worried about how Malin would handle meeting Lydia, if she were still in Sarhan, but he didn't want to address the guilt he felt for leaving her there. Elowen was right; there wasn't a better option, and a rational person would likely see that. Lydia was not a rational person; she was a psychotic pixie of a red-haired woman who was prone to fits of anger and thoughts of sex.

He was concerned about how Malin would handle the news of the assassins after him, even if the only reason they were after him was because of her mother.

The door closed behind him with a soft, final thud as he was halfway down the hall.

Will slowed his steps, reaching inside himself for the magic to locate her. It pulsed faintly, steady and familiar, toward the pull of Malin's signature.

He checked her location instinctively.

Still in the medical bay. Still working.

The relief that washed through him was immediate but short-lived.

She would push herself until nothing was left unless someone stopped her. He knew it in his bones. The thought of abandoning everything else and doing exactly that—duty be damned—flashed hot across his mind.

But he had obligations of his own.

He would work as quickly as possible. If he finished before her... he'd go to her and do just that.

Nothing would stop him.

Shoving the thought aside for now, Will strode to the main deck, forcing focus where his heart resisted yielding.

It took hours, but Will finished the last of the tasks just as the Captain came into view, his boots echoing dully across the battered deck.

There was no ceremony, just a brisk hand-off of status updates traded in clipped, low voices.

The Captain nodded at the report. They remained on track to reach the port a day ahead of schedule. The dead from the pirate skirmish would likely serve as an ample feast for the kraken, which was rumored to be haunting these waters, meaning, with any luck, no more attacks before they docked.

Will added that the water wielder among the crew had managed to scour the worst of the blood from the decks, while the scent still lingered sharply in the damp wood. Some hull damage remained, but nothing beyond what could be mended once they made shore.

The Captain grunted his approval, already turning back toward the helm, his mind no doubt spinning a hundred preparations that Will didn't envy, on just as little sleep as Will was running on.

He barely waited for him to acknowledge.

He turned toward the quarterdeck rail, dragging a hand through his sweat-matted hair, and reached instinctively for the magic humming low and steady in his chest to help him find her.

The pull hit immediately; this was stronger than his lodestone pull usually was, as if his body were tethered to hers.

Malin had moved.

Not the medical bay anymore. She was further down within the ship, down in the passenger cabins. Hope flared hot and sharp in his chest.

Cool night air rolled off the sea, thick with salt and the metallic tang of blood, which no amount of scrubbing could erase.

Will didn't wait. He moved, following the tether in his blood, the magnetic thread of her presence pulling him forward.

Toward her.

The pull led him down the lower corridor, the passage growing narrower with each step. Lanterns swung on their chains overhead, casting broken ribbons of light and shadow onto the worn planks.

Will slowed as he reached the row of passenger cabins, instinct thrumming harder beneath his skin. Malin's magic was close, so close he could almost feel it brushing against his own.

He rounded the final corner and stopped. Her signature wasn't coming from their shared quarters. It was emanating, soft and sure, from behind a different door.

Elowen's.

Will stared at the closed door, his pulse hammering behind his ribs. For a breathless moment, he debated…

Knock?

Barge in?

He considered pacing like a restless wolf until she came out. He wanted to feel his arms around her; he wanted to feel for himself that she had emerged from the battle unharmed, and he needed her comfort after his long day.

He did none of those things.

Instead, he leaned his weight back against the opposite wall, crossing his arms loosely over his chest, his head tilted back. His body was screaming for rest, for her. But he could wait. He would wait.

Breathing slowly, he let her magic wrap around him. It felt warm, golden, and steady.

He closed his eyes and sank into it, feeling the raw edges inside him soften slightly at its touch.

She was alive. She was close.

And soon… soon… he would have her in his arms again.

For now, that was enough.

CHAPTER 4 – MALIN

Seeing her mother coming out of the Captain's cabin, her thoughts immediately pieced together that her mother had spent much of her marriage, if not all of it, as a double agent – Both Government Leader and Resistance Leader. She wasn't sure what she was witnessing.

Mother's chin lifted, her posture brisk and haughty. "It is not what you think," her voice, crisp as cracked parchment, said. "He is a nice enough man, but we were discussing Resistance business."

Malin's exhaustion stripped away the usual walls of politeness she might have built. Her words came out more sharply than she intended. Since her father was after them, they might not be on the best of terms, but… she hardly knew this woman standing before her. It could have been anything. "Well, considering I didn't even realize you were more than Elowen Neldoreth, happily married Chancellor of the Council of Elders till recently, there's a lot about you I don't know. I don't know what to think anymore."

Her mother sighed, a slow exhale as if she were bracing herself against an invisible tide. "You look exhausted. This could wait until morning, if you prefer. But knowing you and your restless mind…" She hesitated, then offered a rare softness. "You'll sleep better if we clear some things now. It is your choice."

Her brain attempted a decision. She was torn, as she was exhausted, but she also desperately needed information. Without waiting for a response, her mother caught her hand, warm and firm, and tugged her gently toward the door to her mother's room.

Malin let herself be led, too tired to argue.

Malin followed her mother into a cabin that was notably larger and far more comfortable than their own. The faint, sweet scent of dried herbs and something subtly mystical filled the air, and just as she'd suspected, the bed against the far wall was draped with unmistakable silk sheets. The small table, with two chairs, sat in the middle of the room. The furnishings weren't lavish, but there was a quiet dignity to them: wood polished smooth, clean linens tucked with a soldier's precision.

Her gaze snagged on the small, framed photograph perched beside the bed. She and Ellie were frozen in a moment of laughter, their past lives already feeling oceans away. It had never occurred to her that her mother would include a picture of her.

They moved toward the table, where a teapot and two empty cups waited. A simple comfort.

"Would you mind heating the water?" her mother motioned to the pot, as she asked in her aristocratic tone.

"Oh. Sure." Malin pressed her fingers to the side of the pot, channeling the flickering thread of magic she still had left. The metal glowed faintly, and then the water began to bubble. She pulled back quickly. "I hope I didn't overdo it. Lady Anariel's still working with me on controlling the temperature."

Her mother smiled, a small, genuine smile. "Considering you've only been learning for a short time, I'm impressed. You're definitely my daughter. It's hard to believe you have only had your magic for such a short time and are already able to do so much."

A compliment. She hadn't expected to hear that. She poured the water over the tea leaves, the soft scent of herbs unfurling between them.

"I could read your mind to gather your questions," her mom said lightly, handing Malin a steaming cup. "But I would rather hear you ask them."

Malin wrapped her hands around the cup, grateful for the heat. She took a careful sip, letting the bitter sharpness steady her fraying nerves.

She still hadn't completely forgiven her mother for not telling her about the magic, about Ellie, and about her father putting Andrew in her life to be her neighbor, confidant, friend, and informant of all their activities. Her mother would have had to know.

Resentment simmered, a bitter bile in the back of her throat.

How could her mother, who could read minds, not have known the truth of Andrew's manipulation, or seen Malin's desperate need for genuine connection?

Surely, she would have seen that Malin could be trusted, that she would have embraced her true self and her powers, rather than wasting a lifetime of ignorance.

Her mother's silence felt less like protection and more like theft of a life she could have led.

While Malin did understand the concern that she might have said something to her father, that understanding felt thin against the years lost. She had always wanted a closer relationship with her, and the weight of all the times she was kept in the dark now felt like a crushing burden, a barrier she wasn't sure she could ever truly dismantle.

After all the chaos during the escape from Media, the fighting with the pirates, and almost losing her daughter, she felt it was time to focus on heartfelt conversations and opportunities to earn trust, rather than dwell on hurt and the past. The last deep conversation they had was their first, back in Media, right before they left. She felt they had begun to bridge some of those hurts then.

As tired as she was, she was feeling like she didn't want to let opportunities pass. This conversation was dual-purpose. She attempted to address some of her questions and foster their relationship. She took a deep breath before starting.

"I left behind everything I knew; my home, my closest friends… without a farewell, the job I loved, and a clinic full of patients with an understaffed team," she expressed her frustration.

"I never imagined my life would turn out like this. I have spent most of my twenty-nine years carefully planning life to find that all that planning feels like it was for nothing." She vented, knowing that it wouldn't change things.

Her mother didn't interrupt.

Malin hesitated as her mother's gaze, a blend of curiosity and concern, seemed to search the depths of her soul.

She took a deep breath, with the scent of old wood around them. "I can accept that you hid my magic and the fact that Ellie had powers. I'm disappointed, but I do understand there were other reasons… Even with that, I have so many questions. Not just about Will," she began, her voice tinged with the weight of recent upheavals.

"But everything. The rapid changes, the dangers we've faced, and… Caelum." She paused, the name of her late fiancé hanging between them like a specter of her past.

"I just married Will," she said finally, her voice low. "The way I feel, I feel like it must mean I truly love him. I know in my heart he's a good man. But…" She swallowed hard. "I barely know him. You read his mind when we were with Gorek and Lysa. You told me you were… okay with him. When I removed my chip and gained my powers, you were the one who told me that he had willed my soul to live through the transformation process when I gained my powers. I wouldn't be here today without him. That puts a lot of positives in his favor."

She stared down into her cup, words snagging against the heaviness in her chest. "But now I realize he pretended to be a teacher to get to meet me. I found out he was a top Resistance asset. A rogue and probably an assassin. Some of the stories…" Her breath hitched. "They don't sound like the man I know. It confuses me." She looked up, the vulnerability raw in her voice. "Who is he? Really?" She took a long breath, allowing herself to consider her words.

"You saw his mind. I was so completely wrong about Andrew, and he lived next door to me for nine years. I thought I knew him, only to find out he worked for Daddy and was placed there to watch me, to make sure that I didn't take my chip out, to make sure that neither Ellie nor I had powers. I thought I knew Daddy, too. But he's the one chasing us now."

The words burned. She forced them out anyway. "I feel that I love him… but I don't think I can trust what I feel anymore."

Mom set her teacup down carefully and reached across the small table, gently placing her hand over Malin's.

"My child," she said, her voice full of quiet grief. "I'm so sorry you're carrying this doubt. I would have fought tooth and nail at that ceremony if I thought Will was a bad fit for you and Ellie."

She squeezed Malin's hand, grounding her.

"I could tell you the missions of the operative I once knew as Hawk, who we now know as Will Hawkson. The successful missions were numerous, and there were almost no unsuccessful ones. They were thefts, cons, assassinations, and worse." She paused, letting the weight of that hang between them. "But everything he did was to save innocent lives. He was the best the Resistance had. The most trusted, and the most dangerous to our enemies."

"Yes," she continued, "Will has a checkered past. There are things in his history that will surprise you. But they are things he should tell you himself. Not me. You may not agree with some of my views, but much of what Will has done for the Resistance was always for a purpose, and many of the things he did were carried out under my orders, although with many layers of authority between us. One thing I learned with him as one of my operatives is… He has his own sense of justice, and he will carry out whatever actions he feels are within that justice. He took orders into consideration, but he held to a code. That is more than I can say for some of the other operatives I had working for me… The one thing I can count on is that Ellie, Zee, and you are people he would do anything for, no matter what it would take… You would be safe, and he is someone who has the specialties to keep you safe."

Her ice-blue gaze didn't waver.

"Caelum was a significant part of your life, but there were parts of it you were not aware of. His was a chapter that ended far too abruptly and tragically. His role in the Resistance was much like Will's, although he did not possess the same skill sets or code. I'm so happy you are finally moving on after all these years."

Malin nodded, but a wave of resentment washed over her, chilling the warmth of her mother's touch.

'Moved on' felt so final. The words felt hollow, almost insulting. How could she 'move on' when her entire world had been ripped out from under her in a matter of weeks? Had she really moved on, though, or just jumped into a trauma bond relationship? How could this be a healthy relationship?

"Caelum and I met the first week of college," she began, her voice tight with suppressed anger. "We were together for all my college years, getting my medical degree. Years, Mom. We built a life, slowly, carefully. He was more than just my partner; he was my anchor. Losing him shattered me. I spent over a decade piecing myself back together, denying myself anything that felt like that kind of love again."

Her gaze was accusatory. "And now," she practically spat, though her voice remained low and strained, "just when I thought I'd finally pieced myself back together, Will came crashing into my world. He's wonderful, truly. But it all happened so fast."

"This has been weeks… My magic, our escape, this… unexpected journey towards something unknown. My gut instincts are screaming at me to follow him, to marry him, to trust him completely, even though my logical brain, the brain that has guided me my entire life, has no data, no evidence, no time to analyze anything at all!"

"I'm sure you know that Will and I have something called a soul-bond. I'm still not even sure what that is. These matching tattoos have just chosen us to be together. It feels so artificial, like I'm being forced into it." Her words faltered as she struggled to articulate the whirlwind of emotions and events that had defined her recent days.

"Malin," her mother's voice softened, "change, especially the kind influenced by magic, has a way of tearing through life like a storm. It upends everything, often leaving us disoriented... However, remember that storms also bring renewal. What feels like upheaval now may be the magic guiding you toward a new beginning."

The ship creaked beneath them, a subtle reminder of the journey they were on. "So, you are worried that the feelings you are experiencing are not your own," her mother continued, "but the feelings given to you by magic."

"Yes. Exactly," Malin admitted, a small smile breaking through her uncertainty. "He grounds me, not like Caelum did, but in a way that feels... right for who I am now, not who I was. With him, I've discovered strengths I never knew I had and faced fears I would've shied away from before I found my magic. The powers within me tell me that we are bound together. I can feel the connection. I long for it to be real, and yet, the speed of it all terrifies me. I feel like I'm scared of being forced into something."

Her mother squeezed her hand in silent solidarity that spoke volumes. "Magic has its own rhythm, my dear. Sometimes, it pushes us into the fray, not to engulf us, but to reveal our true capacities. Trust your heart, Malin. Trust the magic within you."

"It chose Will for a reason. In this last week, your magic has made such improvements, so much faster than is typical. I think that could be because you trust it. Magic is drawn to those who listen to it and embrace it."

"You were faced with a choice: either make this change or risk losing your daughter. Despite all the technology in the city, her powers were intensifying, and it was only a matter of time before the city discovered Ellie, even with my vigilance. I had already started planning to leave with you both, wanting to keep her safe, even against your will, if necessary. I even planned to ask Hawk for help, as he has a reliable reputation for safe transportation. I think it was inevitable that you would have been thrown together. Destiny was going to throw you together, one way or the other. There's no point in mourning something that wouldn't have lasted." Her pragmatic motherly instincts emerged.

"I remember feeling much as you do about the soul-bond," she said.

Malin shook her head. She didn't understand what she meant. "What?"

A wistful look overtook her face as she fell into memories. "Lady Anariel had a cousin, Aldrik Rauno, who would visit with her as I was growing up. He is almost eight years older than I am, so he was not interested in a young child like me, but I had a crush on him. As he was so much older than I… we never had that kind of connection. Just a little girl's pining. In his teens, he went off adventuring."

Malin tried to understand how this connected to the soul-bond.

"By the time he got back, I had met your father, we had married, but things weren't going well. I realized early on that your father was not a fan of magic, but I hoped that would pass."

Malin set the cup down, her hands tightening.

The words spilled before she could pull them back. "Did you ever love Daddy?"

Her mother sighed again, but this time it sounded more like sorrow than impatience. "I thought that might be one of your questions," Mom continued, her voice gentler now as she picked up her cooling teacup. "Yes. Once. When we met, your father was dashing, and we had much in common."

"We really were in love… or I thought we were in the early years. I had hoped to share my powers with him and have him join me in the Resistance, but that did not happen. We had a child, but that child had been born with magic. He had her chipped, and she died. That alone did quite a number on our relationship." Her eyes were staring off into a memory.

Malin remembered her Mom mentioning a lost child before, but the full weight of it, the cold reality of *why*, struck her anew.

"He never knew about my work with the Resistance back then. Over time, his ambitions grew. His work at Masoncore consumed him. Then, my duty was to stay close to him, since your father had taken a position dealing with technologies to suppress powers. He became more valuable to the Resistance as an asset. He was to be a source of information, a means to an end, not a husband."

She paused, sipping her tea, her eyes clouded with a distant sorrow. "When I became Chancellor, he considered it a victory for us both, for his business, and his reputation. Over the years, our marriage became… convenient for both of us. Beneficial. But it was barely a marriage. It did, however, put me in the perfect position to acquire those plans for the city-wide magic suppression system his company was developing. Unfortunately, they found out before we left."

"It's those plans that are the reason we have Media on top of the monsters and pirates, breathing down our necks, though," Malin pointed out, the weariness in her voice a stark contrast to the fire that had burned within her hours earlier when she set the enemy ship ablaze.

The city-wide magic suppression system her father had been instrumental in developing for Media… was a ticking time bomb for people with magic, and stealing its schematics had painted a massive target on their backs. "It was going to be a dangerous journey to Aloria without them after us. I can't even imagine how much harder it will be now."

Mom's gaze, usually so sharp and unwavering, had softened with a hint of something Malin rarely saw – regret. "It will all be worth it if we can save more people in the city from getting those microchips in them." Her mother's words held a fierce conviction. "Look at you, Malin. Look at the incredible healing you accomplished today, powers you've only had for a week since you and Will removed your chip. Recall it was your flames that stopped the rest of their crew from demolishing our small crew. Imagine the potential unlocked in countless others if they were free from that technological leash. When half of those implanted with the chips die, how can that ever be the right solution?"

Malin nodded slowly, the logic undeniable, yet the present danger felt suffocating.

"It was shortly after I lost the baby when Aldrik and I saw each other again. He has a touch of Elven blood, and there haven't been any known mated bonds across species, until us… When it hit, we couldn't deny it, and neither of us wanted to. I still had a role to play, though, within the Resistance. I had lives counting on me, and by then, I had increased my roles in both Media and the Resistance. It took some work between us, but he understood how important my work was, and he had his own work that he found important."

Her mother bore her eyes into her and grabbed her hand. "It was shortly after, about nine months after, that you were born. I had complications with the birth, and when I woke up, you had already been chipped, but you survived." Tears were welling in her eyes, but she held her head high. "I allowed your father to keep thinking you were his child. There was a chance you were, but in my heart... I've always thought you might be Aldrik's child." Malin searched her face, looking for understanding.

Did she hear what she thought she heard? Malin felt her insides quiver as if someone were playing them like a discordant harp; the barbed tendrils of the admission lashed through her.

Yet another secret was revealed.

The words echoed in her mind, fracturing her past, shattering every memory she held dear.

What about her father? The man who had raised her, loved her, and disciplined her. Was it all a charade? A cold dread began to spread from her chest, numbing her fingers, chilling her to the bone even as a furious heat began to prickle beneath her skin. Betrayal. It clawed at her throat, a cold, bitter hand squeezing her windpipe, stealing her voice.

How much more had been hidden? How much more was a lie? This wasn't just a secret; this was the very core of who she thought she was, shattering inside her, crumbling to dust in her very hands.

"A chance?" The words tasted like ash. Malin's voice came out as a gasping, strangled whisper, then rose, disbelief warring with a bitter edge.

"What do you mean, 'a chance'? So, the man who raised me... my entire life... was it all a lie? This isn't like the magic, Mom! This is about who *I am*."

The familiar sting of betrayal, magnified by this ultimate secret, curdled in her stomach.

"Always secrets. When does it stop? Why are you just telling me now? Does he know?" She could feel the fiery rage building in her gut, the heat from her flame powers rising in her, as the temperature in the room began to increase, the air thickening around them. Her gaze, hot with accusation, bore into her mother's, searching for answers, for anything but the familiar, crushing silence of yet another untold truth.

Malin's raw accusations scorched the increasingly warm air. Her mother's expression, previously resolute, now shifted to one of profound sadness.

"Malin, please," Mom began, her voice low and steady, a deliberate attempt to soothe the rising tempest. "I understand your anger. I truly do. This is a lot, and it's a truth I've carried for a very long time. But you need to breathe, darling. You need to focus. Your magic..." Her gaze flickered to Malin's hands, which were now faintly glowing with a dangerous, unstable heat.

Malin hardly heard her, consumed by the burning frustration. "Focus? How can I focus? My whole life, yet another lie! You think you know what's best, but you keep *taking* things from me! Control, my choices, my past..."

A sharp, almost imperceptible shift in her mother's demeanor indicated her decision. Her hand, which still held Malin's, tightened, and a wave of incredible calm, like water washing over hot coals, instantly seeped into Malin's core. The angry heat coiling in her gut, the sharp edges of her frustration, and the burgeoning warmth of her flame powers all receded with an abruptness that left her gasping.

A fresh surge of indignation quickly replaced Malin's initial relief. "Mom!" she protested, pulling her hand away, the sudden coolness a stark contrast to the burning emotions she'd just been stripped of. "Don't do that! Don't just *turn it off*." The words were an accusation, a raw wound where control had been ripped from her. The anger, though diminished, was still there, a stubborn ember flickering in the dampness of her forced tranquility.

Mom's eyes softened further, brimming with unshed tears that mirrored Malin's emotional turmoil, yet her voice remained steady. "I had to, darling. You were losing control, and we are on a wooden ship." She motioned to the melted spoon seated on the table by her hand. "Your magic, when untamed by such strong emotions, can lash out. You're still learning. I couldn't stand by and watch you endanger yourself, or worse." She paused, her gaze holding Malin's. "Now, please. I know this is difficult, but let me explain everything, from the beginning."

Malin stared, caught between the lingering frustration of having her emotions quelled and the genuine concern she saw in her mother's eyes. The abrupt calmness was disorienting, leaving her feeling hollowed out, but the undeniable truth of her mother's words about her uncontrolled magic resonated.

She was a danger. To herself. To others.

She took a shuddering breath, the air now feeling strangely cool against her throat. "Fine," she conceded, the word clipped, but the embers of her rage still glowed beneath the surface. "Explain."

Her gaze softened further. "I didn't tell you before, Malin, because I wasn't *certain*. There was always a chance you were your father's child. I loved him, in my way, and I didn't want to destroy what little peace we had left. And frankly," she added, a flicker of pain crossing her features, "I was afraid. Afraid of what it would do to you, to us. You were already so hurt, so closed off."

She paused, taking a deep breath. "But when I saw your flames... it became undeniable. You have Aldrik's power, Malin. One of his powers is the ability to control others' abilities, but his primary power is the ability to manipulate flames. As much as the man you grew up knowing as your father always said that magic ran in his bloodlines, I never noticed any powers in him. He says he chipped himself, just to make sure that none showed up, but I am doubtful."

"Does Aldrik know that there is a chance?" Malin asked the question in barely a whisper. The room felt too small. The air was too thick with unspoken truths.

Her mother shook her head. "I'm not proud of it, but... I told him that there was no chance you were his when he asked, so I don't believe so. He had always wished we could have children and had suggested that I take you girls away from that city the moment we knew Ellie had powers. If he had thought for one moment you were his... knowing him... he would have burned Media to the ground to get you out. Just on the chance. He is very much like Will in that."

She reached out, her hand finding Malin's again, this time offering a gentle warmth instead of enforced calm. "I'm telling you now, because you deserve to know the truth. I don't want to hide anything else from you. You are right. You deserve all the truth. And because... he's here and intends to join us in Aloria. We will meet him when we get to Sarhan. And I do not want to keep it from you or him any longer. I will tell him when we get to Sarhan. It isn't something that should be told through messages."

Malin pulled her hand back, her earlier anger now a cold, stark, unyielding resolve. She looked at her mother, seeing not just the woman who had kept a monumental secret, but the woman who was finally, painfully, confessing it.

"I need to know," Malin said, her voice steady, each word deliberate. "From this moment forward, Mom, you tell me everything. No more lies, no more omissions, no more 'protecting' me by keeping me in the dark. Not about my magic, not about my family, not about anything. If there is *anything* else, any other secret, any other truth that affects me, you tell me now. Because if I find out about one more thing you've hidden, one more time you've held back the truth... I won't just be angry. I won't just be hurt. I'll be gone. And I won't look back."

Her eyes, still shimmering with unshed tears, met Malin's unflinchingly. A profound weariness seemed to settle over her, but a quiet, determined strength quickly replaced it. "You're right, Malin," she said, her voice barely a whisper, yet firm. "You deserve the truth. All of it."

She paused for a moment. "The only thing that you may want to hear me admit to is something I don't feel I have the right to tell you. It is Will's to tell."

"Will's hiding something from me?" She was incredulous.

"He isn't necessarily hiding it, but maybe hasn't gotten a chance to tell you. Things have been a bit busy lately. I don't think it affects the direction of our journey, so I do feel it is for him to share, or I'd tell you."

She took a deep breath. "So, no more major landmines for me to find out about? I don't have a sibling hiding somewhere. There is nothing about Ellie or me that I don't know yet?" The way her mother phrased Will's secret, Malin wondered if it wasn't all that important. It was just a test of their new communication.

"There are no more major secrets like this. No more monumental hidden truths that would shake the foundations of your life. And from now on, even the small ones, the everyday ones, if you ask, I will tell you. I promise. I want this, Malin. This bond. This new relationship. More than you know." She reached out, her hand hovering, waiting for Malin's permission.

Taking a breath, Malin reached out and finished the connection as she stood. "Mom. I have always wanted a connection with you. I really feel this was a good start. I am very hopeful. Very tired, but very hopeful. I can't say that I'm good with things, but… I can appreciate that things haven't been typical for us, so maybe I should give some added leniency… We will talk more about this when I've had some time to sleep on it."

Walking to the door, Malin hesitated, then said, "Ellie's doing fine, by the way. She's resting, and Zee… he fell asleep holding her hand."

Her mom's smile softened, a real, aching thing. "I've been in quiet communication with Ellie," she said. "I didn't step into the captain's quarters until I knew she was safe. You were amazing today, Malin. You couldn't have made me prouder."

Malin warmed at the words, the heat blooming in her chest, a fragile, aching thing. She had spent so many years wishing for moments like this, hoping her mother would see her, *really* see her, and that they could sit together without politics or distance between them.

For the first time in as long as she could remember, Malin felt something settled between them, something tenuous and precious. She wasn't sure if it was forgiveness or merely the fragile chance to start over. But for tonight, she could accept it.

When the door opened, the corridor outside her mom's door felt colder than before. Or maybe it was just Malin, feeling hollowed out, her bones aching from more than just magic spent.

Looking down in thought, she moved down the narrow hall, her steps slow and dragging, the ship's faint creaks and the distant slap of waves against the hull the only sounds to accompany her. She found Will leaning against the doorframe of their room, his hair red and crusted with blood, dark staining on his arms, which were crossed loosely on his chest. His head was tipped back, eyes closed, probably not asleep, but still like he had been standing there a long time.

At six and a half feet tall and with broad shoulders, he filled the hallway. He was one of the few people she actually had to look up to, with her five-foot-ten height.

Waiting. He was waiting for her.

The raw ache in her bones, the sheer depletion of every cell, left no room for rational thought, only instinct. And her instinct, battered as it was, screamed for his solid presence. Was it the soul bond twisting her emotions? Was this overwhelming pull just another consequence of uncontrolled magic? Or was this… more?

She didn't know. She couldn't know.

Not now.

CHAPTER 5 – WILL

A soft creak of hinges roused Will from the half-trance he'd fallen into. He opened his eyes and found her standing a short distance away.

Malin. She was there.

He saw the dark smudges of weariness around her eyes, her pale skin, and the overwhelming urge to catch her before she collapsed. But her magic still clung to her. It was faint and stubborn, like the last warmth of a dying fire.

Will reached for her without a word.

Malin came to him, just as silently, slipping into the circle of his arms like she was coming home.

Their foreheads touched. It was a simple, anchoring point of connection. He wrapped her close, holding her as if she were something fragile and infinitely precious, which she was.

The cold bite of the corridor faded against the heat of her body as she pressed into him. The weight of her head against his shoulder grounded him more than any anchor ever could.

The low, real thrum of her heart ran through him. He could feel it echoing against his ribs, stitching together places inside him that had been unraveling all night.

He closed his eyes and breathed her in, salt, blood, magic, and the faint sweetness of her skin. For the first time in hours, the knot inside him loosened.

Alive.

She was here.

And for this moment, that was enough.

"Hey, Sparks," he released the words like a whispered prayer of thanks.

"I'm tired," she murmured into his ear, her voice cracking at the edges. When she touched his face, he couldn't help but press into the caress.

"I know," he said, his voice rough, laced with a tenderness that felt out of place for this battered hallway. "Let's get you to bed, Mrs. Hawkson."

Still silent, she let him guide her. Will kept one arm locked firmly around her waist as he opened the door to their quarters, shielding her from the world with his body as he led her inside.

He didn't want to let her go.

But as he pulled back slightly to look at her, he caught the grim reality: the pale gold of her hair streaked with dried blood, her clothes stiff with it, her skin stained in places he hadn't even noticed.

He needed to feel her skin against him, needing the confirmation that she was truly, wholly here.

He reached for the hem of his shirt and grimaced as it pulled against his side, the fabric stuck fast to a deep, crusted wound he hadn't realized he had.

Malin's hands caught his wrists gently and healed the wound.

Wordlessly, they understood.

They stumbled into the small, battered bathroom, thankful that the large ship had a traditional bathroom in the passenger area, even if the water was limited. The shower was a mercy to them both. It was blunt and practical. Steam enveloped the cramped space almost immediately, wrapping them in warmth. They scrubbed away the blood, salt, and smoke in silence, with gentle, careful, clinical touches.

It wasn't like their other showers. There was no urgency or teasing. This was survival, pure and simple; even communication was limited.

When they were clean, or as clean as a ship's shower would allow, and wrapped in towels, Will tugged her toward the bed, not letting more than inches separate them.

They collapsed together onto the narrow mattress, the world outside their door forgotten to him.

Malin curled into him, her head resting against his heart, her breathing slow and even.

Will stared down at her, his hand slowly tracing circles along her bare shoulder.

Even in exhaustion, stripped of her medical composure and elegant clothes, she was breathtaking. Her resilience and her quiet fire drew him in like nothing ever had.

Even as exhausted as he was, he couldn't seem to stop looking at her. Appreciating the curve of her cheek, the smudge of exhaustion under her eyes, the fierce, stubborn life still burning beneath her skin.

A raw, familiar fear clawed at the edges of his mind. How would she react if she truly knew the 'real' him? The man who had assassinated countless lives, whose personal death tally was so high he'd long since stopped counting. The man whose every kill was a deliberate act of his grim justice, carefully aimed at those he judged truly guilty, regardless of formal orders. It left its mark.

She had already raised concerns when they boarded the ship that they were heading into a pirate town – a den of thieves and killers – and her fears about their family being exposed to it. What would she do when she realized that those were his people, the people he felt most comfortable with?

He was a dangerous man, known for not being crossed, and that reputation might be the only thing that kept them safe in town.

But what if that same reputation made them a target? What if his past caught up with him, seeking retribution against those he loved? The very idea curdled in his gut. It was a foreign feeling and one he was not accustomed to dealing with.

She was amazing.

And somehow, she was his. But was he worthy of her?

Dawn's light spilled through the porthole, golden and soft, waking Will from a restless sleep. He was still propped up on the pillows, his head raised. It wasn't the most comfortable position, but it did give him a clear view of the woman in his arms.

Malin lay naked, her head on his arm, tangled against him, her body still and warm. Her breath brushed against his chest in slow, steady exhalations. She hadn't moved. Even now, the weight of her against him felt more precious than anything he could have ever stolen or fought for.

He was in awe of her healing ability. He had been covered in wounds and bruises, and she had several of her own, but as he looked down at her, they were gone. She must have healed him in her sleep.

Judging by the brightness spilling across the floorboards, the day was already in full bloom. Time had slipped away from him, but time was meaningless against the simple fact that she was still here. The same thoughts from the night before were still with him.

She was still breathing.

She was still his, and he didn't deserve her.

The room smelled faintly of salt, old wood, and the lavender oil she'd rubbed into her wrists to help her sleep. It clung to her skin even now, softening the sharp edge of the harrowing day with a fragile, achingly familiar scent.

He lay there in silence, studying her. He worshiped the curve of her bare hip where the sheet had slipped low, the delicate rise and fall of her ribcage, the loose strands of hair curling against her damp skin from the heat of the poorly ventilated room. Reverence rooted him to the bed. He dared not move, dared not even breathe too loudly, lest the delicate spell of her presence shatter.

Then she stirred.

Malin stretched against him in a slow, instinctive movement, her body pressing more fully into his.

Will's eyes closed, a low ache tightening in his gut, and a pure, primal need stirred within him by that simple movement. Every movement of her body against him was like a fucking prayer.

She opened her eyes and caught his gaze. He'd never noticed the silver flecks in her irises, how the light caught them. So much left to learn about her.

She blinked slowly. Will's arm was still wrapped around her, while his other hand traced her curves. His chest rose and fell steadily as she lay against him. She turned her head slightly to gaze at him, a soft smile playing on her lips.

He loved the way the curve of her back made her ass pop up like that.

"Good morning," she murmured, her voice barely above a whisper.

Will shifted his weight, turning to face her fully. "Morning," he replied, his voice low and rough with unspoken emotion. He felt her finger trace down the line of his rough jaw, the stubble now almost a beard.

"Did I wake you?" he asked.

Malin shook her head. He could feel when his touch sent shivers down her spine.

"No," she said softly. "I was just enjoying the feeling of you next to me."

He nodded, taking her hand in his and bringing it to his lips, pressing a soft kiss against her knuckles.

His breath hitched as his manhood swelled, hot and unforgiving. He moaned, trying to gain control. She must be exhausted after yesterday, he rationalized. He needed to give her space.

What was he thinking, letting them go to bed naked? Masochist.

That was the only answer.

She stretched again and turned her back to him, arching her back like a damn goddess rising from the ashes. His hand brushed against the curve of her breast, his fingers naturally finding her nipple. They swirled with a mind of their own.

Her ass ground into his groin, a precise movement that made him groan. His other hand moved of its own accord, sliding down her hip to grip the curve of her waist, his fingers digging into the softness of her flesh as if he could pull her closer, deeper. He rocked into her instinctively before stopping himself.

"Sparks, I don't think you realize how close I am to the end of my willpower. If you don't want to do more right now, I'm going to need to get up and take a very cold shower. If I stay in this room even a moment more... I'm going to have you moaning, and I'm going to hear that little gasp you make when I push my way in." The words came out in a deep growl, with promise behind them.

He could feel her heartbeat, fast and erratic, echoing in the tremble of her body. She reached back and grabbed hold of his cock. "Take me," she murmured, her voice low and raspy, like she'd been screaming for hours.

His eyes widened, and he hissed through gritted teeth, his hips jerking forward with animalistic heat. She didn't stop, didn't fucking hesitate, just wrapped her fingers around him and squeezed, her grip firm and possessive. She turned to face him, pushing him back on the bed, straddling his waist.

"You're alive," she whispered, her lips brushing his ear now, her tongue darting out to trace the edge before she nipped at his earlobe. "You're mine." His willpower left him completely.

His fingers explored her body, moving one hand down between her legs, entering her to feel the moisture and teasing her clit. Her wetness drove him fucking wild. Her hand on his shaft, she stroked up and down. With each move, he thought he would fall apart. He wanted to be inside her, and he tried to adjust for entry, but she held his hand back.

"You wanna be in charge, Sparks? No complaints here… just don't take too long, or I might forget how to behave." His voice was low, rough around the edges. It was more heat than breath, more promise than a threat.

Her free hand slid up to wrap around his neck, pulling him into a kiss that was anything but gentle. Her tongue was in his mouth, hot and demanding as she ground against him.

He groaned into the kiss. His fingers dug into her ass as he lifted her, her legs straddled across his waist as if she were born to be there.

They were both breathing hard, their bodies were slick with sweat and desire, the air between them thick with a heat that could burn empires to the ground.

She broke the kiss only to press her forehead against him, her breath coming in ragged gasps as she rocked against him, the friction almost too much and yet not nearly enough.

"Tell me," she demanded, her voice trembling with need. "Tell me you're mine."

"Yours," he growled, his hands moving to grip her hips as he sheathed her on him, her tightness enveloping him. He watched her breasts bounce with each thrust. "Fucking yours."

Every time she impaled herself on him, she let out that little gasp he loved. It was like sheer heaven around his cock as she squeezed, rocked, and lifted as she rode him.

Their movements were frantic. Every touch was a raw, desperate reminder that they were alive, that they'd survived.

Her nails dug into his arms as she rocked above him. Their moans mingled as they chased the edge together.

He teased her nipples and brought them to his mouth until he couldn't hold back his climax any longer, but she was right there with him. The feeling was so intense that it left him speechless.

Afterward, they lay tangled in the sheets, the air thick with sweat and the sharp tang of salt still clinging to their skin. Malin stretched lazily across him; her body draped along his like she owned him… and she did.

Will had never felt anything like it before.

It wasn't just the heat, or the way his body stirred the moment he even thought of her… though it did, every damn time. It was something deeper… Rawer. She filled a hollow within him he hadn't known existed.

If he ever figured out which god he was supposed to thank for her in his life. For this… he'd be their devotee forever.

Until then, he'd be hers. Completely.

And he would worship her with every chance she gave.

He tipped his head back against the pillow, still trying to catch his breath. A lazy, wicked grin curved his lips.

"Sparks," he drawled, his voice rough from too much pleasure and not nearly enough restraint, "you sure you don't want to take control more often?'

He felt her release a low, satisfied chuckle against his chest.

"Bossy looks good on you," he added, lifting one hand to tangle lazily in her sweat-damp hair. "I might even start taking orders." He said with a crooked grin.

The afterglow faded into a quiet moment, their bodies warm but heavy against the tangled sheets.

It could have been minutes or an hour; Will lay there in silent worship. He brushed his fingers lazily over the bare curve of Malin's hip, but his worship was straying toward unspoken things. Those questions he left buried under the weight of their need for each other. He owed her answers, and she was not the type that would appreciate hidden information, even if it was for a good reason.

Was his fear of losing her a good reason?

Then he looked at her and realized that she was deep in thought.

He tightened his arms around her, pressing a kiss into her hair. "Sparks," he murmured, his voice low, "what's going on in that beautiful brain of yours?"

Malin was silent for a moment. Then she shifted against him, her voice so small he barely caught it.

"I keep thinking back to that moment when it happened. The fear was so intense," she admitted. "I had just used my power to shoot that flame to their ship, feeling a sense of accomplishment for having channeled my flame so far. When I saw Ellie fall, it felt like a punishment for doing that. The kraken and the other sea creatures that night likely ate those that didn't burn on that ship."

Will stilled, his heart knocking painfully against his ribs.

"I almost lost my baby," she whispered, "I would have never forgiven myself if she had died, but I didn't just kill the one that did that to her. I killed so many in the hours of battle before that."

The breath left his lungs in a slow, raw exhale.

"Zee was fighting him," Malin said, her voice breaking a little now. "Ellie tried to help. She stepped wrong. The man's blade…" she stopped, squeezing her eyes shut. "I was close enough. I stopped the bleeding before it was too late."

Will shut his eyes, burying his face against the top of her head. He could see it, clear as if he had been there; he pictured the blood, the screams, Zee standing over Ellie's crumpled body, Malin's magic sparking to save her.

"You saved her," he said roughly.

"You don't understand. I did all that. I was punished for it, and I feel like I should be ashamed or feel bad about it… But I don't. I would do it all again. I was punished, and I don't feel it was fair. If I should have been punished, it should have been me, not her, but I stand behind my decision. Their ship was larger and had more people. If I hadn't, our ship would have been taken."

"I know you made the right choice. If I had your power, I would have done the same. I don't know if that is good or bad, but I do know it did save lives," he said, in awe of her strength.

It had taken Will years of hard choices and seeing people stand in the way for him to stop concerning himself with the decision at all. He had learned to deal with obstacles accordingly.

But Malin… how could she not see it? Not just her raw power, but her raw courage to make such a brutal decision, and then to wrestle with the moral cost of it afterward. Most people would simply celebrate surviving and saving so many; Malin grieved the necessity of it. That humanity, that ability to mourn the darkness required for survival, was one of the things he loved most about her. It was what made her so utterly, terrifyingly, perfectly *her*.

He held her tighter, feeling her fragile heartbeat between them. Although he had stopped concerning himself with the morality of taking lives, counting only the losses of the ones he cared about, he knew she did, and he hoped he could be an anchor for her, as she was for him.

Finally, Will pressed a kiss against her temple and pulled back, reluctantly. He didn't want to add to her mood by bringing up problems. *Later. He would bring it up later.*

"I know your Mom said she was taking care of them, but we should check on them," he said. "I miss them, and I think it would do us both some good to see them. We land in two days, so we have to get things taken care of."

Malin nodded against him, her head moving slowly and heavily.

Reluctantly, they untangled themselves, pulling on rumpled clothes with slow, careful movements. Will's hands lingered when he noticed tiny scrapes along Malin's side, faint etchings of the battle she had forgotten to heal. He smoothed his palm over them, promising silently: Never again.

When they were ready, he opened the door to the hallway, cool air brushing over their skin.

Side-by-side, they stepped out into the dim corridors of the ship, the scent of salt and ash still thick in the air.

They walked to the medical bay, Will's hand brushing lightly against Malin's whenever the roll of the deck shifted them closer, till he pulled her close at her waist, matching his step to hers. As they got closer, he could feel her tensing in his arms. He asked, "What's wrong? How can I help?"

"It's silly," she looked down and shook her head.

He stopped their walk, turned to face her, and lifted her chin. "It's not silly. It's something you are worried about. Please let me in."

She touched his hand. "I know I had to take a break and recuperate, and I wouldn't trade our time... but if I walk in there to see dead or dying, I'm worried I'm going to be upset at myself for not coming sooner. I'm worried about what I'm going to find in there."

"My Sparks. The number of lives you saved. I think almost every crew member has you to thank for something. You worked until you couldn't. It didn't fall all on your shoulders, and no matter what you find, you did the best **you** could. You are Malin Hawkson, badass, and a talented woman in multiple ways… and speaking of your amazing talents, I'm pretty sure I'm still feeling the effects of a few of them myself." He gave a wink and a crooked grin, "You are someone who gives every ounce of you for everything you do. Although there are some ways I prefer more than others," he winked. "In all of them, you are amazing." His closing remarks included a kiss to her forehead, followed by a quick kiss to her lips, which curled to a smile, just as he had hoped. The feel of her softness and her eager reception threatened to dissolve him entirely.

When they got to the door, Will opened it cautiously, watching her reaction. He felt her tension relax under his touch as she took stock of the room. Her shoulders rose as she took a deep breath.

He joined her breath. The sharp scents of brine and copper that had permeated the air hours ago had given way to the faint, clean tang of sea air and antiseptic.

Taking his eyes off her, he looked around the room, the cramped bay, once a chaotic canvas of crimson, now gleamed under the softened light of the lanterns. Beds, still numerous, held crew resting peacefully, none writhing in agony. Three crew members working in the room greeted them from a distance and continued their work, moving with quiet efficiency. Their hands glowed with a soft, blue light as they levitated soiled rags and scrubbed away the last stubborn smears of blood, working magic to restore order.

Malin slipped out of his hold on her waist and ran to Ellie's bedside, where he saw Ellie and Zee sitting, their heads bent over a brightly illustrated old storybook. The book, with its large image of a Unicorn on the front, seemed strangely innocent in this place. One of the cleaning crew members, noticing his gaze linger on the children, gave him a small, weary smile and a nod in return.

Ellie's face was no longer pale; a healthy flush bloomed on her cheeks, and her breathing seemed soft and even. Zee, leaning close, pointed to an illustration of a creature with impossible wings, his finger tracing its outline.

At the faint click of the closing door, Ellie looked up first. Her blue eyes widened, then exploded with joy. "Mom!" she squealed, dropping the book and launching herself from the cot. Zee, a beat behind her, scrambled off, a relieved gasp escaping him. "Malin!"

A smile erupted when a whirlwind of arms and desperate hugs hit Malin. Malin easily buried her face in Ellie's hair at chin level. With her free arm, she pulled Zee, who was only four inches shorter than Malin, tightly against her side, engulfing both of her children in a desperate, loving embrace.

Will watched with a profound tenderness blooming in his chest. A smile of pure, unadulterated relief lit Malin's face, a radiant sun breaking through the grim shadows of the past day. It was the most beautiful thing he had ever seen.

This was it. This was the family he'd never dared to dream of.

It was the light that filled the dark, empty spaces inside him. The terrifying thought flashed: *He couldn't lose this. He wouldn't. Not to assassins, not to old secrets, not to anything.*

Ellie, still clinging to Malin with one arm, turned her beaming face up to Will. "Will!" she exclaimed, her smile still wide.

Zee pulled away from Malin's side, running towards him, a relieved sob releasing. Will, tall enough to comfortably look over most crowds, leaned down as both children launched themselves at him, their young, strong bodies making a joyful impact. He wrapped his arms fiercely around them, burying his face in Ellie's sweet-smelling hair, easily embracing her small frame, and pulling Zee, who was already nearly at his shoulder, close against his chest. He had his family, alive and whole.

The next morning marked their final day on the ship. He kicked himself for not telling Malin while he had multiple chances.

When they finally stepped onto the upper deck, the wind whipped stronger against them. With years of sailing this route, although barely visible to most, he could see Sarhan's crooked skyline as a distant speck on the horizon. It was jagged, battered, chaotic even from there. The city was like a wound against the sea, lawless and loud, a haven carved out by thieves and rebels who'd chosen danger over chains. Life there was hard, but it was free. The plan was for them to reach the docks early in the afternoon tomorrow.

Will leaned heavily against the railing beside Malin, his arm wrapped protectively around her waist, soaking in the warmth where his body met hers. She stared out at the restless churn of water below, unaware of the storm that raged within him.

He leaned into her, breathed in the lavender, citrus, and vanilla of her hair, and pressed a light kiss into her thick blonde waves, trying to imprint the memory of her against him and of this quiet moment into his mind.

He turned his face into the wind, letting it cut across the raw ache in his chest. Some deep part of him, the part that had survived too many broken promises already, knew better. He didn't want his secrets to steal the trust she had in him, but if he told her and she couldn't accept it, he would lose her anyway.

Delaying would only make things worse.

He turned her to face him and tilted her face up, leaning in for a kiss. The softness of those lips made him melt as they parted eagerly. He wanted to savor this kiss, as it might be his last. He brushed his tongue over the edge, feeling the intoxication, remembering what else those lips could do. He had to pull back with a deep moan, fighting the fires he could feel burning. They were in the middle of the top deck, with the children playing nearby. He leaned in to feel her touch, to calm the raging heat within him, without letting her go.

Once he was in control of his emotions again, he looked her in the eye and cleared his throat.

"I'm not sure there will ever be a good time for this, so I'm just going to say it. I always considered myself a brave man who could handle any adversary… I have stared down a horde of orcs without blinking, yet the thought of opening up to you about some things makes my pulse pound like battle drums. You deserve better from me, and I'm sorry." He could see her eyes darken, and she pulled back a little, though her hand remained linked with his. The darkening of her eyes made him decide to test the waters and start with something simple.

"I don't know if you remember hearing it said once in Media, so I think you deserve to know about Lydia. I don't know if she is even in Sarhan anymore. For all I know, she left on the next merchant ship after I left. If she's here, she is unpredictable, reckless, and likely a little psychotic. If she's here, she might be mad at me, or not. Frankly, I don't know what to expect. She's a pint-sized little fire demon, who isn't someone that I wanted to anger lightly. People were hunting me, and I had to keep her safe, so I left her there, with a job, paid for a room for the month, and gave her enough money so she could stay or pay a fare to Aloria on another ship. She couldn't go with me, and honestly… she was fun, but I didn't think it was a relationship. I only found out that she thought it was when I tried to go."

As he spoke, he could see Malin's eyebrow lift and her lips tighten, but she didn't let go. "It sounds like you did what you could for her, though I don't know all the details, to be sure," she analyzed.

"Right. I did. I tried," he considered going into more. Into why he had to leave her, into the Order of Tamris, into the assassins that were chasing him, but instead he let fear guide him and said, "I was living a different life than I am right now. It was two years ago; a lot has changed."

His throat tightened. Damn it, why was honesty to her more brutal than facing death?

She still hadn't pulled away, but she had stilled, and she was quiet in thought. Her silence was deafening.

"So, I might run into an ex-girlfriend. Do you still have feelings for her?"

"No. Not at all," His reaction was immediate and exactly what she seemed to be looking for, as she smiled.

"She has fire, huh?" she asked with a teasing tone.

She wasn't upset. *Maybe he had underplayed the psychotic part?*

"Not like yours, but she has flames. I told you that you are one of a kind." Given how well she was taking this news, he really didn't think it was a good time to add the information about the assassins. That was what he felt would not go over as well. "You're not mad or upset about it?"

"From the stories I heard of you, I will likely run into a few of your exes. Is there a reason to believe she would hurt me or the kids? I doubt she will hurt you much... As long as you aren't still interested in her, I don't see why there would be an issue," she reasoned. It was the reaction he expected from her.

"I never saw her hurt children. She is a tad bit of the jealous type, but with your martial arts skills and your abilities, she wouldn't stand a chance against you," he offered.

"I'll keep that in mind," she mused playfully, leaning her head on his shoulder to nuzzle his neck.

His bravery only went so far, it seemed. He couldn't bring himself to break this playful spell she was under. He was antsy with worry over how she would react to the assassins, though.

He could feel his pent-up energy. Usually, he would train to stay active.

"Maybe we should do some training for the day," he offered.

"That sounds perfect. I'll go find Lady Anariel to get started," she offered. They kissed quickly as they parted, and she went off into the bowels of the ship.

He gazed off into the distance, wondering what lay in store for them. He had shared about Lydia, but he knew that was not the vital information she needed. He kicked himself for not being strong enough. *How could one woman have such a profound impact on him?*

CHAPTER 6 – MALIN

The ghost of the terror still clung to Malin's skin, a phantom chill against the warm wood of the deck, as she watched Ellie. She hadn't been able to find Lady Anariel, but she left word with Nar, who would ensure she knew they were going to try to train on the top deck. Her daughter lay near the edge of the deck, head tilted into the vast emptiness of the ocean, fingers tapping a carefree rhythm that belied how close they'd come to silence just hours before.

"Here they come, Zee!" Ellie's shout, sharp with a child's delight, sliced through the hushed symphony of wind and water.

Malin's breath hitched. She followed Ellie's pointing finger to the churning depths where sleek, gray bodies erupted from the waves. Dolphins. They moved with a breathtaking, synchronized speed, weaving through the water like living silver. Above them, the Dawn's Beacon's strained canvases creaked and swayed. Her oaken masts seemed to claw at a horizon swallowed by the endless, indifferent sea. The sharp salt in the air, already clinging to Malin's boots, was a constant reminder that they were far from land.

Zee crouched beside Ellie with his hand outstretched to the sea. Malin imagined the unseen connection forming, tightening like a shared breath between him and the slick, gray shapes below. His body stilled, and a subtle twitch in his fingers was the only outward sign of the clicking language he perceived beneath the surface.

It felt like a lifetime ago, not just the other day, that she'd cradled Ellie's broken form, the cold dampness of the deck seeping into her knees as she fought against the frantic flutter of a dying pulse.

To witness this unburdened joy now, this vibrant spark of life was almost unbearable in its brilliance.

"They say the boat can't catch them!" Zee shouted, his laughter bright and clear, weaving through the salty air like sunlight piercing a thin fog.

The dolphins, sleek and swift, dipped beneath the ship's prow again, their movements a playful dare. A flash of gray fluke sliced the surface, sending a burst of cool spray that kissed Ellie's face, eliciting a delighted squeal as she wriggled closer to the edge.

The wind whipped strands of her hair across her laughing face.

Without a word, Zee's hand settled firmly against Ellie's lower back, a quiet anchor of responsibility in the midst of their joy.

She trusted he knew the fragility of life, the swiftness of loss. Malin had heard the sailors' grim warnings of children swallowed by the sea in the blink of an eye. Yet, how could she stifle this pure, untethered happiness? It was a rare bloom in the aftermath of so much darkness.

Still, her feet moved almost unconsciously, drawing her closer, a silent promise to intervene if needed, and close enough she could react. Relief eased some of the tension in her shoulders as Ellie finally stepped back from the precipice.

Then, her mother joined Ellie, a silent sentinel ensuring her granddaughter's continued safety.

Watching Zee's quiet connection with the dolphins, Ellie's effortless grace as she'd briefly lifted a discarded rope, and even witnessing the subtle hum of power around some of the crew, a familiar ache tightened in Malin's chest.

How could Media fear this? This inherent wonder?

Her own hands, still capable of mending bones and closing wounds, felt like a miracle she'd almost denied.

How many lives…

The thought was a sharp pang of what could have been.

Killed for this? For the ability to heal, to connect, to… float?

Then she considered her fire magic, the magic that had leveled a unit of guards in the West Woods as they escaped. The fire that had burned a ship filled with people, to protect her family. They did have reason to be afraid of her magic.

A long, slow exhale escaped her, a silent release of years of buried frustration and disbelief.

Then, she turned.

And stilled.

And there…

Will stood on the sun-warmed deck, stripped to the waist, salt light slicking over the sculpted planes of his back. A soft catch in Malin's breath accompanied the sight of his bronze skin. His features were creased with the marks of hard work and the subtle toll of sleepless nights, while the sunlight caught his damp, tousled hair, igniting threads of gold shimmering within. The scars, though visible, showed courage and strength.

Her gaze drifted down, almost involuntarily, to her wrist.

The silver bracelet lay there, delicate but unyielding. It was a simple braid of silver threads, interspersed with tiny blue stones that mirrored her eyes. The metal warmed from the sun was something personal and precious.

Will had given it to her instead of a ring, slipping it into her palm one night when words had failed him. It symbolized the love he'd known, and the kind he wanted to share.

It had belonged to his mother.

The only thing he still had of her.

And now… it was hers.

His claim on her heart. Not ownership. Never that. But it was a truth she didn't think he could say aloud: *I trust you with the part of me I've never given away.* Said or not, she felt it.

Her fingers ghosted across the bracelet. Even now, the threads felt alive. They were woven not just with metal and stone, but memories, with loss, and hope. A quiet tether that pulled at her even when he wasn't near. Although her heart pulled toward him with no effort, her mind was still working through the connection. It was getting stronger, though; there have been many incidents to show how logically they work together. It was different than Caelum… It might even be better.

She looked up at him again, that innate desire blooming, so quiet and familiar, the way it always did when her gaze found him. It pushed those nagging questions to the back of her mind, to be dealt with on another day.

The way his muscles shifted beneath his shoulders with each movement. It was fluid and efficient. He didn't even realize how beautiful he was. His body was built to endure, to protect, to move through pain without pause.

He was fully absorbed in the task before him; unaware he was being studied.

Next to him stood a tall crew member named Rainer. He had a deep laugh and sea-green eyes. He stood barefoot, grinning, with his palms lifted. A spinning orb of seawater floated between them, held aloft by nothing but magic. Droplets hovered like glass beads around it, catching sunlight in fractured sparks.

Rainer flicked his fingers, and the orb flattened into a disc, then a ribbon, before splitting into two.

Will's gaze narrowed, his hand extending not toward the water, but directly at Rainer. A subtle shift pulsed through the air, thick and immediate, like the silent, undeniable pressure of a storm front building inside a quiet room. Malin felt it, a faint prickle on her skin, a sudden, almost imperceptible *emptiness* in the magic-laden air around them.

The ribbons of water, held so perfectly aloft, stuttered. They didn't unravel; they didn't dissipate slowly. They simply *ceased to exist* in their suspended state, collapsing in a sudden, cold splattering across the deck like forgotten rain.

Rainer blinked, his mouth parting in bewildered surprise, then a slow, incredulous laugh escaped him.

"Did you feel it?" Will asked, his voice rough with something akin to awe, yet steady.

"Aye," Rainer nodded, still staring at his wet hands. "One minute, I had it. Then it was... gone. Like a candle flame snuffed out."

Nullification. The word slammed into Malin's mind, bright and clear, resonating with a quiet power. Rainer's magic hadn't just been exhausted; it had been severed, cut off at its source, not by distance, but by Will's presence.

By *Will himself.* He'd finally done it.

After countless hours of agonizing, clenched-jaw silence, of frustration that bled from him even when he held it tight, he'd finally managed to create a localized nullification field. A quiet, profound satisfaction bloomed in Malin's chest, eclipsing everything else. She knew how desperately he'd needed this win. And he'd earned it. Every single agonizing moment of struggle, every failed attempt, had culminated in this silent, decisive triumph.

Her pride lingered for only a breath before something more dangerous slid in beneath it... curiosity maybe. No. It was longing.

Malin fought to focus, but her gaze betrayed her, snagging again on the tattoos and scars etched across Will's back. They were sharp, sweeping lines inked deep black, wrapped around scars that whispered of unspoken things. A ribbon of runes and glyphs traced his spine, glowing faintly beneath the light, from the base of his neck down to the dimples at the small of his back.

That one particular rune always caught her eye, the twin to the rune that magically appeared the night she got her powers. The same mark that throbbed into her skin, just beneath the crook of her arm. The runes looked deceptively simple at first glance; the design was a spiral, coiled tight like the heart of a storm. But the longer she looked, the more it shifted. Lines layered within lines, threads of ink that shimmered just beneath the skin as if lit from within. The outer curve branched off into twin arcs, curling around the spiral like wings, or like two halves of something pulling toward the center. Closer still, she could make out embedded glyphs, which looked ancient and root-script, with each one etched so small that it was almost invisible.

It was subtle and permanent; it seemed to come alive at his touch, as if the marks reached out to each other.

Although her mother and Lysandra had explained that they were soul bonds, or sigils that didn't mark possession, but noted a tethering. They created a symbiotic existence.

She still didn't understand why it had shown up that night, given that Will and she had only known each other for such a short time. Why would magic choose them like that after such a short time?

Malin tried to center herself and focus on the training she had been working on, but her eyes kept tracking back to Will across the deck.

Breathe in. Focus. Breathe out.

It wasn't working.

Malin made a mental note to ask Lady Anariel about the mark, the elf approached. It amazed Malin how steady her steps were steady despite the ship's sway.

"Are you ready for today's lesson?" Lady Anariel asked, a subtle smile curving her mouth. "Or should I give you a moment to catch the rest of your thoughts?"

Malin flushed, jaw tightening. She compartmentalized her thoughts, so that she could focus on the task at hand. "I'm ready."

"Good," Anariel said, already turning toward the shaded area where they practiced. "Because he will be fine without you watching his every move."

Malin looked away, half-embarrassed, half-grateful. She tried to reclaim the focus that had slipped through her fingers like water.

Malin didn't respond, but a blush crossed her cheeks, and she immediately looked down. Instead, she followed, pretending the elf hadn't hit a nerve.

Anariel's gentle humor pricked Malin's pride just enough to snap her out of it.

"Perhaps we should harness that energy instead. Shall we begin?" Anariel gently guided Malin's hands into place.

Her touch was light but sure, like wind catching a loose thread. She moved with effortless precision, her every motion deliberate and practiced. Malin, by comparison, felt stiff and hyperaware.

"Fire magic draws on emotion," Anariel said. "Letting your thoughts wander might not be the problem. It could be the source."

Malin nodded, though doubt still clouded her. How could she wield something so volatile when she could barely keep her thoughts from circling back to him?

Malin thought back to the West Woods when she blacked out and melted the guards that were attacking them. She wanted clarity and assurances that she was in control. Anariel offered only steadiness, and Malin, for now, forced herself to adapt to that uncertainty.

Anariel adjusted her stance, voice calm. "Let your emotions guide you. Do not silence them. Channel them."

Malin tried.

She felt the sudden spark touch her palm, held at waist level, with a shock, then she willed it higher to eye level and asked it to dance like a cobra to the flute. She then strengthened her request, urging it to lighten from orange to deep red, then to blue, and finally to white. The room became like a furnace.

The fire always came when it was needed, when the fight called for it. Then, it wasn't an effort. It was instinct.

But summoning it without danger, without purpose? That was harder, but she could do it when she concentrated. She had a logical caution with fire and, having seen what it could do, she preferred to keep it contained.

Anariel's gaze lingered on the flame, then returned to Malin with a thoughtful hum. "You are steady enough. More would risk burning through the deck, and I doubt the crew would appreciate that."

Malin let the flame fade, her fingers still tingling with residual heat. "So… now what?"

Anariel stepped back, gaze drifting toward the open sky. "Now we try something less likely to set the ship on fire," she said with a slight smile.

Malin arched a brow. "That narrows it down. I think we have already established that my healing is doing just fine."

The elf's mouth twitched. "Just as some people inherit their hair color or eye color, sometimes magical abilities can be hiding in a person, which are overshadowed by other magics. These abilities stay dormant until called. I wonder what other abilities are hiding within you?" When she said this, it made her wonder if Lady Anariel was aware of the relationship between Mom and her cousin. Of course, she must, but…

"That sounds ominous. Up until a week ago, I didn't even realize anyone in my family had magic, much less a lineage of magic."

"It is not. It just means there is more in you than you realize." Anariel extended her hand. "Let me see."

Malin hesitated, then placed her palm against Anariel's. The effect was immediate.

A ripple, like static under her skin. A soft pressure in her chest. Then, something more profound. Not painful, but invasive in a way she couldn't explain. A presence, calm and ancient, moved through her as if it belonged there.

She inhaled sharply as it left her. "What was that?"

Anariel's eyes had gone distant, unfocused, then refocused. "Astral projection. I stepped into your magical center." As she did, a faint smile touched her lips.

Malin pulled her hand back, unsettled. "You could warn someone next time. That is not cool."

"You would have blocked me," Anariel said, not unkindly, but with a crooked smile and raised brow. "But you did not. Which means you are more open than you think. Maybe we should work on that next time." The matter-of-fact way she said it did not leave her sounding like she felt bad in the least for having invaded Malin's body.

"And?"

Anariel smiled, now fully present again. "Your fire is strong. Your healing is intuitive. But there is more. Something just beneath the surface. Waiting."

She paused.

"I think it is time you try levitation."

Malin blinked. "Levitation?" The word felt absurd in her mouth.

The elf nodded. "Your magic responded to it. Strongly. There is already a thread inside you, lightness. You have just never followed it. Each of the magics speaks different languages that you need to learn so that you can communicate with them; it is like learning new languages. You were able to learn fire and healing well, so now you learn this one."

Malin frowned. "I don't feel light."

"No," Anariel said gently. "Because you carry everything like armor."

Malin looked away with a grimace. That hit a little closer to the truth than she wanted to admit.

"You will need space to try," the elf continued, gesturing toward the open area near the ship's aft deck. "And trust. Especially in yourself."

That part sounded worse than the hovering.

Malin followed slowly, boots thudding against the boards. "So, what… just lift off?"

"Not yet. Let us work on lifting other smaller items before you try yourself," Anariel raised a palm. "Close your eyes. Breathe. You are not commanding the wind; you are asking it. Invite it. Feel the center of yourself loosen."

Malin exhaled sharply. "You make it sound like meditation."

"It is. With consequences."

She closed her eyes and felt how tight her jaw was.

Loosen, she told herself. Trust.

But the basket she concentrated on didn't move. Her mind raced.

She didn't feel the wind. Only the roll of the ship. The flick of sweat down her spine. The weight of everything she hadn't said.

The magic didn't move.

Not even a twitch.

Anariel said nothing. Which somehow made it worse.

Malin cracked one eye open. "Maybe it's broken."

"Maybe," Anariel said, her smile returning. "Or maybe you are still trying too hard, or your focus is on other things."

After hours of quiet repetition, sweat, and more frustration than she'd admit, the basket lifted.

Just an inch. Then two.

It hovered, just barely. It trembled slightly before lowering back to the deck with a soft thump.

Malin released a breath she hadn't realized she was holding.

Anariel, arms folded, watched from the shade. Her expression held a rare softness, touched by something older than approval. "You will be able to do this," she said quietly. "Ellie has the power, and your grandmother had it as a weaker power."

The words landed like a spark on dry kindling.

"You knew my grandmother?" Malin asked, brow furrowing, walking close to Anariel and taking a seat next to her.

Anariel nodded once, slow and reverent. "She was strong. And stubborn. Fiercely so. You inherit your healing from her."

The revelation settled into Malin like an unexpected warmth, spreading slowly across her.

There was so much she didn't know.

About her history. Her family. Her own blood.

"I knew you were friends with my mom, but... how old are you? If that's not rude to ask."

Her voice held a surprised tone, but something else, too. Something quieter. Something she hadn't named yet.

Anariel's smile deepened, unreadable. "I lose track of the years at times," she said lightly, "but I should be... three hundred and twenty-five."

Malin blinked. "Three hundred and..." She trailed off, unable to finish the sentence. The number sat heavily in the air between them, impossible to ignore.

"You don't look a day over thirty," Malin said, her tone wry but soft. "How old can you get?"

Anariel's eyes crinkled at the corners. "I have known a few that are several thousand years old. After a time, some choose more solitary lives or lives in service to nature, but we do age, just more slowly. She held the same unreadable, ageless smile.

"Thank you for telling me," Malin said quietly.

"I know why... deep down... everyone kept things from me. It still hurts. But..." She looked down, trying to breathe past the sting in her chest.

"Of course," Anariel reached across the space between them. Her hand found Malin's; it was steady and grounding. "I hope we can keep our friendship strong. Growing into not just teacher and student… but friend to friend, as I was with your grandmother and I am with your mother."

The gesture settled something inside Malin that she hadn't realized was unsettled.

She saw Anariel's eyes soften with something more than sympathy. It was something like pride. "The women of your line have always carried powerful magic," she said. "Your grandmother, your mother, you. It runs deep in your blood."

Malin hesitated, then gave a slight nod, as she began, "Since we're friends now." Her voice dropped, thick with emotion that had simmered since yesterday's revelations. "I spoke with my Mom yesterday, and I need to talk… about Aldrik. My mother just informed me that he is my *father*." The word felt foreign on her tongue. "He's your cousin. Mom says he never knew the truth?"

Malin watched Anariel's face for a clue that she might be surprised by the news, but didn't see anything. "I suspected when I saw your powers, but only confirmed the connection was true when I projected into you. I am very glad to hear it. As close as I have been to your mother and grandmother, I was never a blood relative to them. Elves believe blood connections are sacred. I'm very happy to have you as Kin'ael, or kindred soul. It is what we elves call cousins."

"Kin'ael. I like that for us."

"Elves are lucky if they are blessed with one child, as longevity does not bring large families. Any blood relation is also a closer connection to our magic. Although I have an older brother, I have no other cousins other than Aldrik. You are truly special to me."

This revelation tempered the feelings Malin had brewing. The look of happiness on Anariel's face was honest and raw.

Though quiet, her suppressed fury had tamed to angst and a raw, aching sense of loss. "My mother kept so much of who I am away from me. All those years… what could my life have been if we had known sooner?" She looked at Anariel with a look of desperation and resentment warring in her eyes. "Surely, with your wisdom, you can tell me: why?"

Anariel reached out, her hand gently covering Malin's where it rested on the table. Her gaze was profound, filled with ancient wisdom and deep empathy. "Things happen at times that they are meant to happen. Do not burden the loss of something before acknowledging that which you have gained from it," she murmured. "I know Aldrik, he will react well to this. He has dreamed of family since he was a boy. He honored your mother's wishes out of his love for her. Elven loyalty, even in matters of the heart, runs deep."

Her gaze softened. "As for why your life unfolded as it did… the world of Media was a harsh place for magic. Your mother believed she was protecting you, even if it meant a silence that caused profound wounds. I would not have made the choice, but I did not have to live with what she did. I will not hold this against her either, though I do understand your pain. A life lived in shadows, for you, felt like a life half-lived. And that is a grief no logic can mend."

Malin hesitated, then gave a slight nod. "Thank you for that. I think you may have been right… I have been distracted by several things that my brain is trying to think through. I need a sounding board. Normally, I'd talk to my best friends, Lira or Awelyn, but…" she trailed off. "And I can't exactly have this conversation with my mom. Would you mind if we go somewhere more private and talk?"

"Not at all." Anariel rose gracefully, already drifting toward the dining room. "Let's take a break. Talk over tea."

Malin followed, casting a glance back at Will. He was still training. Still beautiful. Still utterly unaware of the storm inside her.

The dining room was empty. The sun filtered through the slats of the portholes. They moved in quiet rhythm, pouring water into the ceramic teapot. Malin heated it with a whisper of fire and poured the contents into the cups. Then they sat at a nearby table, the room to themselves, and waited for the leaves to steep.

Anariel cupped her mug in both hands. "What's on your mind?"

Malin exhaled. "A few things. First... Media. We left so fast, I didn't even get to say goodbye to my best friends. I know there wasn't time, and we couldn't risk it, but... Saying it out loud now, I know that there was nothing that could have been done and we can't really go back and change it, but I do feel like a crappy friend. I guess I just needed to vent that one." As if an aside, she added, "I said something to Mom about it, but I didn't get the feeling she really understood."

Anariel only sipped her tea, listening.

Malin stared into her cup. "And the other thing is harder. I'm a doctor. I studied for years. I took an oath to heal, to do no harm." She paused, then said it aloud, the words heavier than she expected. "I killed those guards. Mom's advice was that I did what had to be done, but she was willing to keep me in the dark for years and hide important details from me about my life, so her advice is circumspect, at best."

Her voice dipped lower. "After really thinking about it, the worst part is... I'd do it again. I wouldn't even hesitate. Does that make my magic evil?"

Anariel didn't flinch. "Magic isn't good or evil. It just is. It's the person who wields it who gives it purpose. So… did you have a purpose?"

Malin nodded slowly. "I was protecting the people I love. That part feels right. But when the magic came, it was like... it took over. Like I wasn't the one in control anymore, I let it go too far. It hasn't acted like that since, but for a little while after, I was scared to use, for fear it would take control. You saw what I did in that battle in the woods."

She saw flashes of memories… the fire, the screaming, the bodies. She could almost smell the scent of burning from the memories.

"I've never seen magic act that way until that day in the woods. I didn't know you well enough to know if that was you or not, but now I know it was unusual for you." Anariel set her cup down. "I've heard stories. Rare ones. In times of great danger, magic can protect its vessel… if the vessel cannot."

She reached for Malin's hand again, her touch warm and solid. "If you say that the show of magic power that day in the woods was not you, I believe you."

"Maybe that's what it was," Malin murmured, trying to shake the memory from her spine. "It's all a blur."

"The journey ahead and the dangers you face leave a strong possibility that there will be more opportunities to fulfill that vow," Anariel continued, her voice unwavering as it cut to the heart of Malin's deepest conflict. "And next time, you cannot blame the flames, you must decide where your priorities lie."

Anariel's voice was firm now, but kind. "Your family, including me, would not have made it out of that forest without you. You weren't a monster, Malin. You were a shield. A brave one."

They fell into a quiet moment, the tension thinning just enough to let the silence breathe.

Anariel refilled their cups with calm ceremony, patient as ever.

Malin curled her fingers around the mug again, weighing her next words. "There's one more thing," she said. "It's about Will and me," Malin said, then paused, allowing Anariel to pass on the conversation.

But the elf only tilted her head, her expression filled with interest.

Malin continued. "I know we moved fast... and I don't mean Falcon Flight fast. I mean *lighting*. We've only been together a few weeks, and we're already married. I keep telling myself to judge him by how he treats me now, not by what I don't know, but..."

She hesitated, her hands tightening around the warm cup.

"When I ask about his past, he's vague. *Too* vague. It's like... the more people from his old life I meet, the more like a stranger he starts to feel." She let the words settle between them, surprised by how raw they sounded aloud.

"You need to say that to him," Anariel said gently. "He'll understand. I don't know how human males are, but elven ones? They are terrible at reading body language and worse at mind-reading, even the telepathic ones."

Malin smiled despite herself.

Anariel smiled back, then grew serious. "That being said... I noticed something else. You and Will both bear the bonding rune."

Malin's hand instinctively moved to her arm, to the mark she'd traced a hundred times without fully understanding. Her fingers trembled as they brushed it, and the contact sent a whisper of warmth up her skin.

It tingled with recognition.

Anariel let the silence stretch, her gaze full of quiet understanding. "Such bonds are a rare love indeed," she said softly. "Rare even among elves. Almost unheard of among humans."

"I've heard of it, but still don't quite know what it means," she stated. Her voice was smaller than she liked. It felt fragile and uncertain. "What happens now?"

Anariel leaned in slightly, her presence calm and grounding. "When the bond forms, it chooses you, sometimes without warning, and not always with someone you want to be with. There have been stories of enemies bonding with enemies, and even friends with friends. It hits on a subconscious level first. It begins with recognition, something you both feel but can't explain. However, when it becomes clear that you feel you are in the right place, it deepens and creates the tattoos you have. Each bond's tattoos are slightly different, though basically the same."

She gestured toward the mark she had just below her neck on the right side. "That is the sign. Your souls have begun to align, connecting your will, desire, and fate. Over time, your senses will start to overlap. You will share emotions, pain, even dreams. Eventually, you will be able to reach each other across distance. Speak, even without words."

Malin's thoughts raced. Perhaps some of what she has experienced are shared feelings, reactions that hadn't made sense until now.

She'd already felt him.

"I don't... know how to feel about this," she admitted, staring down at her arm. "It's too big. Too fast. I'm not typically the go with my instinct type of person."

Anariel's voice softened. "The bond strengthens over six months. It is a process. You don't have to make a decision today. However, you should be aware of its meaning. The closer you come to the final connection, the harder it will be."

Malin nodded, though she wasn't sure the motion meant agreement or surrender.

"There are risks you should know," Anariel added, voice shaded with warning. "Once the bond fully matures... if one of you dies, the other may not survive the separation. The trauma can be soul deep."

The words fell like stone. "Am I stuck with it then?"

"No. You can reject the bond within the specified period, but after that, you will always feel like a piece of your soul is missing, a lingering ache of happiness that cannot be filled. In some situations, this could be better than the alternative," her caring words spoke as though she had considered the tough choice.

Malin's heart still beat hard in her chest, but the panic had begun to ebb.

She looked down at the mark again, then at the bracelet once more. The tattoo cast a faint glow but was steady. It felt familiar now, less like a warning than a presence.

She wasn't afraid of it anymore.

Yes, it bound her to Will. But it bound *him* to her, too, and she couldn't think of anyone she'd rather be tied to, at least right now... with as little as she knows.

"So... the one on your neck," she said slowly, searching Anariel's face. "Does that mean you are soul-bonded to...?" She trailed off, unsure whether to say Nar or Khelek.

The question had lived in her mind like a held breath, waiting. She didn't expect Anariel to answer so completely, so quickly.

"When the bond came for me," Anariel said simply, her gaze lost in distant memories, "it came for both of them."

The words hit like lightning.

Malin stared, her breath catching.

She watched as Anariel's eyes settled. "I feel equal love for each, Nar and Khelek, in their own ways." There was no hesitation. No shame. "The depths of my feelings towards them both are immeasurable."

Understanding moved through Malin in quiet waves, unsettling and impossible to look away from. "At the same time?" As she said the words, she regretted it. "Never mind, that is none of my business."

Anariel continued, her voice a soft thread. "Elves do not have the same concerns with those feelings as you humans do. Yes. At the same time, or each on their own. I am theirs and they are mine. Elven soul bonds are more common. But with twins and multiple births… it sometimes moves differently. It claims, and it is to the claimant to decide how it will affect them."

Malin felt that truth settle under her skin.

"Two souls, two colors of fire," her voice was both poetic and precise. "They are brothers who have only had each other for the majority of their lives. Their parents were killed when they were young, and they learned early how to survive with only each other to rely on." She paused, her gaze softening as the memory stirred.

"When the bond came, they chose to share me, rather than risk the other missing a part of themselves and having to see the other with me. It is their brotherly love for each other that makes our trio so perfect."

Malin's breath caught.

"At first," Anariel admitted, a faint smile tugging at her lips, "I could not accept it. I nearly broke the connection. But... they were very persistent. Now, I cannot imagine it any other way."

The way she said it was equal parts fondness and amusement, wrapped in a moment of quiet warmth. Malin could hear in her voice that she held no regrets, only history and truth.

The image curled around Malin's ribs and held tight. She saw not just the bond but also its beauty, symmetry, and power. What she'd once viewed as dangerous and uncontrolled now seemed like something else entirely.

Possibility.

Anariel's words peeled back the veil on a world where bonds didn't suffocate or break but *expand*. A world where intimacy wasn't a threat, it was strength, unity, and willingness.

"When it happens," Anariel said quietly, "it is rare. And powerful."

Anariel's voice was warm, filling the quiet places where Malin's doubts had settled. "When it works," she said, a thread of joy woven into her words, "it is as beautiful as it is complex."

"The bond will take everything you are," she said gently, "and give you more than you ever thought possible."

Malin paused, realizing the full implications of what this meant.

She thought back to Nar and Khelek, the quiet ease with which they stood, and the unspoken rhythm between them. It wasn't just affection. It was *alignment*. Magic braided with emotion. It sounded like power without possession.

She saw how their connection with Anariel didn't diminish any of them; it *amplified* them.

It was a dance, not a chain. *But did the magic make them love each other, or did they love each other, and the love drew the magic?*

It was all so confusing. She would have to think about it. Thinking through things was what she did best.

They began the walk back to the deck with her head spinning in analysis.

Anariel's words had left Malin raw, feeling exposed. Her internal struggle was no longer hidden in shadows but illuminated by something that both burned and clarified. She stood between two selves: the woman she had been, and the woman she was becoming. Between the vows she had made and the promises she hadn't yet dared to keep.

The weight of their magically tangled lives pressed down on her. She thought of all she didn't know about him. Then, she thought of every small detail he remembered, every opportunity he gave to show his feelings, every electric touch, including their touches before the tattoos.

Then she remembered the fierce, undeniable pull he had on her, on her heart and soul. The idea that it might all be just a trick of the runes… it did seem farfetched.

Then, her heart broke with how incredibly patient and caring he was when he said, "But if you need it… If that's how this magic works… then we have that time." He squeezed her hand, his gaze locking with hers. "I love you. And I *know* this is real."

How could she face those choices when each one seemed to break the other?

The depth of it stretched out before her, both wide and uncertain. But beneath the fear, beneath the ache, something else stirred.

Determination.

Small. Fragile. But alive.

She glanced at Anariel, her voice barely above a whisper. "What if I can't choose?"

Anariel met her gaze with quiet strength. "You'll find your own truth," she said. "But only if you're brave enough to face it."

Malin turned from the railing, her steps slow at first, then steadier. Each step carried her toward him, toward the bond, the questions, the answers she wasn't sure she wanted.

But she would ask them. She just couldn't decide if she wanted to bring this to *him* before or after she had decided.

Her heartbeat was fast and hard, every step a vow.

Tonight, she needed to face the truth and give him time to think through things as well.

Hours later, in their small stateroom, she paced, practicing her words. Will had chosen to tell the children a bedtime story after she tucked them in. She heard his steps outside the door and steeled herself by smoothing the front of her tunic.

"They are loving some of the tales of my childhood. Finally, some use to those tales I've collected," he said with such happiness, it made her heart swell, a genuine, warm feeling that almost drowned out the apprehension.

"I'm glad they are getting to hear them. Maybe I'll have to join them sometime. I imagine little Will Hawkson looking just like Zee, but with a little more confidence." The image brought a weak smile to crack the concern that still weighed on her face.

He drew her closer, his arm wrapping around her with a practiced ease that seemed to dissolve the space between them. His tone softened, a low murmur against her ear as he brushed kisses down her neck. "You look upset. Is everything alright? This is our last night onboard and might be our last night in a cabin of our own, maybe we can worry about troubles another night." His touches were like a warm, gentle wave, both soothing and dangerously distracting. They threatened to melt her carefully built resolve, whispering a promise she yearned to believe, but still couldn't fully trust.

She had to force herself, but she grabbed his hand to still it as it cupped her breast, her fingers firm against his. Her breath hitched slightly at the contact, a flicker of pleasure warring with her purpose. She met his eyes, forcing herself to hold his gaze. "As much as that is an excellent argument, Will, I do have concerns, but I also had some huge information today."

"Then let me utterly *dispel* those concerns, my lady, so that we can move on to much more pressing matters," he purred, a rakish smile spreading as his thumb lightly teased her nipple.

She closed her eyes and drew in a deep breath, stilling his hand, so she could think. "First, my big news. Did you know that my mother has a boyfriend? Actually… they have a soul bond, like ours." He stilled, but didn't move his hand from her breast. "It turns out. He's not just her boyfriend. He's my father."

"That is some pretty incredible news. What do you think about it?" He touched her cheek and planted a kiss on her forehead.

"I'm really not sure what to think about it yet. He will meet us in Sarhan, so I'm guessing once I meet him, it will help me process the news." She took a deep, calming breath and closed her eyes, as his finger circled her nipple under her hand.

"I have concerns about the safety of the pirate town with the children. It was one thing when we were going to get off one ship and go straight to another… Now, we are staying inside the town at a Pirate sanctuary."

"I would never take chances with our children, and pirates are not something you need to worry about." As he said this, he chose to take off his shirt, placing it on the edge of the bed beside him. He was not playing fair, with his freshly showered smell of sandalwood and vanilla and tanned muscles inches from her. It was definitely distracting. *Was he flexing on purpose?*

She wanted to believe him, to lean into the vibrant world he offered, filled with its enticing promises and bold adventures that seemed to shimmer like distant stars. Yet, other thoughts tugged insistently at her, anchoring her in a sea of caution.

"It's just Caelum," she mused, her mind swirling with memories of her ex-fiancé, Ellie's father. He died while journeying to remote and exotic locations, much like the pirate port they would be arriving at the next day. Her smile wavered, more fragile than before, as if it might shatter with the slightest breeze. He touched her chin in response. The feeling made her close her eyes and lean into his hand.

He said with his crooked smile, looking up at her, "He didn't have *me* there, did he?"

"I don't know what I would do if anything were to happen to any of you," she confessed softly, her voice tinged with vulnerability. "Even Mom. She and I are finally starting to understand each other," she added, the thought was a delicate balance of joy and sorrow. The memory lingered, bittersweet and poignant, like the fading notes of a beautiful, melancholic melody.

Will sat on the edge of the bed and pulled her to him while she stood, his face at breast level, while he lifted her tunic slowly, giving her time to stop his hand. Her brain warned her she should continue the conversation, but her body was not stopping him, as he removed the shirt, revealing her bare body, except for her bra.

She couldn't help but smile at his arrogance, and she shoved him back, but she hadn't thought it through. He pulled her with him, and she straddled him on the bed. *That did not go as planned.*

His hazel eyes met her gaze with unwavering sincerity. "I've journeyed along this route countless times," he continued, "and I know every twist and turn." His tone was resolute, infused with a promise that lingered in the air as it heated around them. "I wouldn't allow any harm to come to any of you," he vowed, his eyes reflecting a deep, unwavering commitment. The fierce protection shining in them was like a balm to her soul, a silent promise that momentarily quieted her racing thoughts.

Realizing that this conversation would not cover the other topics if she didn't adjust the direction, she attempted to disentangle herself from him. Still, his hands were firmly on her hips and waist, making her movements grind into his increasingly prominent bulge. Her efforts made her heart pound, and it became difficult to remember what other things she wanted to discuss with him as thoughts of what would come next clouded her brain.

Seeing that her movement would make things more complicated for her, she closed her eyes and drew in a deep breath, stilling his hand so that she could think, without moving to clear her head. This raw, undeniable pull of him, even amidst the chaos of her thoughts, was a force she was only learning to name within herself. When she opened them back up and looked at him, he had such a look of amusement on his face that she almost slapped the smile off him. Instead, she chose to give in to the desire he had stoked. *He's right. Worrying right now won't stop it from happening. We will deal with it, whatever it is.*

She lay over him with one hand on either side of his head, with their stomachs touching. He ran his hand down her back. Her bra unsnapped.

"Oops. I don't know how that happened." His husky, playful tone left no doubt that he was aware of what had happened. She could feel the flush of her body responding to his game.

He ran his hands from her shoulders down her arms, pulling the bra straps with them as they slid free. "Well, at least they are out of the way now."

"I really love your breasts," he murmured, his voice was thick with emotion, as his thumb traced soft circles on her nipple as he spoke.

Malin shivered slightly at his touch, her heart racing with a mix of frustration and desire. She leaned into him, feeling the warmth of his body against hers. "I do love that you love my breasts," she whispered, her voice hoarse with emotion. She gasped with pleasure as he pulled her closer to him and placed her nipple in his mouth.

After thoroughly sucking and nipping one, he smiled, sliding her down so he could brush his lips against hers in a gentle kiss that sent shivers down her spine, her sensitive nipples scratching on the light chest hairs and sharp muscles.

The room was dim, lit only by the flickering glow of the two candles, with their wax pooling like a molten desire on the rough-hewn table. The air was thick with the scents of sweat, sandalwood, vanilla, lavender, mint, and musk. They gave her a heady cocktail that made her head spin. His hands were everywhere, rough and demanding, yet tender in their urgency.

She closed her eyes and sighed deeply, relishing the feel of his strong arms around her. She couldn't resist the pull any longer; she needed him. With a soft moan, she wrapped her arms around his neck and pulled him closer, deepening the kiss. Their tongues danced together, exploring each other's mouths in a passionate duet that left them both breathless.

She could feel the heat of him, the hard length of his cock straining against the fabric of his trousers, and it sent a jolt of pure, unadulterated lust straight to her core. They moved to lie side by side, closer to the center of the bed, so his legs were no longer hanging off the bed. They unbuttoned each other's pants and helped each other fully disrobe.

When his pants came off, he pushed her back onto the bed.

"My turn to play," he teased.

She moaned, low and throaty, as he slid his hand down her side, his fingers skimming over the curve of her hip before slipping between her thighs.

She was already wet and ready for him. When his fingers brushed and circled her clit, she gasped, her legs trembling. He chuckled, a deep, throaty sound that sent shivers down her spine. Then, he was kissing her again, his tongue plunging into her mouth with a hunger that left her breathless.

His fingers moved with a practiced ease, circling her in slow, deliberate strokes that made her hips buck against his hand. She could feel the tension building inside her, a coiled spring ready to snap, and she moaned into his mouth, her hands clutching at his shoulders as she tried to pull him closer.

But he wasn't done yet.

And then he slid a finger inside her, curling it just right, over and over until she came, her body convulsing as waves of pleasure crashed over her.

When she finally came down from her high, she was panting, her legs like jelly. He stood, his cock hard and ready. She gasped at seeing him, thick, hard, and glistening.

She dropped to her knees, taking him into her mouth with a hunger that matched his own, wanting to give him the pleasure she knew she could provide. His hands tangled in her hair as she sucked and licked at his cock, her tongue swirling around the head before taking him deep into her throat. He groaned, his hips thrusting forward as she worked him with a skill that left him trembling.

He stopped her efforts and turned her to face the wall. He teased her opening with his hard manhood and pumped. Little by little, he pushed inside, making her gasp at each thrust until he slammed into her faster and harder each time. She thought he would split her into two, but she knew it would be worth it. The pounding continued until she couldn't stop the waves. It was everything she could do not to scream, then he finished.

They collapsed onto the bed together, their bodies entwined as they caught their breath, still connected, one of his hands still holding her breast, as if stuck.

She was exhausted. They could have their talk in the morning, before they go. In the back of her mind, she knew he would do everything to keep her and the kids safe, but even he couldn't stop every danger, and she didn't know enough about the risks to prepare.

She does much better when she can prepare her contingency plans.

She had a nagging sense that he was hiding something, and she couldn't figure out what.

CHAPTER 7 – WILL

Will leaned against the rail, fingers gripping the cold metal until it bit into his skin. He'd woken early, hoping to finalize contingency plans before Malin woke and noticed his apprehension. The problem was that he didn't know what to expect. Salt spray kissed his lips, the taste sharp, bitter, like truths best swallowed quickly. Ahead, the port unfolded in a sprawl of lanterns and silhouettes, each shadow heavy with secrets. A knot twisted in his stomach, mirroring the tightening grip of his fingers on the rail.

He'd fucked this up royally.

Malin's questions echoed in his mind; the softness of her voice was threaded with worry. He'd danced around her concerns and distracted her, offering just enough to ease her fears without lying outright.

He'd told her about Lydia, the wild card, but held back the true venom: the Order of Tamris, the assassins. He knew the truth would shatter her, and he couldn't risk that, not yet, not when her fierce, fragile heart was only starting to trust him. He had to keep her safe, even from his own truth.

She was the best fucking thing to come into his life. He was smarter than this. Why couldn't he just tell her? He knew she'd see through it soon enough; he could almost feel the scrutiny of her hawk-like gaze even now. She was beautiful and relentless. When she uncovered the whole messy truth, that her charming rogue husband had assassins lurking behind every corner, ready to sink blades into flesh, how long would she stay?

Not long, if he had learned anything about her.

He exhaled slowly. Malin's strength was undeniable, a fierce shield around the warmth of her family. It was a sanctuary he wouldn't dare poison, not if he had any choice in the matter. He knew he wouldn't if he had that luxury.

He flexed his hands, easing out the tension, eyes tracing the docks as they crept closer. Too many places for danger to hide. Too many vantage points. Every creak of the ship felt like a whisper of trouble.

His plan reduced their danger by keeping him away from them in public. He would send them to the tavern and stay on the ship. That would give him a vantage point for a short while and ensure anyone after him couldn't tie him to them. He told Elowen the plan, who was going to relay it to Malin.

He was so disappointed in himself.

The big, bad Hawk, afraid of a woman.

They would be coming up from the passenger area soon, and he would see them off soon.

Later this evening, he promised himself. He would tell her when they were safe at the inn. If he stayed on board, ensuring they couldn't be traced to him, they would be safe walking through Sarhan.

He could tell her that night.

Then, if she didn't want him with her any longer, he could help her board and leave if she wished. He knew it was selfish, but it would give him these few hours of happiness; he was confident she would likely ask him to stay away and stop traveling with them once she found out.

The mask of the cocky charmer, always within easy reach, felt heavier now, harder to hold in place. He squared his shoulders anyway. Malin deserved a hero, not the hunted. But fuck if he could give her anything better than a shield built of lies and half-truths.

He pushed off the rail, with his jaw tight and gaze steady on the shoreline ahead. Danger might be waiting, and before Malin and

Ellie, his plan would always be to meet it head-on and go out with a fight, taking as many with him as he went. After all, trouble was the one thing Will Hawkson knew intimately. He had always prided himself on being other people's trouble; being the hunted was a new and unwelcome position.

The next hour of docking involved heavy labor, as injuries from the pirate attack had left the ship short-staffed. The captain stood high on the quarterdeck, barking orders, his arms raised as he directed the wind currents with his powers to assist the docking. As they drew closer, the heaving and mooring lines were thrown or levitated to secure the ship.

About half an hour after docking, he noticed Malin standing on deck, checking to make sure Ellie and Zee's belongings were together and secure. Each child carried their own bag. Her travel outfit, much like his, would allow her to blend in and hide if needed. He admired her smooth adaptation to all these changes.

With his head wrapped in black and his face covered, he was sweltering on the open deck. He encouraged Malin and the children to cover themselves similarly. They agreed but hadn't yet. The fewer people who knew they were there, the better. With his height and build, dressed in black, he imagined he was somewhat intimidating. There were times when it was an asset. He would still stand out, at least this way, they wouldn't automatically realize it was him.

He watched as Malin, the children, Lady Anariel, and the brothers prepared to disembark. Despite arriving a day early, even with the pirate attack, he needed to ensure their belongings were transferred to the Inn's secure storage for the onward journey to Qenya Stin Haven. The ship would dock in the morning, so he had to stay behind and oversee the transfer… or at least, that's what he was telling himself.

"Ellie, listen to the adults and use the invisibility on you and Zee if there are problems," he said, kneeling and pulling her into a quick hug; she leaned into him.

"Yes, sir," she took him by surprise by placing a delicate kiss on his cheek.

"Zee, you are the man in charge till I get there. I trust you to keep Ellie safe." He reached out for a hug, and Zee readily accepted.

"You're going to meet us there soon… right?" his small voice held a tremor of uncertainty.

"That is the plan," Will murmured, his voice thick with emotion. "Even with all the support, Sarhan is a pirate town. It's not safe, and after being apart for so long, even a little separation feels like too much." Zee and Ellie immediately wrapped him in a tight hug.

Anariel then drew the children away, giving him a private moment with Malin. He seized the opportunity, pulling Malin into a deep embrace and holding her close, as if imprinting her touch on his memory.

Images of that caravan replayed in his head. He closed his eyes, pushing it back to hold onto the present. He didn't want to imagine his grief if he caused any harm to her.

He pulled his face covering down, wanting her to see his sincerity. He stepped back slightly, holding her gaze. "Sparks… I know you wanted answers. Sorry, I had to leave early this morning, and I've been vague. Tonight, you'll know everything. It's only fair."

Malin's lips pressed into a thin line. She didn't quite meet his eyes, her gaze drifting past his shoulder.

Her voice was even, almost too calm. "I see."

Will's gut clenched. He knew with women that 'I see' could mean anything from 'I understand' to 'I'm meticulously cataloging your failures.' Sparks was not a typical woman, so it could mean she is simply still thinking.

He had given her *some* answers, but her silence spoke volumes. The air around her felt subtly warmer, a quiet tension humming just beneath her skin. This wasn't exhaustion; this was anger, banked and waiting. He had seen it enough times from past relationships.

He was losing her. Not to an enemy blade, but to his own silence.

He swallowed, forcing himself past the immediate issue of Lydia, into the real danger.

"I didn't mean to gloss over your concerns," he forced out, trying to bridge the chasm that had opened between them. "You should know that Sarhan is not a safe place, and while you are with me, it is even less so. Once you reach Sanctuary, find the innkeeper, Zane. You'll recognize him; he's Corben's brother, the innkeeper from the West Woods." His anxiety made him add more details than needed. "I find it curious that Zee's mom, Felicity, named him that. She grew up with the brothers; she always teased that they were like brothers to her. I'm betting she named **our** Zee after him."

He kissed her forehead.

"I remember Corben. I did some thinking too. I do think we will be fine. We aren't a band of powerless travelers. We are going with Nar and Khelek." Malin defended. "I'm going to hold you to your word. We will talk... Tonight," she said, their heads bowing together.

"I do know your strength and abilities, but it doesn't mean I like sending you to danger without being with you, by your side."

"Then you better hurry. We will meet you in the tavern. Two hours. Don't make me punish you," she said playfully, her confidence and humor a potent spark between them. He loved hearing that side of her.

His lips found hers, and his tongue traced their delicate outline. A soft sigh escaped her as her lips parted, a silent invitation he eagerly accepted. She pressed closer, her hands gripping his waist as their tongues danced in a familiar, intimate rhythm. A spark ignited between them, a heat that threatened to consume them both. He reluctantly broke the connection.

"If it wasn't so dangerous, we'd have a room of our own tonight," he growled, a frustrated sound escaping him. "You do something to me I can't even explain."

The captain called him. He was the first to release their embrace, placing a light, loving kiss on her swollen lips before securing her face covering. "Two hours."

He pulled away, their fingers lingering for a moment before breaking contact. Malin turned to the children, glancing back at him once more before focusing her attention on them and directing them to begin their walk. He watched them as they made their way onto the dock, headed towards the town.

The captain stood next to a short crew member. "Sorry to disturb you, but Mario said that there are some people in town acting suspicious." They both turned to look at the man.

"I see them pulling coverings off women and children. They're holding one of those devices that Media uses. Look there." He pointed to the far dock for another merchant ship, where three men with short hair were accosting a mother and her child. They held up a digital tablet to their faces and walked on.

Luckily, they were headed away from the path his family had already taken. Malin and the children had already reached the end of the docks.

"I'll be back." Will quickly took off down the gangplank and along the dock, toward the suspicious men. He pulled down his face covering and whistled.

When they turned, he winked and ran. Luring them away from Sarhan's thrumming docks, he darted into the narrow, shadowed alleys. Tenacious and sure, the trio followed, their heavy footfalls echoing against the stone. Their eagerness was palpable. Will drew them further, careful to keep their fury close, his path as relentless as their pursuit. He pressed deeper into the city's underbelly, his thoughts brushing past the dangerous thrill of another hunt.

Midday sun flickered through the high buildings and tight alleyways, casting shifting shadows. The labyrinth of alleys and catwalks stretched before him like an unwritten map; its twists and turns etched into memory from years of similar pursuits. Each corner brought with it a calculated decision, a risk that might lead to freedom or entrapment. Yet Will's every step was measured, a dance of confidence and cunning.

The alley, a maze of widening and narrowing passages, led him past shuttered potion shops and the ghostly outlines of once-vibrant marketplaces. The sweet scent of herbs and aged wood mingled with the sharp, metallic tang of nearby industry, creating an unsettling yet oddly familiar atmosphere.

Their shouts grew louder, charged with both frustration and determination.

Will glanced back, saw them fanning out to cover his possible escape routes. He smirked, turned sharply, and headed toward the western outskirts where the city's underbelly of corruption was in full bloom, an area he knew well.

Flashing a glimpse of himself around another corner, Will knew the guards would follow.

Past a row of derelict structures, Will slowed just enough to taunt the men with his nearness. He could sense their anticipation building, a coiled spring ready to snap. The docks were far behind, leaving only silence and shadows for company. His heart raced, not from fear or exertion, but from the sheer exhilaration of drawing them into his web.

He ducked into a narrowing passage between two warehouses, its entrance obscured by the long reach of vines and neglect. The perfect place to disappear. He pressed himself flat against the stone, listening to the closing footsteps and voices converging.

He felt the hum of danger in his veins, the whisper of violence promising its quick and perfect release. Then he was a blade slicing through air, a streak of lightning against dark stone. His arms were pure sinew, with unwavering purpose and lethal precision.

One guard's hands clawed at his throat as a crimson stain blossomed between his frantic fingers; another staggered back, his eyes glazing over as a dark bloom spread across his chest. The last man lunged, too late, and Will was already there, coiled and wrapping, a slow-breathing predator, his grip tightening like a closing snare.

The thrill, the exquisite rush of bodies in motion, sang through him as he locked the man's arm, sending his weapon clattering into the shadows.

Will pulled him close, his grip unbreakable and utterly controlled. He felt the struggle and fear tremble through the guard's frame, the desperate flailing of someone realizing how badly they'd misjudged their opponent. The bound man let out a pained wheeze, breath finally escaping after what must have seemed an eternity.

Will surveyed his handiwork for a moment, two fewer dangerous people to come after his family. The two bodies lay crumpled in widening pools, blood staining the slick alley with dark patches. He drew a long breath, felt the air fill his lungs, and awareness flooded back from the heightened edge of confrontation. He pulled a length of cord from his bag, secured the surviving guard's hands with the same practiced ease as he'd disarmed him.

A sigh slipped out, almost a grim chuckle, and he pulled the dazed man to his feet. The guard's eyes were wide, still half stunned, as Will dragged him toward the other end of the alley, away from the spreading blood and the darkening forms of his fallen comrades.

Will shouldered his captive through Sarhan's labyrinthine alleys. The air hung thick with the mingled scents of spices, unwashed bodies, and the distant tang of the sea. It was a stark contrast to the sterile air of Media. Each twist in the narrow passages was a familiar echo, a muscle memory from a lifetime of similar pursuits in this chaotic city. He navigated the uneven cobblestones. The sounds of distant music and hawkers' cries were a constant undercurrent to his grim purpose.

Reaching a chipped-blue door tucked between a spice merchant's stall and a flickering lantern shop, Will rapped out a five-beat cadence, a secret rhythm in Sarhan's noisy symphony. The door creaked inward, revealing a scarred grin that split a weathered face.

A thick, calloused, and familiar hand reached out, pulling them into the dim interior. The room was small. The air smelled of stale ale and something metallic. He noticed a single, oil-burning lamp casting long, dancing shadows on the rough-hewn walls. The center of the room held a small table and two mismatched chairs.

"Will, my friend! Good to see your face again," Homer's voice was a low rumble, the Sarhan accent thick. His eyes flicked to the captive, a silent question in their depths. "Here on business, as always, I see."

Will gave a tight, almost predatory smile. "Glad you're here, Homer. Got two bodies in the alley by the Serpent's Kiss. Need them gone."

Homer's grin widened, a flash of something sharp. "Consider it done." He moved with a surprising quietness for his size, disappearing back into the Sarhan night.

Will turned his attention to the guard, whose gaze darted nervously around the claustrophobic room. "Now, you're going to adore your new accommodations," Will said, his voice deceptively gentle. "Not quite Media's plush interrogation suites, I'll grant you. But trust me, they can be… equally effective at loosening tongues."

He gestured towards a heavy wooden door in the back wall. The guard swallowed deep. He knew what awaited him.

The adjacent room was stark. A single, bare bulb cast a harsh, unforgiving light on a bolted-down wooden chair. The air smelled of fear and old sweat. Will efficiently secured the man, the rough rope biting into his wrists.

"Let's not waste each other's time," Will began, his voice hardening. "How many others are with you? And what exactly do you know about their plans?" His first punch was a calculated tap to the jaw, a sharp warning. The guard's head snapped back, a grunt escaping his lips. A grimace touched his mouth, thinking that was all to expect.

The second punch Will delivered with his full weight landed with a sickening thud against bone, the sound echoing in the small room.

The door creaked open again, and Homer stepped back in, wiping his hands on a stained rag, his expression neutral. He nodded once at Will, a silent acknowledgment.

Their movements became a brutal rhythm, a grim dance punctuated by the guard's ragged breaths and muffled cries.

Homer's scarred knuckles, encased in brass, cracked against the man's ribs, a wet, sickening sound. The flickering bulb above seemed to pulse with each blow.

Time in the small room warped and stretched, measured only by the relentless cycle of question, blow, and the strained silence that followed. The sounds of Sarhan outside faded into a dull hum, the world narrowing to the harsh light and the suffocating tension. Will knew his window was closing; every minute he risked discovery and drew the attention of his hunters, and he needed to meet his family.

He watched the guard closely. The initial defiance in his eyes bled away, leaving only raw, pleading desperation. Shoulders slumped with each unanswered question. The man's gaze darted towards the door – a silent, futile plea.

Will felt nothing but a cold, controlled focus. His pulse remained steady, his hands calm. He could almost taste the man's breaking point on his tongue, a bitter, metallic anticipation. *You chose this.* The thought solidified his resolve. *You came after them.*

Any debt to this man was paid the instant he threatened his family. Pity was a weakness Will couldn't afford, not for a man who had forfeited his right to draw breath. Death was his only destiny; a foregone conclusion Will was simply facilitating.

"How long should we continue before we just kill him and give up on finding anything?" Homer's voice was a rough scrape, breaking the quiet with its demand.

Will said nothing, kept his gaze at the guard, who was crumbling now, breath coming in shallow gasps.

The captive finally broke, his sobs unspooling into a thread of names and numbers, plans whispered like a desperate confession.

Will listened, each word mapping new risks and rewards. He let the guard's secrets spill out, imprinting every detail with a mind trained to see connections others missed. There were only a handful of others with them, but more were expected tomorrow afternoon.

He stepped back and took a long breath. The room seemed to expand around him, the tight grip of tension easing. The bulb swung slower now, a fading metronome.

The guard slumped in the chair, more exhausted than wounded.

Homer moved in, his scarred knuckles delivering brutal blows against the guard's weakened state.

Will turned away, the metallic tang of blood heavy in the close air. He found a basin and pitcher in the corner and splashed water onto his hands, scrubbing away the crimson stain. The rhythmic thudding and the guard's ragged gasps were a grim soundtrack to his cleansing.

Then, a sudden, desperate surge of movement. A strangled cry from Homer, followed by the sickening *thunk* of steel meeting flesh.

Will spun around, water still dripping from his hands. The guard, eyes wide with manic energy, stood over Homer. His scarred grin was now frozen in a mask of death, Homer's own knife buried deep in his chest.

Before Will could fully process the betrayal, the guard lunged, desperate, fueled by adrenaline and fear.

But Will was faster. Years of survival had honed his reflexes to a razor's edge.

He moved with brutal efficiency, intercepting the guard's clumsy attack. His larger frame and superior strength made short work of the desperate man. A swift twist of the wrist, a sickening crunch of bone and sinew. The guard's knife turned against him, driven deep into his heart. The light in his eyes flickered and died.

Will stood over the two bodies, his breath coming in measured rasps. He glanced down at Homer, a flicker of something akin to regret crossing his features. "Damn shame," he murmured, his voice low and devoid of any genuine warmth. "Homer was a useful bastard. Malin's going to kill me for being late."

He knelt beside Homer; his movements were swift and practical. He retrieved a sleek data pad and a small, encrypted comms unit from an inner pocket. Then, he efficiently cut off one of the guard's fingers, used to access the equipment, and any usable currency. With the finger wrapped in the sash, he tore off the guard, and he left the building quickly, without a backward glance at the carnage he left behind.

Re-securing his face covering, he retraced his steps through Sarhan's labyrinthine alleys, his earlier grim purpose now sharpened by the need to return to the Dawn's Beacon.

He sprinted the last stretch to the docks, the familiar creak and sway of the ship a welcome constant in the chaotic city. He descended quickly to their quarters, the data pad and the guard's meager belongings heavy in his pocket. The image of Homer's lifeless eyes had already faded into the background of his brutal existence.

Will found Elowen in the captain's cluttered quarters, her posture sharp and focused as she spoke in low tones with the ship's grizzled commander. He stepped into the doorway, the lingering scent of blood and sweat clinging to him.

Elowen's sharp gaze flicked to him, initially cool and assessing. Then, her eyes narrowed, "A bit disheveled. Problems?"

"There was a complication," Will stated, his voice rough. He extended the comms unit, the data pad, and then held out his bloodied finger. "The access key."

Elowen took the items without a word, her movements precise. She examined the comms unit briefly, then nodded to the captain.

"Thank you, Hawk," she said, her tone utterly neutral.

After turning the items over in her hands, her gaze returned to him, a flicker of something unexpected in her ice-blue eyes.

"You look like shit, William," she stated plainly, her aristocratic tone unwavering even as the words hung in the air.

Will paused, not moving. The sudden levity in Elowen's eyes, that unexpected flash of something human, had cracked a more profound truth within him.

Then, a corner of her mouth quirked upward in a wry smile, and she actually winked. "And you better not tell Malin I said that either."

Will blinked, a genuine surprise rippling through him. The unexpected levity from his formidable mother-in-law was disarming.

He looked at her, truly looked at the woman who had, for decades, pulled his strings, sent him into the darkest corners of the world. A hesitant smile touched his lips. Maybe, just maybe, there was more to Elowen Neldoreth than cold calculation, or perhaps his charm was finally wearing her down.

"Understood," he murmured, a touch of amusement in his voice.

"Go clean yourself up," she instructed, her tone shifting back to a more practical note. "Malin will likely appreciate it."

"Before I go," he said, his voice rougher now, all trace of amusement gone. "There's one more thing. About Malin."

Elowen's expression sharpened instantly, the warmth receding, her gaze like ice. "What about her?"

"I promised her the truth tonight. All of it. The Order of Tamris. The assassins who are here because they're hunting me for *your* mission, for the Tomes. The ones who wiped out that caravan." His voice dropped, raw with accusation and fear. "She values honesty above all else. She's just beginning to trust me, to build something real with me. If this comes out... if she realizes the constant, brutal danger I bring to her, to the children... I will lose them. I know it." Will's jaw clenched, his knuckles white at his sides. "You needed me for your missions. You used me. Now, you will help me protect my family from the consequences of those missions. You will help me keep them. I expect nothing less."

Elowen's eyes met his unflinchingly. A profound weariness settled over her, but was quickly replaced by a quiet, determined strength. "You're right, William," she said, her voice barely a whisper, yet firm. "Their safety is paramount. And your family's loyalty is valuable."

She paused, her gaze holding him. "I don't have an immediate solution to make the issue vanish, but I will consider every resource. This is a problem we will solve. Together. I think you might not be giving her enough credit. I think you need to consider which is more dangerous for you, keeping the information from her or telling her."

Will nodded, the tight knot in his gut easing fractionally at her commitment. He knew that was the best he'd get from her. *For now.* He retreated quickly, the brief exchange with Elowen replaying in his mind. A sliver of his preconceived notions about her had cracked.

The water ran pink and brown as he scrubbed the grime and blood from his skin in the cramped sink.

Twenty years of this. Twenty years of the Resistance's brutal necessity.

He'd been seventeen when he'd first taken a life on their command, and countless others had followed that first necessary act, directives likely coming straight from Elowen.

Now, though, there was Malin. The children. It wasn't that they changed the fundamental work of ending threats, but they sharpened the focus to a razor's edge. Every enemy he'd eliminated before had bought lives. Now, the lives he fought for were the very air he breathed.

Seeing Malin again… the thought was a potent mix of longing and a fierce protectiveness.

But beneath the excitement lurked a gnawing anxiety.

He had to tell her about the assassins, about the very real danger that had followed them to Sarhan. He knew the news would terrify her, might even make her regret their impulsive marriage, might make her want to run. The thought chilled him.

He scrubbed harder, as if he could wash away the inevitable, but the truth remained, a leaden weight in his gut. He had to face her, and he had to tell her.

CHAPTER 8 – MALIN

The heavy wooden doors of the Twin Harbor Tavern slammed open with a gust of salty air, the sound echoing through the suddenly hushed room. Every head, including Malin's, snapped towards the entrance.

"A burly figure, his face grim and coat covered in dust, stood silhouetted against the midday sun before stepping into the dimly lit interior. Malin's breath hitched.

It's not Will.

It felt like an eternity had passed since Will had left, promising to be here within two hours. Without the phone she'd left in Media, time had become murky and unreliable, but the sun's lower position in the sky suggested it must have been over three hours. Maybe her worry was skewing her perception.

The time had given her plenty of opportunity to admire the look of the tavern itself, as it seemed to breathe with a life of its own. Sweet pipe smoke, thick and curling, snaked through the amber shafts of light filtering from unseen windows. Mismatched lanterns cast a warm, uneven glow on the weathered tables, their surfaces etched with the history of countless tankards and tales. The air was heavy with the mingled scents of spiced rum, rich, meaty stew, and the sharp tang of salt-cured meats, underscored by the exotic, lingering fragrance of incense burning in a far corner.

The gentle creak of the ancient wooden beams overhead and the muffled cries of gulls from the nearby harbor were a constant, soothing drone, a stark contrast to the unease churning within her. Strange items and dark, intriguing artifacts adorned the ceilings and walls, some glinting with faint, imperceptible magic, others bearing the honest scars of journeys across vast oceans.

She shifted in the semi-circle alcove booth, the worn leather creaking beneath her. Lady Anariel, on the other side, had a look of patient thought on her face. Her gaze flickered back to her children, their small hands now petting the large, orange-striped cat that had decided it was their guardian near the long wooden bar. According to Zee, the cat had never met someone who truly understood him and was immensely enjoying their conversation.

A small measure of gratitude warmed the knot of anxiety tightening in her chest at their happy entertainment.

She hadn't ordered anything, as she wanted to wait for Will. She left the barmaid a generous tip to ensure there was no ill will. The boisterous lunch crowd had thinned, leaving a comfortable lull.

Her gaze swept across the tavern's patrons. A group of rough-looking men and a petite woman with vibrant, fire-red hair were engrossed in a boisterous game. Their laughter and shouts cut through the tavern's low murmur, drawing cautious glances.

The rest of the clientele seemed ordinary enough: merchants and locals seeking respite, accompanied by several different species. As Media was all human, she'd only read about other species. She tried to acclimate herself, keeping her mind busy as she learned to identify them.

Nar and Khelek had found some elves they had met before and decided to sit with them. Lady Anariel sat in a chair nearby, seemingly lost in thought.

"So, the tall people with slightly green, thick skin are orcs or half-orcs. Right?"

"Yes. Those people are orcs, though, with thick skin, it could be a number of other species. Orcs tend to have very short tempers, so keep that in mind if you ever have any dealings with them," Lady Anariel offered, a hint of disdain in her tone.

"The very short people. Those are dwarves?"

"Not all of them. Elves can also be small; it depends on their lineage. Several forest elves are on the smaller side. I am from a line of High Elves, a descendant of the House of Trillim, in the region of Namarie, where my people, the Mellyrn, reside." She responded proudly. "Those miners at that table are dwarven. They are cunning and shrewd. I have never known a better negotiator, and their ability to craft metal and rock is almost as good as the mountain elves."

Behind the long, sturdy bar, crafted from the salvaged hull of an old ship and gleaming softly under the lamplight, stood a man whose sheer size was arresting. He could only have been Zane, Corben's twin, the innkeeper she was meant to meet.

He towered, not quite Gorek's formidable height, but taller than Will, his shoulders so broad one wondered how he navigated doorways. A shock of dirty blonde hair framed a face that held a startling familiarity, falling into his eyes as he poured three drinks at once. His wide smile mirrored Corben's, the twin she'd met at the West Woods Inn on their journey to the coast.

She'd meant to introduce herself when they arrived, but the innkeeper had been overwhelmed, and she knew proper introductions would come when Will finally arrived.

Malin's eyes kept returning to the thick wooden doors to the right of the bar. Will should have been back by now.

Things could have come up, she told herself, but the reassurance felt hollow.

But the memory of his farewell still clung to her: the desperate grip of his hand and the way his voice had caught; it felt ominous. It had felt like a final goodbye. It chilled her to the bone.

The high-ceilinged room, which had been bustling moments ago, suddenly felt vast and cold around her. The semi-circular alcoves along the walls deepened into shadowy recesses, each one seeming to harbor a fresh, unspoken fear. Even the large central fireplace, accessible from all sides, offered no genuine warmth against her growing dread.

As if summoned by her worry, the tavern door swung open again. This time, it was Will. He strode in, pulling the face covering from his features, his eyes quickly sweeping the room. Her heart leapt in a desperate, foolish flutter she tried to quell.

His quick scan halted, freezing on a woman beside the door, surrounded by a rough-looking group. Her fiery hair glowed in the flickering torchlight, making it impossible to miss her. A hush fell over the clamor of the tavern. The crowd's attention shifted palpably. The air crackled with anticipation.

The woman turned from her table, approaching Will with a predator's grace and speed. Her petite size barely reaching his chest, she wrapped her arms around his neck, pulled herself up, and planted a deep, fierce kiss on him, leaving the onlookers in stunned silence.

Malin's stomach clenched at the sight of the woman's lips on his. *Could this be the Lydia that Will had warned her might be here?* His reaction, she decided, would tell her how she would handle this.

To his credit, Will yanked her off immediately, almost throwing her back.

The red-haired woman stumbled, then delivered a sharp, low punch to his groin that made him suck in a breath.

"Let's see how your balls of steel feel with you waltzing back in here after leaving me stranded here for two years. Two years, Will!" she snarled, her eyes darkened like storm clouds, and the room was suffused with the acrid stench of something burning. "And not even happy to see me!"

The tavern noise died abruptly, all eyes on the scene as it unfolded with brutal clarity.

"Lydia. Wow," Will replied, his voice laced with careful wariness. "It's great to see you again, and it looks like you're doing pretty good for yourself." He motioned to the jewels on her arms and neck.

"I earned these, no thanks to you," she fumed. She watched his eyes look towards Malin, and then she noticed Zee, and her eyes got big as saucers. "Oh. I see what you've been up to. You had a family the whole time we were together? The boy is a little you. Cheeky bastard!"

The tavern held its breath, the tension thick. They seemed to be waiting to see how the moment would resolve.

Will's gaze shot to Malin's face, flickering between apology and tired familiarity.

The woman's eyes followed him, snapping to Malin, "You obviously ain't here for me. He's all yours. You ought to find out about him sooner than later, though, or he'll leave you high and dry like he did me," she spat toward her.

Malin couldn't blame her for being upset under the circumstances. She was glad Will had given her a little heads-up that he might encounter his ex. She had not expected this reaction, though. The way Will explained it, it sounded like he had good reason, but she only heard his side of things. That encounter suggested a far messier truth. From the looks of that encounter, there is more to the story.

Lydia motioned to her table of ruffians, and they were on their feet instantly, falling in behind her as she swept towards the door, leaving no doubt who was in charge.

The room hummed with speculation, the air crackling in the wake of Lydia's departure. The tension and the warmth improved.

Malin watched with narrow eyes, taking in the scene and its unsettling implications. Her mind worked furiously to connect the pieces, and she felt like she had walked into something far more perilous than she had anticipated.

Will visibly regrouped, shaking off the encounter, and started towards Malin. Only to be waylaid again. This time by the barmaid, her ample bosom threatening to spill from her bodice, a knowing smile on her lips. Without a word, the woman reached out and gave his crotch a firm squeeze.

"If you aren't wanting Lydia," she purred, "I've gots a room for ya, Will."

Malin heard his quick reply, "No, Suely. Thanks anyway."

The barmaid's pout was momentary, replaced by a slow smile of pure appreciation. She seemed to openly admire him as he walked away from her.

She thought of the kids, so she glanced over. They stopped petting the cat and were watching with wide eyes. Their young faces reflected a mix of confusion and curiosity as they tried to process what had just happened.

She turned back to Will. Her face was carefully blank. He was on thin ice, and it was cracking fast.

He moved toward them, his steps purposeful but slow. As he got closer, Ellie braved a wave, and Zee mirrored the gesture, albeit less confidently, yet still hopeful.

Malin could only muster a cold, unblinking stare. *What do I even say?*

Then he was there, and all her carefully constructed strategy evaporated. He hauled her from the seat, pulling her tight against him with one arm, so tight she could barely breathe. His mouth came down on hers, a hungry, immediate claim, his other hand cupping her rear, a possessive weight. Heat flooded her cheeks, embarrassment hot and stinging, as the tavern erupted in a roar of cheers and whistles.

She stiffened, her body locking in shock. She was about to kick his leg out from under him and send him to the ground, until she heard it.

"Please," his breath was a rough whisper against her lips, his grip tightening.

Please. A flicker of understanding pierced the confusion.

He was performing for the room. Likely trying to keep that rogue mask he told her about in place. A bold, outrageous game. And strangely… not an unpleasant one. *He should have warned her about this.* She would save the martial arts leverage maneuver for another day.

She'd absolutely make him pay for the public spectacle later, but for now… she relaxed. Melted into the kiss, the noise of the tavern fading. When his lips finally left hers, her mouth tingled, felt swollen, and her legs were unsteady.

As soon as she relaxed, the hooting got even louder.

Will turned, still holding her fiercely at the waist, his chest swelling. "My wife!" he boomed. He flashed a grin at the barkeep. "Zane! This rounds on me!"

The look of pride practically radiating off him made her heart weak, but that didn't mean she enjoyed the embarrassment of it all. The shouts and back-slapping continued as he finally settled beside her, drawing her against his solid warmth.

When the din had died down, she put a sweet smile on her face and raised an eyebrow, "You do know you will pay for that little spectacle… Right?"

"So worth it!" he chuckled and winked at her.

Lady Anariel stood, said her welcome to Will, then excused herself to sit with Nar and Khelek.

Alone with him, she asked, "So, what was that about? Just maintaining your notorious reputation?"

Will smiled sheepishly, showing his dimple. "Well… there was that, but I also wanted no questions from anyone in the room about who I was with."

Will's arm tightened around Malin's waist as she scooted further into the booth to make room. Then, her gaze shifted to the two kids still lingering cautiously by the bar with the cat.

"Zee, Ellie," she called, her voice soft, inviting. The two children approached the booth cautiously, their eyes wide and darting between Malin and the boisterous tavern patrons.

Will watched them, quiet tenderness softening his gaze. He stayed seated in the booth, turning slightly as they came to stand before him. Their eyes were nearly level like this, and something in his steady presence caught her off guard. It amazed her how effortlessly fatherly he seemed, even after just a few weeks of practice.

She noticed Zee shift his weight, his gaze fixed on Will, a flicker of uncertainty in his eyes. He didn't say anything, but the slight furrow in his brow and the way he subtly mirrored Ellie's leaning posture revealed his uncertainty. He looked like he wanted reassurance, but the words seemed to catch in his throat, lost in the lingering tension of the room.

Ellie tilted her head, her bright eyes studying Will with a thoughtful frown. "So…" she began, her voice carrying a hint of innocent confusion, "why did that lady kiss you? And then that other lady? Are people here just… kissier? How do I tell them I don't want them?" She looked over at Malin, then back at Will, clearly trying to piece together the strange social dynamics of this new place.

Will let out a low chuckle, his eyes crinkling at the corners as he looked at Ellie. "No, Bright Eyes, people aren't just 'kissier' here. It's… complicated." He reached out and gently took her hand, his thumb stroking across her knuckles. "That lady, Lydia, she's someone I knew a long time ago, before I met your mom. We were… close, once." He glances at Malin, a flicker of apology and genuine affection in his gaze. "And Suely… well, she's just being Suely. She's overly friendly, but I told her no, remember?"

Will then focused his attention on young Zee, leaning in close. "I know that was a bit... overwhelming back there, but everything's going to be okay. It's just a bit of my past catching up with me. It doesn't change anything about us, about our family." He offered him a reassuring wink.

Then, addressing both children, he added, "And Ellie, if anyone *ever* tries to kiss you without asking, you tell them a firm 'no,' and come find me or your mother, okay? We'll handle it if you need us to. No one gets to do that unless you want them to. Understand?" He emphasized the importance of consent in a way that felt appropriate for their age.

Looking over at the large, orange cat now lying comfortably on the bar top, Will said to the children, "So, I see you've made a new friend?"

This change of subject worked, and the children eagerly launched into a detailed description of their encounter with the large ginger cat. Their conversation was abruptly cut short by a booming voice standing beside them.

"Hawk! Leave it to you to make an entrance!" The barkeeper was just as tall as Will, but with shoulders so broad and muscular they seemed to bulge with power.

He pulled Will into a bear hug that looked like it could crush the wind from him.

"And you brought my namesake nephew with you, too! Felicity always swore she'd tell you about him one day. I'm surprised she let you bring him here, though..." His voice trailed off as he registered the shock on young Zee's face and the ashen pallor that had overtaken Will. "What's going on? What am I missing?" He glanced at Malin, realizing Will was speechless.

"Zee is your nephew? You... my closest friend for decades... you're related to Felicity?" The shock in Will's voice was laced with a raw edge of betrayal.

"What happened to Felicity? She hasn't written in a while, but that's not unusual for her. I could never figure out that contraption she sent," Zane asked, a flicker of genuine concern in his eyes.

"The city found her and her husband. The Resistance was able to get Zane out, just before… It was about six months ago. I only found out he's my son a week ago. Your sister? You helped me pick out the ring! Why didn't you say anything?" Malin could hear the fury surging within Will, hot and sharp.

"She was adamant about telling you herself, when she was ready… You know, Felicity. Corben and I were afraid to cross her. You know better than most," Zane offered apologetically.

Turning to Zee, he said, "Your mom sent me pictures of you all the time. I was so proud when I heard she'd named you after me. She always said the guy you knew as your dad was fantastic, took you to all those ball games, and played every game imaginable with you." He knelt and placed a large hand on the boy's shoulder.

"I… I think I remember seeing some of those pictures. They were by her bed. I asked her who it was, and she said it was my Uncle. Wait… does that mean the innkeeper outside Media is my Uncle, too?" Zee asked, his brow furrowed in thought.

"Yep. My twin brother, Corben. And there are four other older brothers, over in Gosual, near the East Draco Mountains…. I am so damn glad to finally meet my only nephew." He stood and turned back to Will, "And I'm just as glad to finally tell *you*. It's been killing me to keep it in."

"Stew for everyone!" Zane boomed, waving to the barmaid. "Any nephew of mine is probably starving after that journey." He clapped young Zee on the back, a little too hard, making the boy stumble slightly, but Zee's face was becoming more relaxed.

"And speaking of journeys," he continued, turning to Malin with a mischievous glint in his eyes, "you wouldn't believe the trouble this one," he gestured to a visibly stunned Will, "and I used to get into. We met on the *Qenya Stin Haven* when we were just pups, barely thirteen. That whole summer was one disaster after another, but by the gods, it was fun!" He chuckled, shaking his head. "Remember that time with the fermented fruit and the Captain's prize parrot, Hawk?" He winked at Will, clearly trying to inject some much-needed levity into the tense atmosphere.

"I don't think anyone needs or wants to hear about that," Will offered, his faint blush an apparent attempt to shut down the conversation.

"On the contrary," Malin interjected with a raised eyebrow and a playful smile. "Please, Zane, do go on. I'm *dying* to hear some of these stories. Will can consider it partial payment for earlier," she finished with a playful smirk.

The barmaid arrived then, skillfully maneuvering a large tray laden with steaming bowls of stew and thick slices of bread. As the savory aroma filled the air, Ellie scooted around the booth to sit next to her mother, with Zee settling in closely beside her. Zane, the barkeeper, took the seat directly across from Will, his wide grin promising a treasure trove of embarrassing anecdotes.

For the next hour, Zane's booming laughter and Will's occasional, frustrated sighs punctuated the tavern's low murmur as the barkeeper regaled them with tales of their shared youth.

Malin listened intently, a genuine smile touching her face as she caught glimpses of the younger, perhaps wilder, man Will had been.

Zane was launching into a particularly outrageous story about a stolen fishing net and a very angry dockmaster, his laughter echoing through the tavern. Ellie and young Zee were giggling, their earlier unease seemingly forgotten in the face of these colorful tales. Will alternated between groaning theatrically and a small, genuine smile that softened the lines around his eyes.

But as the laughter and boisterous storytelling filled the air, Malin found her thoughts drifting.

This Will, the mischievous boy who'd sailed the seas and brewed questionable concoctions, was a far cry from the dangerous rogue she'd glimpsed before.

He was also different from the reserved, watchful man she'd first met in Media, burdened by secrets and a survival instinct. Yet, beneath the playful exterior, she still saw glimpses of the fierce loyalty and protectiveness that had drawn her to him.

The comfortable camaraderie between the two men and the genuine affection he showed towards the children felt real and undeniable. But the layers were becoming more complex, the facets of his past more numerous than she'd ever imagined.

Who is this man I've married?

A swirl of confusion and a strange, burgeoning affection stirred within her. The answer, she suspected, was far more intricate and intriguing than she could have ever guessed.

The tavern's usual chaos quieted, a ripple drawing her gaze to the doorway. A figure stood there, casting a long shadow. It was her mother, but… unlike anything she had ever seen. This wasn't the cloaked Chancellor. This hardly looked like her.

Tight, tailored leather clothed her, moving like a second skin.

Her silver hair, usually bound up, was a cascade of intricate braids, framing a face that looked younger, stronger. She looked fit, toned, utterly unlike the woman Malin had known all her life. This was not how he left her on the ship.

When she heard her mother was the leader of the Resistance, this was what she had expected. But the idea that the two were the same person was difficult to comprehend.

The locals were staring. Perhaps Mom didn't realize what a dangerous place this was. Malin considered asking Will if he could provide her with some protection or a display of force.

Before she could, a drunk man made the mistake of grabbing her rear as she walked by. Her mother's movements were so quick that Malin almost missed them.

With one hand, she grasped the hand on her rear and squeezed. With the other, she placed a strategically aimed punch to his throat. He immediately released her, grabbing his throat. She continued walking as if nothing had happened.

She could hardly believe what she had seen. Could this be her mother? She looked over at Will, his jaw slack, eyes wide. This was unexpected to him as well.

When her mom got to the table, Will's voice caught as he said, "Zane, I'd like you to meet my new mother-in-law, or as you might know her, Elowen, the leader of the Resistance in Media."

What was he thinking? That information wasn't supposed to be shared with just anyone? Was it?

"Ms. E!" He was on his feet, moving fast, and then he hugged her with a full-on bear hug, picking her up off her feet.

With Will's wide eyes, Zane's reaction wasn't what she or Will expected.

The moment stretched... then was shattered by a loud crash near the door. The same drunk had sent a barmaid's tray clattering to the floor. Zane flushed, offering Mom his seat. She smiled warmly and genuinely, kissing his cheek and adding a quick hug before he hurried away.

"Rooms? How many?" he asked, looking back.

"I'm staying elsewhere, but they need two rooms," Mother said, her voice clear and authoritative. *At least her attitude hadn't changed.*

"You got it, Ms. E." Zane nodded as a fight broke out on the other side of the bar. "I'll take care of it and drop your keys off to you. It appears I've got work to do. I'll talk with you later."

With that, he headed to the fight. His presence alone quelled most of the commotion, and he knocked the instigator out with one hit to the jaw. With broken tables, mess to clean up, and patrons to tend to, it didn't look like he would be back anytime soon.

"I found three Media enforcers on the docks. They were looking for a woman and a child," Will said calmly, looking at her as he said it.

"What if they followed you or came in here? Are they still out there? Should we be concerned about more?" Her eyes widened, sweeping the tavern for more hidden faces.

Will placed his hand on hers, his touch a comfort. She met his eyes as he added, "They are not an issue anymore. I was able to get one to admit that there are more coming tomorrow. As long as we board before midday, we should be fine."

What did he mean, they weren't an issue? The realization hit her.

She pulled her hand away. "You mean… You killed them?"

"Yes, but they would have been an issue for us if I hadn't, and I needed to find out how many more were." His calmness was calculated. *Who could say such a thing so casually?*

"Malin. You know it was necessary. I appreciate you keeping our family safe," Mom said, patting Will's hand.

What kind of reality had she stepped into? Her mom didn't see any issue with the casual discussion of killing people.

She noticed her mom looking around the room, then a smile bloomed on her face, almost glowing. This had to be another dimension. Her mother simply did not get doe-eyed looks.

Then she noticed Will's face. He had turned away, seeming hurt by her words. She reached over and touched his hand, drawing his eyes to meet hers.

"Yes. I know. I'm sorry to overreact. It's all just so new to me." She placed her hand in his again. "I do appreciate you keeping our family safe," she said, her smile genuine. This brought a smile to his face, and he sat up, shoulders squaring slightly.

"You aren't staying at the inn?" Will asked her mom. "Would you like an escort to your next location?" He offered.

"That will not be needed. My friend is here to escort me." Mom gave a sly smile, her gaze drifting towards a striking, tall man sitting alone at a table in the corner. His silver hair gleamed in the candlelight, a stark contrast to his all-black attire.

Friend? Did she mean her father? Her mom uncharacteristically fingered the hem of her vest, her eyes darting to him with a flush in her cheeks. It had to be the man her mother had spoken about on the ship. Her real father.

She hadn't realized she would meet him so soon.

CHAPTER 9 – MALIN

Malin touched her hair, realizing that it was likely out of place, not the look she had hoped for when she met him for the first time.

Malin asked, her voice hesitant, "Do you think… I… could meet him?"

The man rose from his table and walked towards them, a broad smile on his face, though she noticed he smoothed the same place on his vest multiple times. *Maybe he was as nervous as she was.*

"Yes. I do think that would be a good idea," Mom said warmly.

As he approached, they all stood. Malin held onto Will for strength, noting her father was tall, almost as tall as Will.

She'd only known about this for a short time, but she'd been wondering what kind of man he would be.

She thought she noticed something strapped to his legs, but they blended almost perfectly with the all-black outfit; she couldn't tell what it was.

When he approached, he wrapped his arm naturally around her waist, with a look that spoke of hunger. "Ael'an. Del'an sil'en nandor," he said, as he drew her into a passionate kiss, then released her, leaving her flustered.

"I would like to introduce you to Lord Aldrik Rauno of the House of Trillium, Former General of the Merlyyn." Mom's tone held a note of… something. Amusement, or was that giddiness? Was her mother nervous?

Malin had never seen her mother nervous, making it hard to identify the feeling. Then again, with butterflies in her stomach, Malin felt somewhat anxious about it herself. She told herself it didn't matter what he thought, but… the little girl in her worried he wouldn't like her… that she wouldn't be enough.

"Aldrik, I'd like you to meet the family," Mom, composing herself, gestured gracefully. "First, I'd like you to meet Ellie and Zee, the grandkids." Ellie offered a small, polite wave, while Zee gave a quick, almost imperceptible nod.

"This is Will, the new son-in-law, and of course… Malin." She motioned to each of them in turn.

As the man drew closer, his height was commanding. He first extended a hand to Will for a handshake. As their palms met, Malin's eyes watched from beside Will and quickly scanned his features. A deep scar bisected his cheek, stark against the sharp angles of his smooth face, framed by long, wavy brown hair pulled back with a tie. The scar didn't detract; instead, it lent him a rugged, formidable edge. Not at all what she expected.

A strange sensation washed over her. The constant hum of magic within her had stopped. *Could that be him doing that?*

Ellie climbed out of the booth to stand by her, tugging on her shirt.

"It is lovely to meet each of you finally," Aldrik said, his voice a smooth baritone as he grasped Malin's hand and pressed a kiss to the back of it. His touch was warm and comforting, his olive skin a contrast to her own paler, though tanned, hand.

"I was beginning to think she was going to keep me a secret. I've heard a great deal about Ael'an's girls for a long time. I was pleasantly surprised when I received the message that she would meet me here and that I would be joining you on your trip to Aloria. You wouldn't believe how happy that makes me." A genuine warmth filled his tone.

When he met her eyes, she noticed that his eyes were very similar to the violet hue of Lady Anariel's eyes.

"Will, do you think you could get the kids upstairs. They look tired, and I have a few things I would like to discuss." Her mother asked.

Lady Anariel must have been watching, as she appeared at her father's side. "Kin'ael. So nice to see you again." She said, as they clasped hands and touched foreheads in greeting.

She then looked to her and said, "I am happy to get the children prepared for sleep and watch till you come, if you would like." Her smile and honest offer made Malin's shoulders relax. She had been hoping Will would be here for this.

As if instinctively knowing what she needed, he moved behind her and placed his hands on her shoulders, providing the strength she craved.

"Thank you," she said, then turned to the children. "Kids do what she says and get some sleep. We have a long day tomorrow." She kissed and hugged each child, and then Will did the same.

Ellie allowed Aldrik to kiss her hand, but Zee quickly stuck his hand out for a handshake, making his preference clear. The kids then followed Anariel dutifully as they went out of sight.

When she knew they were entirely out of range, she said, "Aldrik, I know you don't know me, and I just found out about you, but… as you'll learn, I'm a very practical person, and I've had more than enough chaos in the last month. I'm nearing my breaking point of speaking in my mother's political ways… Politics was never my strong suit." She blurted the words out before fear could temper them. "I found out today that you are my father. Lady Anariel had to astral project into me earlier, and she confirmed. I am your daughter."

She could feel Will's grip on her shoulders tighten. Aldrik's face paled, as did her mother's. It didn't look like her mom had counted on her bluntness tonight.

The surprise was strong in his voice, but he managed to keep a smile on his face as he asked, looking at her mom, who could not meet his eyes. "What?"

The tone of her mother's voice changed to a higher pitch as she interrupted, "I wanted to tell you in person. It wasn't something I wanted to say telepathically. I suspected when I saw her powers were like yours. I was going to tell you tonight." Her face was ashen, her shoulders slumped as she spoke, her gaze fixed on the floor.

This was not the Mother she knew: not the Chancellor of the High Council, not the Resistance leader she was getting to know, and certainly not the woman who had nearly dropped a man just moments before. It had to be because of Aldrik. *What kind of man is he?*

He patted her hand but didn't take his eyes from Malin. With a stern tone aimed at Mom, "We will discuss this tonight. We cannot change the past, and I won't let this affect my future." Then, his tone shifted to one of warmth and affection, a smile breaking out on his face, revealing his bright white teeth. "I have a daughter. That has been a dream I gave up on decades ago. I will not let past choices interfere with my future happiness."

So far, he was saying the right things.

"I'm very glad to hear that. I currently have one parent who I now know isn't even my parent, and another who's gone to great lengths to avoid me for most of my life. I've only recently gotten to know her, though she has been doing everything she could to try to mend things… and it has been appreciated… I hope we can start over." She motioned to the booth in the alcove, "Care to join me for a talk?" She sat on the side closest to her, making room for Will to join beside her.

She tried to get comfortable in the seat, but couldn't until Will draped his arm over her shoulder protectively. She felt the tension in her shoulders drop with his presence.

Mother slid into the booth delicately, making room for Aldrik at the end. The color had still not returned to her face, but she seemed more composed.

"I can't say that I knew about this, though once I heard you had received flame powers, from her recent messages, I began to suspect. Getting Ana… I mean, Anariel… to use her powers to confirm was one of my ideas to verify. I'm glad to hear she used it independently. Ana's confirmation aside, this direct line of questioning is starting to make you sound even more like my daughter, as I know you didn't get that personality trait from Ael'an." His deep baritone voice carried a swell of happiness that made it clear the news was precisely what he'd been hoping for.

"I am more than happy to be as direct and open with you as you feel comfortable. The idea of having a child in my life, much less a grandchild, means more than you can possibly know. I love this woman more than I thought I ever could, but politics are not one of my favorite traits about her," his face glowed with feeling as he spoke.

As he said it, Mom's lips grew thin and quivered, and he gently caressed her cheek, yet smiled. "I have used my nullifying powers, so she cannot have conversations without me. I'm sure she is upset that she cannot complain to me about this either, with you listening, but this… is an important conversation, and once she has gotten over her initial feelings, I am sure she will understand."

Malin was in awe of his candor. It was far better than she could have hoped for.

"Ael'an. Why don't you tell 'our daughter' about me?"

Before she could speak, Malin spoke up, "What does Ael'an mean?"

"Ah! Noor'wyn. That is Elvish for my soul love." He smiled a crooked smile at her mother that drew a reluctant smile back from her. She raised her eyebrow at the new word. He smiled and continued, "Noor'wyn... Well... the direct translation is hard. It is more like my blessed light. It is commonly known as my daughter." The smile on his face was contagious, revealing his bright white teeth.

She mouthed the words, entranced by the idea.

"I've spent much time in Lumara, the Moon Spire city, with the High Moon Elves, making the language second nature."

"It's beautiful," Malin expressed with a smile.

"I told her some of our past on the trip, but I think she would prefer hearing it from you," Mom added.

"If I go over something you already know, please let me know, so I don't ramble. I'm a bit excited," he offered. "I've known your mother since I was a little boy. With an eight-year difference, I didn't pay much attention to her. She was quite a little minx, getting into trouble everywhere. She would run to me to protect her, so I taught her how to fight."

It was then that she noticed his ears. They weren't the sharp points of an elf, nor the rounded shape of a human. She must have been staring too intently, because Aldrik touched his ear and offered a wry smile. "Yes. I'm only half-elf. I assume you know that Lady Anariel is my cousin. That is why she called me Kin'ael. That is a Kindred soul, the traditional word for cousin or family."

"I'm sorry. I didn't mean to..." she apologized, feeling a flush creep up her neck.

"No. It's fine. It tends to come up eventually. I guess that means you are part Elven also," Aldrik replied, his expression open. He continued, "As most young men do, I went off in search of adventure and found it in abundance, and for many years, I was satisfied with that life."

"Ana asked me to travel with her, as Nar and Khelek had some matters to attend to. When I came back, a chance encounter, and our connection was electric. She was recovering from the loss of her baby, crying under a willow tree at the family estate outside of the city." Mom and Aldrik's eyes locked, their connection intense, as if both were reliving the memory.

"I was taking a walk and heard her cries and came to investigate. That brave little girl I had taught to fight was hurting, and I couldn't do anything to help." He touched her face tenderly. "That electrical touch hit us both, like a lightning bolt from the heavens, and I couldn't live without her. She was much more pragmatic than I, and I had duties to perform for the King. I tried to get her to come with me, but the Resistance needed her just as much as my Kingdom needed me. Feelings were there, but duty was stronger."

Tears rolled down her Mom's face. Malin could never have imagined seeing her in such a vulnerable state. What was it about this man that caused such a drastic change in her mother?

He turned to face Malin. "As you said, we are practical people, so hopefully you see that we cannot curse what we missed in the past. Instead, we should focus on the future we can have. I have always wanted a child, and I am at a point in my life where I can be a part of it. The peace accords have been solidified, and there have been years of peace between the two kingdoms. Battle plans have shifted to politics that I despise, so I relinquished my role to another. I am free to join you."

A stifled yawn touched Malin's face as she added, "I'm finding that destiny has plans for us, and it seems everything is working out, not necessarily in the order we wanted, but in the order we need. I look forward to getting to know you better on this trip. I am already seeing where I might get some of my personality traits."

As she said this, Will brushed his thumb on her jawline with the hand resting over her shoulder. She looked over at him to see him looking at her, his eyes wide, staring at her. It flustered her, and she took a sip before continuing. "Do you have any questions for me?"

"I have so many questions, but in my world, actions speak louder than words. My questions will be answered over time. Ael'an has kept me updated on your events, graduations, your work as a doctor, the birth of your daughter, and her powers. I was amazed to hear about your powers manifesting in last week's message." He reached out to place his hand on hers resting on the table.

"It means so much to me that you are willing to learn about me. It's all I could have hoped for. I would understand if you'd like to wait on telling Ellie, though being able to have a grandchild in my life is more than I ever could have hoped for."

"I will tell her about it in the morning. She deserves to know you fully, no secrets." She spat out the words, 'no secrets,' her chin lifted as she stared at her mother.

"Agree. No secrets," Mom nodded, drying her eyes.

Malin lightly nudged Will, signaling she wanted to get out of the booth. He helped her up when she scooted to the end.

"It has been quite an emotional day, and you are right, actions do speak louder than words. I look forward to learning more about you, but so far, I am finding that you are everything I could have hoped for and more." The joy she felt in that moment was intense. She couldn't hold back the broad smile on her face.

When Aldrik stood, he reached for her hand. She awkwardly let him take it, then, on impulse, pulled him into a hug. She could feel his deep, satisfied breath as he wrapped his arms tighter around her. When she pulled back, she noticed tears of happiness that matched her own.

She looked over at her mother. Emotion shone openly on her face. This was not the mother she was used to, but she seemed much closer to the mother she had always wished for.

Malin pulled her into an equally deep hug, adding quietly to her ear, "I'm still not happy about how things happened, but he's right. I could focus on your poor decisions, even if they were made with good intentions, or… I can focus on those good intentions and expect you to work on making better decisions in the future."

She released her and stood by Will's side. Aldrik reached out to Will for a firm handshake, after which Will placed an arm around her waist.

"It's getting late. The ship is expected to dock by dawn, and we should attempt to board as quickly as possible. We can meet you for breakfast, before we go," Mom stated.

"Agree," Will said.

"In the morning, then," Aldrik added.

Her gaze met her Mom's for a fleeting second, a hint of a smile on her lips before she turned. As she watched them leave, she saw Aldrik pull her hand to his lips and kiss the inside of her wrist, then pull her close and swat her rear. This man was utterly unlike what she could have ever imagined and nothing like the man she grew up thinking was her father."

It was time to go. Time to process everything this day had thrown at them.

She was almost giddy as they walked to the room. Will kept her close.

"I like your father," he said to fill the silence.

"I do too." She paused in thought for a few steps, then said, "Noor'wyn. Have you ever heard Elven before? It sounds so beautiful," she asked.

"I know some Fae, a few words in Orcish I can't repeat in front of children, and some trading terms in Dwarven and Goblish. Elven, especially High Elven, is not easy to learn. I might be able to figure out some of what they're saying if I heard it, since Fae is a derivative of it, but no, I wouldn't say I know Elvish," Will explained. It is one of the most beautiful languages I've heard, second only to the sirens—though luckily my deaf friend, Trager, dragged me out of there."

After hearing that, she couldn't help but give her most 'I'm impressed' look. When they reached the door, he held it open for her.

Anariel was sitting at the small table, waiting patiently. "Is all well?" She seemed to be honestly concerned.

"Yes," Malin said with a chuckle. "All is well." She noticed Anariel's shoulders relax at the news.

"I am grateful." She stood by Malin and faced her. "When Elven families part, the traditional greeting is to touch foreheads. Do you mind?" She asked Malin.

"I would love that!" Anariel's face beamed at her response.

Anariel came close to Malin and leaned her forehead, so they touched for just a moment.

"Peace be well. See you in the morrow," she smiled brightly as she walked to the door.

"Peace be well. See you in the morrow, Kin'ael." Malin earned an even brighter smile at that, then Anariel closed the door behind her. Leaving her to wonder if Will would explain his bizarre behavior on the ship or finally tell her what had seemed so important.

CHAPTER 10 – WILL

When the door closed behind Anariel, Will knew it was only a matter of time. He had promised Malin answers, and she thoroughly deserved them. She was brushing her hair on the bed, finishing the night routine that had become so familiar over the past couple of weeks. No flicker of an eyebrow, no subtle tightening of the lips: her face was a perfect, unreadable canvas.

Although he could hope she had forgotten, the chances were good that she hadn't. With the children in the room, he couldn't exactly distract her again either. He had been planning out the conversation all day in his head, but he wanted both of them to be focused on it, so he decided to wait until they both finished getting ready.

Looking around the room, it was small but reasonable. Nicer than the last room Zane gave him two years ago. The air was thick with the scent of salt and damp wood, lightly illuminated by the flickering glow of a single oil lamp on the bedside table closest to the side that Malin had already claimed. Two small cots had been set up near the foot of their bed, and he could hear the even, soft breathing of Ellie and Zee as they had already drifted off to sleep.

He checked the latch on the door, just to be sure. The sounds from the boisterous tavern below were already fading into a muffled hum as business slowed. He took a few minutes to clean and sharpen his knives, as they had been used that day. With everything put away and ready for bed, he lay next to her in the small bed. It was so small that, as expected, his feet hung over.

He placed a folded, worn canvas on the empty side table on his side of the bed. He sat on the edge, admiring Malin's back. *Even in the dim light, the curve of her back was elegant, a silent promise of the warmth he craved.* He had slept in worse places, but none so fraught with the weight of impending honesty. He took a deep breath, steeling himself. It was time.

Malin turned to face him, and her gaze grew serious. He was preparing to start the presentation when she held his hand between both of hers. "Will," she began, her voice low and earnest, "I learned something about our runes. We already figured out they are soul-bonds, but I discovered more about them from Lady Anariel. Nar, Khelek, and she are bonded."

He had his suspicions about the tattoos that had formed on them both, magically, the night she gained her powers. Bonding runes were uncommon, but he never knew humans could get them.

He frowned. "What did you learn?"

She hesitated, her thumbs tracing circles on the back of his hand. "It's… more than just a feeling. The runes form a profound, magical connection. It creates an intense feeling of attachment." Her ice-blue eyes looked like they were searching for something in his. "It's possible… that what we're feeling… the strength of it… The magic itself might amplify it. It is possible that we aren't feeling it at all and it's all magical influence."

He must have been imagining her saying that. It was absurd that these feelings weren't real.

"I can't believe you would even wonder if this was real, or just the magic. We didn't have the tattoos in the nightclub, and I know how I felt about you on that taxi ride. I know how I felt about you when you called to tell me after Andrew had attacked you. Those feelings, the depth of what I feel for you, are not only caused by magic," he blurted out, feeling his heart flip-flop in his chest.

He reached up, cupping her cheek, his thumb brushing lightly against her skin. "Malin," he said, his voice rough with a sudden urgency, "I cannot believe this is artificial, but if it is or not… **You are my religion, and I'm your servant:** you and these kids.

I don't ever want to be separated from you." Then he remembered the Order of Tamris, and added, "Ever… unless you decide you don't want me. The thought of a life without this family is a bleak and empty landscape that I can't bear to think of living in it."

What could he have done differently to show her how he felt? How real this was?

Malin's brow furrowed as she added, "We do still have a choice in things," she said, as she stared at their joined hands. "Lady Anariel said… there's a period of about six months before the bond fully anchors. Then it becomes irreversible. If we were to try and sever it after that…" A visible shudder ran through her. "The repercussions could be… devastating. For both of us."

"I don't need any timeframe. I would brand myself yours right now, magic be damned." He spoke from his heart. "I didn't take those vows at the handfasting lightly. When I make a promise, I keep it."

The faint smile on her face gave him hope, as she looked up at him, with eyes welled with tears. He took a deep breath. It was now or never. He must come clean with her.

"With all that said, there is more you need to know before you make your decision, and it makes this that much harder for me to say. I promised you answers. Before I give them, I would like you to understand better the journey we have in front of us."

He unfolded a large, blank canvas square, smoothing it flat until it filled most of the end of the bed. He smoothed the creases carefully with his palm. Withdrawing a coin from his pocket, he placed it on the top left corner. Instantly, lines and colors erupted from the coin, spilling across the canvas and filling every inch with vibrant imagery, causing Malin to take a sharp intake of breath.

He loved it when it did that.

"It's a cloaking spell. It took me a while to find a vendor who could do it, but it's well worth it. Without the coin, it is just a folded, blank canvas."

It had been a while since he had it laid out in full like this. It had taken him years to hand-draw, but this map had saved him more times than he could count. With a thick wax coating and countless hours of meticulous documentation, it was a one-of-a-kind map.

The canvas was worn thin at the folds, marked with symbols and routes that brought a sharp tug of memory to his chest. He had started building this back when he was sailing the Qenya with Corben and Zane. He added Resistance routes, civilizations, tribes, and hideouts. This map contained highly sensitive information for both sides, and no one on either side knew it existed… until now.

"It took me decades to put this together. Media is here in the Northern Hemisphere of the world," he pointed to the top middle of the map. "We are traveling to Aloria, in the Southern Hemisphere. We haven't even gotten halfway yet, as Sarhan is only halfway to the middle. There are lands on each side of the waters, and we must pass several dangers to get to the safety of the Alorian city." Each place he referenced, he pointed towards.

"What are these other cities?" Malin asked as she hesitantly traced the edges of the old map.

He leaned closer, his arm brushing hers. He felt a jolt of awareness spark between them even in this mundane moment, and he was suddenly conscious of the points of her nipples under her linen top. "That one there, southwest of Media… that's Fellspire Citadel." He pointed to the mountain peaks that dominated the left side of the map. "The old guard from Media fled there after the city's liberation. It's a fortress. Getting in or out is a death trap; the city *is* the mountain." There was a wry twist to his lips as he remembered the one time he'd had to infiltrate it. "It took me weeks of planning to get in there, last time."

Malin's brow furrowed. "So, they're still holding onto the old ways? Slavery?"

"Oh yeah. Bitter as ever, from what I hear." He tapped another point on the map, far to the east. "And that's Lumara. It's the Elven city of the High Moon Elves that your father talked about. Beautiful place, I saw it from a distance on a scouting mission. The whole place glows. We would need to have Elven emissaries visit, though perhaps your father could arrange for us to get in… They mostly keep to themselves. They don't like to get involved in human squabbles."

He could see from her eyes that the enormity of the trip finally reached her as her eyes widened.

"This map…" He trailed off, his voice rougher now. "It's got things on it… hidden coves, trails through the passes, settlements that aren't on any official charts. I've risked my life for decades to build this. There are Resistance safehouses and outposts, where one can go to obtain help, codes, and Dangerous knowledge—the kind of information that has gotten men killed. This is why I have the highest success rate of all of the Resistance Transporters. I know this route better than anyone."

Will's fingers traced a route from the port of Sarhan across mountainous terrain to a point marked with a subtle spiral symbol. "Aloria," he confirmed. "Where Ellie can learn to control her abilities properly. Where we can all live without worrying about the city putting a suppressor in us." His voice softened almost imperceptibly. "Where we might find something like peace. I've never gotten past the port, but I've taken more people there than most."

"I show you this to hopefully prove to you that I have taken this journey many times. I know the dangers. I'm prepared for contingencies."

He tilted her chin to look directly at her. "Your safety means more to me than I could have ever dreamed. I would never purposefully put you in more danger than we are already in, given we have the city of Media's special forces and pirates after us with an already difficult journey we must make, but..."

She raised her eyebrow at him, waiting for him to continue.

"I can't protect you from the chance we'll run into more of my past relationships, as I was not a monk before you graced my life," he flashed her a crooked, disarming grin in hopes it would lessen the next blow.

"As I am starting to gather, you may have been the farthest thing from a monk I have ever met," she scoffed, though a hint of amusement played on her lips.

"Consider it all research," he countered with a wink. "I'm a one-relationship kind of guy now, though. You and these kids? That's my whole damn world."

"Besides," he'd add, a confident grin spreading across his face, "all that 'experience' was just extensive training in pleasing my *one* woman. And I trust you'd agree my skills are being put to excellent use?"

She smiled and blushed. He loved to make her blush, but he knew now was not the time. He took a deep breath to prepare, then let it out.

"A couple of years ago, I stole something for the Resistance, at your mother's orders. It originated from a group of religious zealots, known as the Order of Tamris. They found out it was me and are now after me. They are assassins and they are dangerous."

The words hung between them. He waited, but it felt like a weight had lifted off of him. It was out there. He had said it. This pause while she thought was going to kill him almost as much as his worry about saying the words, but he would give her as much time as she needed to think. Waited for her to go off on him about putting their lives in danger. Waited for her to decide she couldn't put up with it and tell him to leave in the morning.

The silence stretched, punctuated only by the gentle breathing of their sleeping children. Minutes of silence ticked by before she spoke, punctuated by a deep breath before her verdict.

"We already have a whole city after us. Is this that different? I've been spinning around in my head why you acted so concerned about this. I'm sure there must be some difference, but I can't see it." She caressed his arm idly, rather than pulling away as he expected.

That was not what he was expecting her to say.

"What?" He was at a loss for words. Where was the venom or fear that the others from his past hit him with?

She repeated the question more slowly.

"That is a fair question," he said, looking away. His gaze drifted to the intricate carving on the stateroom door, anywhere but her face.

Her jaw tightened, and she took a slow breath as she thought.

In almost a mumble, he responded, "I... I've known about them for a while. The whole time, actually." He swallowed, the back of his throat suddenly too dry. "I didn't tell you because I didn't want to upset you about the dangers of the journey any more than you already were," he said finally, voice rough. "But the truth is... I didn't trust that I wouldn't lose you if you knew. Everyone I've ever loved—truly loved—left once the danger that always seems to follow me became real. Or they died because they didn't leave fast enough."

He continued, "Felicity left with my son before even telling me about him because she didn't want our child to grow up in fear. I can't blame her. I have thought I was cursed since the night my family was killed. Like me being near them had caused them to get caught. Like it was safer if I kept people at arm's length. Here

I am doing exactly what she worried I would do. I am putting my son in danger by being near him."

"You thought I was like everyone else?" Malin's voice cut like flint.

He flinched. "You're more than that. You are the one I didn't want to lose most. The one that I felt I had to protect from this. The one who I wasn't sure I had the strength to be without."

Her breath hitched, so he looked up to meet her eyes.

"Protect me?" she said, the question was laced with a dangerous calm. Her voice was low, strained, and vibrating with a tightly leashed anger. "By treating me like a child? By making decisions about my safety, about our lives, without telling me the full truth? Because you were worried, I would leave?" She leaned forward, her eyes blazing, though her voice remained a fierce whisper.

"At a time when I find out that my whole life has been spent with people 'protecting' me from the truth. Don't you understand, Will? It's not the monsters out there that scare me most. It's the **secrets** you keep. The ones you think you have to hide, even from me." She jabbed a finger towards her chest, each word a sharp stab. "That's what's truly dangerous. Your assumption that I can't handle the truth. That's what breaks my trust. That's what destroys a partnership. You didn't think I was strong enough or loved you enough to stay."

She could have stabbed him with his blades, and it wouldn't have cut this deep.

He opened his mouth, but no words came out. There was nothing he could say at the moment that would fix this. He desperately wanted to fix this.

The silence that followed was heavy, suffocating, punctuated only by the distant sounds of the tavern below. He watched her face, rigid with something he couldn't quite decipher, but it wasn't the fear he expected.

He could see her eyes drooping as she waited for him. He hadn't prepared for this reaction, though in hindsight, he should have. Thinking back, Elowen had even warned him.

He spoke from the heart. It was all he could do. "You are the strongest woman I have ever known, and that is one of the many reasons I love you."

The silence left him feeling so helpless. He kicked himself for not prioritizing truthfulness, even over the danger. He knew her. He should have known what her priority would be. She isn't like the others. She dispatched half a squadron of guards in the West Woods. Bravery against odds was not something she lacked. She wasn't like the others, and he could not believe that it was just now that he was realizing that.

Finally, she spoke.

"I haven't decided on my next steps. I don't like making decisions without all the information. I want to learn more about the Order of Tamris. I want to know why you feel they were more dangerous than our current dangers, but mostly I need to understand why you felt I wasn't different," She spoke in a much calmer tone, one that gave him hope.

He took a sharp breath. That was a better answer than he expected and a much better answer than he deserved.

"I understand," he whispered.

"Surely there is a way to reason with the Order of Tamris. There has to be another way than just running."

A sliver of possibility sparked within him. Resolve it? Could he? Just because no one ever had… it doesn't mean that it is impossible. "I… I will think about it."

He could see the calculations going in her head, then she gave a slow, tired nod. "For now… we survive. We get to the ship. We keep the kids safe. After that… we'll see what's left to salvage."

That was not as promising.

"We will talk more tomorrow after we are safely onboard the ship. After we overcome this hurdle of danger, we will move on to the next. You didn't think I was strong enough and that I didn't love you enough. That is a hurt I will need to think about before we discuss things any further." She reached over and blew out the oil lamp, casting the room into darkness.

She slid into bed beside him, nestling close with his arm wrapped tightly around her. He breathed in the scent of her hair, a familiar comfort that battled with the unease churning within him. Holding her close felt right, even if everything else felt precariously balanced, as if this would be the last night he would ever hold her like this.

CHAPTER 11 – MALIN

A sense of unease settled over Malin as she surfaced from a sleep thick with dreams of Will. Dreams of a shared future, a child with his eyes, Ellie blossoming into a confident young woman with him watching on. Could her magic be offering solace, a glimpse of what might be, or was it merely preying on her deepest longings?

As she stirred awake, the memory of the discussion they had the night before returned, causing those hopeful dreams to spill into burgeoning anger from his lack of trust in her. She felt so torn, as her subconscious sent her hope, while her memory reminded her of his lack of trust in her.

From her angle lying in the bed, she noticed Ellie wasn't in her bed. A prickle of fear replaced the lingering warmth of her dream. Her gaze darted around the room, searching frantically. Her eyes landed on Ellie's boots, still neatly placed by the door where she'd left them.

A wave of relief washed over Malin, quickly followed by a fresh surge of confusion. She sat up, then she spotted them. They were in Zee's bed, two heads rested close together. Zee's arm was draped protectively over Ellie's waist, each child cocooned in their separate blankets, their breathing soft and synchronized. An innocent tableau of comfort and shared slumber. After the dangers they faced recently, she was glad Ellie had a way to feel safe.

Malin's worry eased, replaced by a surge of tenderness. She thought she had heard Ellie having nightmares last night. The pirate attack had clearly left its mark. She'd need to talk to her mother about finding a way to help Ellie process her fear.

Malin woke both kids and got them ready to go. Seeing Ellie and Zee nestled together, seeking comfort in each other, reinforced the fragility of their little makeshift family. She couldn't risk unsettling the morning with her doubts; the chaos of departure would be a distraction enough. Instead, she moved quietly through the cabin, her mind meticulously sorting through what she knew, preparing the words for the difficult conversation with Ellie ahead regarding the Aldrik situation.

As the kids gathered their belongings, she mentally reached out to her mom, hoping she was listening. "Mom?" She felt the presence almost immediately.

"Good morning. From the way that Will is acting, I'm guessing the morning isn't going well. What happened?" Her mother's voice, calm as still water, resonated in her mind.

Malin's thoughts went to their discussion the night before. *"He told me about this Order of Tamris group, and it sounds like he is almost afraid of them. It just sounded like yet another group of people trying to kill us,"* she projected among their mental pathway, then paused to gather her thoughts.

"I do want to know more about this group, but that isn't what is really upsetting me. Why would he have hidden such important information from me? That is what hurts the most. He knows how much I dislike secrets. Can I even trust him to lead us now? Can we even do this trip without him? Is it possible for us to get to Aloria safely if people like that are hunting him?" Her desperation seeped into every projected thought."

Her mother's mental presence solidified, a firm anchor against Malin's swirling fear. *"Malin, listen to me. He is the only one I would trust with this journey. I know his track record for transporting better than anyone, far better than his willingness to share his past, it seems. He is our best chance, even with the Order after him."*

A wave of exhaustion washed over Malin, leaving only weariness in its wake. *"Is there anything he can do to get them to stop coming after him?"*

"I'm checking on some solutions now. There may be options. I can't say they will be enjoyable, but they might offer a way forward," Mom admitted, a rare note of uncertainty in her mental voice. *"But Malin, we cannot have him distracted by concerns about your relationship. He needs to be top of his game, focused entirely on this trip, or we risk our own lives. Look."*

Mom pushed a vivid mental image into Malin's mind: Will, downstairs at the table with Nar and Khelek. He was deep in a strained conversation, his brow furrowed, his movements stiff. He kept glancing towards the stairs to the rooms, his jaw tight. He was clearly distracted; the tension radiated from him, even in the mental image.

"We need to calm his concerns, Malin," her mother continued, her voice resonating with urgency. *"We need his full attention on the dangers so we can board, not the turmoil in his mind. If he's worried about your feelings, about whether you'll leave him... it jeopardizes us all."*

"You want me to lie about how I feel?" Malin projected back, the question tight with a new kind of resentment. The unfairness of it burned.

"No. Not lie, just give him hope. I'm assuming that there is some love there. Focus on that," Mom insisted, her voice softening, tinged with a plea. *"Let him focus on getting us to the ship. When you are on the ship, you will have weeks to work out the next steps. You can deal with your feelings later when we're safe. But right now, we need him. And he needs to believe you're with him, without question."* With that, her presence withdrew, leaving Malin alone with the heavy weight of her mother's words and the chilling reality of their precarious situation.

She sat pensively. It wasn't like she had decided not to keep the relationship; she didn't feel she had enough information to make any decision right now. Her mother was right. Getting to the ship was the priority for now.

She needed to be strong. She did have feelings for him. As she watched the two children switch between playing tag around the room and gathering items, she realized there were so many reasons to take the risks. She would do it. She strengthened her mindset. She would be decisive and strong, long enough to get on the ship and get underway.

When she saw that they had completed packing and were ready, she sat on the edge of the bed. "Ellie. Zee," she began, patting the mattress beside her, inviting them close. "So, I learned some news that might bother you. I just want you to know that I'm here to talk, and I will gladly help you find any answers you feel you need."

Ellie tensed, her small hand instinctively finding Malin's on the bed beside her, before she asked, "Mom?"

"I found out that the man we know as Poppa, isn't my father." She paused to let that sink in. "Do you remember the tall man we met last night?"

Ellie shook her head hesitantly, and Zee grabbed her hand.

"His name is Aldrik. He is Nanna's special friend, and he is actually my father, and your grandfather." Malin was concerned that this would all be too confusing for her.

"Poppa sent those men to try to take us away. He is not a nice man. I'm happy he's not my Poppa. Is Aldrik a nice man?" She asked innocently.

"I don't know a lot about him yet, but as far as I can tell, he seems to be a nice man. I'll let you decide for yourself," she pulled her in for a hug, then pulled her back to look into her eyes. "I want you to tell me if you ever have any issues with any of this. I know this is a lot, but I don't want you ever to feel like I'm hiding anything from you."

"I know, Mom," she smiled. "When can we see him again?" Before Malin could answer, she responded, "Nanna says they are downstairs waiting for us. Are you ready?" She immediately walked to the door.

Maybe this won't be as hard as she thought.

After she made a last check to ensure that there was nothing left behind, they walked down to the tavern together. It was quiet, with the clinking of wooden mugs and metal bowls increasing as they descended the stairs.

When they came down the stairs and walked into the tavern area, she realized that Mom and Aldrik were seated at a larger table on the far side of the tavern, with Lady Anariel and Zane. Will was sitting at a small table in the middle of the room with Nar and Khelek, their heads bent in what looked like a serious discussion.

"Why don't you head over to Nanna. I'm going to go talk with Will.. I'll be right there in a bit," Malin said to the children.

"But that man is there. Aren't you coming too?" Ellie asked cautiously, grabbing her hand, as she eyed Aldrik cautiously.

"I know he's there, and I'll see him in a little bit, but Will needs me to talk with him about something important. It won't take long. We will both be over soon. Nanna can introduce you again," she assured with a squeeze of her hand.

With the assurance, Ellie was more than happy to run to the table, with her excitement to meet her new grandfather.

Zee stayed behind and grabbed her hand, a worried look on his face, "Are we still family? I heard you fighting. I tried not to hear, but... You seemed upset at Will. If you decide not to be with Will, can I stay with you? Even if... even if new people come?" His voice was barely a whisper, his gaze darting to the larger table with the rest of the family and then back to her, a deep-seated fear in his eyes.

Malin knelt instantly, pulling him close, her heart aching for him. "Zee, listen to me. We are family. You, me, Ellie, and Will. That's our family. Nothing changes that. Family can get upset sometimes, but we are always family. No new person, no new news, ever takes that away. Understand? You're stuck with us." She squeezed his hand firmly, letting him feel her conviction. "You go with Nanna, and when Will and I come, everything will still be us. Okay?"

He nodded slowly, still looking unsure, but the tension in his hand lessened, and he walked cautiously over to the table, where Zane pulled him into a bear hug, causing Zee to smile and giggle.

She caught Aldrik's eye and smiled when she saw his broad grin, and he gave a wink and a nod.

Mom must have told him about needing to talk to Will. It would be good to give Ellie time to get to know him. She mused that there would be plenty of time for them to talk on board the ship.

Will, anticipating Malin's arrival, stood and pulled out a chair for her.

"Morning," she said with a forced smile on her face and as cheery a tone as she could muster. Both Nar and Khelek said warm greetings quickly and left to sit with Lady Anariel at her mother's table, leaving her alone with Will.

"Morning Sparks. I couldn't sleep, so I came down to get a few things prepared so I wouldn't wake you." He cleared his throat and continued, "I... I was afraid you had made up your mind and wouldn't want to sit with me," he said with sincerity in his eyes.

She reached over and caressed his hand, "I'm sorry I made you so concerned. You know how I am with decisions. I need to think through them to consider every angle, but please know that you have been the best thing that has ever happened to me, and I don't want to lose that. I don't want to lose our family. I might have overreacted a bit last night, but it felt like an epidemic of hiding things from me. If I accept my mother's promise not to hide anything, I can surely accept yours. I just need you to promise me that you won't protect me by hiding things anymore."

A wince flickered across his face, and he looked away, though his hand never left hers.

She paused, her gaze softening as she considered the next words carefully. "Last night, I had dreams that felt so vivid, so real… Dreams of us and a life together that I would love to have." She met his eyes, forcing her gaze to hold steady, to project a certainty she didn't entirely feel. "I do want this to be real."

Even if it meant ignoring the unsettling gaps and shadows in her past, a voice whispered in her head, but she pushed it down. "I am disappointed that you would have thought that I would have left you over the threat of danger, given what we've lived through the last few weeks."

Disappointed was an understatement. It was a knife twist, a betrayal of my trust in you, and your trust in me. "But I want to understand better why you thought I would be better with you hiding the information than being worried about the danger, because I don't want you ever to lie to me again. Because this foundation, this bond we're building, has to be built on truth, no matter how ugly.

His eyes shot back to hers, glistening with tears he held back, as his thumb caressed her hand.

"It was stupid. I know. Nar and Khelek said the same earlier. I know you better than that and my fear should have been able to see the truth. You know how important I take making a promise, and I promise that I now understand. I messed up, Malin. I let my past and my fear of losing you blind me to what you truly needed from me. From now on, no more hiding. No more 'protecting' you by keeping you in the dark. You deserve better. We deserve better." His voice was rough, choked with emotion, his gaze unwavering as he stared into her eyes, begging for her to believe him. "As far as the trip to the ship is concerned, I think it is best to have me go ahead of the group of you, so that I can…"

He paused, taking a ragged breath. "So, I can ensure the path is clear. It's not a question of protecting… It's a question of drawing the fire away from you and the children. If anyone is watching, they'll be watching for me. If I can draw them out and deal with them before you arrive, it's safer. It always will be."

Honesty was in his eyes, plain as day. He meant it. She could feel her anger and hurt subsiding. She could get through this day because of that. They would talk when they got settled on the ship.

Their further conversation on the topic was halted at the arrival of the blushing barmaid, who had kissed Will when they arrived. The young woman barely met her gaze, diligently serving the plates on her side of the table with a determined focus before retreating almost as quickly as she'd appeared.

A flicker of something, amusement or perhaps a faint possessiveness, stirred within Malin. This was yet another reason she felt that the bond might be more than just magic. An honest smile crossed her lips, and she felt the knot in her chest relax slightly as they stood to join the others.

She glanced across the busy tavern to where Mom, Aldrik, Lady Anariel, Nar, Khelek, and their children were gathered around a larger table, already deep into their breakfast. "It might be nice to eat all together. Why don't we join the others? We can carry the plates over easily enough."

Will's smile widened, a clear relief in his eyes. He quickly scooped up their mugs and plates, waiting for her to lead the way. The tavern's early hour meant the path to the larger table was clear, a quiet progression from their intimate corner.

Ellie spotted them first, her face lighting up as she nudged Zee, running to meet her. "Mom. He is nice," she whispered, though still loud enough that it was easily heard by most.

Mom offered Malin a knowing, gentle smile that spoke volumes, a smile that seemed to hide a subtle amusement she couldn't yet decipher, and both Lady Anariel and Aldrik stood to greet her.

When she finally arrived at the table, Ellie took her seat. Lady Anariel reached out to touch foreheads. Malin, remembering the custom, leaning into the touch, feeling the familiar warmth of kin. As they separated and Anariel sat, Malin looked up, her smile still lingering, and noticed Aldrik's beaming smile. His joy overflowed as he extended his hand.

"Would you mind if we..." Aldrik began, motioning vaguely between them. His brow furrowed slightly, seeking permission.

Malin's mind immediately went to the forehead touch she'd just shared with Anariel. It was intimate, a deep acknowledgment of connection. But to do that with Aldrik, her biological father, a man she'd literally just met and whose existence she'd only just discovered, felt profoundly vulnerable. It was a new, raw form of intimacy she wasn't prepared for, despite her knowledge of customs.

"It's a... family... or..." Aldrik trailed off, seeing her hesitation, and a shade of blush passed across his face as he looked down. He quickly rescued the moment, raising her hand to his lips and pressing a light kiss on top, then releasing it gently.

Malin's lips twitched. A small, genuine smile broke through, softening her gaze. "Well, that's certainly a more... direct introduction than I'm used to. Mom, Dad, and I were not really the close family types, but that doesn't mean this isn't nice," she teased gently, giving his hand a reassuring squeeze.

The thought of embracing this new, sudden family connection, with all its deep customs and unspoken history, sent a flutter through her that was both exhilarating and terrifying.

"But thank you, Aldrik. It means a lot that you're trying, and once we get more comfortable with each other. We can try again. I suppose we both have a lot to learn about being family, especially one as complicated as ours." As foreign as it felt, she knew in her heart that it was the connection she always hoped for in a family.

Will easily settled in beside Zee, his hand finding Malin's under the table for a brief, reassuring squeeze. The clinking of mugs and the low murmur of conversation suddenly felt less chaotic and more like a symphony, a chorus of their strange, beautiful, found family.

The meal was well-prepared and hearty. Zane had platters of meats, eggs, and something he called 'hash'. Whatever it was, it was delicious. The food was not prepared the way they would have served it in Media. It was full of flavor and spices, but such a treat for her mouth.

With the meal complete, they said farewell to Innkeeper Zane, who wanted to see Zee off. Before they left, they said their goodbyes among the group.

"Hey, little guy. I want to hear that you are eating all of your food, so you can grow up strong," Zane flexed his rippled biceps, making Zee smile. "I love how protective you are of your sister there. Corben and I loved Felicity… your mom, so much, and she was known to get into a world of trouble… she met your Da after all. Protecting her felt like a full-time job sometimes. I love seeing how much you are like me. I'm so happy to finally meet you and know if you ever come back this way. I always got a room for you. Maybe one day I'll figure out how to work that contraption and we can talk through it…. Oh, and thanks for letting me know that Leo likes that fish so much and telling him that every time he brings me a dead mouse, he gets one. I had five dead mice and a dead rat by the door this morning. He got six of those fish, as promised." At that last comment, Zee ran into Zane's arms, and Zane picked him up for a deep bear hug; Zee's legs dangled in the air.

She watched a quiet warmth bloom in the Innkeeper's broad chest, evident in the way his gaze settled on the boy, full of an affection as clear and undeniable as the morning light.

She noticed that both had tears in their eyes. If things went well, this might be the last time they saw each other, unless the innkeeper decided to close his business. "When we get settled, we will make sure to get word to you of our location, so you can come visit," she added.

"For this little guy, I just might do that." Zee's smile reached his eyes.

"It was nice meeting you, Zane. I really wish I had more time to get to know you," Malin said.

Zane extended his hand, and they shook, then she stepped back to stand by Zee.

"Will you be heading this way again?" Zane asked Will.

Will pursed his lips and shook his head. "Not likely, but I thought the last time would be it also. I'd rather say till next time and be hopeful, Brother." They pulled each other into a brotherly hug, patting each other on the back.

"Back at you, Brother," Zane agreed.

Before they left for the ship, Will dutifully checked both kids' bags to ensure they were secure, and then, with a heartfelt parting, ensured the children were ready to leave. She felt a flutter of concern now that she had a better understanding of the dangers of both Media in town, the pirates, and the assassins. No matter how she felt, she needed to ensure that Will knew she felt confident so that he wouldn't worry.

When he got to her, she knew what she wanted to say, "You are not going to give me a goodbye. You will be at the gangplank of that ship when I get there, and we will be boarding together." Her words left nothing to chance, and he looked slightly surprised.

"So, it looks like I've created a monster with that Bossy lady attitude," he said with a boyish grin, pulling her close and kissing her forehead, then her lips. *If he only knew that this was a show for him, and she felt nothing like a bossy lady right now.*

She pushed him back, but not hard enough to actually separate, as she tried to hide her smile. The feel of his strong arms wrapping around her, and the scent of leather, vanilla, and a thread of spice from his soap, was intoxicating, making her bite her lip and breathe deeply. He pulled away all too soon, gave a final nod, and turned to face the street alone.

This new certainty, this bold assertion to Will, was a shield she'd summoned for herself. Beneath the surge of confidence, a quiet, unfamiliar fear still whispered. The journey ahead was filled with too many dangers; even the simple walk-through town could be the last.

Her outward bravado that she wasn't worried about the trip was for him, for Will. She needed him focused, sharp, and unburdened by her anxieties. She couldn't afford to let him see the raw knot of apprehension that still coiled in her gut. Not yet.

She needed him to be the immovable force, the steady hand guiding them through the storms to come. Malin watched until his figure disappeared around the corner, the tavern door swinging shut with a soft click that sounded like a lock turning. The scent of his soap was already fading; she was left with nothing but the chilling weight of his absence.

And the sudden, terrifying thought: *What if that's the last time I ever see him?*

CHAPTER 12 – MALIN

The trek to the docks was unnervingly calm, a stark contrast to their heightened vigilance. The trip through town had Malin jumping at every sudden movement, flinching at every loud call. Each of them had donned black headwraps and face coverings, a bared shield against unseen dangers. The morning sun blazed with relentless intensity, drawing the townspeople out in droves, oblivious to the tension beneath the surface. With her head and face swathed in oppressive fabric, the heat became suffocating, rivulets of sweat streaming down her spine, a searing testament to the stifling heat, even during this brief march through the bustling town.

Will had insisted on leaving first, determined to draw the danger away from them and bid them to wait a bit before leaving. Behind him, Mom and Aldrik followed, their faces a mix of fear and resolve. Lady Anariel stood protectively in front of Nar, who held Ellie's white-knuckled grip. Ellie clung to Zee, who in turn held fast to Khelek, each step heavy with apprehension.

She realized after they had left that she had never asked how to tell if someone was from the Order of Tamris. Did they wear specific robes? Carry specific weapons? Did they have magic? So many questions she didn't think to ask until now. Any one of the people walking by them could be the assassins.

Somehow, she'd been relegated to the end of their group. That was a tactical error, in her opinion, as the streets were filled with typical market shoppers and vendors. Every unpredictable jostle made Malin flinch. They made it to the docks without incident, leaving her to wonder if they had Will to thank for that.

As they approached the ship, she remembered hearing that the Qenya Stin Haven was roughly fifty feet larger than the Dawn's Beacon, which was docked opposite it. While the massive merchant vessel was regarded as sturdy and capable of navigating treacherous waters and venturing near the Draco Mountains, the thought of it sailing so close to dragon nesting grounds unsettled her. The increased chance of dragon attacks terrified her.

Up close, the sheer scale of the Haven struck her. From afar, it was just a larger ship. But docked beside the Beacon across the vast expanse of the pier, the difference was undeniable. Where the smaller vessel gleamed with beautiful wood and refined metal, this larger ship was a fortress. Its thick metal hull appeared less built than brutally forged, and its four masts clawed so much higher into the sky that it simply towered over all the others on the docks.

As they got closer, she couldn't help but admire the craftsmanship, with so many runes, glyphs, and carvings all over her. The sheer intricacy of it pulled her gaze, and for a moment, her worries simply faded.

She had been so busy admiring the ship that she hadn't noticed Will, at the dock end of the gangplank, standing next to a compact, muscular man with long dark hair pulled back and simple clothes. The man exuded authority, speaking animatedly as his hands punctuated his words.

Maybe this is the Captain.

From a distance, when the man moved to the side, she saw a shock of fiery red hair, barely visible through the crowd. When she finally got close enough, she could see it was Lydia, the pint-sized beauty.

How utterly different they were, Malin thought, her gaze sweeping over the woman.

Lydia, small where Malin was tall, a raw, exotic beauty accentuated with makeup and glittering jewels, seemed to thrive on standing out, on being noticed. Malin had always preferred the shadows, wanting only to blend in, to be invisible.

A sharp, unfamiliar spark of jealousy flickered within Malin, quickly followed by a disquieting question: *How could Will love her, when he had so obviously been attracted to this woman in the past?*

Just as the thought solidified, a familiar pull tightened in her chest, and she saw Will's head turn in her direction. *Was this their bond?* He was in the middle of a heated discussion between the Captain and the woman, but his gaze found hers across the bustling pier. He motioned for her to join him.

"Captain, it shouldn't matter what he says. You can decide whether to allow me on board or not. Will promised to take me to Aloria, and he better make good on it," the same petite woman who had accosted Will in the tavern said in a raised voice, her hands planted firmly on her hips, her posture defiant.

She moved deliberately, gracefully, until she was directly beside Will. Her hand, with a subtle possessiveness she hadn't realized was hers, found his arm and slid down to intertwine with his fingers, squeezing gently. It was a silent, undeniable declaration, a public staking of her claim. A sweet smile plastered on her face, she caressed Will's arm, while her internal thoughts churned.

"It tis your call Will, but you let her on… I don't want problems," the Captain responded. Now that she was closer, she could see that his pointed ears and chiseled face were flushed. "Will. I have known you since you were twelve. Trouble follows you, and I don't want any more than we will have on this trip. It's dragon mating season, and the Tanniym Crossing will be tough to get through without at least one attack, not to mention that the Orc raiders like to camp there."

"Barnabas. Lydia. This is my wife, Malin. Do you mind if I speak with her about this?"

"Your wife?" Lydia's eyes widened, and her mouth hung open.

"Your… wife?" Captain Barnabas blinked, his flush deepening, a muscle in his jaw working before he swallowed hard. Then, with a visible effort, he collected himself. "That would be reasonable." He recovered quickly, a new, calculating glint in his flushed eyes as he tipped his hat.

A bit of spitefulness rose in Malin, *yes*, and a weary exasperation at Will's continued evasiveness. This woman wanted to ride on their ship. Malin didn't trust Lydia for a moment. There was an unsettling way she carried herself. But a cold, calculating part of Malin's mind weighed the options. Leaving Lydia on the docks for months felt like an unexploded bomb, a problem that would inevitably return unresolved, besides the fact that if someone wanted out of a place like this and they could help them... Why wouldn't they?

Having her aboard, however undesirable, meant she was contained and observable. And it would force Will's hand. This was the fastest, most direct way to get the answers he was so stubbornly withholding, and to manage a volatile situation on her terms. Knowing everything was, in itself, a form of safety. With that thought, a calculated sweetness settled on Malin's features.

Benefit of the doubt or not, whatever story this woman had, whatever past connection she shared with Will, it no longer mattered. She just needed to make sure that everyone understood exactly whose man he was.

"Lydia, there will be other ships. I am happy to pay your fare on that one. You have been here for this long, you don't need to be on the same ship as my family," Will said.

It could have been jealousy, but Malin hoped that it was clear to Lydia that getting on the ship wasn't about getting Will back.

Malin felt the presence of her mother in her head again. "*Is there an issue? We boarded, but Aldrik is ready to head back down to help you,*" Mom telepathically communicated. Malin looked up to the ship's deck, where they looked down, his eyes concerned, her arm holding him back from descending.

"*We are fine. Lydia wants to join our trip. We are handling it just fine. Please let him know that it is appreciated, but we have it,*" she communicated back, adding a wave and smile in their direction on the ship. They didn't move, a silent acknowledgment that he wasn't coming down.

Aldrik's fierce, immediate protection gave her a comforting warmth she hadn't realized she craved. It was a stark contrast to the subtle evasions and hidden truths she'd been dealing with all her life, a simple, unwavering presence.

Will pulled her off to the side, away from the crowds. "This was unexpected," he murmured, his voice low and strained. "I do have some guilt for leaving her here, but Lydia is…trouble and unpredictable. Dangerous even. She has a way of causing real chaos, not just for me, but for anyone nearby. It's not a good idea to have her on board, but ultimately, I feel it is your choice."

She positioned herself so that she had a good view of the little redhead. Lydia stood tapping her foot with impatience, her hand dancing a vivid flame from one finger to the other, as others would idly flip a coin.

She's the fire-wielder that Will had warned her about. The realization hit Malin with a jolt, cementing the vague, unsettling whispers she'd heard from Will's past. *This was the woman from the stories, the ex-girlfriend with fire.* Jealousy brewed hot and bitter within her gut.

She didn't want Lydia on their ship, but… she also didn't want to be the one to deny passage to someone who, by some twisted code, might be owed something. Maybe she could address the safety concerns with some pointed questions.

"How soon is the next ship? Really?" She asked him, her voice carefully neutral.

His jaw ticked, a muscle jumping beneath his skin as he forced out, "Actually, it might be a month or two. It depends on how many ships are still running."

"It doesn't seem very fair to make her wait that long. I don't see a problem with her coming with us," Malin pressed, her gaze firm, "unless you still have feelings for her or there is some other reason, she would be a safety issue for *us* or the kids you haven't told me."

"No!" His answer was immediate and sharp.

"Then what's the issue? You promised her a trip to Aloria. I've never known you to break a promise," she hinted playfully, hoping to ease his tension, to give him an out. He held his breath, seemingly at a loss for words, his gaze distant. She half expected a smart-mouthed response, a deflection. Instead, he just stood there, silently agonizing.

"I really don't think any good can come of this. She is not a typical person. It is a mistake to allow her on, but… I don't think it is a safety issue, more sever discomfort issue. I do feel guilty about leaving her here. I would like to help her, but I don't think this is the best way to do it. I did promise, but…" Will countered.

"So, your promise isn't as good as you said it is?" She raised an eyebrow and narrowed her eyes at him, then spat through pursed lips, "That is good to know. I will keep that in mind."

He put his hands on her shoulders and looked intently at her as he added, "Promises are something I take very seriously, and in other circumstances, I would jump to this, but… I know her, and she's going to make our lives miserable. I still think it keeps my promise if I make arrangements for her to leave on the next ship, but I'll leave this decision to you."

"If promises are important to you, then keeping your promise to her should also be important," she reasoned.

"Promises are important," he said, pulling her in for a quick hug and a kiss on her lips.

Good enough, she thought, a stubborn resolve setting in. She needed to know everything, and Lydia was the fastest way to get it, one way or another. And anyway, he was hers. She was not worried about Lydia destroying her relationship… She was screwing that up all on her own. "Then it's settled."

She strode over to the pair waiting by the gangplank, leaving Will a few steps behind her.

Malin turned fully to Lydia, her gaze unwavering. "If you come aboard this ship, there will be rules. My children are onboard. They are never to be put in harm's way, directly or indirectly. There will be no fire-wielding, no dramatics that could endanger them, and no attempts to unsettle their lives or their father's. Do you understand, and do you agree to these terms?"

Lydia blinked, her mouth opening and closing once before she managed a raspy, "Yes. I… I understand. And I agree."

"Lydia. I can't see any reason why he shouldn't still be responsible for getting you to Aloria, and I understand that it would be a long wait for the next ship." Malin met the Captain eye-to-eye, her resolve unyielding.

She knew Will preferred Lydia nowhere near them, and her jealousy still prickled, but a deeper, strategic impulse drove her now. This was her chance to understand Will's past and to assert her place, clearly and publicly. Besides, her sense of honor demanded a fair resolution. "If you have room," she continued, "I think it would be the honorable thing for her to come with us or go as far as she wants."

Lydia's eyes went wide and unblinkingly fixed on Malin, as if Malin's words had frozen her in place. Then, almost imperceptibly, her gaze flickered to Will, a question in her eyes, almost as if seeking his approval or confirmation.

Malin, catching the subtle shift, cut in before Will could utter a sound. Her voice remained even, but with an undercurrent of steel. "Just so we're clear, Lydia, this is *my* decision. If it were up to Will, you'd be staying on the dock right now."

"We do have the room, if you and your children will share a room. The rooms are of a good size, and I have one room with two beds," he responded.

Malin could sense Will about to use that as his chance to avoid the situation, about to interject with an excuse. She quickly cut him off, her voice smooth. "Then it sounds like the issue can be resolved easy enough."

She then turned to Lydia, a challenging glint in her eye. "Will it take long for you to gather your things? I would not want to hold things up for you, but it sounds like if you can be ready in time, you have a room."

"Everything I need is here," Lydia stammered, motioning to the two large bags lying nearby. A flicker of cunning replaced her initial shock as her gaze darted between Malin and Will. She had obviously not expected it to be so easy, but since she had the bags there, she must have assumed she would get on board.

"Then, it's settled. We will see you on board. Thank you, Captain, for your help." Malin walked away, leaving the Captain, Lydia, and even Will open-mouthed in her wake. Will caught up with her quickly, his stride mirroring hers as they walked to the ship to board.

The gangplank to the Qenya Stin Haven felt like a bridge to another world, solid and unyielding beneath Malin's boots. The moment they stepped onto the main deck, the sheer scale of the vessel enveloped her.

Will leaned in, his voice a low, teasing murmur by her ear. "Just so you know, you decided to invite our fire-wielding, emotionally unhinged associate aboard. Don't come crying to me when she sets your clothes on fire."

Malin allowed a slow, determined smile to touch her lips, though her eyes held a challenge. "It's your clothes you should be watching, Will," she said. She had every intention of winning.

He simply grinned, unapologetic, seemingly unaware of the silent gauntlet she'd just thrown down.

Gone were the polished hardwoods and elegant curves of the Dawn's Beacon. Here, every surface seemed built for endurance. The deck itself was a labyrinth of thick, dark wood planks, scarred and gleaming with countless journeys, worn smooth in places by the relentless churn of the sea and the endless traffic of sailors. Heavy iron rings and cleats dotted the periphery, securing thick, brine-stained ropes that led up to the four towering masts, their sails furled tight like sleeping giants. The air tasted of salt, tar, and a faint, metallic tang of iron, mixed with a lingering whiff of an unidentified cargo.

Below deck, the contrast deepened. The main corridor was a narrower, dimmer tunnel, lit by sparse, caged lanterns that cast long, dancing shadows. The rhythmic groan of the ship's timbers was louder here, a constant, living sound that vibrated through the floorboards. Doors, heavy and bolted, lined both sides, each a portal to a private world. Will, with a casual familiarity that stung a little, led her past several, his hand finding the grip of her elbow as they navigated a particularly tight turn.

In the hall, standing outside one room was Nar, discussing something with Khelek in the first room she passed. Aldrik was standing at the end of the hall by an open door.

"We guessed you'd want to have the kids in the room with two beds, so they are putting their things away now," he said, motioning to the open room on the left.

"Change of plans. It looks like we'll be sharing a room with the kids now," Malin answered. A small triumph flickered within her. This was the direct consequence of her decision, of her taking control. She hoped it wouldn't backfire.

"Malin. I can see this is already shaping up to be an interesting voyage," her mother directed. "Kids. Instead of you each having your own dressers, you need to plan on sharing one," she instructed, directing the kids.

Malin stepped into the room, revealing a cabin larger than any she'd anticipated for passenger quarters on a merchant vessel.

Inside was a room with two decent-sized double beds bolted to the floor, two dressers along the far wall, and a small table between the beds attached to the wall with four chairs around it. Two small portholes were the only source of natural light in the room. Glowing crystals provided the rest.

For a merchant ship, this was surprisingly spacious, almost comfortable. But then, she reminded herself, it was meant for long voyages, for families perhaps, not just single passengers.

Ellie and Zee, momentarily distracted from their excitement by the arrival of their parents, looked up expectantly.

Will leaned against the doorframe, a faint, almost imperceptible smirk playing on his lips. "This looks cozy," he commented, his gaze sweeping over them before meeting Malin's. "Looks like we're all going to be living in close quarters. What fun! It'll only be three or four weeks."

Malin scanned the room, letting the words sink in. Her mouth dropped open as the full weight of the decision slammed into her. Three or four weeks? She had not realized they would be on board for that long. The number echoed in the sudden silence of the cabin, making the already practical space feel even more Spartan. Trapped in close quarters with Will, her children, and now... Lydia would be staying across the hall. Her calculated gamble suddenly felt less like a brilliant strategic move and more like a very long, very enclosed prison sentence. What had she done?

A prison sentence she had, with stubborn pride and an ill-considered sense of honor, inflicted upon herself. Every reason she'd told herself, every strategy, and every asserted claim... even the pretense of fairness... It all now felt like flimsy excuses for a catastrophic error.

How was she going to endure weeks of Lydia's simmering presence, the constant, unspoken tension, the fear of what secrets might spill out, all while trying to maintain a semblance of normalcy for the children?

She tightened her jaw to hold back the emotions she so badly wanted to keep to herself. A bitter taste, the burgeoning regret of her courtesy to Lydia, filled her mouth. She would never admit it.

Will, sensing the shift, gave her a reassuring nod and took charge of the children. "Alright, you two," he announced, his voice booming, "Let me give you a tour of the ship. We'll be here for a while. You know, I used to live on this ship? It was built by Elven metal shapers." He paused, looking back to her, "Sparks, would you like to come?"

"I'll meet you on the top deck later. I'm going to put a few things away and freshen up," she said, glad for a few moments to think.

They walked out the door and down the hall; Will's laughter echoed through the passenger area.

Once the sounds of their laughter faded, replaced only by the muffled creaks and groans of the ship, Malin finally closed the door and inhaled deeply. Her breath felt thin and inadequate. Her mind, usually a clear, analytical tool, raced, tumbling over the morning's activities in a dizzying loop.

The click of the stateroom door, dull and final, was the sound of her last thread of composure snapping. Her mask, that tight, brave facade she'd plastered on to shield Will and the children from her inner turmoil, fractured and fell away.

The salty tang already clinging to the air from the sea seemed to merge with the tears that welled, hot and stinging, then streamed down her face. She wasn't just tired; she was on the precipice of coming undone.

Her decision to allow Lydia on board had been an impetuous, defiant act. A flash of anger at Will's continued silence about the Order of Tamris, a desperate need to assert her own agency in a world spiraling out of her control. She'd made it with little data, less time, and too much pride.

Not her typical decision, at all.

She clenched her fists, the shame giving a bitter taste in her mouth. She, Malin, the planner, the strategist, had behaved like a hot-headed fool.

It wasn't that Lydia was Will's ex-girlfriend that truly chafed. It was the gaping chasm of the unknown. Who was Lydia, beyond Will's fleeting, incomplete mentions? What did "leaving her stranded" truly mean? That simmering rage, that palpable power in the tavern, the ease with which she'd commanded those rough men that were with her. It spoke of a history far more complicated, far more dangerous, than a simple broken heart. Malin knew nothing. And that ignorance, that lack of data, was a suffocating blanket in the cramped cabin.

Her heart hammered against her ribs, a frantic drum against the backdrop of the ship's awakening. She pressed her palms against her temples, trying to still the frantic thoughts.

Surely Will wouldn't have let her on if she were genuinely a threat. He wouldn't risk the children. But then, he'd risked *her* by keeping the Order a secret.

By letting her walk unknowingly into their crosshairs. The thought was a cold, sharp stab of betrayal. She had needed him to be transparent, absolute, and he hadn't been. And now, she'd mirrored his secrecy with her impulsive spite. The doubt, a venomous current, seeped through her veins, not just for Will, but for her judgment. Had she, in her anger, endangered them all?

The ship shuddered, a deep, resonant groan echoing through the hull as the anchor chains rattled up, each clank a jarring echo of the chaos in her mind.

Shouts from the deck above rose and fell, a chorus of distant commands. Ropes creaked, straining against unseen pulleys. She felt the subtle tremor as the colossal vessel began to pull away from the dock, the slight tilt beneath her feet. The distant view from the porthole, once frozen in a static image of wooden piers, blurred into a slow, deliberate movement.

They were setting sail. And she had just invited a seemingly unpredictable enemy into their confined world.

A quiet desperation settled over her. She couldn't sit, stewing in regret and mounting fear. The lack of information was the problem, and she, Malin, the strategist, knew how to remedy that. She needed answers. She needed to look Lydia in the eye, to push past the anger, and discern the truth. The very thought made her stomach clench, but it was better than this agonizing uncertainty.

She had to find Lydia.

CHAPTER 13 – MALIN

Malin pushed onto the top deck, her gaze swept the sun-drenched planks for any sign of Lydia. The sharp sea air, was a welcome shock against her still-flushed cheeks, hitting her with bracing force. The sturdy oak vibrated beneath her boots as the ship gained a relentless, hungry momentum, with the combination of both wind and mechanical power. The distant groan of the hull was a steady thrum, a deep, resonant beat against the rush of wind that whipped through the rigging. Ropes, thick and taut, groaned against their pulleys, humming a taut symphony as the colossal vessel tilted subtly with the surging waves.

Malin gripped the railing, letting the sheer force of the open ocean wash over her, a desperate attempt to cleanse the turmoil from her mind. She breathed deeply and slowly, pulling in the bracing tang of salt, trying to quiet the frantic questions still echoing from the stateroom. Her gaze swept aft, past the straining masts and the billowed canvas, searching for her answers.

And then she saw them. Her pursuit of Lydia was momentarily forgotten.

Near the stern, tucked beside a coiled heap of ropes, Ellie and Zane spun in a dizzying circle, their laughter carried effortlessly on the wind. Khelek moved with them, a silent, watchful shadow, his dark hair streaming behind him like a banner. Nar, usually so stoic, was crouched low, his broad shoulders shaking with silent mirth as he feigned a clumsy chase, letting the children dart just out of his reach. They were playing some wild, wordless game, a blur of motion and pure, untethered joy against the vast, indifferent sky. The happiness on their faces made her heart sing.

The twins were so good with the children that she wondered if having children was something Anariel had considered. It was evident that the children loved spending time with them.

A warmth, unexpected and profound, bloomed in Malin's chest, a fragile tendril of peace amidst the chaos she felt churning inside her. Here, on the boundless ocean, with the ship eating up the miles, her children, her true north, were safe. Protected. Nar and Khelek, ever vigilant, were more than just guards; they were companions, their presence a quiet testament to the unexpected family they'd found. For a precious, fleeting moment, the weight of Lydia, the sting of Will's secrets, the looming threat of the Order of Tamris, somehow receded – even if just for a moment. There was only the wind, the sea, and the undeniable, vibrant normalcy of her children's laughter. It was a lifeline she hadn't known she desperately needed.

Reluctantly, Malin's gaze lifted from the children to the horizon behind them, to the crooked skyline of Sarhan, shrinking rapidly with every surge of the ship. A strange mix of emotions washed over her. Undeniably relieved at leaving behind the shadowed streets, the lingering threat of Media, and the echoes of a past she was desperate to outrun. But beneath it, a faint touch of melancholy. For what, she wasn't quite sure. The lost innocence? The fragile hope for a quiet life? Or simply the last piece of land she'd known, dissolving into the vast, indifferent blue?

Just as the city began to blur into an indistinguishable line, her eyes caught something else. Pulling into the docks they had just vacated was a colossal freighter, sleek and dark, its lines far too sharp, its technology too advanced for anything she'd seen on these waters. It was undeniably from Media.

A chill, sharper than the sea breeze, snaked down Malin's spine. This wasn't just a merchant ship. This was the one. The guards. The pursuit. It was likely the very vessel carrying the enforcers who would have been after them, hot on their heels, had they lingered even a moment longer. The sudden realization was a cold reminder that escape was temporary, and the past was always, relentlessly, gaining.

Then, she felt a sudden, light touch brush against her shoulder. A sharp jolt of unease coiled in her gut, and her hand instinctively snapped up, palm open, fingers splayed in a practiced block. It was a muscle memory from long hours of training. She spun to face her assailant, her eyes narrowing in fierce readiness, then widening in a jolt of recognition.

Lydia stood there, her own eyes wide in surprise, her face framed by wind-whipped locks of fiery-red hair that streamed back like a vibrant beacon in the bright sunlight. She adjusted her stance and settled into an almost languid grace, one hand casually resting on the railing, but Malin had seen the fleeting look of shock.

"So," Lydia began, her voice smooth, almost purring over the wind. "You actually let me come along. I didn't expect them to let me. Thank you."

Malin could tell the politeness was a thin veneer, cracking even as the words left the woman's lips. Her eyes, fixed on Malin, hardened, a faint, almost imperceptible sneer pulling at the corner of her mouth. "What I don't understand is why?" she pushed, her voice dropping to a low, dangerous growl that barely carried over the ocean's roar. "Why'd you do it? To lord it over me? Or just to make him even more miserable?"

A flash of indignant anger flared, hot and defensive. It wasn't about either of them; it was about principle. It was about *her* rules, *her* sense of justice. She wanted to snap back, to remind Lydia who was in charge now.

But as the words hovered on her tongue, she was reminded of another voice, her mother's gentle yet firm reminder of openness and truth, which echoed in her mind. And her silent vow, made just moments ago in the stateroom, to seek understanding, to gather information rather than let fear fester. This wasn't a battle to win with a sharp retort; it was an opportunity. Lydia had opened the door, though with hostility, but maybe it was because she didn't know another way.

Malin took a breath to steady herself, letting the anger drain with the receding view of Sarhan. "I didn't do it to lord anything over you, Lydia," she stated, her voice calm despite the lingering tension within her shoulders. She met Lydia's cynical gaze unflinchingly. "Will promised you a trip to Aloria. And I believe in promises." She paused, letting the wind carry her words. "But clearly, there's more to your story than just 'Will left me.' If you want to talk about it, truly talk, I'll listen." She wasn't offering friendship, but an olive branch, a path to information she desperately needed.

Lydia's lips curled into a half-scoff, her eyes narrowed, as if weighing Malin's sincerity. She looked as though she was about to dismiss the offer, perhaps even spit out another insult. Then, something in her expression shifted. The tight knot of defiance in her posture seemed to loosen, just a fraction. For a moment, the sharp, assessing gaze softened, revealing a raw vulnerability beneath. It was a crack in the carefully constructed façade, and suddenly, the dam began to break.

Lydia's voice, though still rough, lost its hostile edge, replaced by a raw, brittle tremor. "He just... left me," she whispered, her gaze dropping to the churning water below, avoiding Malin's eyes.

"We had just pulled off this amazing heist. He said he couldn't take me with him. He didn't give me a choice. He left me with some money, a job as a barmaid, and then he was... just... *gone*." A bitter laugh escaped her, devoid of humor. "Nemilos, the Captain of the Hain pirates, came, and he doesn't give you choices. At least none you will like," Her hand clenched on the railing, knuckles white. "He is awful." She finally lifted her head, her eyes, though still red-rimmed, now burned with a desperate, haunted plea. "I just needed to get away. Any way I could."

Malin listened, every word a cold splash of water on her earlier anger toward the woman. Her initial judgment of Lydia, the 'crazy ex' narrative she'd unconsciously adopted, was shattered. The sharp accusation in Lydia's voice, the genuine terror flickering in her eyes, resonated with the sound of chilling truth. The look in her eyes must be real.

To be forced to be a pirate's mistress seemed horrific. While they were waiting for Will in the tavern, she had learned about the Hain pirates. They were known as some of the most heinous pirates.

If Will knew this, would it have affected his decision to let her on board? Surely, he wouldn't have left her in Sarhan for months, knowing what she would be subjected to.

A new, unsettling weight settled in Malin's stomach. This wasn't just a scorned lover. This was a victim. And in that realization, her perspective on Will's guilt shifted, profoundly and painfully. He hadn't just "left" Lydia; he had, however, unintentionally, abandoned her to a fate she had no means to escape. A different kind of anger began to simmer in Malin, directed not at Lydia but at the depths of Will's unspoken past and the horrifying consequences of his choices.

She saw not a woman driven by spite, but a survivor. Another person, just like herself, trapped by the brutal, uncaring realities of a world that cared nothing for choice or consent. The raw vulnerability, the utter lack of agency in Lydia's confession, mirrored the helplessness Malin herself had felt so many times.

Lydia had poured out the story and some hideous details of her torture. It was appalling.

As Lydia spoke, Malin noticed a subtle shift in the air, a drop in temperature that pricked at her unnaturally warm skin, and the wind began to whip with more vigor, tugging at her hair and clothes.

Could a storm be coming?

As Lydia finished her story, Malin's eyes, still fixed on the woman's haunted face, suddenly flickered. Beyond Lydia's head, the sky had darkened, an unnatural, bruised purple black that seemed to swallow the midday sun. It was wrong, a sickening hue that made a shiver, cold and involuntary, run down Malin's spine. She could feel the flame power within her rise a defensive heat against the encroaching chill.

The playful sounds of Ellie and Zane, just moments ago so vibrant, were now swallowed by the rising howl of the wind. She saw Nar and Khelek, their faces grim, already encouraging the children to leave, sweeping them swiftly towards the stairs leading below deck.

And then the first drops began to fall. Sheets of ice-cold water, near freezing, turned what had been a warm, beautiful day into a sudden chill. When they landed on Malin's skin, they hissed. Steam rose, a tiny, almost imperceptible plume, as the water boiled on contact, instantly vanishing. The familiar warmth deep within her flared to protect her from the cold, the constant, protective embers of her fire shielding her from the sudden, drastic temperature change.

Lydia, her face still etched with the raw pain of her confession, suddenly gasped. Her eyes, wide with surprise, fixed on the steaming patches on Malin's skin. Before Malin could process this exposed truth, a tiny flicker of orange light appeared between Lydia's fingers, small and controlled, like a candle flame against the gloom. It danced, as she played with her power, a silent question in her gaze as she watched Malin. Malin debated revealing her own. Then, she decided there was no harm.

She smiled, a genuine, unburdened smile, as she met Lydia's stunned gaze. In answer to Lydia's unvoiced question of flame power, Malin raised her hand, creating a fist-sized sphere of pure, incandescent fire within her palm, which cast a flickering, golden glow on her face and warmed the rapidly chilling air around them. It pulsed, alive and vibrant, before she closed her hand, and it vanished, leaving only the memory of heat.

"You are not the person I expected you to be when I saw you," Lydia said playfully, a wry twist to her lips. "Will may have a type after all."

For a heartbeat, all animosity, all past hurts, all accusations seemed to dissolve between them. There was only shared surprise, a silent acknowledgment of a dangerous, elemental kinship, and an unexpected moment of humor. The brief, intense connection hung in the air, a fragile bridge built on a shared, fiery secret.

Then, the ship lurched, a more resounding, more violent groan, as the waves outside surged. The wind screamed past the deck, suddenly ferocious. Without a word, their shared gaze broke, replaced by an urgent, mutual realization. The storm was here. They turned in unison, scrambling towards the nearest companionway, seeking the relative safety of the ship's interior.

CHAPTER 14 – WILL

Rounding the corner from the passenger area, Will spotted Nar and Khelek, their faces grim, with Ellie and Zee tucked close beside them as they headed towards the dining room. The ship groaned, a deeper, more ominous sound than its usual creaks, and Will felt it in his bones. The air, already sharp with salt, suddenly tasted different, as if it were thicker, charged with an unseen static. Years of sailing, of reading the sky and the shifting moods of the ocean, told him what was coming.

It was more than just a storm; it felt like a beast waking, with the sudden onslaught of rain and winds.

Nar's dark eyes met Will's, a knowing glint within them. "Storm's brewing," Nar stated, his voice low, easily cutting through the ship's growing symphony of groans and creaks. "Weather's turning fast."

Khelek, ever the more direct one, added, "And... *the* other storm may be worse. Malin's still on deck…. With Lydia."

The implication hung heavy in the air: they were talking. *Great.*

Will's jaw tightened. He should have known. Should have anticipated Malin's directness, her need for answers. He'd hoped for more time. He swung towards the door leading to the top deck, a new knot of dread forming in his gut.

The thick glass panel showed the immediate reality: sailors, usually moving with a practiced, almost leisurely efficiency, were now scurrying, their faces grim. Lines were being secured, and sails were rapidly furled. Their movements were sharp, urgent, mirroring the sudden escalation of the wind already screaming outside. He'd seen that look on men's faces too many times to mistake it. Whatever was coming promised to be brutal.

He pushed the heavy door open, stepping out onto the lurching deck just as two figures, battling the sudden gale, were already scrambling towards the companionway leading below.

Malin. And Lydia.

They were damp, steam rising visibly from their forms in the chilled air, their hair plastered to their faces. They were far drier than he would have expected given the sheets of rain he'd just seen, but they were moving with a synchronized urgency that surprised him. He held the door open, bracing against the wind that tried to rip it from his grasp, waiting for them to reach the relative shelter of the interior.

As they burst through, wind-whipped and dripping, Will managed a quick, "Rough weather out there, ladies."

Lydia stalked past him first, her eyes, though wild with the storm, held a chilling intensity as she met his gaze. It was a pure, unadulterated evil stare, full of a venom he hadn't seen from her in years.

Malin followed; her movements were more deliberate. Her eyes flickered to him for a bare second, a fleeting side-eye glance. It wasn't accusatory, not precisely. It was... knowing. A deep, unsettling understanding that he didn't quite comprehend, but which sent a jolt of unease through him, far more potent than Lydia's open animosity.

What lies did Lydia concoct to make Malin act like that?

Suddenly, a deafening crack ripped through the air above them, followed by the roar of a monstrous wave. The ship seemed to buckle, lurching violently to starboard, a gut-wrenching shift that threw everything off balance.

Both women, already reeling from the sudden onslaught, were launched forward by the sheer force of the ship's shudder. Instinctively, Will's arms shot out, catching them both in a tangled, jarring heap against his chest.

Lydia's rigid form pressed against one side, Malin's against the other, their combined weight nearly sending him off his feet.

He held them for a moment, steadying them as the ship slowly righted itself, the sounds of shouting sailors and creaking timbers filling the air.

He glanced between their stunned faces, a fleeting, almost sardonic twist to his lips. "Well," he said, his voice surprisingly even despite the recent jolt, "Looks like this voyage is going to be *very* hands-on."

"Get your hands off me!" Lydia hissed, shoving herself away from Will's grasp as if his touch burned her, her eyes still blazing with a mix of fury and storm-wildness.

Malin, meanwhile, didn't push away, but a sharp, assessing look replaced her shock. "Indeed," she murmured, her voice laced with an irony that belied her damp appearance. "Quite the welcome."

She then turned, heading towards the corridor leading to the passenger rooms without another word, Lydia stalking rigidly beside her.

Will instinctively moved to follow Malin, his hand reaching out. "I'll walk you to our room, Sparks."

Malin didn't even glance back. "I'm perfectly fine, Will. I can find my way." Her voice was cool, dismissive.

Will stopped, his hand falling to his side. *Right.* The message was clear. He was not welcome. Not right now. He watched them disappear down the dimly lit corridor, the sound of Lydia's angry muttering fading with them. A sigh escaped him, part frustration, part resignation. This was going to be a long voyage.

He knew this was just a passing thing. Once Lydia's true colors shone through to Malin, he would have her back.

The common room hit Will with a blast of warm, damp air, thick with the scent of cooking stew and wet wood. A stark, almost jarring contrast to the screaming wind that still howled outside. He braced a hand against the doorframe, letting his eyes adjust, scanning the swaying room for familiar faces. His earlier conversation with Malin still churned in his gut, leaving him edgy and restless.

He found them instantly. In the center of the room, near a glowing crystal, Elowen sat next to Aldrik, her hand resting casually on his arm as he intently watched Ellie and Zane, who were enthusiastically trying to teach him the rules of a card game. Aldrik's brow was furrowed in concentration, but a soft smile played on his lips, and Elowen beamed at the scene, radiating a serene sweetness that almost made Will gag.

Across the room, nestled in a cozy corner, Nar, Khelek, and Anariel were huddled together at a small table, their heads close, their laughter soft and conspiratorial. It was a picture of effortless romance that somehow only amplified Will's current agitation.

His gaze returned to Malin's mother and Aldrik. He needed a distraction, an anchor, or perhaps just a reason to move. Pushing off the doorframe, Will strode towards them, the subtle roll of the ship underfoot a familiar rhythm.

As he neared, Elowen looked up, her blue eyes meeting his. A flicker of recognition, then concern, passed through them.

Ah, so that's how it is, she thought, her voice clear in his mind despite her lips remaining still. *Your thoughts are quite… loud, Will. Come, let's talk somewhere less… public.* With a graceful nod towards Aldrik and the children, she rose. "Aldrik, darling, keep an eye on them for a moment. Will and I need a quick word." She then turned, already gliding towards an unoccupied table in a quieter alcove, leaving him no choice but to follow.

Once they were seated, Elowen's gaze softened. "So, tell me, what troubled thoughts are swirling in that troubled head of yours?"

Will leaned forward, resting his forearms on the table. "Elowen, with all due respect, I really don't want to have a *relationship conversation* right now."

Elowen nodded, a slight sigh escaping her. "Believe me, Will, I don't particularly enjoy listening to them either. Which, as it happens, brings us to why we need to work on this." She gestured between them. "You need to learn how to shield your mind from me and others. It's a skill you possess; you just haven't learned to wield it."

She leaned in, her voice dropping to a low, instructional tone. "Here's what you'll do. First, focus. Imagine a wall, a thick, impenetrable barrier between your thoughts and the outside world. Feel it solidify, layer by layer. Now, I'm going to attempt to read your mind, just a simple surface thought. Your task is to concentrate on that wall, on keeping me out. Don't push me away, just hold your thoughts in."

"I never met a mind reader before now who was willing to share this. Give me a minute. I'll get it. There is no way it is that easy."

Will closed his eyes, focusing on the warmth emanating from his core, the part of him that felt most fundamentally *him*. He pictured a wall, not of stone or metal, but of pure, shimmering light, growing outwards from his mind, solidifying with each breath. He imagined it absorbing all external intrusions, deflecting them like waves against a shore. It felt strange, like flexing a muscle he didn't know he possessed.

He felt Elowen's presence, a gentle probe at the edge of his mental barrier, like a curious finger tapping lightly on the light wall. He concentrated harder, pouring all his will into maintaining the shimmering shield. He wasn't pushing her away, just holding his own.

A moment passed, then another. Elowen's brow was slightly furrowed in concentration, but then a slow, pleased smile spread across her face.

"Good," she murmured, a genuine warmth in her voice that was not telepathic. "Excellent, Will. You felt it, didn't you? The pressure, and then… the resistance."

They continued working on it for a few more tries before his attention was drawn to the doorway, where he saw Malin and Lydia walk in, both now dressed in dry clothing. They were laughing and talking boisterously until Malin's eyes caught him, and they dropped to a whisper.

This is not going to be an easy trip. He'll be dirt until Malin finally sees her for who she is. He just needs to be patient.

Elowen followed his gaze, her expression turning thoughtful. "Speaking of mental defenses," she said, her voice dropping slightly, "it's quite concerning how strong Lydia's are. I've attempted to read her thoughts, even just fleeting impressions, and every attempt has been completely blocked. Either she's a natural, which is rare, or she's had to learn how to build those defenses so strongly out of necessity."

Malin and Lydia, seemingly oblivious to the unspoken exchange, approached the larger table where the children were still engrossed in their card game with Aldrik. With a shared glance, Malin and Lydia took seats next to each other, on the same side of the table as the children, with Malin next to Ellie.

Will's eyes scanned the remaining chairs. There was only one spot left, directly across from Malin, next to Aldrik. With a mental sigh of resignation, Will walked over and took the empty chair, the creak of wood beneath him echoing the uneasy shift in the room's atmosphere, while Elowen took the seat beside Aldrik.

A sharp pang of confusion, followed by a deeper throb of frustration, settled in his chest. Malin would barely look at him. This curt dismissal, after the brief, unexpected flicker of hope he'd felt seeing her laugh with Lydia, was a cold shower.

Just then, as Malin leaned in slightly towards Lydia, Lydia's eyes flicked to his. A brief, almost imperceptible flash of subtle triumph, a sliver of satisfaction, danced in their depths. It was a look he caught for only a moment before it vanished. Her lips twitched, a faint, knowing smirk playing on her mouth, visible only to him.

A surge of cold suspicion washed over Will. He saw it now, clear as the sea spray on deck. The wedge that Lydia was undeniably, actively driving between Malin and him. He knew Lydia. That subtle, almost imperceptible smirk, the glance of triumph, wasn't just about getting on the ship. It was about poisoning Malin's mind, perhaps everyone's mind, with carefully placed doubts and half-truths about his past, twisting every word and action. She was sowing discord, trying to isolate him, to turn his own family against him. He felt a familiar, chilling dread; this was Lydia's specialty, and he knew he had to stop her before it was too late.

But how?

As long as Malin believed the half-truths, he felt powerless to stop her plan, a cold dread tightening in his chest. *How could he fight a ghost from his past, a weapon crafted from whispers and doubt?*

"They surrounded me," she whispered, her hand rising to flutter nervously at her throat. "Big, cruel men, smelling of brine and blood. Some of the nastiest pirates out there. Anyone who knows Nemilos, the Captain of the Hain, knows you don't cross him."

She should have been an actress; she was quite good at captivating people.

She spoke of the constant fear she felt, her hand instinctively going to her arm as if re-living some past trauma. "They forced me," she continued, her voice barely above a whisper, "to join them. They told me I had a choice: become... the Pirate Captain's mistress or the whole crew's." He watched her eyes, though wide and seemingly vulnerable, subtly scan the room, cataloging every sympathetic nod, every furrowed brow.

A knot tightening in his gut. His eyes, honed by years of reading people, caught the subtle tells others might miss. Despite the dramatic words and the carefully modulated tremors in her voice, there was a profound lack of genuine emotional depth in her recounting. Her pain sounded rehearsed, every beat perfectly timed for maximum impact. He saw no real tears, no unbidden flinches of memory, only a practiced melancholy that settled unnaturally on her features.

He waited, dread pooling, for the inevitable pivot back to him.

"You have no idea what it was like," she went on, her voice dropping again, hushed and chilling. "The captain... he has a temper. Beatings are common. Sometimes, for sport. And his eyes... they'd gleam with a demented pleasure in our fear." She shuddered, a full-body tremor that looked utterly convincing. "I had to be his. Every day. Every night. There was no other way to survive. What else could I do?" She paused for effect before pointing to him, "Will abandoned me to that life. There was no other way to survive." She looked around the room to ensure she had their attention. Her gaze snapped to Will, sharp as a whip. "He just left me there, thinking only of his own escape."

And then, just for a flicker, when one of the crewmen at the next table murmured a sympathetic "Terrible thing, that," Will caught it: a brief, almost imperceptible gleam of satisfaction in Lydia's eyes, a calculating glint that vanished as quickly as it appeared as she scanned the room for further reactions.

He noticed her glance frequently at Malin, her gaze holding a silent plea for shared outrage, as she tried to reinforce their supposed alliance. The whole performance was a carefully constructed lie, and Will felt a cold fury begin to simmer. Her story wasn't just too perfect; it was a carefully curated weapon... against him.

Will was about to speak up, to defend himself, to tear apart the lies that were twisting his past into something unrecognizable.

The protest was already forming on his tongue, a hot, angry retort ready to fly.

But before he could, Nar's calm, deep voice cut through the tension, standing next to the table. "Will's a good man, Lydia," he stated, his dark eyes steady, unwavering. "He takes care of his own."

Khelek, standing next to him, leaned forward slightly, gestured to Ellie and Zane, who were quietly listening, their small faces thoughtful. "He's been a great father to these two," he added, his tone firm.

A grizzled crewman, his face weathered by years of sun and spray, nodded slowly. "Life at sea's got two sides to every story, miss," he grumbled, his voice low but clear. "And choices ain't ever easy out here."

Others murmured in agreement, their gazes shifting from Lydia's dramatic performance to Will, a collective, unspoken vote of confidence that both surprised and quieted the rage building within him. They weren't excusing his past, but they weren't buying into Lydia's singular, damning narrative either.

Lydia stood, "I can see I'm not wanted. I'll move to where I am more welcome," as she moved to sit by the small group of sympathetic crewmen, who were more than happy to receive her.

Will watched her go, a cold knot tightening in his stomach. What poison had she whispered to Malin? He'd seen the look in Malin's eyes before she'd stormed off. He hoped he had imagined the flash of revulsion and flicker of disgust that cut him deeper than any blade.

He knew Lydia. He knew how she twisted words, how she painted a picture of him that was just *close* enough to the truth to be believable, yet entirely false in its intent. He had enough baggage he was ashamed of on its own. Had she revealed the bounty on his head in several places, making him out to be a mere criminal? Had she described his work against the Order of Tamris as something purely monstrous, omitting the desperate reasons behind it? Or worse, had she detailed the *types* of jobs he'd taken, the ones that paid well but cost him pieces of his soul? He cursed internally. Whatever it was, it had struck a nerve, precisely because he hadn't yet been able to tell Malin everything himself.

To expose Lydia would mean tearing open old wounds, truths that he knew Malin would want to know, but that she might not like if she got into the details. He had vowed not to hold anything back, so like it or not, he would tell her, but he wanted to tell her.

It would be better if it came from him, rather than her. If he did nothing, Lydia would continue to poison Malin's perception, driving a wedge deeper and deeper, and potentially putting his family at risk. He needed to find a way to talk with her, before the lies took root.

The mugs of clear broth, accompanied by dried meats, bread, and crackers, were served, barely enough to fill them.

The ship's violent lurching made every bite an exercise in precarious balance. The rest of the meal was relatively quiet, with only the occasional flinching as a particularly large wave slammed against the hull. The giggles and snickers from the crew indicated that Lydia was sharing some raunchy jokes. Knowing Lydia, she was working on lining up her fun for the night.

The common room door swung open, and the Captain strode in, his face grim, the storm's palpable intensity seeming to cling to him like static. He didn't waste time with pleasantries. "Listen up, everyone!" he boomed over the rising din. "This isn't just a squall. This is turning into a proper gale. Prepare for a rough night. All crew batten the hatches and prepare for a blow. It's probably better if the passengers stay in the common room, at a higher point on the ship than the rooms."

Crew members, already moving with practiced urgency, began handing out heavy, canvas life vests. The coarse material felt cold in Will's hands as he accepted one, watching as Ellie and Zee, their eyes wide with fear, looked between him and Malin. With practiced ease, he knelt, securing Ellie's vest first, his fingers deft with the unfamiliar buckles. He moved to Zane, pulling the straps tight but not painfully so, murmuring reassurances as he worked. His gaze lingered on their pale faces, a fierce, protective instinct overriding all other concerns. His family was as safe as he could make them, at least for now.

Malin, despite the tension crackling between them moments before, moved with the same desperate speed to help the children and checked his work on Zee's vest. He quickly strapped his own, the buckles biting into his ribs.

He then pushed himself to his feet, his jaw set as he turned towards the ship's bridge, knowing he needed to speak with the Captain.

Pulling Barnabas aside to speak without others hearing, he looked directly at him, his voice cutting through the growing chaos with a sharp edge. "Captain, I hate to ask. It has been a while since I've heard of an attack, but… Do you think this is a natural storm... or a Cetus? It seems odd that the weather changed so quickly." The word, a whisper of ancient dread, hung heavy in the air, drawing a collective gasp from some of the crew in earshot.

It had been years since he had been part of *Cetus* attacks. The monstrous beings of the deep, essentially water dragons that could control storms, were capable of conjuring tempests with a flick of a fin, of swallowing ships whole. They hunt in pods, and if this fury was their doing, then the ship wasn't just battling the elements; it was fighting a sentient, malevolent force. He had lived through two such attacks, on different ships, over his life, and both those ships had sunk. One of those ships was the Qenya Stin Haven, whose crafted thick metal hull was designed with these monsters in mind.

The Captain's gaze remained steady, unrevealing, even as the ship lurched violently beneath them. "Regardless," he stated, his voice firm, "we sail through it. Keep your wits about you. Look out for your shipmates, and yourselves." His eyes flicked to the portholes, then back to Will. "And keep an eye on the water."

Frustration clawed at Will at the lack of a direct answer, but he understood the unspoken implication. The threat of a Cetus, combined with the sheer physical brutality of the storm, was a chilling prospect.

The ship lurched again, the roar of the wind outside mirroring the tumultuous realization within him. The Cetus, if it came, would rip the ship apart, destroy them with brute force.

But Lydia… Lydia would work from the inside, a slow poison, dismantling trust, twisting loyalties, and tearing apart the very fabric of his life with a far more insidious, equally destructive power. He had always fought the monsters he could see. He hoped he was wrong about the one on the outside, a beast of the deep. The other, he knew, was on board, a creature of whispers and fire, and at that moment, he wasn't sure which one he feared more.

CHAPTER 15 – MALIN

Lydia's final barb was a poisonous dart aimed squarely at Will's character, "You lot better stick together in that storm. Knowing Will, he'll be long gone when the real trouble starts." It seemed to hang, vibrating with malice, in the common room's stale air, as she and the group of crewmen separated for what sounded like a visit of her room.

Even though she had stormed out moments ago, trailing the Captain and most of the crew as they went topside to brace for the brewing storm, her words lingered like a bitter aftertaste.

Malin sat across from Will, who seemed lost in thought, his gaze fixed on some unseen point beyond the grimy porthole. She was equally distracted, her mind a churning mess of questions Lydia had so carelessly flung. What was true? What was a deliberate twist of venom? The uncertainty was a heavy weight in her chest.

Nar and Khelek's unexpected defense of Will, though brief, had offered a different perspective, a sliver of light in the murky accusations. As awful as the choices he supposedly made were, perhaps they truly were the best, the only options he had.

It was good to hear the others speak up for Will. She knew Lydia for brief moments, but she knew Will down to his depths. He wasn't perfect, but he wasn't as bad as she made him out to be.

Malin knew that agonizing calculus all too well. There were countless times in the medical clinic when she'd had to choose between treating and saving a handful of patients or just one. She had always chosen to save as many as possible. Every life was meaningful, but if you had to choose between one and many strangers… the many always won… or did it? Knowing Will's past, however grim, it was likely he had been born from a similar, brutal necessity.

But then her gaze fell on her children. They were in their pre-teen years, and more mature than most of their age, but she watched the subtle tightening of Ellie's shoulders, the way Zane's hand, gripping his spoon, turned white at the knuckles. They might not understand the nuances of Lydia's accusations, the complex web of adult betrayal and consequence. Still, they understood the sharp, angry tone, the abrupt, chilling shift in the room's atmosphere. They understood tension.

A cold dread seeped into Malin's gut. She could sense their discomfort, their innocent worry, as clearly as if they'd spoken it aloud. The sheer horror of Lydia's description of Will made Malin's stomach clench. This was not okay. Not in front of them. Not anywhere.

She is trouble. The thought cemented itself in Malin's mind, unyielding. Any lingering hope of friendship, any fleeting camaraderie she'd felt with Lydia during the storm's initial fury, evaporated like mist in the sun.

The way Lydia had spoken, so carelessly, so maliciously, so *loudly*, in front of the children, and about an act so utterly monstrous... it was unforgivable. Malin's most pressing fear wasn't the distant thunder; it was the venomous woman she had foolishly allowed to remain on their ship. Lydia was a threat, far more insidious than any storm, a viper allowed into their sanctuary.

Will, sensing the lingering atmosphere, quickly suggested a game of cards, pulling a worn deck from a nearby shelf. Malin forced a smile, joining in and trying to focus on the simple rules and the children's earnest attempts to win. But her mind refused to settle.

She then tried to reconcile her thoughts of Will and death. The way he talked about killing the Media guards in the tavern had been matter-of-fact, not out of love for the action, but out of grim necessity. He could be cold about death, yes, but that didn't necessarily mean he harbored bloodlust.

She recognized that Lydia was trying to get under her skin, to drive a wedge between them, but that didn't mean there wasn't a kernel of truth to her words. Will himself had said that he used to be another man, a man she would not have liked if she had met him then. Could that truly have been who he was? The question gnawed at her, a silent unease growing alongside the external threat of the storm.

Just because it was who he was in the past doesn't mean that is who he is now. She thought back to how he was with Ellie and Zee, how thoughtful and caring he had been to her, how fiercely protective of all of them.

The words burrowed deep, igniting questions she needed answers to. *Why had he hidden his past? What else was he keeping from her? Could he truly be capable of such... callousness?* She had seen him being caring and nurturing too many times. Her mother had seen inside his thoughts and had reassured her that he was a good man. It was all too frustrating, as the conflicting thoughts ran through her head.

A faint warmth began to bloom in her chest, spreading outward. She noticed the slight beads of sweat on Will's forehead, the way the air around her seemed to shimmer. It wasn't the ship's stew warming her, but her power, reacting to her agitated state. The room felt... hotter.

Just then, a voice brushed against the edges of her mind, soft but precise, cutting through her mounting distraction. *Malin.* It was Mom. *Perhaps, it would be better if you stepped away for a moment. You and Will could talk until you feel relaxed.*

She pushed her chair back suddenly to stand, "I'll be back. I just need to take care of a few things." She noted the worried glances of Ellie and Zee, but her mother and Aldrik were flanking them with distractions."

Across the table, Will gave her a worried glance and stood, "I'll help," he offered, following her to the doorway.

They got out of the dining room and into the hallway, closing the door behind them, when they noticed the sounds. They were faint at first, but as they moved toward the passenger rooms, the sounds intensified. The sounds of heated, passionate sex.

"It sounds like Lydia found a victim," Will said rakishly.

"What does that mean?"

"I didn't think it mattered in your decision, since I was not planning on helping her with her issues, but she is a bit of a sex addict. I have no doubt she found at least one, if not more, to keep her going for a while. There were several guys at the table."

Her jaw hung open, and he reached up to her chin and closed it, with a crooked grin on his face. "You seemed bent on letting her on board, so who was I to stop you?" he teased.

Malin's jaw tightened, a cold knot forming in her stomach. The sarcasm in his voice, sharp and cutting, sliced through the already frayed remnants of her composure. *Bent on letting her on board?* He made it sound like a childish whim, not a calculated risk she'd taken, motivated by a desperate need for answers and a twisted sense of fairness he himself had invoked. *Maybe she had been a bit bent and not thinking clearly.*

Her eyes, burned with a mix of hurt and indignation, but mostly directed at herself for not thinking through the decision. She wanted to scream, to lash out, to demand why he still held so much back, why he constantly pushed her into a corner where she was inclined to make these inferior choices. A tremor ran through her, making her hands clench at her sides, a physical manifestation of the storm brewing within her.

"I'm sorry. Let's talk about this… away from all of this," he offered, his voice softening.

Every justification she'd given herself for allowing Lydia on board now felt flimsy and reckless. She had invited a menace to their already rocky relationship onto their ship, into their lives, on the last words, a sudden vulnerability cutting through her anger.

He tightened his grip, his gaze unwavering. "Because I was trying to protect you, Sparks. And the children. Not from *me*, but from the complications of my past. From people like Lydia. She is dangerous, far more so than you realize. Her kind of madness makes her unpredictable. I didn't want to bring that into your world, into our lives. I didn't want to burden you with it, or worse, put you in harm's way by making you a target of those who still seek to exploit my past." His thumb stroked her arm, a steady, soothing rhythm. "And as for the dock… I panicked. I saw her, I saw the threat she posed, and I reacted out of instinct to shield you from her. My sarcasm earlier was born of frustration, of feeling powerless when you brought her onto the ship. Not anger at you, but fear for what she represents."

Malin listened to the roar of the storm around them, a fitting backdrop to the turmoil in her heart. His words, stripped bare of his usual flippancy, resonated with a desperate honesty.

She still didn't have all the answers, not by a long shot, but his admission of fear, of wanting to protect her, began to chip away at the walls she'd erected. She saw the lines of exhaustion around his eyes, the slight tremble in his hands, and realized he wasn't just deflecting; he was genuinely afraid and frustrated.

"Protect me?" she yelled in the wind, the edge leaving her voice, replaced by a weary understanding. "By keeping me in the dark? Will, that doesn't protect me, it makes me vulnerable because I don't *know* the danger. I need to know. I need to understand."

A faint, almost relieved smile touched his lips, despite the seriousness of their conversation. He squeezed her, and that familiar sparkle returned to his eyes, softening their darkness. "You're right," he admitted, his voice a low, charming rumble that cut through the storm. "You're absolutely right, Sparks. And I promise, I will. How about, let's get through the biggest issue, the biggest fear, and then I will sit for the rest of our days and bore you with those tales, but for now, we have larger issues at hand. I need you to trust me."

He leaned down, pressing a soft kiss to her temple, his lips cool against her heated skin. The sheer sincerity in his gaze, coupled with the familiar comfort of his touch and the undeniable pull of his charm, began to unravel the tight knots of anger and fear in her chest. She still didn't like the secrets, not one bit. But he wasn't reveling in death. He was trying to protect her. A foolish way, perhaps, but a caring one, nonetheless. For now, in the howling embrace of the storm, with his strong arms around her, that was enough. She leaned into him, letting the wild wind and the steady beat of his heart begin to calm her.

Will pulled back slightly, his expression now etched with a grim determination. "There's something else, Sparks. An idea I've been turning over in my mind, a way to make things right with the Order truly. To get them off our backs, permanently." He took a deep breath, the salt air filling his lungs. "It's dangerous. More dangerous than anything I've faced in a long time. But I remember an ancient artifact of the Order of Tamris, hidden deep within the Fellspire Citadel. If I could get that artifact for them, if I could return it… It might be enough to make them drop their pursuit. To finally leave us in peace."

Malin felt a dread seep into her bones, quickly followed by a staggering realization. He wasn't just talking about appeasing an old enemy; he was talking about risking his life, everything, not just for his freedom, but for *theirs*. For *her*. He was willing to walk into untold danger, to face down whatever horrors awaited him in that citadel, all to sever the ties to his past that threatened to unravel their future. He was willing to risk *everything* to make things right between them. The depth of his commitment, the sheer magnitude of the sacrifice he was contemplating, hit her with the force of a physical blow.

"Didn't you say that that Fellspire place was a fortress?"

"Yes. It is almost impossible to get into, but…" he gave that crooked grin she found so endearing. "I've done it once before… though I'll have to find another way, as I won't be able to sleep with ten women to get the right passcodes again. I'm sure there are other ways to get the passcodes. That was just the easiest way to get them at the time."

She couldn't help but realize how incorrigible he was. How could she be mad at that grin?

Just as she was going to tell him that she forgave him and that they were good, a noise…

A loud bellow accompanied by a series of clicks and a high-pitched call.

Will's head snapped up, his eyes wide, no trace of charm left in them. "I know that sound," he yelled over the winds, his voice tight with grim recognition, as he walked her to the door to the companionway, then used the ropes along the walls to pull himself along. "I need to talk with the Captain. Please, Sparks. Can you tell Nar and Khelek that this is a Cetus attack and they need to prepare? They sound far off right now, so I don't know how much time we have. I love you and want to continue this conversation, but…" He was too far for her to hear the rest over the roar of the winds.

What in the world was a Cetus? She recalled hearing something about a sea creature, but there were so many others that she received a warning about… What was coming?

The raw urgency in his eyes, the shift in his posture, the primal terror in the sound itself. It all screamed danger. Malin felt his worry. It was a *Cetus attack.* The words echoed in her mind, a monstrous counterpoint to the fragile peace they had just found. Her children, her beloved, vulnerable children, were in the common room with her family. That is where she should go. Fear, sharp and paralyzing, threatened to consume her.

This was not a time for emotions, not for the delicate dance of their relationship. This was a time for action, for survival. Her logical mind, honed by years of making quick decisions and devising strategies, clicked into place. The conversation, their future, everything depended on getting through this.

Pushing off the railing, she turned towards the companionway, the thought of Nar and Khelek, of getting their formidable skills ready, the only thing propelling her forward.

As she went, she noticed a crewman out on the deck struggling with a rope that had snapped, whipping wildly in the gale, threatening to tear loose completely. He was straining, his face contorted with effort, clearly unable to manage it on his own. Without a second thought, Malin relayed the warning to her mother, knowing Mom was likely listening intently to their bond. *Cetus attack. Heading to help a crewman with a rope on deck. Will said to tell Nar and Khelek to prepare, they will know what to do.*

She reached the crewman, grabbing hold of the thick, sodden rope just as another monstrous wave crashed over the deck, sending a fresh deluge of icy water over them. Her muscles screamed with the effort, the coarse fibers biting into her hands, but she held fast, her focus entirely on keeping hold of the rope. The crewman grunted in surprise, then gratitude, as her added strength helped them regain a measure of control. They were actively working on the rope, bracing themselves against the violent pitching of the ship, when a sudden, jarring impact slammed into her from behind. A sickening crack echoed in her ears, sharper than the storm. Her grip on the rope went slack, and her world spun into an abyss of cold, crushing blackness.

CHAPTER 16 – WILL

Will burst onto the ship's bridge, the heavy door slamming shut behind him, cutting off the immediate roar of the storm to a muffled howl. The space was a maelstrom of activity, lit by the eerie glow of storm lanterns swinging wildly from the ceiling. Navigators shouted readings, helmsmen wrestled with the wheel, and the ship groaned in protest beneath his feet. Captain Barnabas, his pointed ears flattened against his head by the wind, stood braced against the central console, his face grim, his gaze fixed on the churning chaos visible through the reinforced glass of the viewport.

"Captain!" Will bellowed over the din, fighting his way through the scurrying crew.

Barnabas didn't even need to turn. "You heard it too, then," he rumbled, his voice strained. He finally tore his eyes from the storm, his gaze meeting Will's, reflecting the same cold dread. "It's a Cetus. Small pod, but they are hunting and I think they we are the prey."

"Any idea how much time we have?" Will asked, his heart hammering against his ribs. He gripped a support beam, steadying himself as the ship pitched violently.

Barnabas shook his head, his knuckles white where he clung to the console. "Not enough. It's moving faster than any I've seen. We're doing what we can no sails only mechanical power, trying to turn hard into the waves, minimize broadside exposure. But this isn't just about riding out a storm, Will."

His eyes darted out the window to section of snapped rope that lashed dangerously wild in the wind.

"The mainmast is loose. I had a deck hand on it, but… If that goes, it would mean trouble."

He looked back at Will, a desperate plea in his storm-weary eyes. "Will, I need that rigging secured. Can you help us?"

"Happy to," Will responded, already moving towards the snapping rope. He glanced at the main viewport, then back at Barnabas. "But Captain, you need to be aware: I heard the Cetus sounds to the starboard side. We're sailing right towards them. We need to cut hard, move away. Now."

Just then, the ship lurched violently, a bone-jarring impact resounding through the hull as if something immense had slammed into them. The floor beneath Will's feet bucked, sending a fresh wave of shouts through the bridge.

"Blast it all!" Captain Barnabas roared, struggling to maintain his footing. He fought his way back to the viewport, peering into the churning darkness.

"Shaped Elven metal is among the strongest in the land," he bit out, his voice hoarse but firm. "We've stayed afloat through too many other attacks for this to be our end. We can make it through, Will, but it's going to be a hard one. If we lose that rigging, though, we are dead in the water."

"I'm on it!" Will roared back, already heading towards the door not waiting for another word.

He burst out of the bridge, the icy wind and stinging spray assaulting him instantly. He raced across the lurching deck, dodging frantic crewmen and snapping lines, his eyes fixed on the mainmast. He found the rogue rigging. It was a thick, splintered rope lashing wildly, held by three smaller crewmen whose faces were pale with strain, their feet slipping on the slick deck. Their grip was failing.

Without hesitation, Will slammed into position beside them, grabbing hold of the coarse rope, his larger frame and sheer strength immediately making a difference. With a combined grunt, they dug their heels in, slowly gaining ground, inch by painful inch, against the wind's tearing force. They were making progress, the rope slowly coming under control, when out of the corner of his eye, he saw her, then she disappeared. Surely, he wouldn't imagine seeing Lydia.

What is she doing here? he thought, a spike of cold disbelief cutting through the adrenaline.

She was standing near the rail, too close to the edge, watching them with an unnerving stillness. He needed to focus on the rope, she would get inside, if she were smart.

Just then, a monstrous wave, black and frothing, crashed over the ship's bow, a liquid mountain that engulfed them all. Will's lungs burned, the icy water trying to rip the rope from his grip, threatening to drag him into the churning abyss. He gritted his teeth, muscles screaming, barely able to stay attached.

As the water receded, gasping for breath, he lifted his head, his vision clearing enough to see them. There, in the churning, phosphorescent depths just off the starboard side, were the creatures. A pod of immense, dragon-like sea creatures, their heads unmistakably draconic, with front, finger-like flippers churning the water, and long, powerful tails lashing against the hull. They were not just swimming; they were actively working in concert, pressing their massive bodies against the ship's side, trying to flip it.

He knew they were large and dangerous, but if they felt their prey would fight back, they would leave. If Malin were here, her flames might have scared them off. He yelled to the crew near him, "Do you have any powers that could hurt them?"

The crew shook their heads negatively, as they worked to get the rope under control.

In that heart-stopping instant, a flash of memory ignited in his mind. He remembered the harpoon gun, mounted on its pivot nearby, usually shrouded by a canvas cover. He hadn't thought about it in years. It typically took two people to operate, one to aim, one to load the heavy harpoon and ready the charge, but the crew were working the rope. He was the only one available. With a surge of adrenaline, he rushed to gun.

With a desperate, primal yell, he tore off the sodden canvas cover, exposing the weapon. His hands, driven by instinct, snapped open the breech and slammed a heavy, barb-tipped harpoon into place, the familiar click echoing even over the storm. He didn't bother with the usual second hand for stability, his muscles screaming as he locked the firing pin back with a strained click. He planted his feet on the impossibly slick deck, ignoring the sway, and with a grunt of pure effort, swung the gun to aim, the foresight of the barrel blurring into the chaotic, wind-whipped darkness.

He fired.

The harpoon shot forward, a dark streak against the chaos, burying itself deep into the closest creature's flank with a sickening thud that vibrated through the ship. A deafening shriek of pain ripped through the air, momentarily drowning out the storm.

The Cetus thrashed violently, its immense tail lashing the water into a frothing maelstrom.

But the reprieve was fleeting.

The roar of the injured creature quickly muted to a suffocating gurgle as a colossal wave, taller and more furious than the last, rose from the depths. In its last attempt before death to take out the prey, the Cetus launched itself onto the ship.

All Will saw was a moving wall of black against the stormy sky, and for a heart-stopping second, time seemed to stretch as the black wall came into view, as the large body of the creature came crashing down onto the ship with the force of a falling mountain. Will could see the harpoon sticking out of its chest, black blood pumping out. The deck bucked and groaned, and Will, still braced over the now-unmounted harpoon gun, felt the world tilt violently.

The ship tilted, causing the large creature to slide off the deck.

A sickening lurch ripped his feet from beneath him. He slid, a helpless rag doll, across the impossibly slick planks, his fingers scrambling, desperate for purchase that wasn't there. His hand slapped against the cold, wet rail, a fleeting hope, before the sheer momentum of the wave's impact tore him away. He plunged into the churning, ink-black abyss.

The shock of the icy water was immediate, a brutal punch to his senses. It stole his breath, his vision, and for a terrifying instant, even his fear.

Disoriented, unable to see or feel anything but the crushing cold, the only thing he still instinctively clung to was the heavy harpoon gun, a lead anchor in the swirling chaos pulling him down. He gasped, the frigid water invaded his lungs, and knew instantly he had to release the gun, as his life preserver pulled him to the surface.

Once at the surface, he frantically clawed for anything else to grab hold of.

The churning, icy water muted the roar of the storm to a suffocating gurgle. The ship became a rapidly receding shadow above him, a distant silhouette against the madness.

He wasn't alone.

In the brief, terrifying chaos, he saw the flailing forms of several other crewmen, dark shapes against the phosphorescent glow of the deep.

He watched, horrified, as powerful jaws, lined with needle-sharp teeth, wrapped around a crewman only a few yards away, dragging him under with a final, choked cry. Panic surged, cold and stark. He had to get to safety, out of the water, *now*.

His eyes, burning with salt and desperation, frantically scanned the churning surface. Floating nearby was a shattered piece of wood, wreckage from one of the destroyed lifeboats.

A slender hope.

If he could reach that meager piece of flotsam, bobbing half in and half out of the water, he might find a place to hide, a chance to avoid their notice.

Kicking with all his might, fighting the current that sought to drag him under, he strained, every muscle screaming in protest. He reached it, his numb fingers closing around the splintered wood.

Not that this was a safe place, but it was a safer place. Unfortunately, it also left him with no view of what was going on around him.

He held on, forcing himself to limit his movements, to become just another piece of debris in the monstrous sea, hoping against hope he had escaped their ravenous hunt. Typically, once one in the pod fell, the others would leave, but that could be minutes or hours.

After moments that stretched into an eternity, he dared to look around him, floating in and out of the water as the waves tossed him. The relentless waves and winds had blown him far from the ship. He faintly saw a flickering light in the distance. It had to be the ship, but there was no way he could get back to it safely in these treacherous waters. He was on his own, adrift, but at least he was away from the immediate threat of the Cetus and their attacks, as he didn't see any near him.

As the ship seemed to be moving, he hoped that Malin and the kids were fine, that he had stopped the attack, and that once they noticed he was gone, they would come for him.

Suddenly, a massive wave crashed over him. The icy waters engulfed him, ripping him from his purchase on the debris. He was thrown from the wreckage, tumbling in the water, disoriented, desperately trying to determine which way was the surface, which way was air. His world went black.

CHAPTER 17 – WILL

Will woke coughing up seawater and with a rasping burn in his throat. The blinding sunlight above told him that hours had passed, though he didn't know how many. He lay sprawled on rough, dark rocks, the sharp edges digging into his back. The air was thick with the scent of salt and something else – a sweet, unknown fragrance of tropical flora carried on a warm breeze. He pushed himself up, every muscle protesting, to find himself alone on a rocky beach.

The shore was a jagged crescent of volcanic rock, slick and dark, giving way to a dense wall of vibrant green jungle. Towering palms, their fronds impossibly broad, swayed lazily against a sky so intensely blue it almost hurt to look. The waves here were gentler, lapping at the rocks with a steady, rhythmic hush, unbothered by the stir of a storm.

He stood up to get a better look around. There was no sign of a ship, no splintered wreckage beyond the rock he clung to, no distant smoke, no faint sails. No one in sight, no sign of campfire or civilization. Just the relentless, indifferent beauty of a distant shore.

With only a few other pieces of debris, he hoped that he had been the only casualty. Malin had gone down to the family, so surely, they were fine and looking for him. He wouldn't allow himself to consider any other alternatives. He would bide his time till they found him. He concentrated on Malin, following the soul-bond. It was miles away, surely on the ship. They would be looking for him. It was only a matter of time. He would need to stay near the shore.

After he stripped off his clothes and shoes to let them dry, he had traveled these routes for years, so if he could get his bearings, he might be able to figure out where he was and how to find help. His map was left in his bag on board the ship, so he would need to go by memory.

He found a tall, straight stick and plunged it into the soil vertically. He marked the location of the longest shadow. He needed to wait. In his head, he began counting.

The sun was high, baking the rocks and making the air shimmer. His lips were parched, cracked, and burning, a torment that eclipsed even the ache in his bones. He had no idea if it had been hours or days since he was swept overboard, since the Cetus.

Will's stomach growled, a sharp, insistent demand that pulled him from his daze. He was stranded. There were miles of coastline. He needed to prepare a fire that he could use as a signal fire and wait, but exhaustion from that little activity wore on him, so he sat to catch his breath.

There had to be edible plants in the tall foliage nearby.

Pushing himself to his feet, he stumbled towards the dense tree line. A quick check as he got closer revealed some familiar fruit hanging heavy on the branches, a small victory. They were on the sour side, but undeniably edible and filled with juices. He quickly gathered a few, biting into one with a grateful, if wincing, sigh. The tart juice was a welcome shock to his parched mouth.

It reminded him of a time when he and the twins had been shipwrecked near Aloria. They must have been fifteen years old and alone on that island for at least three months before they were rescued. They had learned a lot about survival from each other on that trip. It had not been the last time those skills had been put to use.

His internal counting reached 1,500, a mental rhythm he maintained to track time. He checked his makeshift sundial and marked its progress. He now knew his east-west orientation, a small but crucial piece of information. They hadn't even made it a whole night out of Sarhan before the storm hit, and the heading he knew they were on would have placed them somewhere off the Coast of Kanata. He donned his dry clothes and shoes, grateful for the boots on the rocky shore.

Kanata, a vast wilderness that spans the continent, was known for its smaller, scattered tribes and towns, which were home to a diverse array of species. Determining exactly where he was on that huge coastline was his immediate, daunting challenge.

With the dense forest, camping close to the water meant that anyone could be watching him, but if he camped too close to the tree line, he'd be easily ambushed.

He found a flatter section of rock, picked up another sturdy stick, and began to draw, etching the contours of the coastline he could see into the damp sand. Perhaps laying it out visually would spark his memory from the detailed maps he'd studied countless times aboard the ship. Each curve and inlet he replicated was a desperate plea to his mind, hoping for a flicker of recognition, a clue to his location in this wild, beautiful, and utterly isolating landscape.

As he gathered wood, he stopped to pee against a tree, and a shiver ran down Will's spine. A presence, light yet unmistakable, settled in his mind, then a familiar voice, clear as a bell, echoed within his skull. *William.*

Will got some on his feet. He shoved the wood aside and muttered aloud, *Well, isn't this just a grand reunion. You do know how to make an entrance, Elowen.* A sarcastic grin, thin and strained, touched his lips. *Though, I must say, barging into a man's thoughts when he's relieving himself is a new level of intrusive, even for you.*

You were thinking rather loudly, dear boy, Elowen's mental voice retorted, a dry amusement threading through her tone. *Besides, I needed to confirm you were alive. The ship… we've run aground. On a reef, it seems, and the Captain says that even high tide won't release us. We're safe for now. Aldrik, Anariel, Nar, Khelek, and the children are *here. But tell me, William. Is Malin with you? I can't reach her, and that concerns me greatly.*

Will's blood ran cold. The sarcasm drained from him, leaving him hollow. If Elowen, with her powerful telepathy, couldn't reach Malin, it was a terrifying sign. Panic, stark and visceral, clawed at his throat.

No. She's not, he rasped, his voice raw. *I sent her to warn Nar and Khelek. She should have been down in the common room.*

Please, not her. Not Malin.

William, calm yourself, Elowen's mental voice urged, though he could feel the tremor of her concern. *Remember, your bond with Malin is… unique. An early soul bond, forged deeper than most. You may be able to find her through it. Close your eyes. Reach for her.*

He did, squeezing his eyelids shut against the harsh sun. He pushed past the chaos of his fear, past the dull ache of his body, and reached out with every fiber of his being. He focused on the familiar warmth, the spark that was uniquely Malin. A faint, almost imperceptible thread, stretched thin across the vastness, shimmered in the depths of his mind. Yes. He could feel her. It was a faint, persistent tug in the direction of Northwest of his current location.

She was alive.

He opened his eyes, determination hardening his jaw. He would head straight to Malin.

I feel her, he thought back to Elowen, the relief a palpable wave, quickly followed by a grimace. *It's… uncomfortable, knowing you're in there, Elowen, right in my head, but I am grateful to hear from you. Thank you for reaching out. I'm glad to hear you're with the kids .*

I understand, William, Elowen acknowledged, a hint of genuine sympathy in her tone. *But use the shields we practiced. I won't be able to reach you then. And…* Her mental voice turned grave, a chill seeping into his thoughts despite the warm air. *When I reached for you, I felt another presence at first. Faint. But distinct. Someone else with a power like mine is nearby. Be careful. You are not yet at the level to be able to pick and choose who to let in, so your only option is to let everyone in or block everyone out. If it is safe, drop shields at dawn and dusk. I will attempt to reach you then.*

He could feel her leave his mind. A relief, though having the company wouldn't have been so bad.

Finding Malin was his top priority, so he decided to begin his trek following the direction his pull to her wanted him to go. Elowen's warning about others in the area made it even more of a reason to keep moving, especially since he couldn't sense them.

Not wanting the wood to go to waste, he gathered it to take with him. He then took off his shirt, fashioned it into a bag, and placed the rest of the fruit and some of the wood inside, strapping it to his back.

He decided to walk the shore until he felt the pull change direction. He walked for over an hour when he heard a voice call out from the tree line. He recognized the voice. Lydia. She ran to him. "Will. I'm so happy to see you!"

Will's gut twisted. Lydia. One of the last people he wanted to see.

Just when he thought he might have a moment of solitude, the universe, in its infinite cruelty, delivered her directly to him. Her declaration of happiness grated on his ears. He kept his expression carefully neutral, allowing none of the irritation bubbling inside him to show. His priority remained Malin.

"Lydia," he acknowledged, his voice flat.

He could hear her stomach churning, a loud, undeniable gurgle from her midsection. Instinct, or perhaps just a primal need to silence the unpleasant noise, took over. He unslung his makeshift shirt-bag and pulled out a piece of the sour fruit. "Here," he offered, holding it out.

Lydia snatched it, gobbling it down with an almost feral hunger, juice dribbling down her chin. For a moment, she looked less like the dangerous manipulator he knew and more like a desperate creature.

Once she'd devoured the fruit, some semblance of her usual composure returned, though her eyes still held a frantic glint. "Will," she repeated, stepping closer, "What happened? I thought... I thought I was alone. What about the ship?"

He ignored her questions for the moment. "What were you doing on deck, Lydia?" he asked, his voice low, a controlled edge to it. The image of her standing near the rail, watching, while he and the crew fought for their lives, still rankled.

Lydia waved a dismissive hand, a hint of her old arrogance returning. "Oh, my toy, you see, he wanted to do something... dangerous. And I thought, well, sex on a deck in the middle of a storm? How terribly amusing. I had just finished when I saw you on deck." Her lips curled into a familiar, unsettling smirk. "I was merely enjoying the view, watching your muscles ripple as you wrestled with that rope. Quite the show, until the big wave hit."

She shuddered, a genuine shiver this time, then looked at him with an unnerving intensity. "It was terrifying, Will. One moment, I was watching you, the next... I was just in the water. I thought I was going to die."

Will's jaw tightened. *Sex on deck. Watching his muscles ripple.* Her casual disregard for the peril, her self-absorption even in the face of death, was infuriating. And the way she framed it, as if his near-death struggle was mere entertainment... it confirmed every dark suspicion he'd ever harbored about her. He needed to find Malin, and this woman was going to be nothing but a distraction.

"Do you know how we can get back to the ship or where to go from here?" Lydia asked.

Will ignored her questions and kept walking.

"You just going to go off and leave me to fend for myself again?" She tried to gain his sympathy, but he could see her ploy.

"If I left you, Lydia, I'm... *off-handedly* sorry," Will said, the sarcasm thick enough to cut with a knife. He pushed past her, moving towards the tree line, scanning the dense foliage. "Honestly, though, I never wanted to see you die." He risked a glance back at her, his expression grim. "I've had too many people around me killed because of the folks who are after me. I figured leaving you in Sarhan, even if it felt like abandonment to you, was a better fate than the alternative." He paused, a flicker of genuine irritation crossing his face.

"In fact, I thought I was doing you a favor by leaving you there. I even got word to Zane to help you with getting on any ship you wanted out of the port." His voice hardened, a dangerous edge returning. "But he said you told him to 'Get Bent?'"

Lydia flinched, her eyes widening slightly, but quickly recovered, a defensive glint appearing. "He didn't want to help. How could he? By that time, I had already been claimed by Nemilos. If he had stepped in, Nemilos would have burned down Sanctuary to get to me. Zane didn't need that, and you know it," she spat.

Realizing that the stories of Captain Nemilos Kaku were infamous for his ruthlessness, she was probably telling the truth about what he would have done to Sanctuary if she had gotten help. Her decision to stay with him probably saved more lives than she knows.

He started walking. If she wanted to keep up with him, that was her choice. He wasn't going to force or ask her to, but he would attempt to help her... this time... if she chose to accept the help.

"Clearly," Will scoffed, resuming his pace along the rough shoreline. "Look, Malin might have some misguided soft spot for you, but I don't. I'm heading out. You can follow if you want, but don't expect me to hold your hand. If you can't keep up, I'm leaving you behind." He didn't wait for her decision; he just kept walking.

A moment later, he heard her scrambling footsteps behind him. "Fine!" she snapped, her voice still rough but audible. "Just try to lose me, Will. You know I'll find my own way."

Will didn't dignify that with a response. He just kept walking; the rhythmic crash of the waves against the shore was a brutal reminder of the world they were stranded in.

His focus remained singular: Malin. Every step was a prayer, every glance towards the distant northwest a desperate hope. Lydia was a burden, a complication he hadn't wanted, but for now, she was simply part of the landscape he had to navigate to reach his wife.

The sun was a bleeding wound on the horizon, painting the churning sky in hues of orange and bruised purple. As it dipped below the jagged silhouette of the rocky shore, Will noticed a dark, still pool of water trapped between two large boulders. The light was fading fast; it was too poor to make out its contents.

He pulled one of the smaller logs from his makeshift shirt-bag and held it out to Lydia. "You could be useful for once and light the end of this so we can actually see something."

"Now I'm needed. Oh, joy," she drawled, but a flicker of interest, perhaps even boredom, crossed her face.

She cupped her hands around the end of the log, a faint, reddish glow appearing between her palms. It took a moment, the damp wood resisting, but then a small flame flickered, caught, and began to burn steadily.

When the torch truly lit, casting dancing shadows, Will exclaimed, "Nice! We're stopping here to eat."

The light illuminated the shallow pool, revealing a large, startled fish trapped within. Without preamble, he took the two other logs from his bag and placed them on a large, flat rock, forming a makeshift grill. He then arranged three small stones around the budding fire, placed another flat rock on top, and with swift, practiced motions, took out his knife, quickly killed the fish, dressed it, and laid it on the heated rock.

"If you can maximize that flame, this will cook faster," he offered, without looking at her, his focus entirely on the meager meal.

He felt her eyes on the fish, breathing in deeply, and could almost hear her stomach rumbling again. Lydia's flames were so much weaker than Malin's; even at full power, her fire was a dull, angry red, nowhere near Malin's brilliant, cleansing white. Even still, her focused heat did cook the fish a bit faster. They ate in near silence, the sizzle of the cooking fish and the distant roar of the ocean filling the void between them.

Will stiffened, already cleaning his knife on a patch of grass. The chill of the night had begun to settle, seeping into his bones. It was a good thing he'd gathered that wood, as he desperately needed his shirt now.

He shook the shirt out, damp but relatively clean, and pulled it back on, letting the familiar fabric shield him from the cold.

"That's no fun. I was enjoying the view," Lydia purred, looking up from her seat on the ground, her eyes glinting in the firelight.

He ignored her comment, refusing to engage.

The silence stretched, thick and uncomfortable, broken only by the rhythmic clapping of the waves against the shore. Finally, Lydia broke it, her voice surprisingly soft. "I do like her. I didn't want to, but she has a way about her. I don't know too many people like that. I don't know what she's doing with you, but…"

"I will not be talking about Malin with you," he clarified, his voice flat, dismissing the very notion.

A slow, deliberate smile spread across her face. She hiked up her skirt, legs spread wide, leaving no barrier for a full view of her. "You sure you don't want just a little taste? You seemed to like the fish just fine." Her voice was a low, suggestive whisper, designed to crawl under his skin. "For old times' sake and all," she added.

Will felt a hot surge of disgust, the casual vulgarity a stark contrast to the peril they had just faced.

He turned away, the desire to put distance between them overwhelming. "That is not on the menu, ever," he stated, his voice a low growl, his stride lengthening quickly as he began walking away from the makeshift camp.

She scurried to catch up, her bare feet surprisingly agile on the rough ground. "Never say never, my pet," she said, her voice breathy, and reached out, touching his arm as she almost stumbled.

He instantly grabbed her arm, his grip harsh, and shoved it off him. The venom in his voice was undeniable. "I am not your pet anymore." The words hung in the cold night air, and she took a surprised step back, her smirk finally faltering.

Then he felt it. He had paid so much attention to her; he hadn't been paying as good attention to his surroundings as he should have. He could feel people with powers nearby.

Why couldn't he see anyone?

"Hold on. There are others near here." He looked around, but couldn't see anyone, but he could feel their powers. "Why can't I see them, but I can feel them?"

Lydia let out a cackle that cut to the bone.

Suddenly, he felt an odd sensation, like a buzzing through his whole body. He could no longer feel the powers of Lydia or the people around him, as he had.

"How?" He couldn't see them, and he couldn't sense them. He swung at the air.

He could hear deep laughter all around him. He was surrounded.

His eyes were betraying him. He tried to raise his mental shields, but he couldn't. He tried to nullify the powers around him, but it didn't work; they must have been stronger than he was. He couldn't tell how many people surrounded him. He was powerless.

As he looked around, the moon was beginning to cast its faint, silver glow when, just as he was about to round a particularly jagged spur of rock, the world shimmered and fractured. It wasn't a physical shift; his feet remained firmly planted on the rough, uneven ground, yet suddenly, undeniably, he was on the ship and he could feel the sensation of the sea. The cold, damp air of the tropical beach vanished, replaced by the familiar scent of salt and tar, the metallic tang of blood, and the oppressive weight of the storm. He could feel the ship moving, vibrating with the familiar hum of its engines, the distant shouts of crewmen, but it was subtly wrong, like a memory warped by fever.

"What is going on?" Will demanded aloud, his voice echoing strangely in the illusory space, drowned out by the phantom creak of timbers. How had this happened? What magic was this? Was he losing his mind?

Then, cutting through the ghostly sounds of the ship, he heard it. Lydia's high-pitched, evil laugh, a sound that clawed at his nerves, sharp and undeniably real within the illusion.

"Nemi, I thought you were never going to get here. Would've gone hungry if it weren't for Will," he heard her sticky-sweet voice, seemingly just to his left, clear as day. Yet when he spun, there was no one there.

The deck stretched empty before him, the rigging stark against a nonexistent, impossibly calm sky. His heart hammered, a frantic drum against his ribs.

Could she be talking about Captain Nemilos? The pirate she was running from?

Lydia did not have these powers. There was someone else here doing this. *It must be him.*

He could hear the sound of a slap making contact with skin, followed by a body dropping to the ground. "You dared try to leave me."

"No. No, my love. We have a bond. I knew you could find me. You said we are bonded. This… this is my ex. The one what left me in Sarhan," He could hear the begging in her voice. She was scared.

"This is the one? I had promised you could have some fun with him if we ever found him. We shall see when we get back to the playrooms," Nemi said.

Playrooms do not sound fun.

Why couldn't he see them? He gripped his head, grappling with the impossible, the sheer disorientation making his stomach churn. This wasn't real, but it *felt* real. He swung his fists wildly in the direction he'd heard the voices, striking only empty air, futile blows against a deception. His foot caught on an unseen rock, and he lost his balance, tumbling awkwardly onto the hard, uneven beach, still physically present. The illusion flickered, the ship's sounds momentarily replaced by the harsh reality of the crashing waves and the feel of abrasive stone, before snapping back into place with a sickening lurch.

He lay there, panting, the ghost ship rocking beneath him. The cold sweat of fear mixed with the dampness of the beach.

His mental shields. He needed to raise his mental shields, as Elowen taught him. He concentrated, then the images of the ship disappeared, replaced by the rugged coastline and rocky shores, waves crashing. He saw Lydia, and a group of pirates surrounded him.

He felt a crack to his head, and his world went black.

CHAPTER 18 – MALIN

Darkness. A throbbing, relentless ache pulsed behind Malin's eyes, a drumbeat of pain. She tried to think of her medical training, but the world felt fuzzy, with trouble digging into her memories. The world swayed, not with the familiar roll of a ship, but with a dizzying, disorienting spin. She coughed, a dry, ragged sound that tore at her throat, and the salty taste of seawater filled her mouth. She was half in and half out of the water on a beach of brown, sharp rocks mixed with vibrant pink sands.

She forced her eyes open. Blinding sunlight stabbed at her, forcing them shut again. When she finally managed to squint them open, she saw a blur of vivid green, then the endless blue of the sky. She was lying on something hard, gritty, and uneven. Slowly, agonizingly, she realized it was a beach.

Fear, cold and sharp, cut through the disorientation. Her head throbbed, a dull, insistent thrum that resonated with every beat of her heart. A tentative hand went to the back of her skull, and her fingers were slick with blood. Then, a searing pain shot up her right leg. She looked down, her breath catching in her throat. Her leg was twisted at an unnatural angle, the bone clearly broken.

Panic flared, raw and desperate. Not now. Not like this. She tried to push herself up, but a wave of nausea swept over her, coupled with a dizzying rush that sent spots dancing before her eyes. The world tilted precariously.

She tried to remember what happened. She was working the ropes with the crewman. Things were going well, then she felt a crack in the back of her head. She couldn't remember anything after that. Surely, Will and the family will be looking for her. It is only a matter of time. She reached out with her bond to find Will.

He wasn't close. The kids were with the family, in the safest hands possible. Will had gone to the Captain, so once he realized she was not on the boat… surely, he would have convinced them to turn around to get her. They would come to get her any time.

Just then, her stomach retched, over and over until she was dry heaving. The saltwater and bile left a bitter taste in her mouth.

Through the haze of pain and disorientation, she heard sounds. A soft, rhythmic clapping of water, then something else. She heard voices. Low, guttural, utterly alien. She blinked, forcing her vision to clear, and saw them. A group of figures emerged from the dense tropical foliage at the edge of the beach.

Her first instinct was fear, but she knew that if she didn't get help soon, she would die. She hoped these beings would help her.

They were short and slender, their skin a mottled green-gray that blended unnervingly with the shadows. And then she saw them: gills, delicate slits visible on their necks, flaring faintly with each breath. Their eyes were large and dark, unblinking. They carried no weapons she recognized, but their very presence, their unnatural stillness, sent a fresh jolt of terror through her.

They spoke again, their language… a series of words mixed with clicks and soft grunts, entirely incomprehensible. She didn't know what they were, but they were unlike anything she had ever encountered. *Didn't she have something in her ear that was supposed to help with that?*

Her healing magic, usually a reliable comfort, felt sluggish, distant, and overwhelmed by the sheer extent of her injuries and the disorienting blow to her head. She could feel it working, a slow, deep thrum beneath the pain, trying to knit bone and close wounds, but it was a battle.

The faces of the gill-creatures swam before her, their alien features growing larger, closer. The world began to spin faster, the light dimming at the edges of her vision. The last thing she registered was their dark, unblinking eyes, before the welcoming blackness claimed her once more.

Malin woke to the scent of dried herbs and the persistent, throbbing ache behind her eyes. Her hand instinctively flew to her head, finding it wrapped tightly in soft, unfamiliar bandages. A wave of nausea swept over her with the slight movement, and she squeezed her eyes shut, fighting the urge to vomit.

Her medical training immediately kicked in, cataloging the symptoms even as her brain felt sluggish, like mud. The throbbing pain, the nausea triggered by movement, and the overall sensation of her mind being foggy and disconnected. It all pointed to a diagnosis that wasn't just a bump on the head; it was a concussion. Even the faint, familiar voices of her magic, usually a vibrant hum beneath her skin, were muted, barely a whisper within her, a sure sign of her body prioritizing basic functions over anything complex.

Where was her family? Surely, they were on their way to her. She tried to reach out to her mother, but her head hurt too badly to think. She could feel Will's presence, but it was far away.

She became aware of other bindings: her right leg felt stiff and unyielding, wrapped securely in a splint, and her left arm was equally immobilized. She noticed that her bracelet was still on her uninjured arm. Someone was treating her, then. Someone had found her, and they were treating her kindly, hadn't stolen from her, and were in the process of healing her. She might not know where she was, but she was safe. She felt a slight fuzziness in her head, and the pain that she should feel from whatever injury had caused her to be immobilized was gone. She surmised that she must have been drugged.

She opened her eyes again, taking in her surroundings. She was in a small, circular hut. Bunches of dried herbs hung from the wooden rafters and walls, their shadows dancing in the dim light filtering through cracks. The bed was far too small, her feet dangling unceremoniously off the end of the rough wooden frame. The room itself was sparse, clearly crafted from local wood, and carried the rich, earthy smells of a village, with damp soil, exotic blossoms, and distant cooking fires.

She realized she was no longer in her clothes but dressed in a simple, reddish-brown linen shift, the color of the packed dirt floor beneath her. Her stomach grumbled in a loud, undeniable protest for its emptiness.

A shuffling sound drew her gaze to the entrance. She looked up, hoping to see a familiar face.

A small, ancient woman hobbled in, leaning heavily on a gnarled wooden cane. Her face was a map of wrinkles, her eyes dark and wise as they focused on Malin. She was short and slender, her skin a mottled green-gray that blended unnervingly with the shadows, just like the people Malin had glimpsed on the beach. And then Malin saw them: gills, delicate slits visible on her neck, flaring faintly with each breath. Her eyes were large and dark, unblinking, fixed on Malin with an unnerving stillness. She moved with practiced ease, approaching the bed and gently checking the bandages on Malin's head. *The healer,* Malin surmised, a flicker of clarity piercing her confusion.

She had so many questions for her, but her brain wouldn't cooperate in asking them. Where was her family? She felt for Will through their bond, and he seemed far away. She tried to move and threw up off to the side of the bed. Her world felt so fuzzy.

The woman straightened, then extended a gnarled hand holding a wooden cup. It contained a steaming liquid that looked like a deep amber tea and smelled surprisingly sweet.

Hesitantly, Malin took the cup. The taste was delicious, warm but not hot, coating her dry throat with a soothing comfort. She drank it down greedily. As the last drop left her lips, the world became woozy, spinning faster than the ship ever had. Her eyelids grew heavy, and she had no strength left to fight the pull.

The darkness, soft and welcoming this time, consumed her once more.

Malin woke again, the lingering fog in her mind finally lifting. This time, she could feel the splints were off her arm and leg. She cautiously touched her head; it was no longer wrapped, and the relentless drumbeat of pain had blessedly ceased. She stretched her arm, gingerly testing the joints. It was sore, stiff from disuse, but not hurt. A wave of relief washed over her, just as she reached for the bucket by her bed and vomited. The sudden movement must have caused it because of the concussion.

She uncovered her legs, pulling back the thin linen shift, to see that they looked completely normal, their skin smooth and unbroken. Someone had changed her clothes again; she was now in a soft, grey linen shift, a stark contrast to the reddish-brown one.

How long had she been out? The question pulsed in her mind.

Hesitantly, she let her long legs swing off the side of the bed. They touched the cool, packed dirt floor easily and, surprisingly, without pain. Her right leg, the one that had been so clearly broken, felt only a dull ache, otherwise normal. She decided to try to stand. She was wobbly, her muscles weak and uncoordinated from prolonged rest, but she could stand. She took a moment, balancing precariously, to look around the small, circular room.

She reached out for Will through their bond. He was still so far away. Surely, he could tell where she was, just as she could tell where he was. Why didn't he come to get her? She hoped he wasn't hurt, also. The rest of the family would have no way to find her or even know she is there. She reached out her thoughts to her mother, but nothing happened; she didn't understand how that power worked. Maybe this was normal.

She was alone and hurt. A panic set in, a tear slipping down her face.

There was a tall shelf crafted from rough-hewn wood, filled with an assortment of containers and woven baskets holding dried herbs and unfamiliar remedies. Books, scrolls, and a variety of strange, intricate objects she didn't recognize were tucked among them. A small step ladder stood near the shelf, suggesting a regular need to access its higher reaches. There was a second, empty bed on the opposite side of the hut, covered with a simple woven mat, and a small, low table with two miniature chairs beside it, carved from dark, heavy wood. She recognized some of the plants hanging from the rafters as medicinal, a familiar comfort in this alien place. She was thankful that she had spent so much time helping Caelum study for his degree in Medicinal Horticulture while they were in college.

A sudden wave of dizziness and vomiting hit her, forcing her to sit back down on the bed before she could explore further. As her head cleared slightly, her thoughts, no longer dulled by pain, began to race, then drifted to memories. Maybe it was the drugs, but she was racked with memories.

She closed her eyes, remembering those many nights in college. While she had been learning to be a doctor, Caelum, her brilliant, kind Caelum, was learning to make medicine. She had helped him study for so many of his exams, poring over ancient texts and complex formulas late into the night. They had started as friends, the four of them—Awelyn, Lira, Caelum, and herself—inseparable ever since their first year at the academy. Friendship had been the bedrock; her focus was solely on getting her degree. It wasn't until their third year that she even realized he liked her, and then her fourth before she finally admitted she liked him back.

A faint shuffling sound pulled her back to the present. She quickly dried her face with the rough linen sheet, trying to compose herself. The same ancient woman who had brought the tea earlier hobbled back into the hut, this time with a tray laden with a steaming bowl of stew and another small cup of liquid.

Malin eyed the cup cautiously. She would have to make sure it wasn't going to sedate her again. She needed answers.

"You are awake," the old woman said, her voice raspy, thick with an accent Malin couldn't place.

"Hi. You speak my language," Malin replied, then grimaced internally. It sounded silly, even to her ears. *Of course, she spoke the language. She just spoke it.*

"We have met your kind before," the woman stated, her dark, unblinking eyes assessing Malin.

Malin realized with a pang of embarrassment that she still didn't know her name. "Thank you," Malin said, her voice a little stronger than before. "For everything. I'm Malin. I don't think I ever properly introduced myself."

The woman's dark, unblinking eyes held a knowing glint. "I am Khun MorBaan," she said, her voice raspy but clear, with that thick, unplaceable accent. "I am the village elder and healer."

Malin hesitated, a question burning on her tongue. "Khun MorBaan," she began, "if you don't mind me asking... what species are you? And the people I saw on the beach? I have never seen anyone like you before."

Her lips curved into something that might have been a smile. "We are the Gill-Kin Fae, or as some outsiders call us, the Marid."

The revelation settled in Malin's mind, a new piece of the puzzle of this strange world. "Gill-Kin Fae," she murmured, testing the words. She understood the gills, the mottled skin, the almost aquatic grace.

"I've heard of Fae before, but I didn't realize they were like you," she said.

"For the Gil-Kin, Heitsi-Eibib, an elf of the high ones, fell in love with the oceans and then fell in love with a creature of the sea. Out of their love came the Marid." Her explanation seemed straightforward enough.

"How are you feeling? With as badly injured as you were, we expected you to be here for weeks, not days."

"It has been days?" Malin's eyes widened, her surprise genuine. Her healing magic truly was incredible, even when her head was still scrambled.

"Yes. Four to be exact. Do you know how you came to be on our shores?" she asked, her gaze unwavering as she placed the tray in front of Malin. She looked up, her wrinkled brow furrowing slightly with a worried glance. "The tea is only tea this time," she added, as if sensing Malin's apprehension.

Four days. Malin struggled to remember the chaotic events that led her here. "I was traveling on a ship with my family. We were in a terrible storm… and then… Will thought there was a Cetus attack." She took a hesitant bite of the stew. She couldn't make out the ingredients, but the rich, savory flavor was incredible, warming her from the inside out.

"Did you find any others?" She was afraid of what the answer would be.

"No. It has only been you," the old woman confirmed, a note of quiet sorrow in her voice. Malin released the breath she held.

"We have sent words out to the other human we know. He may be able to help you reconnect with your loved ones again. He will be here this evening or in the morning."

The mention of another human sparked a fragile hope. "Your healing is faster than normal," the healer continued, her expression shifting to one of profound curiosity. She reached out, checking Malin's pulse on her neck and gently touching her forehead. "Is this magic? We have met some with magic, but no one can heal as quickly as you. It is incredible."

A voice outside the hut spoke then, guttural and resonant, a string of strange words with clicks and grunts, just as Malin had heard when she had first landed on the beach.

"I'm still learning about this stuff, but I thought that my humm worm universal translators in my ears were supposed to be able to translate. Is something wrong?" Malin asked with rising concern.

"Calm down. It is possible that they were damaged in the injury or that they do not understand our language. We are a tiny tribe with very few of us left," she said wistfully. "We will take care of things. You are healing well, and soon you will be able to find your family."

The old woman's head snapped towards the sound. "They need me. I will be back. You can leave, but I recommend you stay here for now. It will make the transition easier until the human arrives," she explained, already turning to hobble out.

Malin watched her go, and a sense of unease settled over her. She did not like the idea of feeling like a prisoner, even a well-treated one, but she was so tired, so utterly drained, that it didn't sound like the worst idea to stay and continue healing. Taking slow, deliberate bites of the nourishing food, she reached out with her mind, desperately seeking her mother. She got no connection, only the vast, empty expanse of her thoughts. Surely, Mom would reach out to her if she were looking for her, if she knew she was alive.

But Malin didn't fully understand how the power worked. Perhaps it was the distance, or maybe her mother had to reach out first, from her side of their bond. She could only hope that they had made it through the storm without issues and were frantically searching for her, but how would she ever find them?

She finished the stew, placed the empty tray on the small table, and sank back onto the bed. Her body ached with a profound weariness, now that the immediate threat was gone and the adrenaline had faded. She closed her eyes, and this time, in her own accord, she fell asleep.

This time, when Malin awoke, the throbbing behind her eyes was entirely gone, replaced by a dull ache that felt like progress rather than injury. Her body was sore, but she showed no apparent signs of pain.

A tray of fresh fruit and a bowl of steaming, fragrant porridge waited on the table. On a chair, neatly folded, was a clean shift in the reddish-brown color of the packed earth floor. She felt a surge of strength in her limbs, a lightness in her step. Confident now, she pushed off the bed and walked around the small hut, stretching her newly mended arm and leg. Her body felt remarkably whole, though stiff, a testament to her unique magic and the diligent care of Khun MorBaan.

Only moments after waking, her improved consciousness acting like a beacon, she felt it: the unmistakable brush of her mother's mind in her head. It was faint, distant, but undeniably there.

Malin. Are you alright? We've been so worried. I kept trying to reach out, but I couldn't find you. The concern and worry in her mother's mental voice were thick, almost palpable.

Malin's relief was a dizzying wave. *Mom! Yes, I'm… I'm doing better now. I got hit in the back of the head when I was helping secure a rope. It was a nasty blow, but between my healing and the Marid village healer's care, I'm on the mend.*

Then, her anxieties surfaced. *How are the kids? Will? Is everyone safe?*

The kids are a little shook up, but they are holding on strong, Mom replied, a steady presence in her mind. *The ship is stuck on a reef, but fortunately, it remains intact. The crew is working on getting it off, but until then, we're camped on shore.* A moment of hesitant silence stretched before her mother's mental voice returned, tinged with a fresh layer of concern. *The rest of us are hanging in, but… we haven't heard from Will. He went off looking for you, but I haven't been able to reach him for days. He could have his mental barriers up, or… He sensed your location and said he had gone searching for you before we lost connection; perhaps you should try to sense his.*

Will is missing? The words slammed into Malin, eclipsing the relief of knowing the others were safe.

Her thoughts spun, a fresh wave of panic threatening to overwhelm her. She pushed it down, centering herself as Lady Anariel had taught her. She reached out, extending her mental tendrils, searching for that familiar, infuriatingly evasive presence that was uniquely Will. Yes. There! A distinct pull, a faint pull in the swirling chaos of her mind, tugging her in a clear direction. It had to be him.

You can sense him, so you know he is alive, her voice confirmed, a thread of hope. *Lydia is missing too. We haven't seen her since the attack. Lady Anariel received news that something had happened to her parents, so we decided to head to Mellyrn on foot. We can get transport from there to Aloria, if needed. It is over two weeks of hiking, but it makes the most sense. The stranded ship is a target for pirate attacks, and we don't have supplies here to stay camped with the crew for much longer, and honestly, I don't care for sleeping in tents much longer.* There was a dry wit in that last thought, a familiar touch of her mother's personality. *If I knew where you were, we could certainly get you on the way. Finding Will is your best chance, as he will know the routes and how to get to Mellyrn. Find him. Can you tell me about the people you are with?*

Malin described the people and what she knew about them.

The sheer weight of it all descended upon Malin. All the challenges all at once: the missing loved ones, the vast, unfamiliar wilderness, the daunting journey. She felt herself breaking down, the accumulated stress of the shipwreck, her injuries, and now the uncertainty of her family's scattered fates, hitting her with full force. *Mom. What do I do? I don't know where I am. I don't know how to travel in the jungle. I've lived in Media my whole life and never left the city walls! How am I supposed to find him? How am I supposed to get back to you and the kids?* Her mental plea was raw, edged with desperation.

The connection wavered, not ending, but her mother didn't respond immediately. Several tense moments dragged by before the connection surged back, stronger this time, brimming with purpose. *Aldrik almost beheaded a crewman who wouldn't respond fast enough, but he believes he may be able to get to the village you are in. It is the opposite direction from Mellyrn, so we can't detour for you. The kids and I are going to head to the kingdom with Nar, Khelek, and Lady Anariel, where they will be safer. Mom's voice softened, almost a chuckle. Bless him, but your father is worried about his daughter and seems to want to move mountains to ensure your safety.*

Hearing that help was coming to her… and her father, of all people… helped calm her panic, a fragile warmth spreading through her.

With thick emotions swelling in her thoughts, *Please let him know how much that means to me,* she mentally expressed her gratitude, a profound wellspring.

The crew told him that he is about a five-day walk from you. Are you sure that you can hold out until then? Elowen asked, a faint tremor of worry still in her thoughts.

Yes. They are good people. I don't think that will be a problem, Malin thought, genuinely. She felt safe and cared for.

I will keep trying to check in with you. Elowen's mental voice grew more serious. *At this distance, we both need to be open to communicating simultaneously. There are others out there with similar powers to mine, though, so you need to keep your wards raised, or risk intrusions. Try to keep them raised and lower them only around midday, sunset, and sunrise, if you feel safe. I will also try to reach out then. Be safe, Malin, and know that we will do everything we can to keep your children safe. I love you.*

I know you will keep them safe. Mom. I love you too. Thank you so much, and please let Ellie and Zee know that I am thinking about them.

Her heart felt immeasurably lighter, knowing that they were safe and being cared for. She didn't think there were better hands for the kids to be in than with Nar and Khelek, whose loyalty and strength were absolute. With that, she could feel the connection gracefully end, a lingering warmth in her mind.

Her father is coming to protect her. It was an odd thought to consider him her father, given the complexities of their new relationship, but his actions and genuine worry proved his claim.

Five days. She could wait here that long. The other human would be here soon, as well, so she wouldn't feel so utterly alone. A sudden feeling of calm settled over her, profound and unexpected. Until then, she would keep herself busy learning about this new culture.

She finished the food on the tray and changed her shift. She brushed her hair with her fingers and braided it, using a small piece of string she found on a shelf to tie it.

As she finished, Khun hobbled in, carrying a fresh bundle of herbs. As the late afternoon sun began its slow descent, "Come, you are strong enough now. Let me show you our village," she offered.

The sunlight, even softened by the evening, was still too bright for Malin's head injury, causing her to squint, blink, and often instinctively cover her face with a hand. Khun MorBaan walked at a measured pace, her cane tapping a gentle rhythm on the dirt paths. As they walked around the village, Khun pointed out various structures or huts similar to the one she was in, larger communal buildings, and strange, intricate traps set for fishing. She introduced Malin to several people they passed, few of whom could speak Malin's language, but all offered solemn, dark-eyed gazes.

They came to a large, communal fire pit in the middle of the village, where a massive pot bubbled, filling the air with savory scents. Gathered around it were three of the Current Keepers, a council of respected elders. The one with the most ornate clothing was skinny and slightly taller than the others, with movements that were precise and deliberate. He managed to speak a halting greeting in her language. Another was a plump, jovial woman whose laughter rumbled like distant thunder, her skin a deeper green. The third was of average size in both height and weight, but striking, covered in very colorful scales that shimmered under her simple clothing, with delicate corals attached as adornments to her hair and garments.

Malin observed them, her analytical mind absorbing details even as a profound weariness began to creep back. She noticed that the roles and contributions to the community seemed more important than gender or physical appearance. There was an easy, flowing hierarchy based on wisdom and skill, rather than on gender, status, or wealth. It was a refreshing contrast to the societies she was familiar with.

A small group of children, all with their subtle gills and large eyes, ran past, chasing some brightly colored insect, their laughter bright and unrestrained. No parent followed them, and no one shouted commands. Malin asked Khun about it. She explained that while children spent more time with their immediate family, they were raised as part of the entire village, cared for and taught by everyone.

"I have a daughter and a stepson," Malin said, the words heavy with a sudden surge of maternal worry. "I'm really worried about them. This is the longest I've been away from my daughter. She would have reached out to me by now if she could." Her concern was palpable, a fragile thread woven through her newfound calm.

A wave of profound exhaustion rolled over her then, pulling at her like the tide. Khun MorBaan seemed to notice immediately. With a gentle touch to her arm, the elder guided her back towards the healing hut. It turned out that the other, empty bed Malin had seen earlier was, in fact, Khun's own. Khun MorBaan gently tucked her in, adjusted the woven blanket, and Malin, too tired to resist, closed her eyes.

The soft, unfamiliar sounds of dawn stirred her, a gentle rustling of leaves and distant bird calls, but Malin merely snuggled deeper into the rough sheets, instinctively scrunching her long legs to fit into the small bed. Her body felt whole and rested. It was a profound relief after the agony of only a few days ago.

Then, a familiar voice, hushed and filled with concern, pierced her peaceful awakening. "Will she be okay?"

It was a voice she hadn't heard in years, yet it resonated deeply within her memory, pulling at something long buried. She tried to place it, a frantic mental search that eluded her.

Her eyes fluttered open, blinking against the soft, filtered light. She must be dreaming. This was a cruel trick of her subconscious, a longing too deep to be real, rooted in the memories of loss she had from the day before. The eyes looking back at her were impossibly blue, set in a face that was achingly familiar, yet older, etched with subtle lines she didn't know.

This was the voice and face of her lost love, Caelum. She felt her world tilt, and her skin tingled with discomfort.

She barely breathed out, "Caelum." Her breath hitched. "You... You can't be here? You're dead," she spat as she sat up quickly, the words raw, disbelief warring with a desperate, burgeoning hope. She shook her head a few times, as her eyes could not see what was clearly in front of her.

She blinked several times, hard, willing the vision away, but he remained. His light blond hair, just like her own, fell to his chin, slightly mussed, complementing the day or two of stubble that dusted his jaw. When she finally realized it was not a trick, not a lingering hallucination, she slowly and tentatively reached out, her hand trembling. Her fingers brushed his cheek, feeling the rough stubble, the warm skin. His blue eyes, still that striking, impossible color, stood out against his tanned skin, reflecting a mixture of wonder and profound relief.

"Is it really you?" she whispered, her voice fragile as she tried to dispel the thick ache in her throat. Her heart hammered, not with pain, but with an overwhelming surge of disbelief and desperate hope, even as a cautious part of her worried about being tricked.

"Malin. I never thought I'd see you again." He pulled her to a stand, then into a deep embrace. His strong arms wrapped around her, crushing her gently against him. He was only an inch or two taller than her, a familiar height that sent a jolt through her.

A flood of memories hit her with the very scent of him: the smell of sweat, earth, and a faint, sweet hint of his familiar vanilla soap enveloped her, a sensory anchor to a past she thought had been irrevocably lost.

He had always said he wanted to save people, the only way he knew how. As Media, their beloved city, needed rare medical ingredients, he would travel the world, braving distant lands, in search of unique medicinal plants to protect its inhabitants. She had hated his trips outside the city, the gnawing worry that he would never return, but she knew his work was so important to him, so vital for the lives of countless people. When he finally proposed, she had just passed her medical exam, the ink barely dry on her certificate. They were planning a short engagement and a small wedding, a quiet affair. They had meticulously planned and joyfully lived their lives. Days after the proposal, he had planned a significant trip to procure medical supplies, a necessary but lengthy expedition. He would be gone for two months. When he came back, they would marry.

Life, however, had other plans for her. The day she found out she was pregnant with Ellie was the very same day she found out that he had died. It was only weeks after he had proposed. The memories were still so raw, even after all these years. She could feel the hot, familiar sting of tears pouring from her eyes, tracing paths through the dust on her cheeks.

He pulled back, holding her at arm's length, his gaze searching hers. "When they sent word to me, saying a human was here, injured… I never dreamed, not for a moment, it would be you."

Tears welled in her eyes, blurring his beloved face. "You're alive! How? What happened?" The questions tumbled out, urgent and desperate, each word a desperate claw at the years of grief and unanswered prayers.

Caelum's smile was bittersweet. "It's a long story, Doc. We have plenty of time to catch up." His use of the nickname he gave her in college, that familiar, tender "Doc," tugged at her heart and, against all odds, helped her begin to accept that this might really be him.

"Khun said you were healing quickly. When they reached out to me, they told me the human was injured so badly they expected you to be in recovery for months." He looked at her, truly seeing her, a hint of awe in his gaze.

A spark of defiance, of newfound power, flared within her. She pulled her hand from his, letting it hover between them. "I… I was chipped. And I got my chip out not long ago. I have powers now. I can heal, but I also have this," she said, her voice firm with conviction. She concentrated, and a small, crimson fireball ignited in her palm, a miniature sun glowing fiercely in the dim hut, its heat a familiar comfort. Then, with a thought, she extinguished it, plunging the space back into soft shadows.

He stepped back, his eyes wide. "Malin," he breathed, a genuine shock in his voice. "That is… incredible."

The excitement of seeing him was instantly tempered by a cold, complex question that arose within Malin: *Why?*

What had truly happened to him, to keep him away all these years? The man she had mourned, the man who was the father of her child, was here, breathing, looking at her.

Should she tell him he is a father? No. Not yet. She needed more information, far more, before she risked Ellie.

Malin pulled away, a stark, emotional distance growing between them despite the close confines of the hut. "Why didn't you come back?" she questioned, the words sharp, edged with years of pain, abandonment, and resurrected hope. "Why did they think you were dead? Why didn't you try to even get word to me, to anyone?"

The silence that followed was heavy, broken only by the distant, rhythmic pounding of the waves against the shores nearby.

Caelum shifted, his gaze flickering, a subtle discomfort in his posture. "Malin, it's… complicated. After I left for that last supply run, things went wrong. Very wrong. I was captured, held in places I couldn't escape, couldn't send word to you. I barely survived. They made sure I couldn't communicate, and I had no way to know if anyone would even look for me, or if it would put you in more danger. I had found out that Media had orders to kill me on sight, so I knew I couldn't come back. I didn't want to risk your safety by sending you a message." His voice was low, carefully modulated, but there was a guardedness in his eyes that Malin couldn't ignore.

She felt his answers were vague, filled with evasions about dangers he couldn't fully speak of, about believing it was safer for her not to know. *Once again.* Another man who thought it was protecting her by hiding information from her. Just what she needed.

Something within her, a primal, maternal instinct, cautioned her. Her mind, usually so quick to forgive, now bristled with a deep-seated distrust.

"And you?" he asked, his expression carefully neutral, his gaze searching. "What happened? After I left... what happened that made you leave Media? Was it the powers?"

Malin met his gaze, weighing her words. *How much could she reveal? How much should she?*

The excitement of seeing him warred with the insistent whispers of caution. She had learned the hard way the cost of misplaced trust, the danger of truths carelessly shared. "My powers made it too dangerous, eventually. My mother left with us." It was the simplest truth, the most basic. Enough for now.

"Your Mom left Media?" His eyes widened.

"She told me you were in the Resistance," Malin stated.

"So, you know she was the leader of the Resistance. That is huge."

"It was a pretty big surprise to me also." She considered telling him about the role the man she thought had been her father had played but decided against it for now.

"Can I take you somewhere? I travel extensively and would be able to get you anywhere you needed, even Aloria."

"I have someone on their way here. He will be able to help with that, but..." She paused at his disappointed look. "Having another person would be great. First, we must go find someone."

She wasn't sure whether she should tell him she was married, and she would need to look for her husband. Maybe she would hold off. She might need his help to find him.

"So, you have a plan?" he asked.

Plan? Malin's thoughts raced. The man she had loved, mourned, the father of her child, was alive. He was standing right here. But the life she had built since his supposed death, the love she had found with Will, the bond she had formed with the man who was now a father to Ellie, a partner to her… it was all suddenly, terrifyingly, at stake. How could she reconcile the past with the vibrant, demanding present?

Could she truly trust him, this ghost from her past, this man who claimed to have loved her, yet hid so much? And if she could trust him, what did that mean for everything else?

How would she tell Ellie? How could she possibly navigate this without shattering the tentative, precious family they had become? The thought of telling Will, of seeing his reaction, sent a pang through her heart that was sharper than any betrayal. She was supposed to be forging a future with him, with their children.

Maybe if she gave herself time, if she got to know him again, truly, this insidious, distrustful feeling would dissipate. Or maybe, it would simply confirm her deepest fears. The path forward was a dark, tangled forest, and she had no map.

CHAPTER 19 – WILL

The jolt of the horse's gait ripped Will from a shallow unconsciousness. Raw agony was his first sensation, not thought. Rough ropes bit into his wrists, drawing blood with every desperate flex of his bound hands, then dug deep into his ankles and upper thighs, constricting like venomous snakes. His arms, wrenched behind his back, screamed in strained protest, the muscles already cramping. He was draped stomach-down over the animal, his chest taking the relentless, jarring brunt of every single one of its steps, each impact jarring his teeth, rattling his bones.

A thick gag choked him, the coarse fabric scratching his raw tongue, filling his mouth with a taste of dust and desperation. A blindfold stole every sliver of light, leaving him in suffocating, absolute darkness. He felt something else. Something he had never experienced before. There was a buzzing in his consciousness that emanated from the bite of a needle or barb piercing his flesh on his neck. It was attached with a rough band or leather strap wrapped tightly around his neck.

Where am I? What the hell happened? Panic flared as he reached out with his powers to identify who was near him. Nothing. Just the increase in the disconcerting buzz, causing a cold tendril of fear to squeeze his gut.

He tried to shift, to test his binds, but the movement only amplified the pain, sending a sharp jab through his ribs. The horse beneath him was a powerful beast, its heavy hooves thudding a rhythmic, almost hypnotic beat against what stounded like a packed dirt path. He felt the strong ripple of its muscles beneath him with each stride, the scent of horse sweat and dust filling his nostrils.

Other sounds slowly filtered in. The jingle of bridles, the creak of saddles, and the low murmur of voices. Too many voices.

His heart hammered a desperate rhythm against his ribs.

Then, a scent cut through the dust and horse: Lydia's perfume. The familiar, cloying sweetness that used to bring a rush of warmth now sent a chill straight to his bones. Lydia. This was her doing.

He tried to stretch the ropes to see if he could break them, but they were too tight. The horse's every step nearly winded him, pressing into his chest. He had never had a love of horses, as few were built for his dimensions.

"He's up," a deep voice near him said gruffly.

The horse stopped, then rough hands lifted his torso and removed his gag. He took a much-needed gasp of air, savoring the cool morning breeze.

"Well, well, well," Will rasped, his voice rough but laced with a familiar sarcasm. "Took you long enough. Was beginning to think I'd have to file a complaint about the travel accommodations."

A snort of laughter broke through the tension, coming from one of the younger, lighter voices nearby, as rough hands ripped him off the horse, letting him fall with a thud on the moss-covered ground. He heard a popping sound from his shoulder, accompanied by intense pain. His shoulder must have come out of the socket again. It had been over eleven years since the last time. He centered his thoughts, forcing shallow, quick breaths, to ride through the pain.

"See? Graceful even bound," Will continued, twisting his head slightly in the direction of the laugh. "Now that's comedic timing. Good choice, kid. A natural." He then shifted his attention back towards the deeper voice. "Perhaps Mr. Gruff Man here could use a few lessons on delivery. You really undersold the 'He's up' line, you know? No flair, no pizzazz. It's all in the presentation."

With that, he got a punch in the side.

Worth it.

A sudden, heavy hand clamped his jaw, lifting his head. He tried to fight it. He had been in enough of these situations to know that they were probably about to drug him. Not many were willing to risk giving him opportunities to escape. It's what he would do. He tried to keep his jaw muscles tensed and locked.

Like it or not, a cool, metallic rim pressed against his lips, and a sickly-sweet liquid was forced down his throat.

He tried to hold this liquid in his cheek so that he could spit it out, but they knew that technique and held his nose and sealed his mouth, until he was forced to gag it down, while he struggled futilely. He felt four hands lift him back on the horse. The last thing he registered was the insistent thud of hooves fading, fading…and then, black.

Will surfaced from the blackout into a world of new pain. At first, it felt like he was floating weightless, with his arms out to each side, but as he moved, his left shoulder wrenched in the sockets, and the sick weight of his own body pulled at his ribcage and wrists. Metal cuffs cut grooves into his skin. His legs were spread and shackled, in a standing position, holding his body up, but even that wasn't easy. The belt was still wrapped around his neck. When he moved, barbs embedded into him. There was a buzzing feeling emanating from those barbs; every time he reached out with his powers, the buzzing became painful.

The gag was back in his mouth, this one thicker and fixed tight by a leather strap at the back of his neck. He tasted dried blood, probably his own.

His eyes were uncovered now, and a slow look around revealed a large room, lit only by a few dangling lanterns, casting a jaundiced light on the wooden walls. The floor was damp and sticky in patches. A large bed lay on the other side of the room, by a desk piled with papers and objects, and a chair.

Lydia was there, to his left. She was naked, arms shackled in front of her, her breasts clamped to a board by metal screws. Blood ran in thin lines down her belly, glistening as it caught the lantern light. Her face was twisted in something halfway between agony and ecstasy; her lips were bitten raw, her jaw slack.

He was likely in this position because of her. He had no sympathy for her. She was getting what she deserved.

A naked, tall man with long, dark curly hair tied back neatly at the nape stood behind her, hands gripping her hips. He was built like a barrel, with silver rings on every finger and hair so black it almost disappeared in the dark of the room.

Each thrust sent a ripple through Lydia's spine, her head knocking back against his chest.

"Now," the man said, his voice a lazy purr with the clipped edges of Sarhan's highest caste. "That's what happens to bad girls. Isn't that right, my pet?"

She moaned, but her response was lost in the sound of her body slapping against the board.

The man grunted, finished with a last, brutal surge, then let Lydia slump forward against her restraints. He wiped himself with a strip of linen.

Lydia whimpered. "Yes, Nemi."

With trembling fingers, she undid the clamps on her nipples, letting them spring free with a wet snap. Blood welled around the edges, and she massaged it into her skin, finally bringing some to her lips. She sucked her fingers, eyes never leaving Nemilos.

Nemilos turned his attention toward Will. "Welcome, Mr. Hawkson," he said, like a host greeting a guest to a dinner party. "I apologize for the accommodations. We didn't realize we would have guests. Lydia has told me of you, and I must say you do have a reputation. I had promised her that I would give her opportunities to play with you."

Will tried to answer, but the gag made it a wet choke.

The man approached, stopping just close enough that Will could see the lattice of scars along his forearms, the faint blue veins under pale skin.

"My name is Captain Nemilos Kako of the Crimson Wake," he said. "I suppose you've heard of me?"

Will rolled his eyes, which seemed to upset his captor. He traced a long fingernail down the muscles of Will's bicep.

"Your reputation also has preceded you… The famed Hawk of the Resistance. I'm surprised we haven't run into each other formally until now. I'm sure you noticed that your powers don't work. A little gift from the prisons of Fellspire Citadel. Apparently, they need to remove powers temporarily from people in prison, and they devised that little device I have attached to your neck. It works similarly to the microchip that Media uses, but with more finesse, providing a slightly different frequency, and will not induce death… to most people. We got lucky with you. I can see I'm going to have a lot of fun."

Will arched an eyebrow. He had heard about the technology but hadn't realized it had been scaled down to the size of a large pendant.

Nemilos smiled with all his teeth. "Lydia spoke of you with… fondness. My pet has been having some challenges lately. I blame it on this rainy weather, but… I told her that if she wanted you as a pet, we could arrange that… after you are broken. In case there are better options, I've also reached out to some of those groups who seem to have an interest in you… a number of them…

impressive… We shall see if their offers are worth giving up my pet's new toy."

He reached up and stroked Will's cheek, tracing a line from his jaw to his earlobe. Will jerked away, but the chains did not allow for much movement.

Nemilos leaned in, lowering his voice. "We'll have plenty of time to get to know each other. For now, let's dispense with pleasantries. I have spent a lifetime learning to break people." He walked back over to the edge of the bed and took a seat.

"I want to see what my canvas looks like. Take that shirt off him," he said, his thick, heavy accent.

Lydia tottered over on unsteady legs with a knife in hand. She undid the buttons of his shirt with slow, shaking hands, peeling it off his shoulders. She ran her tongue along the sweat-stained hollow at his collarbone. He tried to turn away, but the chains held him still.

He noticed all the scars and bruises on her body. He almost felt sorry for her.

Lydia rubbed her hands over his chest, then licked and sucked his nipples.

"Good girl," he said.

"Should I take off his pants too?" Lydia asked, her voice small yet hopeful.

"Not today, my pet. We must save some fun for tomorrow; today, you work for your reward." He gathered the large whip on the table in his hand, letting the long thong hit the floor, then he walked behind him, so he couldn't see what he was doing.

Lydia pouted but followed orders and finished removing his shirt. She then sliced what was left of the shirt off, leaving him shirtless in the chill room.

When she finished, she dutifully returned to where he sat on the bed with his knees akimbo. She dropped to her knees and began pleasuring him.

Will tried to turn away, but the chains didn't offer much.

His voice was suddenly cold. "Here is the game." He stopped her, and she wiped her mouth. He motioned for her to lie on the bed. "For every time my little pet strokes the toy, you will get the whip, until she has climaxed. Simple enough?"

Will glared, then nodded once. *This could take a while with her,* Will thought, remembering their history.

Nemilos clapped his hands. "Excellent! You remember the rules, don't you, my pet?"

She nodded and smiled. Nemilos fetched a large, wooden phallus from a shelf. From a distance, Will could see that it looked smooth and slightly larger than average. He placed the toy into a hole in a bench.

"Begin," he said, as he walked to stand behind Will.

Lydia straddled the low bench, raising her hips and sinking onto the toy. One plunge and one lash with the whip. The first lash was a firebrand down Will's spine. He sucked air through his nose, refusing to give Nemilos the satisfaction of a scream.

Each downward plunge earned her a grunt from Will, her hands clawing at her thighs. By the fifth stroke, Will was biting through the gag to keep from yelling. Blood was trickling down his side, pooling at the waist of his trousers.

He turned to Will, admiration in his eyes. "Still conscious. Impressive, but she has several strokes left."

She upped her tempo. The next five lashes came in rapid succession, turning Will's back into a mass of welts and open wounds. Another five… or was it six. He just knew it was pain. Excruciating pain.

He couldn't hold it in any longer, but the gag wouldn't allow sound to escape. He tried to scream when the stroke hit his chest.

"I think this would be so much more fun if I could hear you. Let me help you with that gag," he said as he let Will spit out the hard mouth covering.

The strokes continued. He lost track of the pain, but it seemed her enjoyment was nearing its peak. He said, "Slower, my dear. Savor it."

Lydia obeyed, and the room filled with her gasping, animal noises, followed by the crack of his whip and his scream.

At stroke twenty or was it thirty, Will started to fade. The pain was too much, the world flickering at the edges. He saw Lydia in double, her face split by shadow and sweat. He tried to focus, to count, but the numbers slipped through his fingers.

His legs were having trouble holding him, and his shoulder felt like it would rip off.

Eventually, Nemilos relented. He stood beside Will, cupping his chin in one hand. "I think you're ready," he said.

Aiming for Nemilos, Will spat a clot of blood onto the floor, as the pirate was expecting it and dodged.

He laughed. "That's the spirit…. Lydia, you need to clean him."

"No. I think I'm good. No cleaning needed. I think this color of red really goes with my eyes," he forced out.

"Gladly, Nemi," she walked toward Will completely naked, teasing the tip of her nipple as she went.

She licked the blood from his back, her tongue slow and deliberate. As much pain as he was in, every touch was electric, white-hot agony.

Nemilos watched, stroking himself. When Lydia finished, he pulled her to him and kissed her roughly and hard, then dragged them behind him.

"You are a witch, and I can't get enough of you." He lifted her, pressing her body against Will's back as a wall. He could barely stand on his own, but the pressure on his shoulder was intense as he had to press back against her to stay upright.

"You know, walls would be a lot easier," Will ground out.

"You did so well," he cooed, ignoring Will, as he slammed into them. "Now show me how much you want it."

"You mean how much she wants to touch me, more like it." The pain in his arm was killing him, but he wouldn't give this madman an ounce of pleasure from his pain if he could help it.

Every thrust threatened to rip his arm off. As much as he wanted to continue commenting, he could not do anything without risking a scream being released. Every moan, lick of the blood, and squeal she gave seemed to turn Nemilos on more. Her hands wrapped around his front to tease his nipples, then she was able to move lower, so she could reach Will's waist. She shoved her hands down his pants to grab his cock. It seemed to be dual-purpose. Something to hold onto, and the thrusts allowed her to stroke his length repeatedly.

He couldn't vocalize the scream for their pleasure, but he was screaming internally.

He hated them. He hated them both, and he would make them pay. He just had to hold on.

The pain in his arm was so intense that he thought it would be enough, but his body had a mind of its own. He realized he had to concentrate not to let her touch get to him, but some things couldn't be controlled. Finally, Nemilos finished, and he walked to the bed, turned, and surveyed the room. His eyes landed on his partial erection.

How could his body betray him like this?

"My pet. You have teased your toy. Let's see what you can do with that toy in your mouth."

"Of course, she wants me. I think she remembers that thirty-six-hour fuck feast we had that night in Sarhan after the heist. I think she had trouble walking for almost a week after that. I can't blame her. It is not reacting to her, though," Will choked out through the pain.

"It seems he is not ready to have the gag removed yet," he said as he walked over and forced the gag into Will's mouth again.

She flashed a smile at Will as his eyes went wide. She kneeled down, unbuttoned his pants, and pulled his cock out. His wriggling in his chains did nothing but make her more interested and cause his shoulder to scream, so he concentrated on calming himself down. He tried to think of every sickening thing he could to make his body not respond.

Her tongue found him, and she licked and sucked over and over, then took him into her mouth. He didn't know how she could take so much of him in without choking. As much as he hated it, it felt amazing. He hated that his body had betrayed him like that. He should have been stronger than that.

As much as he tried to hold back, with the pain he felt, he couldn't, and he ended up climaxing in her mouth against his will. He was mad. Mad at them, but mostly at himself. The pain was so intense, yet his body had responded.

Nemilos clapped at the show. "My pet. This one is going to be fun to break. You can see it in his face. He hates that he just climaxed." He paused, watching Lydia lick the stickiness from him. "I think we need to move your toy into the other playroom. Make sure he is fed before putting him away."

She moved to the desk in the far corner of the room, where a tray with a bowl and cup was already set. Then, she picked up a long metal object about the size of her hand and added it to the tray. She carried the tray over and set it at his feet. Then it sounded like she dragged a chair behind him.

Will struggled to make sense of her words, his mind racing. Then he felt her hands gently brushing his shoulders and jawline, and suddenly, the gag dropped to the ground.

"What has he done to you?" he asked. His voice, dry and raw, was a mix of confusion and concern. She climbed down from the chair, tore off a piece of bread, and held it out to him with anticipation. Even with her diminutive stature, she had to stretch upward to reach. She dragged the chair in front of him and stood, now looking down from a slight height advantage.

"He made me better. He and I are connected. He said." Her eyes, wild and weary, stirred a complex mix of pity and frustration within him.

He had always known she was a little off-kilter, but it was clear Nemilos had transformed her into something extreme.

"I like this view," she remarked with a strange satisfaction.

"If you can let me out of this, I can get us both out."

She fed him morsel by morsel, her actions both caring and unsettling. When she tried to slide her finger into his mouth, he attempted to bite it. She giggled, countering with a kiss, but he managed to bite her tongue. As she pulled away, her bloody mouth twisted into a broad smile, and she licked her lower lip.

"Drink some water. We need you to rest and be strong for tomorrow. That's my reward day. I get my toy," she said, pressing a cup to his lips. He tasted it reluctantly.

"Let me go. I can get us both out of here," he pleaded, his voice tinged with desperation.

"Silly toy. With that shoulder, you aren't getting out of here until Nemilos breaks you or kills you." Her words were laced with a wicked gleam, yet he could sense a hint of disappointment beneath.

"Finish eating like a good toy," she teased, her fingers trailing lightly over the raw lashes on his ribs.

"I'm not your toy," he growled, defiance lacing his voice.

It was then that it dawned on him that he could check for Malin. She was still far away. He could only hope that she and the others would bring back up and get him out of this. He just had to hold out.

"Oh, but you are my toy. Nemi said you were going to be my reward for being good from now on, so I don't leave again."

So that was why he was trying to break him. He wanted his toy. When the Order or Malin finds out he's here, it might not go as well for them.

"You don't understand, Lydia. If the Order finds out I'm here, they will not be bargaining for me. They will wipe all of you out to get me," he hoped logic would win out.

"Someone thinks highly of themselves," she teased.

He could see his words were going nowhere. "Why are you doing this?"

Lydia giggled. "Nemi says we are soul-bonded. He had us get matching tattoos. I didn't realize how much more fun I could have until I met him."

"You didn't look like you were having much fun."

"What do you know?"

The food and drink gone, Lydia reached onto the tray for the small metal object and placed it on his arm. "I'll get Doc to set your shoulder. We won't be able to play with it for a while, but you'll like it tomorrow."

He heard a hiss and a bite of something as she injected him with something, and his world spiraled into chaos, the effects of a hallucinogen taking over, before darkness enveloped him once more.

When he woke up, he was at Malin's house. He was lying in her bed naked. There was an odd haze covering his eyes, and an exhaustion weighed on his body. His head spun, as if he were drunk. On the side table were bottles of liquor. Had he and Malin been drinking? He tried to move, but nothing. Then he noticed the silk ribbons that held him to her bed frame.

He tried to access his powers, but they were no longer there. He heard a noise in her bathroom.

"Will. Are you awake and ready for more? Already?" He heard Malin's voice, but it didn't feel right.

"What's going on?" he asked.

"Silly. We just got married. I had hoped you would have remembered that. Ellie will be at Mom's for another week. We have the house to ourselves," she explained, as she walked into the room with that little lingerie number he had found before…"

His head was spinning. It didn't feel right.

"The boss says you need to stay put while I work," she said as she straddled him.

"You know I like to play. Let my hands free and we will both enjoy," he said, feeling his erection growing.

She didn't say another word. Instead, she just slid onto him and began riding. It didn't feel right. It felt good, but not as good as it should have.

He remembered his mental wards and tried to raise them. When he did, his world changed in flashes. The room was dark and hard, and this wasn't Malin. This was Lydia.

He was disgusted. "Lydia! How? Get off me."

The image went back to Malin's bedroom.

Malin laughed over him as she rode up and down on him. He was confused. What was going on? His head spun, and his whole body felt fuzzy.

Then he heard the voice, a deep baritone, Nemilos, "Someone taught our little toy to raise his shields. Hum. This will be fun."

The illusion dropped, and Lydia was riding him and about to climax.

He screamed a deep guttural scream of frustration as she finished and slid off him, with Nemilos walking over to them both.

"Nemi. He was fun, but you are better," she purred. "Your turn, my love," she said, as she pushed the gag into his mouth.

The pirate bent her over Will's body and thrust inside her. They undulated over and over against him. With every thrust, he imagined stabbing them with a knife. Finally, after what seemed like a marathon and several positions, they finished.

Then Nemilos pulled a blade out and proceeded to make hundreds of little cuts all over his body, poured liquor over it, and had Lydia lick it off. The pain of the cuts was bad enough, the liquor made it burn unimaginably, but Lydia made him feel ashamed. It was a feeling he wasn't used to. He noticed the pirate watching him intently, perhaps looking for weaknesses.

It would be what he would do.

When they were finished playing with him, the injection knocked him out.

He had lost track of day and night. It looked like sunset, but sometimes, he woke up in a memory; other times, he woke up in a dream. Most of the time, it was a nightmare.

He didn't know if full days passed or hours between sessions. He had found a pattern: Sessions with pain and physical torture were usually followed by sessions with mental torture. The last time he had enjoyed a quick round of punches, cracking more ribs, and more of the whip. The round he had woken from would be mental torture.

He was in a constantly drugged state with his head fuzzy and spinning. It was Nemilos' illusions that were the worst torture. The worst had been when his eyes were forced open and the many illusions that made it look like Lydia was Malin, and he was forced to watch as she was tortured, raped, and worse. He would not accept that it was actually Malin, no matter how real it felt, and he cursed the machine on his neck that took his powers, so he could not find her on his own.

He was familiar with physical torture. This wasn't the first time he had been forced to endure those, including waterboarding, whips, punches, and cuts all over his body. The sexual assault by both of them and the toys were also new to Will.

He wanted to kill him and make him pay for every indiscretion. It was only a matter of time before he was able to get out of there.

The sound of humming came from the bed, where Lydia's tuneless, low hum threaded through the haze of pain and exhaustion.

Will blinked, expecting darkness, but a lantern had been left burning near his face, its glass blackened in places, so the light splayed into weird, geometric patterns across the walls. His head still swam from the cocktail he had been given before.

He tried to move. His left arm was still bound to his body, the one that had come out of the joint. It was strapped tight against his side, useless. His other wrist was cuffed to a new set of iron rings; this time, bolted to a table. The belt was still around his neck with the barbs sticking into him. His head throbbed with every heartbeat. The layers of wounds on his back stuck him to the surface, pulling and tearing whenever he tried to shift. He was completely naked, exposed, and vulnerable, but at least the gag wasn't in his mouth. The shoulder pain wasn't as bad as he expected, as it had been put back in the joint and had been healing.

He turned his head at the sound of papers moving.

Near the table, Nemilos was seated behind a desk, leafing through a stack of dog-eared papers. He looked up when Will stirred, his lips curling in a cold smile.

"Back with us," Nemilos said.

Will spat blood onto the tabletop. "Sorry to keep you waiting," he managed, through a raspy throat.

Nemilos set the papers down. "I've kept myself busy. Don't worry about that, but it's time to play. If I remember, today is my pet's turn to play."

She emerged from a shadowed corner, still naked, but cleaned up for the most part. She came to Will's side and rested her chin on the table, inches from his face.

"My toy is awake," she cooed, licking the edge of what he realized was a freshly shaven jaw.

Will recoiled, but the manacles held him tight.

Nemilos rose and moved to stand at the head of the table. "You're a stubborn one. I don't believe I've ever had someone last over a week like this," he mused. "I like the challenge. But you…" He reached out and stroked Will's hair, almost affectionately. "You're something special."

Will turned his head, fixing Lydia with a glare. "You're enjoying this."

"Because you were so good for me yesterday and screamed when I asked, I have a special treat today. Let's see what fun we can have? To make sure we have his full cooperation, I think he needs a dose of fun," He nearly purred.

Nemilos motioned, and Lydia crawled up onto the table with a small handheld injector in her hand, straddling Will's hips, then she pushed it to his arm.

He felt the injection of something biting him. This felt different than the usual concoction. His head still spun, but it was as if every nerve in his body was alive and feeling amazing.

She leaned forward, whispering in his ear, "You're gonna love this." She teased as he felt his erection engorge.

"What did you put in me?" His head spun, but he wasn't falling asleep. He just wasn't in control of his body, and all the pain he was in faded away, and even trying to move his neck or fingers didn't work. They removed the gag, but he couldn't say anything. He was not in control of his own body. He screamed on the inside.

"Do you like it? It's one of the Alorian court's party drugs. Quite convenient. Hours of pleasure and many releases. My source was able to get them today. I thought we would put them to use today." Nemilos dosed himself, then immediately began touching himself.

Will tensed, bracing for pain or darkness, but his world changed. He was back in Media in the bedroom with Malin. Malin was above him, not Lydia. How did he get here? Was he dreaming?

"Just lie back. I'll take care of everything," he heard Malin say.

Nemilos nodded. "Proceed." The sound was so far in the distance that he almost missed it.

Her lips, tongue, and hands explored all over him. She was an expert and relentless. This can't be Malin. Naked and grinding on him.

Will tried to dissociate, to go somewhere else, but his body betrayed him. He fought every instinct to respond. Right before he could feel his climax coming, the world changed. He was back in the demented playroom with Lydia riding him like a horse yet again.

Right before Will was to climax, the pirate calmly told her to stop. Lydia sat back on her heels, licking her lips. She grinned up at Nemilos, who was visibly pleased.

"My pet," Nemilos said, stroking her hair. "He has been so fun to play with. You can see it in his face. I think we will both have you this time." He climbed onto the table and pressed Lydia against his chest, then he thrust into her, while she was already impaled on him.

She cried out, but he waited, and she dutifully pushed herself up and down on them, riding them both.

Will's cheeks burned. He wanted to scream, to smash the table, and bite through his tongue. Anything to spite them.

She kept working until both men climaxed, then she made noises like she had cum.

"What fun would you like next?" She asked dutifully.

"My eager little vixen. Come." She walked over to him. First, he plunged his fingers into her, pulled them out, and tasted them. Then, he slapped her, making her nose bleed.

"You didn't cum. My pet. Making him pop was fun, but I like to see you happy."

"I'm sorry, Nemi. You know how to make it happen so much better." The words seemed to be precisely what he wanted to hear, as he bent her over Will's waist and plunged into her yet again.

This time, she grabbed hold of Will's cock and between her hand and her mouth, she teased until all three of them climaxed at the same time.

"Oh, my pet. I didn't even realize I wanted that to happen. You know me so well. I think it is time to get him ready for the next round. What do you think?"

Lydia climbed off the table and started gathering up cuffs and leather straps.

Suddenly a knock at the door.

"They know not to bother me," he seemed vexed. He cleaned himself off and put on his pants. Will could tell he was starting to gain control over his body again.

Lydia didn't bother covering herself as she opened the door when he motioned that he was ready.

A short, large pirate took a couple of steps into the room. "Sir, I know you didn't want to be disturbed, but I do think this might qualify as something you would want to know. We have had several of our sentries go missing. It is too many for them to be runaways, and we are operating on the three-person patrol rule."

"Are there any signs as to who it might be?" Lydia slid next to the pirate and began rubbing herself against his leg.

"If it is the Order, we are all dead now. Either that, or it's my wife. Either way, you won't like the outcome," Will rasped, forcing the words out.

Nemilos took a moment to think, then shoved her away, almost gently. "We can keep him like this one more night. I have work to do. You are not to play with your toy without me."

She pouted but agreed to obey. As she buckled Will's cuffs tighter, she murmured in his ear, "I told you never say never." As she said it, she used her flame magic to singe the hair off of his chest, leaving blisters by his nipples.

That was something he did not miss. She always liked the fact that blisters make the skin so sensitive. *Great.*

She produced a metal syringe from the desk and, with an apologetic grimace, jabbed it into his thigh. The plunger depressed with a hiss, and icy fire spread through his veins.

Will barely had time to curse before the world fell apart in a swirl of color and static. He felt the table fall away, the cuffs unhook, then the darkness swallowed everything.

Chapter 20 – Malin

The hour before dawn was never silent in the Marid village. Even in sleep, the air rippled with the breath of the wildwood and the pulse of distant surf, the wind whispered secrets through the fungal towers and the high-rooted trees. Malin rose in darkness, slipping from her cot before the hut's thin walls even hinted at morning.

This morning, as every morning had been, she got the same nauseous feeling. At first, she had thought it was the concussion, but she had fully healed from that. Her magic kept the morning sickness at bay. She was pregnant. She wondered what other effects magic would have on her pregnancy. She wished she had it the last time she was pregnant with Ellie. It would have made it so much easier.

She gathered her hair into a tight knot, wrapped herself in a loose shirt, and a pair of loose linen pants, then padded barefoot over the mossy planks that wound between the tents.

She searched for Will along their soul-bond, stretching her awareness out across whatever distance separated them. Will's presence hadn't moved since she woke up. He wasn't moving, or if he was, it was in impossibly small increments, like someone confined to a single room or building. He was alive, she could tell that much, but more was still a mystery. She remembered that Lady Anariel had said that soul bonds can eventually communicate through their bond, and try as she might, the connection remained silent.

She moved in silence, weaving through snoring Marid, sidestepping a sleeping child curled with a fat-tailed squirrel. Her breath ghosted in the cold. The village's glow-fungi blinked low and blue in the predawn, and when she stepped beyond the outer ring of dwellings, the world became a deep well of green and black. Recalling that her mother had said dawn and dusk, she waited patiently to hear from her mother, leaving the channel clear, just in case. It was such an odd feeling to look forward to hearing from her mother each day, but she reached out each day at the prescribed times for any chance of news about her family.

She had never been away from Ellie for so long. This longing for her child was pulling on her, though hormones might have been part of that. She missed Zee also, of course, but for eleven years and ten months, she had never been away from her more than one night.

She found her clearing, a short walk from the sleeping huts, bounded by iron-rooted thorns and spongy, copper-colored lichen. She had been coming here each of the last three mornings. The surface underfoot was perfect: yielding, but not so soft as to throw balance.

The exercise would help her keep her mind off things.

Malin began with a warm-up. The daily practice had become a sequence ingrained in her body. Malin let her mind go flat, breathing in through her nose, out through pursed lips, sinking deeper into the rhythm of her limbs. Ellie was only five when she asked to learn, but they did it together. Back in Media, it became a bonding ritual that helped to ground her in the mornings. Back then, Malin had considered it a good exercise and found it mentally clarifying. Now that her life seemed to be constantly in peril, she felt the need to focus on the moves and how they could help her. With every turn and extension, she felt the accumulated muscle memory: the need to be ready, to help protect herself.

She tried to lose herself entirely in the movement, but she couldn't. Every few minutes, she paused to reach out with the thread of her bond to Will and mentally to her mother, constantly tugging at her thoughts like a child yanking a sleeve.

If he were coming for her, shouldn't he be on the move by now? Shouldn't she sense urgency, or at least a shift in the direction of the tether between them? She was worried. He would have been there if he could. His not coming meant he was likely in trouble. He needed her. Instead, he was still. It was concerning. Malin closed her eyes, tried to breathe away the panic. The world around her was filled with distant bird calls, the gurgle of a stream over rock, and the faintest tremor in the ground as something massive padded through the undergrowth. She opened her eyes and forced herself back into the pattern, this time doubling the speed, demanding perfection from every transition. When she finished, heart pounding, she dropped to one knee, steadying herself against the earth, noticing that she had earned a school of younglings watching her from the edges of the clearing. When she looked at them, they scattered away, giggling. It brought a much-needed smile to her face.

The horizon was beginning to brighten now. The jungle's strange foliage caught the first light and refracted it, painting the clearing in bruised purples and molten golds. Malin rose, wiped her hands on her tunic, and set off for a cooling walk back to the village, letting the sweat evaporate into the heavy morning air.

On the way back, she skirted the ring of tents. It was easier to avoid the small talk that greeted an early riser, especially since she didn't know the language. She nearly missed him at first: a tall figure ducking out of a conical hut near the far side of the village, moving quickly and with uncharacteristic stealth.

Caelum.

His hair was still damp, his tunic half-buttoned. For an instant, Malin thought he'd seen her, but he kept his head low, hands deep in his pockets. The hut he'd left belonged to Clorsha, a Marid woman Malin had met the day before while tending to a cut on a youngling's arm. Clorsha lived alone, a fact everyone in the village had proudly attested to. It wasn't her business if he was involved with her. It was just unexpected.

Malin kept her face blank but filed the observation away for later. If Caelum wanted privacy, she would give it to him. She'd find a time to ask.

She headed back to her hut to clean herself up.

By the time the village was awake, the air had thickened with humidity and the promise of midday heat. Malin found Caelum waiting for her by the outer walkway, hands behind his back, looking every bit an eager instructor. His face was already sun-browned and streaked with sweat, but he grinned when he saw her, teeth white and sharp in the morning light.

"Ready for your next lesson in medicinal herbs of this area?" he called, voice carrying easily over the lazy burble of the village.

She joined him with a nod, and together they followed the moss-lined path that wound through the tall fungal spires and down toward the narrow ribbon of beach where the jungle met the endless, green-tinted sea. The tide was low, exposing shelves of pinkish rock slick with brine and dotted with strange, spiky anemones.

Caelum launched straight into lecture mode. "This shoreline is a microclimate," he said, crouching to point out a cluster of waxy blue shoots threading up between two slabs of driftwood. "See these? Solaferra root. It is highly toxic to most mammals, but Marid uses it for pain relief in microdoses. The trick is to boil it first, then neutralize it with a base. If you get the ratio wrong, it'll shut down your lungs in seconds."

Malin knelt beside him, peering at the plant with practiced clinical detachment. "Looks like the stuff that grows along the roads in Upper Media. We used to have to clear it out of the schoolyard. The teachers said it could kill a dog."

Caelum smiled, pleased. "Exactly. But here, it's medicine. Or poison, depending on who you're trying to help." He straightened, brushing sand from his knees, and gestured for her to follow.

As they walked, he pointed out other flora and fungi, rattling off genus names and Marid colloquialisms with the easy confidence of someone who had spent years cataloging every oddity of the borderlands. Malin found herself responding in kind, matching his knowledge with snippets of her own: the astringent leaf that made a natural coagulant, the tiny red berries that could knock a child unconscious in minutes, the bark that cured toothaches but caused debilitating nausea in large doses.

It was frighteningly easy, the way they fell into the rhythm. It reminded her of late nights in the medical school, bent over Petrie dishes and dissecting trays, competing to see who could memorize more symptoms before falling asleep at the table. There was a comfort in it, almost a sense of time travel, back to when everything was possible, and the world was simple.

Occasionally, Caelum would brush against her as they moved through the narrowest sections of the trail. At first, Malin wrote it off as a coincidence. The path was rough, with poor visibility, and they both walked with long, careless strides. But by the fifth or sixth contact, she noticed how he seemed to linger, letting his arm touch her a heartbeat longer than necessary. Once, he placed a steadying hand at her waist when they navigated a slippery rock, and the pressure of his fingers burned long after he'd let go.

Each touch brought up memories that she had buried in the pain of loss. She remembered the feelings of their friendship that had grown stronger over the years, the plans they had discussed, and imagined the life they could have had.

She was now married to Will, although she had previously questioned their relationship. Those questions left the moment she realized how much she needed him by her side, and once she realized that she was carrying his child. They would have the family he always wanted.

Caelum was the past, and as wonderful as those memories were, they were not as strong as what she had with Will. She pretended not to notice, focusing on the plants. He seemed content with the game, continuing his monologue as they worked deeper into the wild.

About an hour in, they reached a shallow ravine, where the sun broke through the jungle canopy and painted the world in searing white and living green. There, half-buried in shadow, grew a single, enormous flower: petals bright red, stalk thick as a child's arm, and stamens curling like gold wires.

Caelum stopped abruptly, drawing a sharp breath. "That's a bloodshade blossom," he said, reverent. "Never seen one this close to the coast before."

Malin crouched for a better look. "I thought they only grew on high cliffs."

He shook his head. "That's what the books say. But the Marid have a dozen legends about them. They use it to mark coming-of-age ceremonies, grind the petals into a paste, and paint it on the forehead. Supposed to protect the mind from enchantment. It's highly psychoactive." He knelt beside her, voice dropping to a near-whisper. "Want to see something cool?"

She shrugged. She didn't know what to say. All she wanted was for Aldrik to get there, so they could leave to rescue Will.

He produced a small knife, flicked the blade open with practiced ease, and cut a sliver from the petal. "Watch," he said, holding the piece in his palm.

Malin leaned in, and he moved his hand so close to her face she could see the tiny veins in the flesh of the flower. As the seconds ticked by, the cut edge began to ooze a silvery fluid, which bubbled and hissed in contact with the air.

"Exothermic reaction," Caelum explained, his breath warm on her ear. "You could use this as an emergency heat source. Or a weapon. The fumes…" he leaned even closer, "will make your head spin if you're not careful."

She could feel the heat from the reaction, and her head felt a little fuzzy. She was immediately drawn to him, almost hypnotically. It was overwhelming how quickly the air between them had filled with possibility and threat. Malin stepped back, shaking her head as if to clear it.

"I'm married, Caelum," she said, keeping her voice level, but feeling her head spin.

He smiled, not at all embarrassed. "So, you've said. I'm just sharing botany." He set the petals aside and stood, stretching the muscles in his back. She couldn't stop looking at the way they flexed. "I didn't mean to make you uncomfortable. I hope it didn't cause a reaction."

"Good. I'm feeling a bit unwell now. Maybe I should go back to the hut," she said.

"I'll look out for you. Let's head back just in case there is a reaction." She hadn't told him she was pregnant. She wanted Will to be the first to know.

They walked on, the conversation shifting to other topics, such as the failures of Media's educational system, the best way to treat a gut wound in the field, and the languages he spoke, since he knew Marid well. But the air between them never quite relaxed, and Malin caught him stealing glances whenever he thought she wasn't looking.

Halfway back to the village, Malin decided to address the other thing that had stuck in her mind. She waited until they were alone in a shaded hollow, with only the rasp of insects and the far-off call of a hunting bird for company.

"It isn't any of my business, and you are welcome to see who you like… I saw you this morning," she said, keeping her eyes on the path ahead. "Leaving Clorsha's hut."

He didn't respond at first, and she turned to see him frowning.

"That wasn't me," Caelum said. "Must have been someone else."

She stared at him. "You're the only tall human male in three kilometers. And you were wearing that shirt." She gestured to the tan tunic, still half-unbuttoned.

He bristled, jaw tightening. "Maybe you saw wrong."

Malin thought back to the moment. She could replay it in perfect detail. It was his gait, the way he ducked his head, the flash of his hair in the blue light. *What purpose would there be for lying about this?*

She let it go for now, but said, "I didn't realize Clorsha had company. She told me she preferred to be alone."

"She does," Caelum snapped, a little too quickly. Then, softer: "I was just helping her with something."

She knew he had been there. Thinking back to their college days, she recalled that there were a few times she thought she had seen things, but he had assured her she hadn't. Back then, she had started to think she was crazy or hallucinating for a little while.

Malin arched an eyebrow but didn't press further. Perhaps loss allowed her to forget some of those negative aspects of their relationship. It seemed she dodged a bullet after all.

They finished the walk in uneasy silence, both of them lost in their internal thoughts and calculations.

As they neared the village, Malin took stock of what she had learned. Caelum's knowledge was as sharp as ever, his charisma intact, but she was seeing the cracks now. The way he guarded his secrets, the flickers of defensiveness when challenged, the hunger that always sat just beneath his surface charm.

It was funny, she thought, the way memory protected us from our heartbreak. How easy it was to forget the little things that made someone dangerous, or irresistible, or both.

By the time they reached the first ring of tents, Malin had resolved to keep her distance, at least for now. There were too many questions and too much at stake.

She watched him disappear toward the trading post, then ducked back to her hut, needing a moment to herself before whatever came next.

Evening came with the hush of a storm waiting offshore. Malin found Caelum hunched over a fire pit near the edge of the village, his knuckles raw from splitting kindling and his hands blackened with charcoal. He had arranged the logs in a textbook pyramid, built a feathered nest of dry moss and tinder at its heart, and was now attacking the pile with a flint and steel, striking sparks until his fingers trembled.

She watched him for a minute, arms folded, before stepping closer. "Trouble?"

He didn't look up. "Something's off with the wood. Too wet, or maybe the air's too thick. I'll get it."

Malin knelt beside him, examining the setup. "It does look like it is perfect. It's probably too wet."

She could almost feel his pride radiating off the arrangement, as if the act of making a fire with his own hands was a point of honor.

After the tenth failed attempt, he cursed under his breath. Malin reached out and touched the log with two fingers. A spark flared to life, licking up the side of the kindling and catching hold instantly. Within seconds, the whole pyramid was ablaze, the heat a sudden, welcome shock against the cool night air.

Caelum jerked his hand back as if burned. "I had it!" he snapped, voice sharper than the firelight warranted. "Gods, Malin. You didn't have to…"

She blinked, caught off guard by his anger. "Sorry. I'm a flame starter. You knew that." What could have triggered that outburst? It was very childish.

"I said, I had it." He stood abruptly, fists clenched at his sides. For a moment, his face was lit from below, eyes dark and wild.

The moment passed. He exhaled, deflated, and ran a hand through his hair. "It's fine. I'm just tired."

She nodded, unsure what else to say.

They cooked in silence, skewering pieces of dried fish over the flames and roasting tubers scavenged from the jungle's edge. The food was bland but filling, and by the time they finished, Caelum's mood had mellowed. He leaned back, letting the warmth of the fire soak into his bones, and stared into the distance where the jungle faded into the black ocean.

"You ever think about what would have happened if we'd stayed in Media?" he asked, voice low.

Malin picked at the remains of her fish. "I just left Media a little over a month ago. It's pretty fresh in my mind."

He smiled bitterly. "You were always better at that than I was. Moving on."

She shrugged. "I don't know about that. I only moved on from you a little over a month ago."

They sat like that for a while, listening to the crackle of fire and the faraway cries of nocturnal predators.

At last, Caelum spoke again. "It was probably for the best that they found out about me," he said. "I never really fit in at Masoncore. And with the Resistance... I always felt like they were using me, not valuing what I could do."

Malin remembered the old arguments, the late-night rants about hierarchy and wasted potential. She saw now how much of it had been pride, but also something deeper… a need to be seen, to matter.

"What about now?" she asked.

He glanced over, eyes catching hers. "Now? The tribes I deliver to appreciate me. I'm the only one who can get them what they need when they need it. Out here, I matter." His tone was defensive, almost challenging.

Malin sensed he wanted her to argue, to press for some admission of regret or loneliness. Instead, she said, "I'm glad you found a place."

He seemed to relax a bit, his gaze drifting back to the fire.

A lull settled, and Malin felt the familiar ache of missing Will even sharper now, after her day with Caelum. She let herself drift, lowering her mental defenses and searching for the tether to her mother. It came easily, a pulse of sensation in the back of her mind, a warmth like sunlight through closed eyelids.

Are you safe? she thought, broadcasting it into the void.

Her mother's voice answered almost instantly, bright and steady. *We are well. Zee and Ellie are sleeping. The journey to Mellyrn is smooth. So far, there are no incidents.*

Malin let out a breath she hadn't realized she was holding. *And Aldrik?*

Faster than expected, Mom replied. *He will reach your location tonight, if not sooner. The man is relentless.*

Malin smiled to herself. *Is he… okay?*

He is Aldrik. He does not permit himself to be unwell. There was the faintest undertone of affection, or maybe exasperation.

Malin hesitated, then asked the question she'd been dreading. *And Will? I haven't felt him move in days.*

The pause was longer this time. *No new information,* her mother said. *His status has not changed. But if there was news, you would know.*

They spoke of random things. She missed hearing her voice. After so many years of disconnect and so many secrets, she had every reason to cut contact, but the little girl inside her that always wanted to have her mother's love was so pleased to finally be getting it. With final words of how much each other missed the other, she felt her mother's side of the connection close.

Malin closed the connection, letting the warmth linger for a moment before pulling her mind back into the present.

Across the fire, Caelum was watching her, head tilted. "Thinking about your family?" he asked.

She nodded. "Always."

He studied her for a while, then shrugged. "You're lucky. Most people who leave Media have nothing left but bad memories."

She didn't answer, but she felt the weight of his words long after they'd cleared their bowls.

After the meal, the sky darkened to indigo, and the Marid village shrank to a constellation of dim orange points, each marking a fire, a lantern, or a clutch of low conversation. Malin and Caelum remained by the embers of their fire; the world reduced to flickering heat and shadows that curled around the shapes of their bodies.

Caelum showed her where the village stored its celebratory drinks. He had found cups of a local drink that the Marid elders enjoy, a fermented and spiced fruit. It was sweet and savory at the same time. Given the baby, she agreed to try a little, but she didn't plan to drink much. It was quite good, and she only had the one drink before she could tell she was feeling the effects, if not already drunk. She decided to switch to water. Her head was spinning slightly, and she slurred a few words.

They sat close together, sharing the log bench in silence, with him slowly moving closer. He said it was to keep their conversation private.

Caelum broke the silence with a gentle nudge. "Remember that time in Advanced Pathologies when Professor Len said your report was 'almost as clever as it was insubordinate'?"

Malin snorted, the sound unexpectedly loud in the quiet. "He meant it as an insult. I think."

Her head felt fuzzy. Fuzzier than the little she had to drink should have made her feel. She saw villagers drink the stuff all day without issue; maybe it only reacted to humans.

"Maybe. But you laughed all the way through his critique." Caelum leaned in, and his shoulder pressed against hers.

It was an old, familiar touch, one they'd shared a hundred times in student lounges and research libraries. This time, it felt charged, as if the story's memory carried a latent voltage.

He shifted closer, with their legs touching side-by-side. "That was the first time I realized I loved you."

She smiled, wary but not unfriendly. "That was before we even had our first kiss. How could you know that then?" She could hear her words slur, even though she changed to water. *What was in that drink?*

She attempted to stand and felt the world tilt. She would just sit here for a little bit. *Why was she so dizzy?*

"You are pretty special. You don't even realize how amazing you are. I just knew," he blushed with a soft laugh, as he stared at her lips. "I think that was always meant to be. We just got there slower than most. I didn't care how long it took as long as you would have me. I've never forgotten about you and often wished things had been different. I even considered facing the wrath of your father and heading back to Media to steal you away."

The talk turned to other memories. To old classmates and teachers, the endless cycle of exams and failed experiments. Malin let herself relax, or maybe it was the drink. It encouraged her to let the nostalgia cushion the sharp edges of the present. That small amount of drink warmed her thoughts. When she looked at him, she saw the boy he'd been, not just the man he'd become. It was as if she were transported to the past.

He reached for her hand, entwining their fingers with practiced ease. The skin-to-skin contact was immediate and electric, but also deeply, heartbreakingly familiar. The fuzzy feeling within her centered on her emotions and the electricity of his touch.

"Malin," he said, voice low. "I know things are different now. But I don't think I ever stopped…" He broke off, searching for the word, then let it hang.

She held his gaze. "Please. Don't say it." Her rational brain was telling her to let go, but that part of her brain was muted by the fuzziness and the electric feeling of his hand in hers.

He nodded, silent. The only sound was the pop of sap in the fire and the distant hiss of the tide.

He turned to face her, eyes soft in the gloom, and leaned in before she could stop him.

She was taken off guard, at first, motionless. The kiss was slow and hesitant at first, his lips warm against hers, his hand tightening on hers as if anchoring himself to something irreplaceable. That vibrant electric feeling exploded within her, asking for more.

For a moment, she let herself be kissed. She remembered the taste of his mouth, the way his heart always seemed to race ahead of his intentions. This didn't feel right, as strong as that electric feeling was that was obstructing her rational side, her magic kicked in. She could feel her magic push against the chemicals, talking to her and waking her up from his trance.

When she realized what was happening, she broke the connection, pushing his hand away. "I don't know what was in that drink, but I told you," she said, pulling back to ensure the message was clear. She let the silence stretch, then spoke with calm finality. "We've talked about this. I'm married now and we are never going to be again."

Caelum recoiled, hand slipping free. "I know. I'm sorry. I just…"

"I know?" she asked, softer than she felt. "Then what was that, if you know? You don't know me anymore. You know the little girl who used to fall for you and wasn't strong enough to realize how badly you treated me. I may have forgotten… pushed some of that back… because of my grief of being without you, but… that's not who I am anymore. I will not accept another slip." Her warning was thick, and if he didn't grasp it… Ellie or not… she would not hesitate to show him what a bad idea it is to cross her.

He stared into the fire, jaw clenched, but after a moment, he nodded.

"I am leaving tomorrow," Malin said. "To go find my husband. If you don't think you can handle that, Aldrik and I will go alone." To punctuate her feelings, she released a white-hot fireball into the dying fire.

He didn't answer right away. When he did, his voice was harder, the old pride resurfacing. "You know, we would be married by now. If things had gone differently."

She shrugged. "But they didn't. You chose to leave me alone when you could have come back for me. You could have gotten word that you were alive and that you wanted me to join you. There were lots of things you could have done over the course of the last eleven years, but instead… You chose to let me think you were dead, and I have moved on."

The words hung between them, heavy as stone.

Caelum reached down and picked up a pebble from the ground. He held it between his thumb and forefinger, then, with a flick of concentration, let it float into the air, spinning slowly in the space between them. The gesture was casual but deliberate, a subtle flex of power.

Malin studied the pebble, then looked back at him. "When did your powers emerge? The telekinesis. We have been together for days. Why didn't you show them to me before?"

He hesitated, then set the pebble down. "I always had it. Just learned to hide it better than most."

She frowned. "Were you chipped?"

Caelum shook his head. "No. Never needed it. I was careful."

Her pulse raced. "More secrets and lies withheld from me… for my own good. I'm sure. Will it ever end? At what point am I strong enough to be told the truth?" She probed further. "I'm so tired of the people I love protecting me from what they think is too much for me to accept."

He looked up, shadows deepening the hollows of his eyes. "Your father found out about my powers… about my role in the Resistance. He was my manager at Masoncore. He made it clear I wasn't welcome back. Not just at the company, but in your life."

Malin stared at him, eyes widening. "You told me you were captured and couldn't get word back. Which is it?"

"I didn't want to immediately tell you that the fake death and your loss of me was all your father's doing until I knew where things stood."

"We have been together for days. You had time. Why now? I didn't know he was involved. Given how he is currently trying to kill my family and capture us, it is believable." Her chin trembled for a moment as she realized how real the story was.

He nodded, pain visible but unspoken. "He sent a team to meet me on one of my medicine gathering trips. He granted me my life but said if I ever set foot in Media again or contacted you, he'd have me killed. Said you deserved better."

She absorbed this in silence, with her mind racing.

Caelum ran his hands through his hair, clearly agitated. "I snuck into Media once. I tried to check on you. But you were always being watched by Andrew. I used to work with him, then he got the job with your father. He was always there with you."

"Andrew was just a neighbor. Why didn't you get a message to me?" she asked.

"Andrew was more than just your neighbor. He was your father's successor in the company, and his right-hand man for some of his more back-alley work." He met her eyes, and for the first time, she saw real fear in them. "You had just gotten your clinic job; you were doing so well… You didn't have powers. Why would you have wanted to leave Media? To run the risk that Fellspire goons would trap you and make you a slave or worse? I am not a fighter. I wouldn't have been able to protect you. My life wasn't a life that you would have done well with… always traveling, making my own questionable deals. It was better for you to stay in Media."

She said nothing but stood and took a step away. She could still feel her head spinning from the drink, but not as severely.

After a moment, Caelum also stood, brushing dust from his pants. "I should go," he said. "Before I say anything else stupid."

She turned to head to her hut. She hadn't gotten more than a few steps before she saw him. At the far end of the path, where the high-canopied fungal spires dipped into the silver-lit marsh, a lone figure moved with the deliberate economy of a soldier in unfamiliar territory. Tall, black-clad, his silver hair pulled tight into a severe queue. Malin's heart stopped, then thudded double time.

Aldrik. Her real father.

She felt her knees go weak, threatening to buckle, but then the realization took over, and she started walking fast, then running, her boots splashing through the moist ground as her arms pumped.

He looked up, caught her gaze, and everything else melted away for her. He dropped his pack and started toward her, and for a moment it was just the two of them, covering the distance in an awkward, desperate sprint.

They met in the middle, collided with an embrace that nearly knocked Malin off her feet.

Aldrik wrapped his arms around her and pulled her tight, burying his face in her hair. They held like that for a long time, not speaking, barely breathing, two points of gravity locked together.

When they finally pulled apart, he studied her face, as if searching for cracks, then touched their foreheads in Elven tradition. "Noor'wyn, you look strong," he said. "Your mother had me worried about you."

She smiled, blinking back the heat in her eyes. "I'm so happy to see you. When I woke alone… I didn't know what to do. You look like you haven't slept in a while. Are you alright?"

He laughed, the sound gravelly and real. "I am here now. As soon as I heard… nothing was going to hold me back from helping you. Sleep can wait." He pulled back and brushed the dirt and mud from his clothes. "Travel and worry about you, does that. I did not just find out about you, only to lose you so soon."

A shadow moved behind them. Malin turned to see Caelum, hands jammed into his pockets, watching the reunion with a face that didn't know how to arrange itself. It was equal parts longing, envy, and wariness.

Aldrik caught the look and straightened, though he put his arm protectively around Malin's shoulders.

"Caelum," Malin startled. "I'd…"

Caelum jumped in, voice brittle. "I can't even touch your hand, but this guy, you run straight into his arms. Isn't he a bit old to be your husband?"

Malin snorted. "Caelum… this… is Aldrik. He's my birth father."

Aldrik offered a hand, polite but guarded.

Caelum hesitated, then took it. They stayed connected for longer than she expected, then Caelum winced before the connection ended.

"Your father?"

"Yes… We will be leaving in the morning to get my husband. If you still want to go. Until then, Aldrik and I have some talking to do. Good night." Her dismissal was straightforward and left no room for discussion.

Malin felt a sudden, almost dizzying calm come over her, like a pressure had been relieved somewhere deep in her chest.

Aldrik's arm still slung over her shoulders, she said, "Let's go inside. I want to hear everything. I asked Khun to set up a hut for you. I'm staying with her in the medical hut. I'll walk you to yours, where we can talk after you clean up. No offense, but you could use a bath." They both broke into a smile and laughed at that as Aldrik pulled his shirt to his nose and took a whiff.

The tension broke, and she led them away.

Caelum took a few steps to follow, then Caelum, true to form, stormed off into the darkness, his muttered farewells sounding suspiciously like curses aimed in the general direction of Clorsha's hut.

Good riddance. For now.

This was the conversation she truly craved.

For the first time in days, she allowed herself to believe that things might turn out all right.

CHAPTER 21 – MALIN

After Malin showed Aldrik to the wash pool and his hut, she gave him some time to clean up, promising that she would be right back. She figured he would likely be hungry, so she grabbed some bowls of stew and some cups of the local brew for them to celebrate his arrival. She would stick to water, though she might take a few sips in celebration. She thought she recalled an Elven tradition about arrivals that included toasts, and she recalled how Aldrik appreciated sticking to traditions.

She gave him an hour or so to get ready, while she packed for the morning. She tapped on the light wood of the door. Aldrik quickly opened it, his hair wet, and clad in the clean clothing Khun had laid out for him. The pants looked more like tight, long shorts on him, and the shirt would likely rip when he took it off, but Khun had already shown up and taken his clothes to be washed.

The quiet creak of the hut door shutting behind her felt like a breath held and finally released, sealing Malin off from the stress of Caelum's raw envy and the chill of the night. Aldrik's hut, tucked away on the very edge of town, was small but offered the perfect privacy Malin had arranged.

He settled into a high-backed, wooden chair, gesturing for Malin to take the one opposite him. The room was warm, with an earthy scent and a faint, pleasant aroma of woodsmoke from the fire burning in the courtyard nearby, a stark contrast to the emotional whirlwind outside with Caelum. The moon, now past its zenith, cast long, silver streaks through the tall window.

"So," Malin began, leaning forward, the tension she hadn't realized she was still carrying beginning to ease in his presence. He reached over and placed his hand on hers, resting on the table.

"How are you? Your mother said that you had been hurt."

She filled him in on the events of the last few days as he ate the meal, avoiding any conversation that might let him realize she was pregnant. Will should be the first to know.

He lifted the cup with the same drink that had gotten her drunk, gave it a smell and a sip, and said, "This is not a drink that is a good idea to have right now. Why do you have it?"

She didn't understand the question, "I thought it was an Elven tradition to toast an arrival. Do you not drink wine? Caelum said it was like a wine, but with local fruit. It was as close as I could find."

"I drink wine with no issues. This is Gares Isa, also known as a love potion by some tribes," he said, his surprise evident.

"A what?" She couldn't believe her ears. He had tried to drug her. "That is a step too far!" Heat flushed throughout her body, and the air temperature became like a sauna. "Caelum. Caelum did this. He showed me the bottles."

"If you need help killing him, I am happy to help. A little more information would be appreciated first. So far, it sounds like a fair bit of justice, though." She couldn't tell if he was joking or if he meant it, with that crooked grin, but it made a bit of her anger melt away.

"I could use your guidance on this."

She took a cleansing breath. "I guess since he is Ellie's father, we probably shouldn't kill him off so quickly, though that is what I'm contemplating at this moment. What do I do about him? How do I even *begin* to navigate someone like him? My instincts are screaming at me not to trust him, and some are saying to kill him," she joked, though there might have been some truth in there also.

"Since getting my magic, I have started to appreciate my instincts." She dumped and rinsed the cups, replacing them with the water in the pitcher on the table.

"Ellie's father? You said he was dead."

"I thought he was." She took another deep breath and added, "This is why when I say that even this short time as my father, you have been the most honest and true parent I could have asked for. You are the only one who hasn't tried to protect me by hiding things from me."

He scrunched his forehead at her words and brushed his fingers with his thumb.

She continued, "It was my father... I mean the man I thought was my father... What do I call him now?" After a beat of thought, she continued, "I'll call him Dad... found out that Caelum has powers and that he was working for the Resistance and told Caelum that he would kill him if he ever came back for me. He never knew about Ellie."

Aldrik thought silently for a moment, then spoke, "I can't fault your Dad for wanting to kill someone like that. Mind you, I would easily kill him for many other reasons, but only after giving you the final choice, though. He should have only made the threat after discussing it with you."

He paused, leaning in a bit and added, "I would love it if you would be willing to call me Aeladar. It means 'father' in Elven, so you don't have to feel confused about what to call us... As long as I can have you in my life, I don't care what name you choose for me, though," he said, with a broad, honest smile and wide eyes.

She walked over and threw her arms around him. The feeling of acceptance and hope that he brought to her life meant a great deal to her. Her world had fallen apart and was still in the process of rebuilding, but this man was the foundation she hadn't realized she needed.

"Thank you. Aeladar." Tears were rolling down her cheeks, which he reached up and caught with his fingers.

"As far as the next part, you might not be as happy with that advice, but..." he paused and steepled his fingers, his gaze distant, considering.

"Caelum... yes. A difficult young man, clearly, and I will be watching him more closely now. Your instincts are likely right, Noor'wyn. I've seen enough of the world to know that. My initial thought? Untrustworthy. Certainly, we need to watch him closely. But... once he learns the full truth. Once he knows he is a father... that will be the true test. It will reveal the kind of man he truly is. Or the kind of man he *could be*." They retook their seats, their hands finding each other in the middle of the table.

He paused, a faint, almost melancholy smile touching his lips. "When you told me I was your father... my first thought was what I would have done if I knew earlier, and how ill-equipped I would have been to raise a young girl. A soldier, constantly on the move, in the thick of a centuries-long war. No place for a child."

Malin immediately bristled, shaking her head. "Don't say that. Compared to... well, compared to what I *did* grow up with, you would have been a godsend." The words tasted bitter on her tongue, a raw honesty that she rarely let surface.

Aldrik's gaze softened, a flicker of understanding in his eyes, as he stopped her before she could finish. "Perhaps. But my point stands: it would have been a challenge. A constant battle against circumstances, against duty. But..." he leaned forward, his voice firm with conviction, "I would have found a way. I would have insisted you be with me, likely on the battlefront outside Lumara, where I was stationed, despite the dangers. It would have been a battlement, yes, but I would have carved out a space, made it safe for you within those walls. At worst, if it truly proved impossible, I would have insisted on visiting you as often as possible and stepping away from the battlefront more often. Any Aeladar would. It's… a powerful bond."

He sighed, a deep, resonant sound. "That thought… that very possibility, helped me to understand better and appreciate your mother. She might not have told me precisely because she knew I *would* have insisted on that very thing. She would have known that I would have found a way to be in your life, no matter the cost, no matter the war. It's one of the reasons I have… forgiven her. Completely."

He looked directly at Malin, his expression earnest. "This is why you must tell Caelum about Ellie immediately. It is the only way to know. The true measure of a man is not in his words, but in how he acts when faced with undeniable responsibility, especially one as profound as fatherhood."

The crisp sounds of the new morning filled the hut as Malin moved about, her body feeling almost fully restored. Khun MorBaan had laid out the clothes Malin had arrived in, now cleaned and dried: the familiar sturdy breeches, a fitted tunic, leather vest, and her worn but comfortable boots. Changing back into them felt like shedding a temporary skin, a return to her true self.

Once dressed, Malin took a deep breath. The conversation with Caelum wouldn't be easy. She found him outside the hut, gazing out at the churning sea. She pulled him aside, away from the casual curiosity of the Gill-Kin Fae.

"Caelum," she began, her voice low, the words carefully chosen. "First, I know you tried to drug me. It was reprehensible, and if it hadn't been for this next part, you might not have made it out of this village alive today," she said menacingly.

She smiled as she heard him gulp and saw him take a step back. "I see now that was clearly a mistake… I was excited… and wanted to take the easy route to make things work with us…" he stammered, slowly stepping farther and farther away.

"Don't worry. I'm not going to kill you, though I have to admit the thought did cross my mind," she explained through tight lips.

"You might not, but… What about him?" She felt his hand touch her shoulder and turned to look at Aldrik, standing behind her with a stern look on his face. She elbowed him lightly and smiled, loving his protectiveness.

"There's something you need to know… Something important." She looked directly into his blue eyes and revealed, "I have an eleven-year-old daughter. She's… she's yours. You have a daughter."

Caelum's face, usually so composed, fractured. His jaw slackened, and his eyes widened, a mixture of shock and disbelief warring in their depths. He said nothing, simply staring at her as the enormity of her words settled over him.

Malin continued, needing him to understand the depth of her past commitment. "And, I thought you were dead… Even right up until Awelyn's birthday, I hadn't even considered moving on. Not truly. My love for you, then, was absolute. I believed you were gone, forever, and that my love for you could never be matched. That was until I met Will. I am with him completely. Do not attempt any advances again."

A strange expression crossed his face then, a subtle shift that Malin couldn't quite decipher. It was almost a possessive glint, quickly masked by a wry smile. "So," he teased, his voice low, laden with a disturbing insinuation, "if something should happen to this husband of yours, we could raise our daughter together." His gaze lingered on her, clearing his throat.

Malin recoiled, a cold shock running through her. The implication, the casual dismissal of Will's life, was abhorrent.

"No," she stated flatly, her voice firm, leaving no room for misinterpretation. "Absolutely not. That's not the case at all."

She met his gaze directly, determined to convey the truth. "I feel like *we* have grown apart. Years have passed. I'm not the same person I used to be. Although it has been nice to reminisce over the last few days, we were in a relationship in our youth. One that would not work for me in who I have become now."

Her heart hammered, hoping he understood. He was looking at her, but she couldn't tell if he genuinely believed her.

"I love my husband. Will and I may not have had the years of buildup that a relationship typically has, but I can't imagine a person who is a better fit than he is. There will not be a you and me, ever." With that, she began to walk away, leaving Aldrik and Caelum standing there. When she realized that Aldrik was hanging back, she waited and listened.

Aldrik drew Caelum closer. Their voices were too low to decipher. Then, Aldrik's voice grew, becoming stern and unyielding. She distinctly heard him say, "I will be watching you, Caelum. You understand me? If she wants you to go, you will go." The words were a powerful warning, a promise of consequences.

A small, grim satisfaction settled in Malin's heart. Aldrik had her back and was watching. If Caelum decided to join them, this journey would indeed be a test. *She wondered what kind of a man he really was.*

Aldrik met her at her hut when he was finished. Kuhn was shuffling around the hut as she finished her packing.

She pulled a project she'd been working on for days from her bag. She didn't have a lot of skills, but she remembered something that Ellie and she had done occasionally. She had woven a necklace out of flowers. Her skills weren't great, but she hoped the sentiment would carry through. The daisy chain, with its white and yellow petals, was simple but held together well. She'd spent a couple of quiet hours weaving it, each knot a silent prayer of thanks for the life, warmth, and healing she'd received.

Kuhn, ever graceful, turned from tending a cluster of pearl-oysters, her gills flaring softly as she registered Malin's presence. Her eyes, deep and knowing like the ocean itself, regarded Malin with a calm, accepting gaze.

"Kuhn," Malin began, her voice a little softer than usual, "I... I wanted to give you something." She held out the necklace. "It's a small token, to show how much I appreciate all you have done for me."

Kuhn took the delicate garland, her webbed fingers surprisingly gentle as they brushed the petals. She tilted her head, observing the simple beauty, a faint, almost imperceptible hum vibrating in her chest.

Then, Malin took a breath, recalling the sounds she'd painstakingly memorized. She met Kuhn's gaze, offering her deepest sincerity. "Cam on long tot bạn," she said, the syllables feeling a little strange on her tongue, yet deeply meaningful. "I think that means, Thank you for your graciousness. I hope I didn't kill it."

A slow, serene smile spread across Kuhn's face, revealing rows of small, sharp teeth that somehow looked entirely kind. She looked at the necklace, then back at Malin, a silent understanding passing between them. With a fluid movement, she fastened the necklace around her neck, the bright petals a vibrant splash against her shimmering green-gray skin, then pulled her in for a hug.

"You did well. You learn quickly. Heitsi-Eibib sent you to us, it is he we shall thank," Kuhn said with a pat of her hand. With that, Malin left the hut, with her packs of supplies for their journey, provided by the Marid.

Aldrik was waiting outside the door of the hut for her, ready to go. "I heard from Ael'an. She says the children are well and they are on schedule to get to Mellryn, though they have had to take some longer trails to avoid issues, but she wouldn't go into details. Just so you know, it is not only you she is that way with, though I will have an easier time making her regret it. Working together, we may have a hope of breaking her from that bad habit," he said with a sly smile. "Before we go, I want you to wear these," he handed her a set of three black knives in a sheath. "You wear them at your waist or hip."

"Thank you," she said as she strapped them onto her waist, with him watching. "Kuhn had given me this," she pulled out the long wooden blade embedded into a staff that could be used as a walking stick. "I have never seen a wooden blade that was as sharp as this."

"It's ironwood. A local specialty," Aldrik offered.

She looked around for Caelum, and just as she had given up, he turned the corner and walked towards them, with his pack on his back.

When he got to them, he said, "I understand that we will not be a thing, but… I have no family. I thought I was alone in this world, but now you tell me I have a daughter. I'm not sure what kind of a father I will be, but I would like to find out. Can't promise much more, but I would like to get a chance," he admitted, his voice raw with hope.

Aldrik gave Caelum a curt nod, a silent acknowledgment of the uneasy alliance, then clapped him firmly on the back. "Good. Let's move. You said Northwest? Right, Noor'wyn?" he said, already striding forward to take the lead on the winding trail.

Two days later, the dense, humid jungle had become their world. Aldrik, a silent, formidable presence at the front, cut a path with practiced ease.

Malin's initial excitement at Aldrik's return was tempered by the relentless, stifling heat and the ceaseless buzz of insects.

"Why couldn't my magic power have been shooing away insects or moving faster? I was not designed or trained to walk in jungles," Malin lamented, leading to both men just laughing.

She felt the steady, undeniable pull of her soul bond to Will, guiding her every step, keeping Aldrik headed in the right direction. Caelum followed, collecting plants for his bag. They walked in silence for the most part.

"Doc," Caelum finally puffed, wiping sweat from his brow. "Where are you getting these directions? We've been walking for two days without a path or map. I know this area, and there are some not-so-nice elements around here. Is this another of your new magic powers?" His tone held a hint of genuine confusion mixed with sarcasm.

Malin stumbled over a gnarled root, nearly losing her footing. "Something like that," she muttered, pushing aside a tangle of hanging vines. In her exhaustion, she decided now was the time to be direct. "It's a soul-bond, Caelum. With Will."

Caelum stopped dead in his tracks. She looked back to see the casual curiosity drain from his face, replaced by a storm of emotions: shock, disbelief, and a flash of something akin to hurt. "A soul-bond? Humans don't get soul-bonds," he repeated, his voice low, almost a whisper. "But... isn't that where... when one of them dies, the other can also?" His eyes, fixed on her, were wide with an unsettling mix of apprehension and accusation.

"I'm Aldrik's daughter, so I'm obviously not a full human, but some humans do... since Will is a full human," Malin retorted.

Aldrik, at the lead, paused ahead and turned slowly. His gaze, calm but piercing, settled on Caelum. "That is the case. A true soul-bond is a deep and rare connection. What affects one affects the other, even unto death," he stated, his voice resonating with quiet authority.

A heavy silence descended, filled only with the chirping of unseen insects and the rustle of leaves. Malin could feel Caelum's eyes staring at her back as she walked. They had encountered many animals on the trek, some dangerous and some not. Caelum had been surprised to see her healing power in action, but he was grateful for it when she had to deal with his snake bite.

"If this is a place with not-so-nice elements, then that would explain where Will is. That would be the only reason he wouldn't have come for me," Malin surmised.

"What do you mean by 'dangerous elements'?" Aldrik asked Caelum.

"I've avoided the area so I can't confirm, but rumors say there is a pirate encampment nearby," Caelum responded.

She wished her levitation power had been strong enough to lift her so that she could fly over all of this. She was, by no stretch, a natural jungle hiker. Her entire life had been spent within the orderly, paved streets of Media. This wilderness was beautiful, but relentless.

They continued hiking, and the air was thick with unspoken tension. Suddenly, Aldrik held up a hand, freezing them in place.

Malin's senses sharpened, and she heard it too now: the crunch of footsteps, the low murmur of voices not far ahead. These sounded rough, and they were unconcerned about being overheard. Either Media guards, raiders, or pirates.

"I think there are three of them, judging by the distinct thud of their boots on the jungle floor," Aldrik whispered to Malin as they crouched behind the fallen log nearby.

Before Malin could react, Caelum simply *vanished*. One moment he was there, standing beside her, the next, the air where he'd been shimmered faintly, and he was gone. Invisible, including everything he was carrying.

"That's one of Ellie's powers," Malin breathed, more to herself than to anyone, a surge of pride and concern washing over her. "What should we do about them?" she whispered to Aldrik.

"I'd like to question them, so we know what lies ahead. How far away do you think he is now?" He offered.

"We are getting close. This feels like it did when we were getting into Seaborn, so about a town away," she said.

"All the more reason to question them, then. We just need one. I'll be back." Aldrik jumped into action, his black blades out, ready for action.

Malin got their attention, giving him time to surprise one with a knife to the throat. One began walking towards her menacingly. "Hey, my pretty. Once we get rid of that man of yours, we can have some fun."

"You think he's the only one you have to be worried about?" She threw an attack of punches and kicks that dropped him to the ground, then she whipped him around with his elbow and wrist at precarious angles behind his back, while she put all her weight on his back. He was begging for her to let him go. She looked over, and Aldrik had already felled the other, and he was walking over to her, wiping the blood on the bushes before putting his blades away.

"Nicely done, Noor'wyn." His smile was ear to ear.

"Now, sir. Talking like that to my daughter was not a good idea. I am in a benevolent mood right now, though, but I want to get our excursion over with as quickly as possible. I am warning you now that you had better tell us what we want to know quickly, or you will not like the consequences." The venom in his deep voice made it clear he was not someone to be trifled with.

"I'll tell you what you wanna know," the pirate spat out quickly.

"What lies that direction?" Malin asked, pointing in the direction they were headed.

"That's… that's where Cap'n Nemilos got his base. We got some big prizes he's ransoming off to the right bidders right now. We just waiting for the right offer. He's playing with him now."

"What does playing with him mean?" Malin asked, her heart palpitated in concern.

He held up his left hand, showing he only had a thumb and two fingers left. "Cap'n likes pain. I was gonna leave, but he makes us travel in groups of three. I tried to leave twice before, and each time he made me play a game… I lost." He said, wiggling his fingers in the air.

Caelum reappeared behind Malin, making the pirate jump.

"You've been forthcoming. You say you want to leave. You tell us how to get into the stronghold and where he has his prisoner. I'll be generous and hand you some coins before sending you on your way," Aldrik offered, as he helped the man get to a normal sitting position.

The pirate then broke down the whole layout of the complex and all the details for ingress and egress. When he was done, Aldrik helped him stand. At almost six inches taller than him, he looked quite foreboding when he said, "I have a power that can find anyone I want. If you have been untruthful, there is nowhere you can go that I will not be able to find you. Are you sure you do not have anything else to add?"

"No sir."

"Then be on your way," Aldrik said, removing the sword and knives from the pirates' bodies.

When the man was out of earshot, Malin asked, "That is some power. I didn't realize you could do that."

"I cannot... but he does not know that." He gave a crooked smile like Will's. *She always heard that women fall for a man like her father, but…*

She rechecked his location. He hadn't moved in hours. It almost seemed like he might be sleeping.

She turned to Caelum. "The invisibility power. Ellie has that too," she said.

"She does? So, she got both of my powers. That is fantastic," he said with an extra swing to his arms. Shortly after, she noticed him whistling the little tune he used to save for after he passed a big exam.

Since she first told Caelum, this was the first question he had asked about Ellie. The silent tension in the jungle held a new, complex layer, but first, they must get Will.

CHAPTER 22 – WILL

Will woke to find himself naked, as per usual. The days and nights had slipped with the pain and the drugging. Had it been two days, a week, or longer? His head was still swimming with whatever they were plying him with, but he had some of his faculties with him. The gag was in his mouth again, likely due to the string of insults he spat out the last time it was removed.

His left arm was immobilized; he was hanging again, secured by straps around his waist, neck, legs, and arms. His legs were spread quite far apart. His right arm and neck were attached to the wall with adjustable straps to change his position. How many days had this been going on? He had cuts and bruises all over his body and the iron taste of blood in his mouth.

He had noticed the two rooms meant different types of torture. The room with him hanging was typically more of the physical torture. He would take that any day over the mental tortures.

To the left, Nemilos and Lydia were having sex. She was bent over the table with a black leather belt around her neck. He was holding the other end of the belt like a leash. At second glance, he realized that the pirate had something strapped around his waist. Looking closer, it was a phallus strapped to his waist and legs. He stopped mid-thrust when the pirate noticed that he had woken.

"Oh, good. You have decided to join the party. You will like this party. Won't he pet?" Nemilos seemed eager to share his idea of fun.

"Yes… It will be fun, and I will get a very special reward with you if I do a really good job." The slight shake in her voice let him know that this would not be fun for either of them.

He walked close to him and touched his arm, then his face where the gag was. The smell of leather, bourbon, and blood was thick, almost sickening. "So first, I want to ensure that we are on the same page in how this will go. I want to hear you, so I am going to remove this gag, but if you can't behave, I will have to put it back." They were face to face, with Will's legs spread apart, dropping his height by a small amount, just low enough to be shorter than Nemilos.

As he released the gag from around his mouth, the pirate's voice was thick, as he purred in his ear, "I'm going to make you mine. You will bend to me," as he rubbed his cock against Will's.

What the hell does that mean? He knew Nemilos seemed to want to be the alpha and took great offense that Will had not broken yet, but surely he didn't mean what he thought he meant.

As he stepped back away, Will looked down at Nemilos' equipment and snorted a laugh. It earned him a punch in the gut, but it was worth it. His equipment was of average size in comparison. *Maybe that was his issue. He had jealousy issues.*

"I'm going to show you what you can expect if you choose not to play along and be good," he growled, then threw a few more deep punches to Will's ribs. He had to admit, they were brutal punches. One after another, they came. When they finally stopped, he thought he could count on at least three cracked ribs, though maybe more.

"Now that I've got my workout in, I want to show you my new toy, courtesy of Media. Their offer was not good enough, but I was happy to kill their representatives and take their toys in exchange. Maybe next time they will offer more," he said with pride in his tone.

Or maybe they will just send more people and wipe you out next time, though Will felt like Media wasn't that interested in him. He was a nuisance, but not that high on their list.

"I played with this with a few of the guards before they left us. I now know not to turn it up too high, but it's fun. You'll see," Will thought he noticed Nemilos get hard just thinking about it.

This will not be fun, Will thought.

He brought out a machine the size of a large backpack, complete with long cords and clamps. He strapped them first to Lydia's nipples and pressed a button, shocking her. She straightened and shook, dropping to the ground, gasping.

"Oh, what fun. That was on the first level, too. I can't wait to see how you will do." He walked over to where Lydia had fallen and stood waiting till she stood up for him. He removed the clasps from her nipples, giving each one a lick and a suck, then he moved to Will.

With clamps in hand, snapping as he went, he walked to Will. Caressing a hand along his hip, he moved between his legs and lifted his cock to move it out of the way, clamping first one, then the other to his testicles. The snap of the clamps threatened to make him scream, but he fought with all of his being. He would do everything in his power not to let this psychopath win.

When the first shock of electricity hit, he felt like someone had taken a hammer to his groin. He tried not to scream, but he let out an involuntary whimper when it stopped.

"That was level two."

When level three hit him, he couldn't stop the scream. Will stayed conscious for as long as he could. The last level he remembered was five.

When Will woke up, he was groggy. They kept him strapped down naked on the table again in the 'pleasure' room, though at least this time he had a thin muslin sheet on him. At least he wasn't leaning over the table again.

Once he had been able to get out of his leg strap and kicked Nemilos, it felt like a little bit of retribution for the indignities he had suffered.

His left arm was immobilized, but he could move his fingers, and any struggling hurt. After so many days of this, he was starting to see through the cracks in the illusions. They had been messing with his mind. It was hard to tell if he was actually in the room he was in, if he was waking in a memory room, or a room of their design. Nemilos was torturing him, not for information, but for fun.

The longest physical torture he had endured was four months. Luckily, he was saved before he broke, but he was close.

Those torturers had never included the use of Malin against him, though. Punches, electric, whips, cuts… he could withstand that. The latest illusion was making Lydia look like Malin and doing horrible things to her. Lydia played along perfectly, and every scream and wound looked and felt so real.

Something had happened within the last day or two; he didn't have magic, but he could feel their soul-bond, and he knew that it was not her, but they didn't know that. Reaching out, he could feel that she was closer. He hoped she was bringing others with her, but it was Malin who kept him strong.

Lydia's reward was always the same, it seemed. Playtime with him, as she called it. Every time, he tried to keep his mental wards up, so that he could convince his body that it wasn't Malin, but Nemilos was too strong. The day before, he had heard Lydia speaking with him about all the groups that had bounties on his head for one thing or another. He was sure it was only a question of time before someone's price was good enough for the pirate to accept the trade. If he hadn't been rescued before, his only hope was that the trade included him being alive. It is much easier to transport a dead body than an alive one, from experience. If they had been stupid enough to send word to the Order, they were all doomed.

He didn't know what happened to everyone else. He assumed that the children were fine. Nar and Khelek were the best protectors he could hope for, and they would keep the children away from any rescue efforts.

It was Malin who weighed on his mind. She would come for him, and knowing she seemed to be getting closer, he only hoped she had enough people with her to get him out without getting caught herself, or the torture that he had only been imagining could become reality.

They hadn't had a lot of time to get to know each other, but he had heard the stories of General Aldrik Rauno. There was a reason the High Elves of Lumara had decided to broker for peace after hundreds of years of fighting and winning. General Rauno had taken over the Army about ten years before. His cunning, strategy, and fighting ability were legendary. If they could get him free, he might not be at his best, but the thoughts of what he would do to both of them were enough to keep him looking forward to trying.

They would come for him. He just had to hold out.

The walls of the playroom were lined floor to ceiling with shelves. Each shelf bore a neat array of whips, paddles, metal hooks, wooden plugs, rods, clamps, and things that defied easy description. A rack of knives gleamed beside a coil of a black whip his back had become intimate with. Someone had arranged the toys with an obsessive symmetry; even the bloodstains on the table seemed part of the décor.

The air was wet with the scent of disinfectant, sweat, and a syrupy perfume that drilled straight into his memory. Lydia.

She was there, lounging on a massive bed pushed against the far wall, watching him with hooded eyes. A muslin robe clung to her body, but it had slipped to expose one breast, nipple still marked from the clamps and bruises on her body.

Some of the illusions he was forced to watch must have actually been happening to her. He almost felt bad for her, except that she had been given every opportunity to release him, and she had just laughed.

"He was there for her reward, and she liked having her reward," she would say.

She watched him for a long, silent minute, her hand working between her legs beneath the cloth. The rise and fall of her chest told him she was close. Her gaze never left his.

Will tried to say her name, but the gag turned it into a grunt.

Lydia grinned. "Awake at last," she purred, fingers still busy. "You were moaning for hours. I was pretending it was my name."

He struggled, testing every strap in turn. It was pointless— Nemilos had tied him with a sailor's precision, all knots doubled and set just out of reach.

Lydia arched her back, shivering. "You should see yourself," she said. "So desperate. So helpless. If I closed my eyes, I could almost believe you were enjoying it."

He locked eyes with her, trying to project hatred, but all he saw reflected was hunger.

She finished, shuddering once, then rolled onto her side, facing him. "It's your turn, you know."

He tensed, bracing for her approach. She walked over with the injector in her hand.

He felt the sting of the drugs, then the buzzing as it took over his system, and he could feel the numbness in his body begin.

She let her hands roam over his body, every touch of broken bone, cut, or bruise felt painful, though he could tell the drugs were kicking in when the pain subsided. When he stopped wincing at her touch, she removed his gag and returned to her place on the bed. She laid there, fingers painting circles in the wet spot between her thighs.

"My turn?" Will managed, his voice raw from the drugs and the screaming.

She licked her lips. "You were always so clever. Always running away from yourself. But here you are."

Will's mind was fraying.

He saw double: the honest Lydia and a ghostly echo, her silhouette rimmed in white like an overexposed photograph. Were these memories or real, drug-induced, or both?

They were in their room in Sarhan at night on the Sarhan docks, their warm bodies pressed together, the salt on her skin. That had been a lifetime ago. Then he was brought back to reality with the sting of the bloody whip that had plagued him so many times. He looked up to see Lydia's smile at the end of it.

She climbed on him and straddled him, gyrating against his limp form, as she force-fed him small bites of food. He didn't realize how hungry he was.

"Maybe you can have more to eat if you let me play. Just me. No illusion," she coaxed.

He was not playing the game she wanted. "I'm not really hungry right now," he said, as his stomach growled loudly.

She swung her legs off him. "He'll be back soon," she whispered. "You should try to relax," she purred in his ear as she replaced the gag.

Will tried to scream at her, to beg or curse, but the gag stole the words. He could only glare as she bent over him, her robe falling open with each step.

She leaned over him, her breath hot on his cheek. "Nemilos likes to break things," she said. "But I just like to watch. You will be broken. Nemi finds you a challenge. He's never had someone last so long. He is having to come up with new games." She flicked the sheet away, exposing the wounds on his stomach. Her hands traced the lash marks, lingering over each fresh cut.

Will bucked, trying to shake her off, but she only laughed. "Stronger than you look. You're lucky he didn't flay you alive that last time with those kicks."

She plucked a clamp from the shelf, holding it up to the light. "Should we see what you can take?"

He thrashed harder, and she straddled his chest, pinning him with her thighs. Her hands moved with clinical precision, attaching clamps to his nipples, then lower, until every nerve in his body sang with pain.

"There," she said, admiring her work. "Beautiful."

A shadow flickered in the doorway. It was Nemilos, returned from wherever monsters go to rest. He wore a velvet robe and sipped from a cut-glass bottle.

"Ah, you're awake," Nemilos said. He poured a splash of liquor onto Will's wounds, watching with pleasure as the alcohol seared.

"Are you ready for another day? I'm impressed. I've never had someone last so long. You are a real challenge for me." Nemilos asked, his tone soft as a lover's. "I like it."

He nodded at Lydia, who smiled, retreating to her bed, curling up to watch.

Nemilos circled the table, fingers drumming along Will's skin. "You're not going to die," he said. "Not yet. But you are going to beg for it."

Hours went by of torture. Waterboarding was easy, he had managed that often enough. The punches were getting harder to take with so many of his broken ribs. With a constant soak in alcohol and salt that covered his wounds, his skin felt like it was on fire. Ripping his nails out was so cliché.

Dizzy with the drugs in his system, to control him, probably helped him last through the pain. He began to wonder if Lydia was supposed to have given him that dose before Nemilos came in? Surely, he would have broken much sooner if he wasn't so numb from the drugs.

Will's mind lurched, reaching for something—anything—to hold onto. Malin, her face, her voice. He tried to focus on it, to build a wall between himself and the pain. But she felt impossibly far away.

He closed his eyes, bracing for the next blow. As brave an act as he was trying to put up, he knew he was close. The only solace was the feeling that Malin was getting closer.

In the end, there was nothing but the cold and Lydia's laughter echoing in the small, dark room until his world went black.

CHAPTER 23 – MALIN

Aldrik had left to scout the pirate encampment, promising to return as soon as he could. Both her concern and the oppressive humidity of the jungle seemed to thicken within Malin with each passing hour.

She and Caelum were hidden in a small, cramped cave Aldrik had found. It was uncomfortable. Her feelings, which started as memories of their past attraction, had now evolved into disappointment. Caelum hadn't asked about Ellie. He hadn't asked to find out what kind of things she likes, what his daughter looks like, or what similarities she shared with him.

Malin was waiting and left wanting.

Malin paced, her anxious footsteps wearing a shallow track in the dirt floor.

The air inside had been cool and damp, smelling faintly of wet earth and distant decaying leaves, but Malin's concern stirred her flame power, raising the temperature in the space. She was sweating. Every rustle of foliage outside, every bird call, sounded amplified, making Malin's nerves hum. The only steady sound was the drip-drip-drip of water from the cave's ceiling into a shallow pool, a monotonous rhythm that did little to soothe her frayed edges.

Caelum, meanwhile, seemed restless, constantly shifting in and out of sight, practicing his invisibility.

"So," he began, breaking the tense silence, "Ellie has powers now, you said? Like... what kind?" His voice held a genuine curiosity, the first she'd heard regarding their daughter since his return.

He leaned forward, eyes intent, questions about Ellie's personality and habits tumbling out.

Malin, despite her unease, found herself describing their daughter, a small warmth blooming in her chest as she spoke of Ellie's bright curiosity and burgeoning magical abilities with her telekinesis and invisibility.

Suddenly, there was a disturbance in the undergrowth at the cave entrance. A shadow fell across the opening. Malin, still on a hair-trigger from days of flight and injury, didn't hesitate. A surge of protective instinct, sharpened by the thought of Will, made her act. A searing fireball erupted from her palm, shooting toward the silhouette.

"Malin. It's me." Aldrik's voice, calm and steady, with a hint of a smile, cut through her fears.

Embarrassment, hot and swift, flushed her cheeks. "Aeladar! I'm so sorry, I didn't…" She scrambled out of the small cave, throwing herself into his tight embrace. His familiar, earthy scent was grounding.

He returned her hug, a brief, reassuring squeeze. "It's alright, Noor'wyn. Good reflexes. I like it." His tone was devoid of judgment. He pulled back, his face grim. "As expected, their numbers are overwhelming. Roughly eighty to a hundred pirates, a combination of species, a few Orcs, some Elves, and almost all are magic users. A direct assault is suicidal."

"I took out guards with my flames. I think we will be able to handle more than you think," she said, the words coming out sharper than she intended. She felt the fierce, crackling energy of her magic at her fingertips, a new, volatile confidence that demanded action.

"You are my daughter. I have no doubts your flames are bright," Aldrik said, creating a small fireball in his hand, its light a stark reminder of the power he had mastered. "Without knowing which building he is in, and who or how Will is being guarded, going in with a direct assault may also lead to them killing him," he explained.

Malin's bravado crumbled. A visceral wave of horror washed over her, so cold and intense it momentarily stole her breath. The words "killing him" echoed in her mind, a nightmare she had fought so hard to avoid. She saw it in a flash of terror: a chaotic assault, and in the confusion, Will, her Will, lost forever. Her hands, which had been flexing with power, now trembled.

"I can't lose him," she whispered, the words a raw, desperate plea. "What if we're too late? What if they hurt him? Every minute we wait…" Her voice trailed off, a lump forming in her throat.

Aldrik's gaze softened. He extinguished the fireball, the small light in his hand disappearing. "We will not be too late, Noor'wyn," he said, his voice a steady anchor in her storm. "But we must be smart. A direct assault is a fight for a small chance. We need a plan to ensure we all get in and out alive, and with him in tow. We need a strategy. We need to know who we are fighting and where."

His calm, clear logic began to seep into her panic, a cool stream against her boiling emotions. It wasn't about her confidence or her flames. It was about Will. And for him, she would wait. For him, she would be smart.

He knelt, sketching a rough map in the damp earth with a twig. "Our plan needs to focus on stealth, misdirection, and precision targeting to rescue Will. I'm fairly certain I've identified the building he's most likely in. It's the largest structure, dead center of their compound. But as soon as possible, Malin, I was hoping you could confirm that with your connection to him. Your options: either get close to check, or risk detection by walking the outskirts of the camp."

Aldrik then looked at Caelum, a glint in his eye. "Caelum, I have a job for you, one I hope you'll accept." He seemed cautiously optimistic. "I need you to use your invisibility to map out patrol routes, guard rotations, and any defensive wards around that central building. We need eyes inside."

Caelum's brows furrowed. "My invisibility... it only lasts for a minute or two at a time, Aldrik."

Malin's eyes widened. She instinctively thought of Ellie, who could now hold the invisibility of several people for almost an hour, thanks to her focused training with Lady Anariel, Nar, and Khelek over the past month. The contrast between Caelum's limited ability and their daughter's burgeoning power was stark.

Aldrik's strategic mind shifted gears immediately. "In that case," he said, his voice decisive, "If you are seen, go undercover as a pirate. You're human, like many of them. Blend in, observe. If they start to question you, use your invisibility to create a distraction and get away. I can gather other critical intel we need from one of the guards."

Caelum's eyes narrowed. "You mean... you're going to torture him?"

Aldrik's gaze hardened, meeting Caelum's without flinching. "They are torturing Will. It seems only fair."

Malin watched and listened, a sudden, chilling realization dawning on her. How much her morality had shifted since leaving Media. Before, such a statement would have horrified her, perhaps even made her physically ill. At this moment, what Aldrik said made complete sense. If anything, she realized with a jolt, she would likely help if it meant getting Will back.

Was it magic, the journey, or Will that had sharpened her edges and stripped away the polite conventions of her past?

Aldrik continued, "Your mother reached out. They're finding Media guards in several places along their route and having to re-route around them. The kids are still doing fine, though. She just might not be able to communicate for a bit, as those patrols seem to be able to track her mental signals. She said they're close to Mellyrn, so she didn't want you to worry."

Malin thanked him, a wave of gratitude washing over her. It was incredibly considerate of him to think to reassure her about the kids when they were planning something as dangerous as a siege.

After going through all the options and discussion of plans, they decided they would launch their attack in the morning, when more of the pirates were likely to be sleeping off their nightly revelries. Exhausted but resolute, Malin went to sleep.

The next morning, the air was cool and damp, carrying the familiar scents of woodsmoke and damp earth.

Aldrik, had entered the cave looking surprisingly chipper. "I tortured the guard last night. Got all the information we needed. Took a few hours, but it was worth it," he said casually. "He also knew where the pirates stashed the Media supplies they took off the captured guards. They included some grenades and explosives. With a little fire in the wrong place, I'll use those for a distraction, giving you two a chance to get inside the compound undetected." His eyes gleamed with a quiet, lethal satisfaction.

Malin's stomach churned with a mix of dread and anticipation. A look of horror was on Caelum's face. Her brain could barely comprehend that they had just made plans for three people to storm a pirate stronghold based on her feeling that Will was in there. She wasn't sure what that meant. *Were they crazy for following her, or did they just believe in her that much?*

If she had heard about this months ago, she would have thought she was insane.

Aldrik turned to her then, his expression softening, a flicker of concern in his eyes. "Malin," he began, his voice low, "Are you certain you are ready for this? You've healed remarkably, but a confrontation is... unpredictable and will likely be very bloody." She could hear the concern in his voice.

She knew he had heard of the pirate attack, but he had never witnessed her fighting. They were up against formidable odds. It's probably reasonable for him to have been concerned about how she would hold up.

Malin met his gaze, her own resolve hardening. "I am, Aeladar," she said, using the name instinctively, the foreign syllables feeling surprisingly natural on her tongue. As she said it, her heart jolted at the instinctive smile that touched his lips, hearing her using his role as father in conversation, "Will is in there. I have to do this. And I'm stronger than you know." A small, determined fireball briefly ignited in her palm, a silent testament to her resolve.

Aldrik studied her for a long moment, a proud, almost relieved, expression slowly replacing his worry. He nodded, a single, firm movement. "Very well. Your conviction is all I need."

He stepped forward, clasping her hands between his, their fingers interlacing. Then, with a solemn tenderness, he leaned in and touched his forehead to hers. Given the danger they were facing, this simple act felt different this time. The warmth of his skin, the faint scent of jungle and earth, was a comfort. It gave her strength.

Overcome by a sudden surge of emotion, Malin threw her arms around him, hugging him fiercely. "Thank you, Aeladar," she whispered into his shoulder, the word a promise of the bond that was growing between them.

He held her tightly for a beat, then pulled back, his eyes firm with purpose. "We will make it through this, Noor'wyn. All of us. You will get Will back, and we will get back to our family."

His words were a tonic, yet a pang of longing shot through her. Ellie. Zee. Her heart ached with a sudden, intense desire to hold them, to say goodbye, to reassure them. But she quickly pushed the thought away, strengthening her resolve. They would get through this. She would see them again. She had to.

Aldrik then turned to Caelum, giving him a brief, almost imperceptible nod. "Stay with her. An hour from now, look for my signal. That's your window. If you leave her or fail to protect her, as you should have… You will have me to answer to." His tone left nothing to question.

Caelum's eyes went wide, and Malin thought she saw him swallow. He just nodded as Aldrik backed away.

With a final, meaningful look, Aldrik melted back into the dense jungle, moving with the silent grace of a hunter. Malin watched him disappear, then turned to Caelum.

This was it.

Together, they plunged into the humid green labyrinth, heading towards the pirate stronghold. They had sixty minutes.

Malin and Caelum were in position, crouched low in the thick undergrowth on the outskirts of the pirate compound. The air was heavy, humid, thick with the scent of damp earth and the distant, stale odor of unwashed bodies and spilled drink. Every rustle of leaves, every unseen insect hum, prickled at Malin's heightened senses. Her heart hammered against her ribs, a frantic drumbeat against the jungle's quiet hum. She kept her eyes fixed on the dim outlines of the pirate structures, waiting.

Then, the world erupted.

A series of deafening BOOMs tore through the pre-dawn quiet, followed by a series of rapid, concussive blasts that shook the very ground beneath them. A fiery orange glow illuminated the tree line on the far side of the compound, quickly followed by the shouts and panicked cries of men.

Aldrik's signal.

"That must be it!" Malin whispered, her voice barely audible over the fading echoes of the explosions. Her body, coiled tight with anticipation, uncoiled into action.

She immediately extended her senses, reaching for the familiar anchor of her soul-bond with Will. His presence was a faint confirmation that he was still in the large building at the compound's center. Aldrik's initial location assessment had been correct. She focused on the task, pushing down the surge of protective fury that threatened to overwhelm her calm.

Around them, the pirate encampment was thrown into chaos. Shadows detached from the barracks, figures spilling out, shouting. Orcs, Elves, and humans, many still half-dressed, grabbed weapons and sprinted towards the multiple points of explosion on the other side of the compound. Their panicked shouts and heavy footfalls grew louder, then faded as they ran, their numbers thinning rapidly around the central structures.

Caelum, phasing in and out of sight with his invisibility at her side, moved with unsettling grace. He would disappear into the shimmering air, then reappear seconds later further ahead in the deepening shadows, his movements a blur as he scouted their path.

As the path cleared, Malin's gaze swept back to the large central building, the location where she could feel Will was. What were they doing to him? She tried to prepare herself for the worst.

A tall figure, distinctive even in the chaos, burst from its main entrance. He had dark hair, pulled back from a stern face, and wore a rich, red robe that contrasted sharply with the rough clothing of the other pirates. He barked orders, his voice carrying an undeniable authority even over the distant din of the explosions, pointing towards the fires.

This, Malin instantly knew, must be the Captain.

A fierce, protective inferno ignited in Malin's chest, the flames building within her as she watched the man who was likely holding Will. There was a heat, a power beneath her skin, threatening to burst free.

Calm down, Malin, she internally commanded herself. Not yet. Not here. Control it. She took a deep, shuddering breath, forcing the inferno to settle, to bank its coals.

Not yet. Soon.

Malin moved like a shadow, Caelum's invisible presence a faint shimmer just in front of her. They slipped through the thinning ranks of pirates, who were still mainly focused on the distant explosions and the commotion at the compound's edge.

The main building, a surprisingly grand structure given its remote location, loomed before them. It wasn't built for comfort, but for command, with its sturdy, dark wood and the slight elevation that gave it an air of importance.

She pushed open the heavy main doors, which yielded with barely a creak, revealing a cavernous interior.

The parlor was a testament to opulence, a lavish display of polished woods, plush cushions, and a library brimming with treasures. The faint scent of exotic spices and aged wood permeated the room. A massive, ornate wooden table, surrounded by heavy, carved chairs that resembled thrones, dominated the center. This was the hall of a man who valued appearance and command above all.

What kind of person is this Nemilos? Malin wondered, a flicker of disgust for his ostentatious display in such a brutal setting.

She didn't linger. Her soul-bond pulsed, a frantic beacon urging her onward. Just beyond the grand room, a short, dim hallway stretched, flanked by two identical, heavy wooden doors. Both rooms were closed to the chaos outside the building.

The first door she approached smelled faintly of iron and decay, a scent that grew stronger with every step. Her hand hesitated on the cold metal handle for a moment before she pushed it open slowly.

The room beyond was dark and barren. It was a dungeon room, no doubt, but empty of people. Yet, the coppery, metallic tang of fresh blood hung thick in the air and the red stains on what little of the floor that was illuminated were a sickening testament to untold recent horrors.

Her stomach lurched, and a chill snaked down her spine. Someone had been here. Recently. Will? No, her bond still pulled her forward, to the next door.

Taking a breath to steady her, she moved to the second door. This one offered no distinct scent from the outside, but a faint, rhythmic thudding, almost imperceptible, reached her ears. She gripped the handle, turning it with excruciating slowness, barely making a sound as she nudged the door open just enough to peer inside.

Her eyes took in a scene that stole her breath and ignited a cold fury that surpassed any she had ever known.

The room, like the first, had high ceilings, but here, the space was filled with an array of disturbing implements. And in the center, chained down on a large, wooden table, was Will.

His body was stretched taut, his eyes squeezed shut, and his head was thrown back, exposing his throat. Straddling him, her body swaying with a sickening rhythm, was Lydia. Her dark hair spilled over Will's chest as she rode him. "Nemi said 'Wait', but with your cock so hard… I just can't help but ride. I can't let the Alorian drugs go to waste. It will be worth a beating or two," she cooed as she slid up and down him.

Malin was about to rush in, a primal scream caught in her throat, ready to rip Lydia off Will with her bare hands. But before she could move, a firm hand clamped down on her shoulder, pulling her back into the hallway. The door to the pleasure room clicked shut, plunging them back into relative darkness.

"Malin. I'm assuming that is your husband," Caelum's voice was a low, urgent whisper in her ear, steady despite the chaos she'd just witnessed. "You need to center yourself. Make a plan before you go into battle."

She could feel the temperature in the small hallway increasing rapidly.

He was right. It took all willpower. Her blood was roaring, her hands trembling, but Caelum's words cut through the red haze.

Will was drugged, with who knows what, and vulnerable. There were weapons near Lydia and Will was in no position to defend himself. Rushing in blindly would only put him in more danger.

She took a shuddering breath, forcing her surging magic back down, banking the flames. *Calm. Focus.*

Caelum didn't wait. He was a shimmer and then gone, a silent dart into the room. Malin counted to three, forcing herself to be patient, then flung the door open.

Lydia, still astride Will, shrieked, a high-pitched sound of shock and outrage. But before the scream could fully form, Caelum appeared and clamped his hand over her mouth. He wrestled her off Will, pinning her arms behind her back.

Malin rushed over to assess Will. His eyes were sealed shut, and he was muttering something to himself, like a mantra. She couldn't make out the words. His legs and right arm were spread out and tied down. His left arm was bound tightly to him, as she would have secured a shoulder or arm injury. *What had they done to him?* He had cuts, wounds, and bruises all over his body; the pool of blood under the table told her that he likely lost a good deal of blood.

She tried to use her magic on the worst of his injuries, but nothing seemed to happen. She would heal him later. Getting him free was her first charge.

There was an odd strap and mechanical device around his neck. She loosened it slightly, but he needed to be up before it could be completely removed.

Caelum's hand over Lydia's mouth, while she struggled furiously. A sudden, acrid smell of burnt hair filled the air, and Caelum yelped, pulling his hand away with a hiss.

"She burned me!" Caelum whined, shaking his hand like a cat that had stepped in water, a decidedly unheroic, almost sissy comment that seemed ludicrous in the face of Will's peril.

Lydia, free of his grasp, scrambled off the table, her eyes blazing with raw fire.

"Surely, you can man up and keep her from leaving at least," Malin said, ignoring Lydia for the moment as she worked to release Will.

With a knife already in her hand, she cut through the thick leather straps binding his ankles, then his one bound wrist, putting the knife away quickly, so she could have both hands free to help him get up.

Will groaned as the restraints loosened, his body sagging. His skin felt clammy, his breath shallow, as though he was feverish.

She felt his hand reach her throat in an instant. With one hand, she grabbed his wrist. With the other, she reached for the belt around his throat, pulling him closer to her, where his fingers wouldn't have as firm a grip.

He was choking her. She struggled for breath, little dots danced in front of her eyes, and she couldn't speak. She kept trying to maneuver out of his grasp. She tried her healing magic again, and it began to glow. She could tell it was healing him. Hopefully, he could tell it was her.

CHAPTER 24 – WILL

Will's head lolled to the side, the world a blurry, nauseating swirl of colors and distorted shapes. The tricks and torture Nemilos had used had increased, escalating in their cruelty. He knew he was near his breaking point. Physical torture, he could take for months, perhaps years. But this level of psychological torment, using Malin against him, painting false images, making him doubt his sanity, was proving unbearable.

He sealed his eyes shut and kept telling himself that Malin was coming. If he said it enough, maybe it would happen.

Lydia had been riding him only moments before, a searing, twisted mimicry of pleasure that branded itself onto his drugged senses. They expected him to believe that Malin would simply walk through that door now. This was the middle of a pirate encampment, a den of cutthroats and magic users. If anyone came, it would have been an army of people, a tactical unit, not just Malin. She might handle most, but not alone. He hated the idea of her finding him like this, knowing what they were doing to him.

He could feel this person, probably Lydia, loosening the chains on his arm. It was obviously another of Nemilos' tests, another cruel game to see if he would fight back again, if his spirit was finally broken.

But he kept trying to get free. He would keep trying to kill them. Maybe next time, he would. He would get out of these playrooms. Every chance he could. Images of Malin and the children, their faces clear and vibrant despite the haze, flashed through his mind, hardening his resolve.

He wrapped his hand around the throat of whoever this was and squeezed, pushing against the drug-induced weakness. Then he heard Lydia's cold, mocking laughter nearby. *No.* He couldn't be squeezing Lydia's throat then. Who was in front of him, if Lydia was over there...?

He was utterly stunned. His mind, still hazed by the drug and the lingering shock of combat, struggled to grasp the reality of her embrace. This had to be a trick, a cruel illusion he'd been so close to destroying.

Suddenly, the buzzing that had haunted him for days, the persistent, hallucinogenic hum, stopped. He could feel his magic return to him, then the warmth of her healing magic. The raw power of the magic all around him was a tangible presence. More importantly, clearer than any thought, he could feel his soul-bond with Malin. This was her, and he was killing her.

His hand released as quickly as his drug-induced neurons could fire. He dropped his arm, and she fell to the ground, clutching her neck, coughing. It was Malin. *It was actually her.* He stared at her, then his hands in horror. *What had he done?*

Still clutching her throat with one hand and pouring her magic into him with the other, she stood, then she threw her arms around him.

"Malin... Is that really you?" he rasped, the words thick with a desperate mixture of hope and fear, horrified at what he had just done to her.

A wave of sickening terror washed over him as the memories crashed back: his hands around her throat, the burning magic, the absolute certainty that she was the enemy, the one he had to eliminate. How close he'd come. How horrifyingly close to killing *her.* The very thought sent a cold shiver through his drugged body, making his blood run cold even as her warmth permeated him.

He tested his lodestone magic, a shaky, almost disbelieving probe. And then he felt it, not the chaotic energy of enemies, but the distinct, familiar hum of their bond, connecting him to her.

And beyond that, the calm, steady presence of the forty or so people with magic around him.

No longer a threat. No longer a buzzing cacophony, but a vibrant chorus of life he was now connected to.

The fight was over. She was real. And she had saved him. A profound, almost unbearable relief began to well up, threatening to overwhelm him.

Her healing warmth was clearing the fuzz from his thoughts. It was definitely Malin.

Will's vision, still hazy, centered on her, and he fought to make sense of the rage in her eyes. This wasn't the Malin who reasoned, who healed. This was a raw, unleashed force.

"You vile bitch!" Malin roared, her voice laced with venom, a primal snarl of protection as she faced the witch. "This is because of you! You did this to him!"

Looking past Malin, Will's blurry gaze settled on a blond man holding Lydia's arms behind her back, her naked body almost shaking with fury.

"Caelum, you better not let her go. Malin rasped out, but it was too late.

The blond man winced, releasing his grip, and Lydia, a wild animal, lunged toward them, something shiny glinting in her hand. It was the injector.

Before he could even try to find a weapon, Malin's hands erupted, not in the orange flames, but in blinding, white-hot fire that engulfed Lydia. She fell to the floor, reaching out to Will, as if he would do anything to save her. The inferno consumed Lydia, tearing a horrifying scream from her throat before it abruptly choked off. The smell of burning flesh and ozone filled the air, acrid and sickening.

Even as Lydia collapsed into a smoldering heap, Malin's furious gaze didn't waver. Her free hand, still glowing faintly, found his chest. A warm, golden glow bloomed within him, fighting against the frigid grip of the drugs. The pain dulled, the nausea lessened.

"You're here. You're actually here." His arms tightened around her, the sheer impossibility of it crushing the breath from his lungs. "I almost... Malin, I almost took your life. And Lydia... the way you handled her... that was incredible."

"I'm not sure I have much fire left after that, but... it did feel good. How are you feeling?" she asked as her hands still glowed with her healing powers.

Then, with no warning, the room went black. Not just dim, but an absolute, suffocating void. He was in a sea of nothingness, the buzzing returning, louder than ever. He heard Malin and the blond man gasp in surprise, their sudden terror a sharp echo in the void. He had lived with this for too long. He knew the cause.

Nemilos.

A deep voice, cold and authoritative, ripped through the fading haze. "I see you have taken my pet, but you have been kind enough to find me a new one."

The thought of Malin having to be subjected to Nemilos' cruelty, to this mind-bending torment, bit into him deep in his soul. *That would not happen.* He prayed she had more people, more allies, than just this Caelum. Malin had said the name, but it couldn't be Ellie's father; he was dead. Even in his drug-induced state, he remembered that.

A slow, predatory smile spread across Nemilos' face as his form began to solidify in the darkness, standing by the parlor doors, in his dark, billowing robe. It was a smile not of surprise, but of perverse delight.

The difference, this time, was crucial: Will didn't have that collar on him, blocking his power.

He forced his eyes open, pushing back against the blackness, pouring every ounce of his will into his nullifying power. The darkness in his head fractured, then shattered. The room snapped back into existence, sharp and clear.

Nemilos stood there, cruel smile still fixed, his hand raised.

Will looked directly at him, a defiant smile spreading across his face.

Nemilos's hand faltered, his eyes widening in shock. As Will focused his power solely on the pirate, he felt the familiar warmth of Malin's healing surge through him, stronger than before, like a tide finally turning.

"Surprised?" Will managed, his voice still hoarse, but laced with a familiar bite. "Thought you had all the fun, did you, Nemi?" The name, used with such insolent familiarity, was a calculated jab. "I assume at this point... we know each other well enough for me to use that name."

He reveled in seeing Nemilos's jaw clench. "I'd like you to meet Malin. My wife. Remember I told you that you wouldn't like to meet her? I think you are about to find out why. I would have her burn you to ash like Lydia, but I would rather see you suffer a bit more."

Then, Will stood. Slowly. Deliberately.

He stretched his naked body, feeling the dull ache in his muscles melting away, reveling in the miraculous speed of Malin's healing. He unstrapped the last of the restraints on his left arm, releasing his shoulder, feeling the joint and muscles knit back to normal. He was still physically underpowered, every movement demanding immense effort, but that raw strength was returning with every beat of his heart and her powers. Nemilos didn't realize Malin was a healer, much less one who could work at this exponential rate.

Nemilos's mouth was agape. "How?" The word was a disbelieving gasp.

He then seemed to collect himself, his eyes flicking from Will to Malin, then to the blond man, assessing the new threat. With sword in hand, Nemilos closed the door and then, motioning for the one Malin called Caelum, who was on his way to the far side of the room, to stand by Malin. It seemed apparent that Nemilos thought he had the physical advantage and that, eventually, Will would have to drop the nullification, allowing him to get the collars on them.

Caelum vanished, a ripple in the air that momentarily pulled Nemilos's gaze.

Will had to refocus, instantly clamping down on his nullifying power, risking a dizzying lurch as the effort tried to overwhelm him. He couldn't afford to lose the only protection he had against Nemilos' powers. They had to buy time.

He might not be at his physical peak yet, but his mouth could certainly annoy. Even with the warmth of Malin's healing, he felt the immense drain of holding the nullification, a cold exhaustion filling his bones, but the satisfaction of seeing Nemilos's face contorted in baffled fury was worth it.

His eyes landed on the collar that had plagued him for days, lying discarded on a nearby table. That was it. That was how they would escape. He didn't know how, but he wanted that collar on that man. Preferably, to extract some torture of his own, but at least to provide them with protection from the illusions and his magic. He pictured the collar on him as clearly as if it were reality.

They locked eyes, and Malin's widened in response, as if she had seen the image of his desire. Her gaze flickered toward the collar.

He nodded, a single, decisive movement. How could she have known?

He thought he had imagined it at first, but he saw a flash of an image of knives at her waist. Slowly, he moved his hand to her waist, and the knives were there, right where the image told him to expect them.

He reached for the knife on her side, causing Nemilos to snap into a guarded position, the sword held ready.

Will, with only a knife in hand, began to circle Nemilos, who was armed with a long, gleaming cutlass. Will deliberately placed himself between Malin and the pirate, counting on Nemilos to assume a naked, uncollared man with a knife was more of a threat than a lone unarmed woman. He didn't know Malin. He had no clue where Caelum had gone, but it seemed he was no direct threat.

He glanced over at Malin, just a quick flicker of his eyes. She had the collar in her hands.

His heart swelled with thoughts of her. How could she be so perfectly dangerous? So perfect for him?

It was an uneven fight, a sword against a knife, much less a knife held by a naked man.

Will jabbed in Nemilos's direction but couldn't risk getting too close. His movements were still sluggish, his body responding with infuriating slowness despite Malin's healing.

Nemilos, confident in his superior weapon and Will's apparent weakness, seemed to be toying with him, a cruel grin spreading across his face as he parried Will's tentative thrusts with insulting ease. The pirate captain was relishing this.

Will needed to change the game. He needed to throw Nemilos off balance, to shatter that arrogant composure. He thought of something, but he had a feeling that Malin would hate it.

"You know, Nemi," Will drawled, his voice still a little rough, but dripping with disdain, "Lydia *adored* me. Said I was the only one who truly understood how to make her cum, and she faked it every time with you. She always told me... how much *better* I was than you. Guess that's why she kept coming back for more, even when you weren't looking. Of course, she wanted to keep me. I could fuck that woman so much better than you could."

He winced as he said it, not daring to look at Malin. He knew it would hurt her, but he also knew that the pirate's alpha male dominance wouldn't be able to take the emasculating words.

As expected, Nemilos' face contorted. The taunt, aimed directly at his pride and perceived virility, struck home. His eyes blazed with uncontrolled fury, and he abandoned his careful, taunting defense. He began to lash out carelessly, his sword strokes wide and wild, driven by raw rage rather than skill. This was the opening Will had been waiting for.

Malin seized the moment. With a sudden burst of speed, she launched herself behind Nemilos, a blur of motion. She landed squarely on his back, her arms wrapping around his neck. The collar, the instrument of Nemilos' torment, was in her hands. Will saw her straining, muscles bulging, as she fought to secure it around his throat, so he continued his jabs with his knife.

Nemilos roared, caught completely off guard. He lurched backward, ramming Malin violently against the stone wall with a sickening thud. Will's heart sank, as he saw the blood on the wall.

Will, despite the returning ache in his limbs, lunged forward, pressing the attack, keeping Nemilos off balance.

But as the captain stumbled back, Malin fell, her grip on the collar lost. She crumpled to the ground, a dark stain blossoming instantly beneath her head. Blood.

Will's world narrowed. Fury, cold and absolute, eclipsed everything. He was on Nemilos in an instant, abandoning any pretense of tactical movement or trying to save him for torture. He drove the knife forward, a desperate, powerful thrust born of pure rage. The blade plunged deep, finding Nemilos' heart.

Nemilos gasped, his eyes wide with shock, blood bubbling at his lips. He clawed at the knife, a gurgling sound escaping him, before his body slumped forward, crashing to the ground.

Will didn't spare him a second glance. He dropped the knife, the weapon clattering on the stone, and scrambled to Malin's side. The scent of blood was overpowering now, a stark contrast to the lingering smell of ozone from Lydia's demise.

"Malin." he whispered, his voice cracking, his hands hovering over her head, afraid to touch.

She lay too still, too pale, a crimson pool spreading rapidly beneath her.

The door burst open. Will, adrenaline surging, grabbed for the dropped knife, prepared to protect Malin at all costs. He came face-to-face with Aldrik.

"She's hurt," Will gasped, the words barely leaving his lips, a raw, ragged sound.

Aldrik's gaze swept over Malin, then over Nemilos' crumpled form. His face was grim, but his voice remained steady, matter-of-fact. "Noor'wyn!" He quickly closed the door and began looking for medical supplies. He brought a cushion from the bed and began applying pressure. Then he looked up at Will, who was already at Malin's side. "We have to get out of here."

Will was focused on Malin. "We have to stop this bleeding first. We can't go anywhere until she is safe."

"She will not be safe until we are out of here," Aldrik countered, his tone brooking no argument.

Will looked around, desperate. His eyes landed on a small, sealed jar on a nearby shelf. It was a course, gray powder Nemilos had used on his wounds when they bled too much, to "keep him in the fun longer," as he would say. It wouldn't heal fully, but it might slow the flow, buy them time to get real help, or for her to heal.

With as severely as she was hurt, he hoped she would recover. He snatched it, ripping a piece from Nemilos' soft robe for a makeshift bandage. He poured the powder generously over Malin's head wound, pressing the fabric firmly. He held her close, cradling her in his arms, feeling the unnerving lightness of her unconscious body.

She was hurt, but she was here.

Aldrik shooed Will's hands away, replacing them with his own to keep pressure on the wound. "Get clothes on. You are not much good like that." His gaze flicked pointedly at Will's nakedness.

Will tore himself away, rationalizing the point with a bitter tang of frustration. Seeing Aldrik was taking care of her, he needed to be useful, not just a liability. He'd seen Nemilos get clothing out of a large, carved chest near the bed. He found clothing that would fit, a hefty bag filled with gold and jewels, and Nemilos' heavy scabbard and belt. The weight of the sword was a comforting presence after being unarmed for so long. He also found a light pack and filled it with useful items from around the room.

Malin moaned, a soft, heartbreaking sound. Will was instantly at her side, adrenaline overriding his lingering weakness. He gently lifted her, placing a tender kiss upon her forehead. It was a promise of rescue, a thank you for being there, and a silent prayer, before carefully shifting her over his shoulder.

Aldrik, now fully armed with a long hunting knife, looked at the door. "I accidentally killed their doctor in the blast. I did not realize it was their medical building. Are you ready? The village we came from is a two-day hike. I do not know if there is anywhere closer."

"I heard them talking," Will grunted, shifting Malin's weight, "about a village one day hike to the South. They might have a healer."

Aldrik's eyes hardened. "We came from the Northeast, so that sounds like a better option, especially since it is in the direction of Mellryn. Do we know anything else about the village?"

"Only that they get their supplies and fresh women from there," Will offered, a sardonic twist to his lips. "I know he can become invisible, but…Where is blondie?"

Aldrik's expression flattened, a dangerous glint in his eye. "He might be afraid I would kill him. I did warn him I would if anything happened to her... He might be smarter than he looks and realized I would follow through."

Will managed a weak, appreciative grin. He recognized the brutal honesty, the unwavering loyalty. He liked that. He liked it a lot.

"You know, Aldrik," he said, his voice dropping slightly, "I think we're going to get along just fine." He met Aldrik's gaze, the hint of a challenge, and a deeper respect passing between them.

Then, with a flicker of understanding, Will's eyes dropped to Aldrik's hand, gripping his hunting knife. Will offered his own, now sheathed, blade hilt-first. Aldrik's fingers brushed his own for a split second, a silent, hard-won agreement.

"Stay sharp," Aldrik murmured, already reaching for the door. "This is where it gets interesting."

"I sense about thirty of them out there, but if I'm carrying her and still not up to form, I won't be as much help as I'd like," Will said.

"I will manage," Aldrik said as they walked out of the building then turned on his flame thrower power, like Malin.

Deadly. He liked it.

CHAPTER 25 – WILL

The humid jungle air still pressed in, but the sounds of the pirate camp had faded to a distant hum. Every jarring step sent a fresh throb through Will's already ragged ribs. They had hiked for about an hour, as fast as his battered body dared, Aldrik setting a brutal pace.

Their escape hadn't been entirely clean; they'd run into scattered resistance leaving the compound, but with both he and Aldrik having nullifying powers and their quiet, lethal efficiency, it was nothing they couldn't handle. On top of his exceptional firepower, Will had been profoundly impressed by his father-in-law's fighting skills as they encountered resistance.

Once they were clear of the immediate danger, Will couldn't wait any longer. His heart hammered with a desperate urgency, eclipsing even the ache in his recently tortured body.

"The kids?" Will gasped out, pain from his cracked ribs screaming with every breath, as he looked at Aldrik.

"Are they... how are they? Last I heard, they were heading to Mellyrn with Malin's mother, Anariel, and my brothers." He winced slightly at his phrasing for Nar and Khelek, one he'd only recently started using as they'd become his closest confidants outside of Malin. It felt odd to say to someone else. Other than Zane and Corben, he didn't have many that he considered almost family. "Are they safe? Did they get there?"

Aldrik met his gaze, his expression unreadable as ever. "Last I knew, the plan was going well," he stated, his voice flat. "I separated from them where the ship set up camp until they could free her. The children traveled with Malin's mother and the others. I communicate with... her," he paused. A flicker of something in his eyes that Will couldn't decipher, "as often as I can, but I have not heard from her in a day or so. Not for lack of trying on my part, hopefully, it is simply distance and interference."

Will's gut clenched. A day. An eternity when his children were involved. "I… I don't even know how long I was in there," he rasped, the horrifying truth hitting him. "I was taken the night I had spoken with her last."

That was ten days ago," Aldrik said, his voice grim. "Ten days they had you. Your endurance is… notable. We moved as fast as we could once Malin reached us.

"We have to assume they are fine," Aldrik said, his voice softer now, almost a rare comfort. "It is what I have learned to do in these situations. Assume the best, so you can keep focused on the task at hand. It is the only way to avoid crumbling when you cannot be there." He clapped a hand on Will's shoulder, a firm, grounding pressure, causing a jolt of pain to shoot down his arm, making his teeth ache. He bit back a groan. "It is what we have to do now, too."

Will nodded, a bitter taste in his mouth, but he understood the logic. Worry wouldn't help. Action would.

He focused on the rhythm of his breathing, which was already ragged. His cracked ribs… a souvenir from Nemilos's tender care. He fought through it, jaw clenched, as he shifted Malin's weight in his arms.

As they pushed deeper into the jungle, moving as quickly as Malin's inert weight and his injuries allowed, his body began to protest in other ways. Small trails of blood began to ooze from the raw lashes and deep cuts, from places where Nemilos' restraints had chafed and torn his skin. The impacts from being used as a heavy bag didn't help either.

He left a faint, disturbing trail, dripping red onto the forest floor. He worried they could be tracked, but he didn't have the energy to do anything about it. He cursed under his breath, slowing just enough to fish out the small jar of powder he'd used on Malin's head. He sprinkled some onto the worst of his scrapes and cuts, pressing it with his free hand, hoping it would clot the flow. It was a brief, inefficient fix, but it had to do.

Aldrik, seeing Will's struggles, stopped abruptly. "Give her to me," he said, his voice firm, leaving no room for argument.

Will's grip on Malin instinctively tightened. "No. I've got her."

A wave of fierce protectiveness surged through him, mixed with a deeper, unsettling feeling. He felt a profound, almost primal need to hold her, to keep her close after everything that had happened. Giving her up felt like admitting defeat, like letting her down after she'd suffered so much because of him. He wasn't about to relinquish the single, tangible connection he had to her safety.

Aldrik took a step closer, his gaze steady, unwavering. "Ael'kin." The Elven term, one Will dimly recalled, meaning something like 'soul kin' or 'chosen family', cut through his reluctance. "You are bleeding. You are injured. Every breath is costing you. I can move faster and safer with her. We have to keep moving." He didn't ask; he stated it as a fact, an undeniable necessity. He was already reaching for Malin.

Will hesitated, his mind screaming in protest even as his body screamed for relief. Aldrik's use of Ael'kin had thrown him off, a potent reminder of the familial bonds they were fighting for. He wanted to refuse, but the cold, hard logic of Aldrik's words cut through his reluctance. He couldn't risk Malin's safety just for his own primal need to be the one carrying her, to hold her close.

He met Aldrik's gaze, saw the unshakeable resolve there. With a heavy sigh that rattled his ribs, he gently, reluctantly, transferred Malin into his waiting arms. The change was immediate. Aldrik moved with an almost ethereal grace, Malin's weight seeming to disappear on his broader, uninjured frame. Will suddenly felt hollow, empty-handed, a deep sense of failure coiling in his gut, as if he'd just handed over the most precious thing he had.

Which he had.

"I believe, I know my Noor'wyn well enough by now to know that she would have burned me alive if I let anything happen to you. For both of our sakes… this is the better choice," he said, a rare, crooked grin touching his lips.

Will could not argue with his logic. The image of Malin's wrath was a powerful motivator.

From this distance, he could see her better. She was still unconscious, frighteningly still. The bleeding from her head wound had stopped thanks to the crude compress and the powder, but she was so pale, almost translucent in the dim light filtering through the canopy. The sight of her, so vulnerable, twisted his gut with a cold dread. If he could have killed Nemilos sooner… If he had been stronger… If he had been paying attention that first night with the fish on the beach with Lydia. He kicked himself for the many poor choices that put her here.

As they passed a small, gurgling stream, its water clear and cool over smooth stones, Will motioned for him to stop. Aldrik knelt immediately, carefully placing Malin down on a moss-covered outcropping near the water, gently elevating her head.

He didn't know when he'd last truly eaten or slept without the haze of drugs. His stomach growled loudly in protest, a hollow ache that mirrored the dull throb in his head. Thankfully, the aphrodisiac they had given him had worn off, though his body still felt raw and exposed. Running in that condition had chafed him terribly, and he didn't even want to consider the possibility of blisters blooming across his inner thighs.

"Tend to her for a moment, while I gather some food," Aldrik ordered, disappearing into the brush.

He opened the bag he had packed from items in the room before they left. He pulled out a cup and a rag.

First, he attempted to clean the crusted blood from the wound and her hair. His eyes scanned the surrounding undergrowth, recognizing the broad, veined leaves of a familiar healing plant, known for its rapid, if temporary, restorative properties. He moved quickly, plucking a handful of the leaves, sifting through them to be sure he had the right ones. Then, without a second thought, he tore a wide strip from the lower edge of his shirt, fashioned a larger, softer wrap, and secured it to Malin's head, pressing the crushed leaves against the wound. The poultice held a faint, earthy scent that mingled with the damp jungle air.

A soft moan escaped Malin's lips. Her eyelids fluttered but did not open. Her color was improving. He was hopeful that it was a road to recovery.

Aldrik returned a few minutes later, holding a handful of small, root-like tubers. "These are edible. Not much, but enough for now."

They ate in silence for a few minutes, the small meal doing little to satisfy their hunger but providing a much-needed boost.

"How's our girl doing?" Aldrik asked, his voice low, concern etching lines around his eyes as he gently brushed a strand of damp hair from Malin's pale face.

"Aeladar?" she moaned, her voice thin and reedy, but stronger this time.

She shifted slightly with her eyelids fluttering open. The bleeding had stopped, and the pale flush on her cheeks seemed almost to hold color.

Aldrik immediately grasped her hand, his thumb stroking her knuckles. "I'm here, Noor'wyn, with Will."

She groaned and instinctively clutched her head.

Will immediately caught her hand, holding it still. "Wait, Sparks. We're here. It's best if you don't move too much."

"Will?" she asked again, her eyes finally, agonizingly, fluttering open. They were still clouded, but they found his face.

"I'm here," he reassured her, his voice thick with relief. "We're trying to get you to help." He squeezed her hand, a silent promise.

Malin's eyes flickered, trying to focus on his face, then on Aldrik's. "I... I can heal myself," she whispered, her voice still weak, but a flicker of her old fire returning. She tried to lift a hand to her head, but Will gently held it down.

"My stubborn Sparks," he murmured. "I know you are healing yourself, but you took a nasty hit. We'll rest here for a moment, then head to the village. Please rest."

He gently cradled her head in his lap, stroking her damp hair away from the crude poultice on her temple, until she rested. She groaned but leaned into his touch.

Aldrik, ever vigilant, was already scanning their surroundings, his hand resting on the hilt of his hunting knife.

"So," Will said, keeping his voice low, his gaze fixed on Malin's pale face, "who was Blondie, anyway? Caelum, you called him. Not that Caelum. Malin said he was dead." The question had been gnawing at him, a raw nerve amidst the chaos.

Aldrik paused, his eyes still sweeping the jungle. "That's him. Apparently, he has arisen," he stated flatly, his voice devoid of emotion. "Cowardly little prick if you ask me. Malin told him about Ellie to give him a chance to want to be a father. I guess it didn't mean as much to him as it should have. That or I scared him off."

"You are intimidating... to the average man," he said with a boyish smile. "But even you wouldn't scare me off those two. Anyone who wouldn't want to act like a father to that little girl doesn't deserve her time anyway," Will countered, a bitter edge to his voice, as he examined his wounds again.

He decided to remove his shirt, once white and now dark red, and wade into the creek. He heard an audible gasp from Aldrik as the clear creek water around him instantly turned crimson, washing off the dried blood. The cool water felt good on his wound-covered body as he rinsed and cleaned the shirt on a rock with the small fist of soap he'd found.

"Maybe you just don't know me well enough yet, but if you could sustain what you endured in that building, without breaking… maybe I don't scare you much," he said, winking at Will.

Then, Aldrik sighed, a rare display of weariness. "If I had raised her, she would never have met that man. I feel like I let her down. I want to make up for as much as I can."

The cool water felt good on his wound-covered body, as he rinsed and cleaned the shirt on a rock with the small fist of soap he found.

Will grunted, "If you had raised her, I might not have met her, and we wouldn't have Ellie. Things happen the way they must at times. You are a soldier like me. We can't stop things from happening that we don't like. How we react to those things and move through them is what shows us who we really are." He reluctantly left the stream, his muscles more awake and without as much of the crusted blood.

Malin was what mattered. He focused on the rhythm of her breathing, the faint pulse beneath his fingers. "She is the strongest woman I know. I think she is even stronger than her mother. She is capable, but we will take care of her, even when she thinks she doesn't need to be taken care of."

"Agreed."

Will nodded, recognizing the need.

He spotted a cluster of wild berries, dark and plump, hidden beneath broad leaves. He cautiously picked a few. They tasted tart, slightly sweet, and a wave of raw energy, however small, rippled through him. He found a few more patches, quickly gathering enough for himself and Aldrik.

Malin moaned again, a little stronger this time. She shifted slightly with her eyelids fluttering open. The bleeding had stopped, and the pale flush on her cheeks seemed a fraction less stark.

"Hey, Sparks?" Will murmured. "You are looking a lot better. How are you feeling?" Aldrik joined her by her side.

She tried to push herself up, and Will helped her steady herself. "What happened? Who was that?"

"That was the great Captain Nemilos Kako." Will confirmed, his voice flat. "He was a damn good torturer. Almost as good as me, better in some ways. I am very glad to see him go. I just wish I had more time to give him a dose of what he gave me." He said while stroking her hair.

"When I saw you hurt… getting to you was all I could think of at the time. "I just wanted to fry him," she said, as she forced out a light smile.

"That's my girl," he said, pulling her close.

Aldrik lightly rubbed her back. "The color is coming back fairly quickly now."

"We have a bit further to get to the village. You lost a lot of blood. It would be best to get there before dark. Are you ready to get moving? I'll carry you," Will offered.

She shook her head, as if trying to shake the dizziness away, "Can you help me up?" She tried to stand but couldn't without his help. Even then, she couldn't stay straight. "Maybe I could ride on your back?" she smiled.

"Deal." Will exclaimed with a dimpled grin.

Aldrik helped Will adjust Malin gently onto his back with her arms wrapped around his neck. Will could feel her body, warm and solid now, less unnervingly limp than before. He swayed slightly, exhaustion a heavy cloak, but the thought of getting her to safety pushed him forward. At his movement, he could feel her healing warmth start.

"No Sparks. You focus on healing yourself right now. I'm fine for now. I've trekked worse terrain in worse shape." He could feel the growing presence of life and magic ahead, stronger now that they had their rest, touching her hands clasped around his neck. "I can sense people with powers this way. We aren't far."

They walked for another hour till the jungle around them began to subtly thin. The oppressive density of the canopy eased, allowing more sunlight to dapple the forest floor. The air, while still humid, held a faint, earthy scent of disturbed soil mixed with something sweet and floral, different from the deeper jungle. Then, a whisper of a path, barely visible through the undergrowth, presented itself, leading to a broader, clearly maintained trail.

Aldrik, ever vigilant, moved ahead, his senses already tuned to their surroundings. "We're close," he stated, his voice low. "I can smell woodsmoke, distant. And... something else. Power, but controlled."

He ached, but his wounds would heal. He worried about how long it would take for the scars she couldn't see to leave him and how close he came to losing... if it hadn't been for her.

CHAPTER 26 – WILL

Malin's color was returning, and she was weakly humming while she rode on his back. The song was the one they danced to in her kitchen, back in Media. He could feel a trickle of her healing magic flowing into him. He knew it would do no good to argue with her about her needing to heal first, at this point… as long as she was also improving.

Nestled within the natural embrace of the jungle lay the village. It wasn't the crude, rough-hewn settlement Will expected. Structures of intricately carved dark wood and thick, woven leaves rose from the forest floor, some built directly into the towering trees themselves. The craftsmanship was subtle, organic, almost as if the village had grown naturally from the earth, the tell-tale construction methods of the Fae, though which ones he still couldn't tell.

As large as the village was, an unnatural stillness hung over it. The sun was getting close to setting, but doors were shut, windows shuttered, and a pervasive silence settled, broken only by the distant, rhythmic chirping of jungle cicadas. It felt deserted.

Will took a few cautious steps into the clearing, Malin's weight a heavy presence. "Hello?" he called out, his voice echoing in the quiet. He tried again, this time in the flowing syllables of the common Fae tongue. "We mean no harm. We seek aid. We have an injured person."

A shutter on one of the larger, tree-bound homes creaked open a fraction, then snapped shut. A palpable wave of fear, almost a physical thing, washed over him. He could feel eyes on them, darting from shadowed doorways and concealed windows. They were being watched, and the watchers were terrified. He had seen this reaction before; they probably mistook him and Aldrik for pirates.

Before Will could try to explain further, a sudden, jarring crash erupted from the far side of the village, followed by a guttural shout. Then another. And another. They rushed over to investigate.

A small, heavily armed, crude, and brutish group of six pirates dragged a terrified woman from a building, and her screams tore through the quiet of the town. She transformed before their eyes into a rat-like humanoid, but it didn't help; they kept pulling.

"Fresh pickings, lads!" one of them roared, his voice thick with malicious glee.

Will's blood ran cold.

He looked at Aldrik, a silent, furious agreement passing between them. He tightened his grip on Malin, the anger that had driven him in Nemilos' chamber flaring anew. He might be exhausted, his body screaming for rest, but he couldn't stand by.

"Stay with her," Will directed Aldrik, his voice low and firm, as he carefully lowered Malin to the ground behind a thick tree root, just out of sight.

But Aldrik held his arm. "You have been through enough. There are plenty of them to go around. I cannot have you monopolizing all the fun."

They both drew their weapons; his blade felt cumbersome and unfamiliar, but the weight was reassuring.

"Will, wait." Malin moaned, stirring against the tree root, her eyes fluttering open, now a little more focused. "I can…"

"Stay down, Sparks," Will cut her off, not unkindly. He wouldn't let her endanger herself again.

Aldrik nodded, his face grim. "Please stay. We will deal with this."

Will didn't wait. He moved, a silent, predatory blur. The pirates, focused on their terrified prey, didn't see him until he was almost upon them. He activated his nullifying power, sending a jolt of disruptive energy towards the nearest pirate, a hulking Orc whose crude axe began to vibrate violently in his hands. The Orc bellowed in confusion as Will swung the cutlass, clumsily, but with all the force he could muster, driving the pirate back.

Meanwhile, Aldrik moved with uncanny speed. He was a whisper of motion, appearing behind another pirate, his knife, a silent flash in the air. The pirate crumpled without a sound.

Will caught a glimpse of Caelum, too, a shimmering outline, disarming a third pirate with a swift, almost playful move before melting back into invisibility.

Still here, then, Blondie, Will thought, a flicker of begrudging acknowledgement. Will gave a little respect to the little guy. They had been hiking hard, even injured, and he had stayed up, hidden though he was. He probably overheard the conversation about Aldrik wanting to kill him.

The remaining pirates, bewildered by the sudden, silent attacks and their magic flickering uselessly, turned on their attackers.

Will, though still weak, fought with a desperate ferocity, fueled by Malin's vulnerability. He parried, dodged, and thrust, using his wits as much as the heavy sword, driving the pirates back from the terrified woman. It was a quick, brutal exchange, fueled by desperation and a shared, silent intent to protect.

Within moments, it was over. The last pirate lay still, defeated by a combined, if uncoordinated, effort. The woman they had been dragging stood frozen, then sank to her knees, weeping.

Slowly, cautiously, doors began to creak open again. The Fae villagers, their eyes wide with disbelief and gratitude, emerged from their hiding places. They were of medium height, slender, with graceful features and eyes that held the ancient wisdom of the forest. Their initial fear gave way to profound awe as they looked from the fallen pirates to the battered woman covered in dried blood.

Will turned toward their focus, and his gaze immediately went to Malin. She stood to the side; her eyes were clear and focused. A small, self-satisfied smile touched her lips as she carefully ran a hand over her temple.

A tiny woman with straight silver hair and sharp, brown eyes, eyes that shone with deep intelligence, approached them cautiously, then said with a deep, respectful bow. "You are not like the others." It was a declaration more than anything, and her voice carried like wind chimes. Her gaze rested on Malin, then Will. "You saved our kin. What can we offer you in thanks? You said you need a healer?"

"I think we have the healing thing down," Malin attempted weakly.

Will moved quickly to her side, "I would feel better if we could get a healer, but... Right now, we could use some food and a change of clothes. If we could also get a place to stay for the night, it would be even better," he added.

Although this dialect for Fae was one he was familiar with, the humm worms - the universal translator worms in their ears - seemed to translate most of it.

Followed by her complaints, he lifted her in his arms and followed the woman with Aldrik behind.

"You know, Sparks. You may be a fantastic doctor, but you suck at being a patient," he said as he kissed her cheek.

This earned him a welcome smile, and her head rested on his shoulder.

She took them to her small house near the outskirts of town, where she gave them two rooms to sleep in. They were surprisingly comfortable spaces despite their humble appearance.

The air inside smelled of dried herbs and cool earth. The lingering pallor had left Malin's face.

As they entered their room and closed the door, she said, her voice firm, eyes fixed on him, "My turn to heal you. You promised… once I was healed."

He stepped back, a grimace fighting his attempt at a smile. "That was the deal."

Her gaze, full of raw pain as it swept over the full extent of his lacerations and bruises, twisted his gut almost as much as the original torment.

She reached for him, her touch already a familiar spark against his skin as she began unbuttoning his blood-crusted shirt. The warmth of her healing flooded him even before her palms settled on his chest, an electric current chasing away the aches.

When she began to unbutton his pants, Will's grin, despite his pain, widened. "Well now, Sparks," he drawled, a suggestive glint in his eyes. "Didn't realize you were in *that* much of a hurry to see all my glorious parts again," he teased.

"I did miss some parts of you, but right now, I need to take care of my patient," she said, smiling, but he could tell her smile didn't reach her eyes. Her hands moved over his torso, a warm, tingling sensation spreading through him. "Almost. Just a few lingering aches, deeper."

Her brow furrowed. "Your ribs. Six cracked."

"Is that all? It felt like more," he said as he ran his hands slowly up and down her arms as she worked.

She focused her energy, and he felt a profound shift within him, a deep-seated ache easing, a dull pressure lifting. His lungs expanded fully for the first time in days, a delicious, liberating breath.

"Better?" she asked, her eyes searching within his for answers.

"Much," he breathed, flexing his shoulders, evaluating the new freedom in his chest.

His physical wounds, the raw gashes, the bruised impacts, the pain from the cracked ribs, even the blisters on his inner thighs… all gone. Her magic hummed beneath his skin, leaving a clean, almost exhilarating lightness.

"Perfect," she murmured, a warmth in her eyes that made his heart skip. "Now, as much as I appreciate the view, I think we should save the full-body appreciation for a time when we're not quite so… hungry, dirty, and well-traveled. Get dressed, love."

"Agree. Another time." She looked away, as she said, "I can't even imagine what they did to you… I just know what I healed, and that was more trauma than one person should ever have to see."

"It is what you can't see that hurts the worst." He touched her hand. The slight caress brought her eyes to his, "It was you who got me through. You are my rock. My love for you got me through. Del'an sil'en nandor, as they would say in Elven."

Her smile touched her eyes, a glimmer of tears in their depths. She looked down at their joined hands. "I never knew what it was to be a rock for someone," she murmured, her voice soft with a mix of wonder and humility. "I never had a rock of my own. All I know is that my love for you has become the strongest part of me."

He turned to get the clean clothes laid out on the bed, and she swatted his ass playfully. He chuckled, the sound deep and full in his chest, so different from the broken gasps of earlier. As he pulled on a fresh shirt, he heard the rustle of fabric behind him and turned to see Malin shedding her tattered garments, her movements fluid and unselfconscious.

When they were both done, they turned to face each other, and Malin snorted, a laugh bubbling up from deep within her. Neither of their borrowed pants reached their ankles, and the shirts looked two sizes too small, stretching taut across their shoulders and chests. But they were clean, and the feeling of fresh fabric against their skin was a luxury beyond measure.

"You're incredible, Sparks. One day, you will wake up and see it… You're too good for me, and I know it, but I will spend the rest of my life trying to be good enough."

"You, my love, have helped me to become someone I never imagined I could be…"

He cut her off, "I know. I'm sorry." He could only think of the fact that her doctor's creed said to take no life, and it was because of him that she did that.

She placed a finger on his lips to silence him and continued, "Someone strong, with powers that make me believe in myself and help me protect the people I love. I became a doctor because I wanted to help people, but now I have the power to protect others from truly dangerous individuals and save lives, like those on the ship. It was you… in my life that brought me this." His heart fluttered.

"I love you so much that the instant I realized you were missing, I felt a piece of me was missing. My heart longed for you when we were apart. Soul-bond or not, I need you to feel whole." His heart skipped a beat.

Their gazes locked, the intensity of the moment deepening the bond between them, a tangible beat that pulsed through his very bones. It was a connection that went beyond magic, beyond touch, a feeling of two souls finally settling back into their rightful alignment.

"Will," she began, her voice barely a whisper, yet it cut through the lingering haze in his mind. "I… I have something important to speak with you about… Before dinner."

His gut clenched. His mind immediately went to danger. Another threat? News of Media? His hand instinctively went to the dagger strapped to his thigh, then he caught himself. No. Her expression wasn't fearful. He saw a slight smile tug at her lips as she read his concern in his eyes.

She took a slow, deep breath, her gaze unwavering. "I'm pregnant," she said.

The world tilted. Time stopped, then lurched violently forward. *Pregnant.*

The word echoed in his mind, sharp and impossible. He stared at her, utterly speechless, his grip on her arms tightening without conscious thought. Her eyes, those impossibly blue eyes, held no deception.

The world shattered, then reformed in brilliant, blinding light. Pregnant. Not a trick. Not a fear. A baby. *Their* baby.

A wave of pure, undiluted joy surged through him, so overwhelming it stole his breath and made his vision blur. Every fiber of his being screamed with elation. He stared at her, utterly speechless, his grip on her arms tightening, pulling her closer until no air could exist between them. He felt like he could lift her, lift the world, and shout the news to the constellations.

"A baby?" he finally managed, his voice a hoarse, incredulous whisper, raw with staggering happiness. "Our baby?"

He crushed her against him, burying his face in her neck, breathing in her scent, trying to anchor himself in this impossible, perfect reality. This was a miracle. This was everything he never knew he wanted, magnified a thousand times.

Then, slowly, as the first rush of ecstasy began to ebb, a cold dread started to seep in. A baby. Here? Now? In this life of constant flight, with assassins at their heels and a world trying to chip away at their very souls? How could they protect another vulnerable life? The thought was terrifying, an unbearable weight settling in his chest.

He pulled back, holding her at arm's length, his eyes wide, the joy still warring with the dawning fear. "Malin... a baby. Here?

Now? With the Order of Tamris hunting us, and Media still out there? This journey to Aloria... It's dangerous enough for us, for Ellie and Zee. How can we possibly...?" His voice trailed off, the questions too immense to form.

Malin's expression softened, a familiar resolve hardening her gaze. She reached up, cupping his cheek, her thumb stroking gently. "We will," she said, her voice quiet but firm, cutting through his rising panic. "We will protect them. Just like we protect Ellie and Zee. We've faced worse, Will. We've already faced the impossible and won." Her eyes, so clear and unwavering, held his. "This baby... It's not a burden, Will. It's hope. More reasons to fight. More reasons to find that peace for us. We'll find a way. We always do."

He stared at her, at the fierce, undeniable pull she had on him, on his heart and soul. He saw her unwavering strength, her conviction, and in her eyes, he found a reflection of his own desperate, burgeoning hope. The terror began to recede, replaced by a profound, almost unbearable relief. Holding her close felt right, even if everything else felt precariously balanced. He'd have to turn his mind inside out, but if finding a solution to the Order of Tamris would help their family, he would fight the God they worship directly if needed. The thought of letting her go, even for a moment, left him undone. It was bad enough knowing that danger was around every corner, but that thought was worse.

Just as he was voicing his hope, a loud, undeniable growl rumbled from his stomach.

Malin's eyes widened, a soft chuckle escaping her. Just then, a matching rumble echoed from her midsection.

Will laughed, a genuine, joyful sound that felt foreign and wonderful after so long. "I guess even world-saving heroes and their patients need to eat," he murmured, gently tracing the line of her jaw. "Dinner is ready, and it would be rude to miss it." He squeezed her hands. "We can pick this up later. All of it. Promise."

She nodded, her smile finally reaching her eyes, a promise reflected in their depths. "Promise."

They shared a brief kiss before opening the door, assaulted by the aromas of food spread out on the table.

Their hosts had prepared quite a spread for them, and the meal buzzed with a quiet warmth. In the center, a low, smooth-topped tree stump served as their dining table, laden with several bowls of unusual, vibrantly colored foods.

Will hadn't recognized any of the ingredients, but the earthy aromas were surprisingly inviting. Their hosts, and her equally short husband, whose dark hair and kind eyes mirrored hers, passed the dishes around with gentle smiles.

Aldrik sat beside Malin, his usual stoic demeanor softened by the glow of a nearby lantern, and Will found himself between Malin and the hosts.

They watched as their hosts completed their traditional blessing of the food. He found it fascinating, as he could see how similar it was to other Fae blessings he had seen, but it also had some very woodland creature-like differences.

As their hosts left the room to finish the ritual outdoors, they asked them to stay and eat.

As the quiet hum of the blessing faded, Malin took a deep breath, her hand finding Will's under the table. She gave his fingers a reassuring squeeze, a silent plea for support. "Aeladar," she began, her voice a little unsteady, drawing his gaze. "Will and I... we have something to tell you."

Will felt the tension rise in the air, a familiar ripple of apprehension, but he squeezed Malin's hand back, letting her know he was with her.

"I wanted to tell Will first, privately." She paused, taking another bracing breath, then looked directly at Aldrik, a hint of defiance in her gaze. "But now we're telling you together. I'm pregnant, Aeladar. We're going to have a baby."

Will watched Aldrik's face. The Elf's serene expression, usually so unreadable, fractured with a profound shock. His eyes widened, fixing on Malin's stomach, then darting to Will's face. For a long moment, silence stretched, heavy and expectant, broken only by the crackle of the hearth and the gentle chirping of crickets outside.

Then, a slow, radiant smile spread across Aldrik's face, transforming his features. It wasn't just happiness; it was pure, unadulterated elation, a joy so profound it shimmered around him like the soft glow of moonlight. He pushed away from the table, not gracefully, but with a sudden, almost clumsy urgency, and in two swift strides, he was kneeling before Malin.

"A Wyn'syl... a baby," he whispered, his voice thick with emotion, his gaze fixed on her belly as if he could already see the new life stirring within. He looked up at Malin, his eyes brimming with unshed tears. "A Del'wyn... grandchild." He reached out, his hand trembling slightly, hovering near her stomach as if afraid to touch. "I... I never thought... I know I have Ellie and Zee, but to be able to have a Del'wyn so small. As I aged, I realized that I always wanted to be a Pir'ion... Grandfather. To hold a little one, to share stories, to watch them grow." He looked from Malin to Will, then back to Malin, a deep, abiding warmth radiating from him. "This is... this is truly wonderful news. A blessing."

He finally, gently, placed his hand on Malin's stomach, a gesture of profound tenderness and acceptance. The joy radiating from him was palpable, filling the small room with a happiness that settled over them like a soft blanket.

Still holding the air of elation, they finished the nourishing but straightforward dinner of roasted root vegetables and a stew of forest game. It was strangely flavorful despite lacking familiar spices. Aldrik opened a discussion of their plan and destination for the morning.

"Before I separated from the group, Elowen said she would bring your belongings with them to Mellyrn. I haven't been able to reach her to confirm, but they should be reaching there soon," he told them, his voice calm, but he could sense some concern in his voice. "We will leave first thing in the morning. Our host has given us maps and supplies for the journey. It is only a two or three-day journey from here, so we will be with them soon."

Will felt a surge of relief so potent it almost buckled his knees. Just a few more days, and he would see them. The thought was a beacon, a blinding light in the darkness that had been his captivity. But with the relief came a sharp stab of concern.

Two or three more days? It felt like an eternity. Every hour they were apart was another hour he couldn't protect them, couldn't confirm with his own eyes that they were truly safe. The waiting was agony. As Aldrik had said, "he had to hold out hope that they were safe."

Hope felt like a fragile thing right now, easily shattered.

His kids had to be safe. The mantra echoed in his mind, a desperate prayer. They were his world, his anchor, the reason he'd endured ten days of unimaginable torment.

He marveled at how profoundly his life had changed in such a short time. Just weeks ago, he was a loner smuggler, drifting from job to job, responsible only for himself. Now, he was a father and husband, his entire world tilting on the axis of *their* needs, *their* safety, *their* very breath.

Every calculated risk, every weary step, every beat of his heart was for them. The thought was both terrifying and the most exhilarating truth he'd ever known.

Later, under a sky ablaze with constellations he knew so well, Will found himself outside the hut. He leaned against the gnarled trunk of a massive tree, the rough bark digging into his back, a constant, dull ache thrumming through his still-recovering body. He watched the distant glow of the village hearths, feeling the cool, still air, but the quiet offered little solace. His mind was a maelstrom of phantom sensations, the echoes of a nightmare he couldn't quite shake.

He felt Malin approach before he heard her, a subtle shift in the air, then the unmistakable feel of their bond radiating towards him like a lighthouse. A familiar warmth enveloped him as she came to stand beside him, then wrapped her arms around his waist, resting her head against his back, his hands lovingly cupping her flat stomach.

His child. *Their* child. A new life, small and fragile, nestled inside her, completely dependent on them. The thought sent a jolt of fierce, protective joy through him so potent it made his vision blur. He would get to watch this child grow, teach them, protect them with every fiber of his being.

He leaned into her, sighing deeply, feeling the solid comfort of her body against his, a balm to his agitated spirit. She turned him gently, urging him to face her. Her eyes, clear and shimmering in the starlight, were a steady, unwavering blue.

"I was so worried about you," she began, her voice soft, a tremor running through it that spoke of her fear. "When I saw... what they were doing... and Lydia..." She swallowed hard, her gaze searching his, not demanding, but offering. "You don't have to share. I'm not sure I even want to know all the details, but... I'm here if you need to talk. All of it."

"You know what kept me going," he admitted, the words raw, tearing at something deep inside him, exposing the vulnerable core he rarely showed. "Every twist of their knife, every hallucinatory horror... it was the memory of you. Your laugh, your stubborn kindness, the way you look at me. You and our family."

He wrapped her close, pulling her tighter, desperate to feel her reality. The soft curve of her hip against his, the gentle rise and fall of her breath – each sensation was a stark, blessed contrast to the twisted, forced sensations from before. "If it had been physical torture only, I would have held out for a good long while," he murmured into her hair. "But he would use you against me, with his illusions. I knew it wasn't you. My mind told me. But it was hard to unsee those things… Lydia's acting skills were good, but not good enough. At first, they had me, and with enough of the drugs, they could trick me for a little bit." He pulled her back then, needing to see her face, to anchor himself in her truth. "By the time it got to her turn with me, I could immediately tell." He paused, savoring the feel of her hands on his arms, pushing the phantom memories away with the undeniable presence of *his* Malin.

"Those eyes," he said, his voice husky with emotion. "He could never get those eyes the right color. I knew it wasn't you just by looking at the eyes."

He carefully lifted her chin, his thumb stroking her jawline. Their lips touched, a tentative brush that deepened into fierce hunger. Her lips parted, soft and yielding, and he brushed his tongue against them, a desperate plea, before he flicked in to claim her mouth as his. He took a deep, shuddering breath, savoring her presence, the taste of her, the absolute, undeniable reality of her, desperate to cleanse himself of every phantom touch, every twisted illusion of another.

He pulled back, a shaky laugh escaping him. "Torture must have really gotten to me. I actually opened my mind to your mother, hoping that I would hear from that battle ax. That tech wouldn't even let her through," He said it teasingly. "But I did. I was... desperate."

Malin's arms tightened around him, pulling him close again. "I saw the rooms, the blood, I can't even imagine what they did… but… I saw what she was doing. And I know you. They couldn't break you. When I cut you loose and you didn't know it was me…" She stroked his back in a comforting rhythm. "You were magnificent. Even tied down, you fought. And then… what you did in there… for me… for us."

"I almost killed you," he turned away, ashamed of his reaction.

"You kept fighting, until you knew it was me. That is all that mattered to me," she assured with a light kiss to his lips.

"And you, Sparks," he murmured into her hair. "You were amazing. You saved me. And then that fire… where did that intensity come from? You torched Lydia to a crisp."

"I… I don't know," she admitted, her voice soft. "It just… came. Seeing what she was doing to you, what Nemilos was doing to us. Something just… snapped. A fury I didn't know I had." She pulled back slightly, looking up at him.

"Is it wrong that it felt so good… To watch her burn." A flicker of something primal, dangerous, but undeniably *hers*, passed through her eyes.

"That's my girl," he said, pulling her close again, a fierce protectiveness swelling in his chest. "Perfectly dangerous."

He closed his eyes, inhaling her scent, the raw scent of her magic, and then they walked together back to the room, hands connected.

She's real. She's here.

When they got the door closed, he pulled her to him. Her lips were parted in that inviting way that made him want to lose himself in them. His lips touched her lightly. Flashes of memories. Kisses with Malin that turned into Lydia's face. He hadn't been entirely forthcoming with her about how effective

Nemilos' illusions had been. It took him several tries before he realized what was happening.

He tried to deepen the kiss again, to lose himself in her warmth, to erase the ugly images burned into his mind. He wanted to feel her, truly feel her, the way he always had. He reached for her, his hands finding the soft fabric of her borrowed shirt, pulling her closer as he sought comfort and release.

But as he closed his eyes, a phantom image flashed behind his eyelids. The image of Lydia's mocking face, her eyes wide with a triumphant, lustful gleam as she rode him, the drug-induced haze, the sickening violation. He flinched, pulling back abruptly, his breath catching in his throat.

Malin's hands went to his face, her touch gentle, concerned. "Will? What is it?"

He shook his head, unable to meet her gaze, a wave of self-disgust washing over him. "I... I can't, Sparks. Not yet. I keep seeing her. Her face. What they did." The words were choked, raw, laced with humiliation, the lingering taint of the forced intimacy, even though he knew it wasn't his fault. "I can't get past it."

She didn't push. Her hands wrapped around him again, holding him tighter than before, her head resting against his chest. "It's okay, Will. It's okay. You don't have to be okay. Not yet. We just... hold each other. We're safe now."

Her touch was a tonic to his soul, a silent promise that she understood, that he wasn't broken in her eyes.

He felt a deep, profound shift within him, a subtle strengthening of the invisible tether that bound them. Her presence was a grounding anchor in the storm of his mind. He could almost feel their magic interweaving, a slow, gentle hum of connection that went deeper than anything he'd known before. It wasn't the explosive rush of their power merging, but a quiet, foundational resonance.

They stood there, under the unfamiliar stars, holding onto each other, the silence broken only by the chirping of crickets and the soft rustle of leaves. She had healed his body, but his mind remained a battlefield, littered with fresh trauma and lingering questions. Yet, wrapped in her arms, he felt a fragile peace begin to settle.

Finally, he spoke, the words were a murmur against her hair. "I saw Caelum in town earlier. He's here. In the village."

He felt Malin stiffen slightly in his arms. He had a feeling that the peace, however fragile, was about to be tested again.

CHAPTER 27 – MALIN

The lingering taste of sweet, roasted root vegetables from the Fae village breakfast still warmed Malin's tongue. After heartfelt thanks to their quiet, hospitable hosts, the first day of hiking had started under a canopy of dappled sunlight, surprisingly well. Every muscle in Malin's body hummed with the restored vitality of her magic, a stark contrast to the crippling exhaustion she'd felt just yesterday. They covered a great deal of ground, the forest floor beneath her boots softening to a familiar cushion as the hours melted away.

As they walked, she learned of the device that had been on Will's neck that stole his powers. She didn't know much about the Fellspire Citadel, but the idea that someone would take away another's powers as punishment, their very essence, felt brutal, almost as bad as Media.

For him to have endured such a violation for so long, her heart ached with a pain that mirrored his own. She knew without a doubt that the powerful emotion swelling within her was pure love for this man. With every silent declaration, every unspoken confirmation in her mind, she could feel their soul-bond growing stronger, intertwining their very beings.

But the physical ease didn't extend to the atmosphere between her two companions. Aeladar, usually a silent, almost ghost-like presence, was clearly on edge. He had not been happy when Will had told him he had seen Caelum in the village battle. He kept mumbling "coward", "If he gets his hands on him…", and "Dran'syl"… which she found out was something worse than coward in Elven, though he wouldn't elaborate for her delicate ears. All of which made Will raise an eyebrow, a slight, knowing smirk playing on his lips. He seemed obsessed, and Will, having seen Caelum face actual danger, wasn't buying all the drama.

Nonetheless, every rustle in the undergrowth, every sudden chirp of an exotic bird, made her father's head snap around, his hand instinctively going to his blade. Will had warned them, his voice tight and low, that his nullifying barrier would catch the invisible man if he dared to follow.

Finally, after hours of grumbling, Will asked, "Why do you think he is such a coward? From what I saw, it seemed like he was doing some pretty heroic stuff, for someone who isn't a warrior."

Aeladar halted, his jaw tightening. He turned, his eyes, usually serene, now sharp with a cold, ancient anger. "At the pirate encampment, I was going into the building to find you. I saw Caelum already outside the building, making his escape, not engaging. He was there. If he didn't even stay to watch her fall, that is cowardice. It is inexcusable for me. If his fear of me was so profound that he chose to flee rather than aid the woman he supposedly loved, the woman who was fighting for your life, the mother of his child... if he abandoned her in that moment of desperate need... then he does not deserve to be an Aeladar to Ellie." Her father's voice, though low, carried the weight of a judgment that Will knew was final.

Whether or not Caelum was Ellie's biological father, Aldrik had unequivocally decided that he did not deserve to know her, not after abandoning them in the chaos of battle.

Malin couldn't fault his reasoning, even if a tiny, complex part of her still wrestled with the ghost of the man Caelum once was. The air between them, once cleared by the immediate danger, now felt charged with her father's simmering fury and the unspoken weight of Caelum's betrayal.

As they walked, Malin noticed Aeladar's posture stiffen further, his keen half-Elven senses seemingly overwhelmed. He abruptly halted, his hand pressing against his chest, right over his heart. A low, guttural sound escaped him, almost a growl. His eyes, usually so composed, were wide with a raw, visceral panic that sent a jolt of alarm through Malin.

"What is it?" Malin demanded, her hand instinctively going to her chest, trying to feel for a reciprocal tremor.

Aeladar didn't answer directly. Instead, he pulled out the folded, leather-bound map their hosts had given them. His fingers, usually so precise, trembled slightly as he unfolded it, his eyes darting frantically across the intricate lines and symbols. He traced a spot with a trembling finger, then looked up, his gaze meeting Malin's with an intensity that made her breath catch.

"Ael'an," he rasped, the single word thick with urgency.

Her mother?

"Something is wrong," he said, pain in his voice.

Malin felt a cold dread settle in her stomach. "What do you mean? Is she hurt?"

"I cannot communicate with her," he said, his voice tight, "but I feel it. A pull. An urgent pull. Not far from here. Not in the direction of Mellyrn." His eyes widened further, a dawning horror on his face. "She is close. Too close. We should be able to speak easily. We could be there in half an hour. Maybe less."

"If Mom's in trouble, let's go," she agreed.

Will moved instantly, his hand on his blade, his gaze already sweeping for danger as he followed Aldrik and her.

The forest around them, previously a comforting canopy, suddenly felt alive with unseen threats. The destination of Mellyrn and the hope of seeing their children faded to a distant point on the map. All that mattered was the desperate urgency in Aldrik's eyes and the silent plea for a soul-bonded companion in peril.

Will didn't leave her side as they traveled. He was like a shadow. It felt so good to have him there, like a part of her had been missing and was finally in place.

Her father moved like a dark wildcat. Malin and Will followed his unerring sense of direction, not on a hike, but in a desperate sprint through the dense foliage. The jungle became a dizzying wash of green and shadow around them, every rustle, every snapped twig, a potential give-away.

After what felt like mere minutes, Aeladar abruptly dropped to a crouch, pulling them down with him. Seeing him in action, Malin finally understood why Will's stories of General Rauno commanded such respect. It wasn't just the raw athleticism or the unyielding determination. It was the love he so obviously carried for her mother, a palpable force that resonated deep within Malin. She recognized it, a powerful echo of the fierce, protective devotion she felt from Will, a stark contrast to the hollow promises of her past.

Through a screen of thick ferns, Malin peered out. Her breath hitched. Below them, in a small, concealed clearing, was a troop formation of Media Guards. Their dark uniforms stood out starkly against the verdant undergrowth. She could hear their rough voices, murmuring about "waiting for larger transport," and "reinforcements."

Then, Malin's eyes landed on it. A large, armored Command vehicle, its dark metal glinting ominously even in the filtered light. It was sleek, heavily reinforced, and unlike any standard Media military equipment she had seen.

"She's in there," Aldrik whispered, his voice laced with venom, his gaze fixed on the vehicle. "I can feel her. They're holding her. Why can't she respond?" She could feel his anxiety and concern.

Malin placed a firm hand on Aldrik's arm, forcing his gaze to meet hers. Her voice was low, steady, a calm counterpoint to his rising panic. "Aeladar. Breathe with me. Focus. You can feel her. That's what matters. Not the why right now. Just the *what*.

Mom's here. She's alive." She paused, giving him a moment to draw a ragged breath. "Her inability to respond means they're blocking her, not that she's gone. Maybe they are using one of those devices that they used on Will." She squeezed his arm, a silent command for him to ground himself.

The stakes had just escalated catastrophically. They had to get her mother before those reinforcements arrived.

Will immediately went still beside them, his brow furrowed in intense concentration as his eyes swept over the scene. Malin knew that look; he was already weighing angles, calculating numbers, seeking weaknesses.

"We have the advantage. We have two flame powers and two of the deadliest fighters I know. If we go in blazing, they might leave in their transport and we will have a harder time getting her back. I would think that a diversion would be our best bet," Will spoke his strategy, earning a nod from her father.

"I agree," Aeladar said.

Her gaze swept over the gathered guards, dismissed them, then snapped back to one figure standing slightly apart, giving orders.

Suddenly, Malin froze. A cold, sickening wave washed over her, making her stomach clench.

It couldn't be.

He was dressed in civilian clothing, but a subtle armored vest was visible beneath his tunic. He had light brown hair and eyes. It was her old neighbor, the man whom her father had placed as her neighbor so that she could watch him. The man whom she had trusted, her Dad's most trusted right-hand man.

Andrew.

The recognition hit her with the force of a physical blow. Andrew, here. This was her father's elite enforcer squad. Given how they had wiped out the last squad in the West Woods in their escape from the city, she could see why they might have thought that reinforcements were warranted. She could feel the flames within her rising, a furious heat replacing the cold dread.

Will, oblivious to Malin's silent horror, began to lay out a plan, his voice a low, urgent murmur. "Here's what we do. Aldrik, you take the perimeter. Disable their comms, but quietly. Malin…" He turned to her, his eyes gleaming with a dangerous intensity. "This relies heavily on you, as Aldrik needs to focus on getting Elowen."

"Andrew's in there," she stated with barely contained fury.

"The Andrew?" Will's eyes widened, a rare flicker of surprise crossing his face. Then he regained his composure. "Stay calm. Let us make a plan."

Aldrik listened, looking from one to the other with raised eyebrow, "Who is Andrew? Should we be worried about an Andrew?"

"Andrew is the person that was placed to live next to her, to pretend to be her friend, to give intel to the city. Andrew attacked her and lost. It is *her* we should be worried about," Will said with a grim satisfaction that made Malin's inner fire burn hotter. "It's not a good idea to do someone dirty like that, especially when she has powers like hers."

"Oh. Don't worry Noor'wyn. He'll get what's coming… today," Aldrik stated with a hard glint in his eyes. "Do you have a better idea that gets Elowen out before that 'larger transport' arrives?" he asked.

The silence that followed was heavy with the unspoken truth. They were running out of time.

"I want to help," a quiet voice from behind them startled them. Caelum. He materialized from the shadows, looking less ethereal than before, but still out of place in his civilian clothes. "I know I screwed up at the pirate compound. It was my first battle like that. I didn't know what to do. Please give me another try." Then looking to her father, "I want to make it up to you."

Aldrik lunged at Caelum, but Will held him back, a powerful grip on his arm. "I knew you were following."

Malin took a deep breath, the fury in her core solidifying into cold, hard resolve. This wasn't about Caelum's redemption, not now. It was about her mother, about revenge for Andrew's betrayal, about getting their family back.

"Thank you. I know what we are going to do," she stated, her voice flat, dangerously calm. "We are going to kill them all. Caelum. You need to go distract them. Go ask the time or something, just get them watching you. Aeladar, you take the left and get into that Command vehicle to get her out. Will, take the right. I'll take the middle and take care of Andrew."

"Who am I to argue with a lady? I'm in," Will said, a glint of wicked amusement in his eyes. "Lead the way, Sparks."

The plan was audacious, bordering on suicidal, but that seemed to be their specialty lately.

They estimated roughly thirty heavily armed, elite special forces guards. They were Media's best... spread out around the clearing. But they had the element of surprise and the burning motivation of family.

Caelum, pale but resolute, melted away into the jungle on the opposite side of the clearing. A moment later, a distinct, rather awkward cough echoed from the tree line, followed by a surprisingly loud, if somewhat nervous, voice calling out, "Excuse me. Could anyone tell me the time? My chronometer seems to have... stopped."

The effect was immediate. Heads swiveled. Guards, who moments before had been idly chatting, snapped to attention, their weapons raised towards the unexpected, civilian-clad figure.

That was their cue.

Aldrik was a whisper of death on the left flank. He cut through the initial line of guards, a silent, black-bladed wraith. His movements were a liquid dance of precision and lethality. Knives flashed, throats were slit, and the elite guards dropped without a sound, their bodies crumpling before they could even scream. He reached the Command vehicle in seconds, a shadow against its armored hull.

She watched as long as she could before it was time for her to move into action. She shot white-hot flames in front of her, engulfing guards who then caused additional chaos by running while on fire.

She got past Caelum, who stood frozen, staring at her. His face, usually so composed, was slack with pure, unadulterated terror. His eyes, wide and fixed on her, reflected the scorching heat of her aura, seeing not Malin, but something primordial and utterly terrifying. He made no move to help, no sound, just a statue carved from fear.

A cold satisfaction bloomed in Malin's chest as she witnessed Caelum's fear. He'd seen her at her weakest, had betrayed her, and now he saw her at her most dangerous. It was a potent, terrifying power, and at that moment, she embraced it. Let him be afraid.

As bullets were fired in her direction, her flames melted them in mid-air. The flames within her grew stronger, encouraging her. The flames surrounding her body formed a protective shield as she took out guard after guard. She glanced to the right, and Will was a whirlwind of controlled chaos. He moved with brutal efficiency, a primal rage fueling his attacks. He was a force of nature, punching, kicking, snapping necks, using their momentum against them. Weapons flew from hands, bodies crumpled, and within moments, a bloody swath showed his progress.

Every kill was precise, economical.

One down. Two down. More.

His side of the clearing became a graveyard of twitching limbs and silenced guards.

Malin heard muffled shouts, a brief struggle, then silence from within the vehicle. Aldrik emerged moments later, her mother lay unconscious, cradled in his arms like a child. He was already retreating into the jungle cover, a ghost disappearing with his precious cargo.

Malin, meanwhile, was a storm of focused fury in the center. She didn't waste time on subtleties. Her fists glowed with raw energy; her feet moved with the precision of her martial arts training. Each blow landed with bone-shattering force. She twisted, ducked, and weaved through the desperate counterattacks, a blur of righteous anger.

Guards came at her with energy rifles, with stun batons, but her rage made her fast, unstoppable. She felt the searing heat of her power, a devastating force in her hands.

Every guard she met became a calculated choice. The lives she extinguished were not just lives, but obstacles. Obstacles to Ellie and Zee's safety. Obstacles to Will's freedom. Obstacles to the future they deserved.

The doctor in her recoiled, an ache of the oath she once held sacred, but the protector, the mother, the *warrior* she was becoming, crushed it down.

There was no room for hesitation, no space for mercy. Only the burning desire to find Andrew, to make him pay, fueled this brutal efficiency. He was not a direct obstacle to safety, unlike these guards. He was the embodiment of a more profound, colder betrayal. He had watched her, pretending to be her friend, all while obeying her father's orders to keep her chipped, to keep her powerless. He was one of the many who had hidden the truth of her life from her, and the thought of his deception now burned hotter than any flame she commanded.

Each incinerated guard became a fleeting memory, replaced by a cold, hard knot in her gut.

Her eyes frantically scanned the faces of the dying, the defeated. She moved through the melee like a vengeful spirit, taking down every man who dared to stand in her way, but Andrew was nowhere to be found.

He was the one she craved.

She saw only terror, confusion, and death in the eyes of the remaining guards. Had he fled? Had he slipped away in the initial confusion?

Suddenly, she felt a hand graze her neck. The unexpected attack came from behind, a low, guttural grunt accompanying the strike. She didn't need to see his face. She knew. She turned to face her attacker.

Andrew.

His hand had burns, and he was holding a metal device, similar to the one that Nemilos had used on Will. He had tried to put one of those devices on her.

Rage, pure and undiluted, surged through her, overpowering the sudden weakness flooding her veins.

Even as her muscles threatened to give way, her training kicked in. She spun, a whirlwind of motion, her martial arts instincts taking over. She pivoted on one foot, bringing her elbow back in a vicious, arcing strike aimed for his head.

He grunted, surprised by her immediate, powerful counter. She needed him to bleed. She needed him to *pay* before she crisped him.

"Hey. Malin. How about we head back to Media, and you can tell us where your mother's drive is? Your Dad says he misses you. He gave us orders not to hurt you." Andrew said it with a slick, self-satisfied smirk, as if offering her a generous lifeline.

His eyes, however, held a glint of genuine confusion at her unleashed power, quickly masked by practiced charm. He truly seemed to believe she'd be relieved that his words were a benevolent invitation rather than a sickening trap.

"I don't think my Dad counted on the fact that I might not want to go back," she offered, her flame power already banked, a controlled heat just beneath her skin.

As Andrew circled her, a small metal device was clutched in his hand. It looked very similar to the one that had been on Will's neck, the very one that had stolen his powers. She felt a cold precision settle over her. She glanced over to see Will had a guard pinned beneath him, his weight on the man's chest, a lazy, appreciative grin spreading across his face.

"Enjoying the show, Sparks. Let me know if you want me to tag in," he called out, his voice laced with a knowing amusement that promised he wouldn't interfere unless necessary.

Andrew lunged first, his movements predictable, clumsy even. His desperate swings with the device were so easy to read; she flowed around them with the grace of her martial arts training, effortlessly dodging each attempt to jab her.

She toyed with him, her feet light, her body a blur of precision as she parried his clumsy thrusts, enjoying the rising panic in his eyes. He wasn't a warrior; he was a manipulator, and in this close-quarters dance, his true ineptitude shone.

As Andrew stumbled back from another parry, Malin called out to Will, "Don't worry, honey. This will be over soon. There won't be a need to tag you in. Take a rest."

The words were a stark echo of Will's casual brutality, and a thrill, cold and sharp, went through her. This feeling, this absolute control, this calm before the strike. It reminded her intensely of him, and a fierce, undeniable wave of love for Will, for the man who had shown her what true power felt like, pulsed through her veins.

In the next thrust, when he overextended, she didn't need fire. Her open palm struck his wrist, disarming him with a sharp crack, the device skittering across the ground. Before he could react, her knee connected with his gut, doubling him over with a strangled gasp. As he staggered, she spun, delivering a precise, bone-jarring kick to his temple.

Andrew dropped like a stone, collapsing to the ground. The look of utter shock and bewilderment on his face as he fell was exactly the closure she needed.

But the fight wasn't truly over. Will, who had watched the entire exchange with a grim satisfaction, suddenly shifted. He dragged the guard he'd been pinning over to Andrew's prone form, and with a swift, brutal efficiency, used his blade to finish Andrew off. The glint of steel was quick, decisive. Will straightened, wiping his blade on the guard's tunic before sheathing it.

"Never liked him," Will muttered, his voice flat, entirely devoid of emotion, as he glanced at Andrew's now lifeless body.

The casual brutality of the act, the simple, cold words, were a stark reminder of the rogue beneath the charming façade. Then, his eyes met Malin's, a flicker of something assessing, almost possessive, passing between them.

She turned to look around at the battlefield. Caelum was staring at her, still frozen in fear, almost unblinking. All the other guards were dead.

"I thought it was a good idea to keep one alive. I wasn't sure if we would need someone to operate some equipment or something." Will's keen observational skills had been at work. He nudged the young guard with his boot, a silent command to stay put.

Just then, she noticed something nearby on the outskirts of the clearing. Aeladar bent over her mother, lying on the grassy hill. They walked over, Caelum trailing far behind them, his face still etched with the horror of Malin's recent display.

"I don't know what is wrong. She can't wake up," he said, his voice raw, looking utterly crushed as he gently cradled her mother's head.

Will turned to the young guard, "You have two options. I can keep you alive, and you can tell us everything we want to know now, or I can torture you. You will tell us what we want to know, and then you won't be alive," he clearly outlined the options for him, his voice devoid of emotion, causing Caelum's face to pale even whiter.

Malin's breath hitched, a faint surprise fluttering through her at the sheer brutality of Will's words, delivered with such dispassionate clarity. This was the rogue, the killer, the part of him she'd only ever glimpsed, a stark reminder of the life he'd lived before her, the very life that had, in part, led them to this chaotic existence.

Only a short time ago, back in Media, such an exchange would have horrified her, perhaps even driven her away. Now, she found herself not just accepting it, but a chilling part of her acknowledged its brutal efficiency. It was a weapon, wielded to protect. This was the cost of their freedom, the price of survival in a world that didn't play by rules she'd once held sacred.

She looked at Will, his profile hard, resolute. He would do what was necessary, no matter how ugly, to keep them safe. And in that moment, Malin realized with a profound certainty that they were better off for him being this way. Her own hands, still vibrating with the memory of the guards she'd incinerated, were testament to how far she'd fallen... or how far she had risen... from her oath to protect life. She could live with this part of Will. She had to because she was becoming it herself.

"I'll talk. It's a new nanotechnology. Experimental, Dr. Neldoreth ordered us to use it. They want to be able to use her powers, so they don't want to remove them, but they don't want her to be able to use them on us. I don't know anything else but that. The computers should show more. Look, I'm new to this group. Please let me live. I just wanted out of Talvi," the guard begged, his eyes wide with terror.

"Let me check out the computers," Malin offered, already moving with purpose toward the Command vehicle. The idea of a new technology, one that could suppress Elowen's immense power without destroying it, sent a chill down her spine.

When she reached the vehicle, the two main screens flickered to life, bathing the interior in a cold, blue glow. A blinking red timer dominated one display: reinforcements would be here within fifteen minutes. They didn't have time to do much investigation. The full details of the nanotechnology would have to wait.

"How do we keep these on? The last one I used needed fingerprints," he asked, pulling his knife out.

"Here you need this," the guard pleaded as he handed over a small object to Will on a lanyard.

The decision was made in a silent, urgent exchange of glances between Malin, Will, and Aldrik. There was no time for deliberation. They would grab what they could, quickly copy the hard drives, destroy what they couldn't take, and leave, carrying Elowen out of there. Mellyrn was only a half-day's walk from here. They could get help there, and Media wouldn't dare follow them once they crossed into the sovereign borders of the Elf territories.

Before they departed, Malin took a page directly from Aldrik's teachings, a cold resolve settling over her features. She walked over to the cowering young soldier tied up on the ground, her expression unreadable.

"You should be very afraid of me," she stated, her voice low, almost a purr, yet crackling with an undeniable power that made the air around them hum.

The guard's eyes darted nervously, acknowledging, "I am. Very."

"Good," Malin continued, her gaze piercing him. Internally, she was smiling.

"Then spread the word. Tell everyone in Media. Tell your superiors, tell your families. Tell them that I can track people. Tell them that if they ever come after us again, if they ever threaten my family, if they even *think* of touching my mother or my children again… I will come after the city. All of it. And I won't stop until every last one of them burns. Make sure to tell my Dad, especially. He is on my list also." Her voice was quiet, but the implicit threat was a roaring flame.

 It was a false promise, but it would likely be taken as deadly and absolute.

With a quick kick to his temple by her, he was down, but alive.

As they walked away from the clearing, with the data module and what little else they could salvage from the Command vehicle, the last sounds they heard were the crackle of flames as the armored vehicle and the dead were consumed by fire.

Malin felt a grim satisfaction. They had taken out an elite squad of enforcers, people who had been the direct cause of so much suffering and so many deaths. But even as the triumph settled in her bones, a deep current of concern ran through her. Her mother was still unconscious, a mystery of nanotechnology weighing heavily on them.

Killing the enemy was one thing.

Saving her family was another entirely.

Chapter 28 – Malin

The rhythmic thud of Aldrik's boots on the forest floor had been a steady, grounding beat for hours. They had to hike quite a distance before the stench of burnt metal and flesh faded from the air.

Malin's own body thrummed with a strange mix of residual adrenaline and the lingering warmth of her magic. She had tried to heal her mother as they walked, but it was as if there was a barrier her magic could not cross. A cold wave of frustration washed over her. Her medical training, honed over the years, was useless here. And now, her magic, which had felt so boundless and powerful against Andrew and the guards, was equally impotent. To stand by, unable to heal the woman she was just beginning to truly connect with, felt like a cruel irony, a stark reminder of the limits she still faced.

Aldrik strode ahead effortlessly, with her mother cradled carefully in his arms. His gaze was fixed forward, his focus entirely on getting her to safety, his hand occasionally adjusting Elowen's head with a tenderness that warmed something deep inside Malin.

It was a casual, unconscious gesture, yet it spoke volumes. Malin had never seen her Dad, a man who measured affection in good grades, veiled expectations, and calculated silences, show even a fraction of such tenderness to her, much less to her mother. She was a Daddy's girl, but she realized that it was meeting his expectations and garnering praise she had looked for with him. It was very transactional.

A sharp pang of longing, swiftly followed by a bittersweet ache, resonated within her chest. This was what a father's love could look like: protective, gentle, unwavering. And it was a love she was only just now witnessing from her biological father, a man who was still essentially a stranger.

Malin was a tangled knot of emotions. Beneath the immediate relief of having escaped Media's clutches and having Andrew out of her life, a deep, gnawing anxiety persisted for her mother.

Mom remained utterly still in Aeladar's arms, her face too pale, too peaceful. The guard's desperate words about nanotechnology echoed in Malin's head. What had they done to her? Could it be reversed? It sounded like Media had a plan to wake her up, so there must be something possible.

Yet, overriding some of the worry, a burgeoning excitement began to bubble as the forest canopy thinned. As sweet as the air smelled, with the scent of unfamiliar blossoms, it was the idea that she was close to seeing the children. She had come far too close to death too many times since she had seen them last.

Malin's jaw nearly dropped when the trees parted with her first view of the castle.

Before them stretched a sprawling expanse of meticulously cultivated farmlands, vibrant green and gold under the afternoon sun, unlike anything she had ever seen in Media's sterile hydroponic towers or Sarhan's dusty plains. As if they grew out of the ground, the outer almost crystalline castle walls of Mellyrn curved gracefully and naturally with the world. The stone held a warm, glowing amber in the sunlight, seamlessly interwoven with massive, ancient trees. It was grand and imposing, yet somehow not overbearing. It felt more like a natural extension of the landscape than a conquering structure.

They passed through the wide, welcoming outer gates, and a different kind of bustle enveloped them. The air hummed with a soft murmur of voices, melodious and warm, distinct from the clipped tones of Media. This was the village.

The marketplace was alive with activity, a kaleidoscope of colors and sounds. Stalls, some carved from living wood, others crafted from gleaming stone, overflowed with produce Malin didn't recognize. There were fruits in hues of violet and deep orange, leafy greens that shimmered like jewels, and an array of fragrant herbs.

Merchants of all species mingled freely: tall, elegant Elves with their serene expressions, robust Humans with their earnest laughter, petite forest Elves, some dwarves, and several Fae.

Malin watched them, a profound sense of wonder blooming in her chest. This was unlike anything she had ever known in Media, where humanity reigned supreme and other species were only whispered about in history books or seen as myths. Here, there was no hierarchy of blood or magic, just a vibrant tapestry of life, coexisting, trading, *being*. It was a living testament to the harmony she'd only ever dreamed was possible.

There were few animal products, as expected, but the sheer variety of plant-based foods was astounding.

The very ground seemed to gleam, not with polished stone, but with a vibrant, living cleanliness. It was beautiful, truly beautiful. Every person Malin saw seemed genuinely content, a stark contrast to the weary, often guarded faces of those in Media and Sarhan. This place radiated peace and prosperity, a living testament to its kind and just rule.

They continued deeper into the village, following a wide, curving path that led towards the castle's core. The path itself seemed to shimmer, faintly luminous, lit by the same soft, internal glow that Malin now noticed emanating from some of the buildings. Ahead, the inner gates of the castle loomed, even more magnificent than the outer ones, seeming to be carved from a single, immense piece of glowing, seamless stone.

As they approached, two Elven guards, taller and more imposing than any she had seen, stepped forward, their faces unreadable, though their eyes held a serene intelligence. They weren't hostile, but their presence was firm, a clear boundary.

Beyond them, within the castle grounds, Malin saw even more activity. Banners in vibrant, natural colors were being unfurled, garlands of fresh flowers draped over archways, and the soft strains of what sounded like distant, celebratory music drifted on the breeze. It looked like they were preparing for a festival of some kind.

A welcoming sight, perhaps, but the heavy weight of her mother's unconscious body in Aeladar's arms was a stark reminder that their arrival was far from festive.

She felt Will's hand on her shoulder, comforting. Looking back, she noticed the same furrow of his brow that she held onto hers.

The anticipation of seeing the kids soon was of the utmost importance to her. Aeladar seemed to know where to go and what to do. Hopefully, they would find the kids along the way.

At the guards' unresponsiveness, or perhaps their too-slow reaction to the urgency radiating from him, Aldrik cut in, his voice a low growl. "Out of my way. Now."

"General... I mean Lord Rauno. We were not told you were expected. Apologies," They quickly moved out of the way, practically snapping to attention.

Aelanar is a bad ass.

He strode past them, his presence an immovable force. The moment they stepped into the castle proper, the sounds of the festival preparations seemed to recede, replaced by the soft hum of the castle's living magic and the gentle rush of unseen water.

He didn't slow as he walked confidently through the halls. "Find the healers! Immediately! Have them meet me in my bedchambers," he commanded the first castle attendants they passed, his voice echoing through the halls.

Even as his orders were being relayed by swiftly moving Elves, Aeladar's gaze swept the grand, living hall.

He stopped another attendant hurrying past. "And where can I find Anariel? Nar, Khelek, and my grandchildren? Bring them to me immediately?" The questions were sharp, laced with a barely contained demand that brokered no delay.

Malin felt a surge of hope. His priorities were exactly where they needed to be. She and Will followed along until they got to a tall door that a servant opened for them.

"Thank you, Jessim. Are the healers en route?" He said, walking into the sitting area, which featured a couch, chair, and four doors, one of which was already open. He then continued into that room.

"Yes, my lord. They should be here shortly," the tall Elf in a long brown robe said, as Aldrik placed her on the large, four-poster bed, adorned with silken sheets, on one side of the room.

He was so careful with her, as he straightened her hair and put her hands in more comfortable positions.

"Damn it! Where are those healers?" he fumed without taking his eyes off her.

A tall man in a white robe walked into the room. He held a bag filled to the brim with medical devices she had never seen.

Aldrik hesitated before moving away, but he did, never taking his eyes off her. Malin watched intently as he performed a medical check, as she would do with an unconscious patient, then he pulled a device she had never seen and placed it on her mother's chest.

"I am Minster Annow. I have never seen this before. We have more healers on their way. If you could give more information about this, it may help," he said to Aelandar. Then to them, he said, "It may take some time. Perhaps you should come back."

Aldrik then turned to them. His eyes were wet, and his brows were furrowed. "The children should be here soon. I would rather not have them see her like this. It would be better if you met them away from here. I will stay with her."

Malin couldn't help herself. She threw her arms around him, tears slipping from her.

"Aelandar. She will be fine. We will figure this out. Media wanted her to wake and get her powers back, so there has to be a way to make it happen. We just have to figure out how they were going to do it," she whispered, hoping that showing him that rationale would help him ground his despair.

Just then, the door to the sitting area opened, and Nar and Khelek were in the room waiting for them. Malin and Will left Aldrik to watch over the Minster and her mother, closing the door behind them. Nar's arm was in a sling, and Khelek's face was bruised, but the look on their faces was what she first noticed. There was no smile. They could hardly hold her gaze, and when they did… they were dejected. All this, she barely registered. What she did register was that she did not see her children.

"Where are the children?" Malin blurted out the question, escaping before she could even greet them. It was the first thing, the *only* thing that truly mattered.

Nar and Khelek exchanged a pained glance, their shoulders slumping with a visible weight. Malin's heart sank, a cold dread seeping into her veins. It wasn't just disappointment she saw; it was the heavy shroud of failure, of deep, personal anguish.

Nar cleared his throat, his voice raspy, thick with unshed emotion. "Malin… we are so sorry. We… we tried." His gaze, usually so steady, was filled with self-reproach, fixed on some unseen point beyond her. "The attack was sudden and overwhelming. We were able to hold them off long enough for your mother to get the children to safety. We ensured that they got away with her. We haven't seen them since." The last words were a whisper, raw and broken, as if speaking of them aloud tore a fresh wound.

Khelek nodded slowly, his gaze fixed on the floor, his broad shoulders hunched. He ran a hand over his face, scrubbing at eyes that were visibly struggling with the memory, his jaw tight. They looked utterly devastated, clearly feeling the crushing burden of a failure that wasn't theirs alone, but one they carried as if it were.

"When we heard General Rauno was seen carrying Lady Elowen into the castle, we hoped the children would be with her," Khelek added, his voice barely a whisper. "But… if you are also looking for them…"

Malin felt a cold wave wash over her, worse than the lingering chills of the Media ambush. It wasn't a wave; it was an avalanche, a crushing, suffocating weight that stole the air from her lungs. Her blood ran to ice, then a different, more chilling terror seized her.

Ellie. Zee. Alone. Lost.

The thought was a searing brand on her soul, a torment worse than any physical wound. Her children are out there somewhere, vulnerable.

She looked at Nar and Khelek, their faces etched with guilt and sorrow, and her heart ached for them. She knew they had fought with everything they had, battling to create that precious window of escape. There was no anger, only a profound gratitude that they had given her children a fighting chance, even at great personal cost. The agony of not knowing was immense, but she knew the twins were as devastated as she was. The only person who held the answers, the only one who could tell them where Ellie and Zee were, was currently lost in the depths of a nanotechnology-induced coma.

Malin reached out, touching an arm of each elf, her voice steady despite the tremor in her soul. "You did what you could," she said softly, her gaze holding theirs, willing them to believe her. "You saved them. You gave them a chance, and that's more than anyone else could have done. Don't carry this burden. We'll find them. We have to."

Gone. They're gone.

"How many were there?" Will asked, his voice low, his hand instantly finding Malin's, squeezing it.

Nar sighed, a weary sound. "About sixty Media guards. Elite troops. Enforcers from Media. Anariel, Khelek, and I held them off for as long as we could. When both Khelek and I were injured." He gestured to his sling. "Anariel had to get us to Mellyrn for healing. Nar … almost died."

"Anariel has troops out looking for the children, searching the area where they were last seen," Khelek managed to add, offering a sliver of hope in the devastating news. "They're the best trackers Mellryn has. They are thorough. They'll find them."

Malin nodded numbly, the vibrant, joyful energy of Mellyrn suddenly fading to background noise. Her children were out there, somewhere, lost. And her mother lay still, a victim of an unknown enemy.

The battle for her mother had been won, but the real fight, the fight for her family's future, had only just begun.

"We must go back to where the Media guards were," Will stated.

"If Mom and the kids had been attacked, she would have done what they did and held them off for as long as she could, so the kids could get away. She would have told them to run as far and as fast as they could," she reasoned. "She would have counted on communicating with them when she got away. They weren't on the transport we hit when we saved her, so they must have gotten away. We need to find where they found her and see if we can find their trail."

"It is near dark, and we have been traveling for days. We know there is a larger transport of Media troops that was on its way. I don't want to rush into any decision," Will weighed in, his practical side asserting itself.

"We have a castle of intel at our fingertips and a General to call on. Let's use the assets we have to find out what we can. If they have trackers out there, they might have already gotten some information. We don't know if Media is still out there... though I like to think Malin's little 'warning' scared them into rethinking their travel plans." Will offered a faint, almost imperceptible smirk, a flicker of his usual cockiness that was quickly swallowed by genuine concern. "Maybe they'll just stay away." His voice held more hope than certainty.

"The children are capable, our walk through the woods showed us they can think on their feet. If anything, Zee can always ask the animals to watch after them. We might even find that Ellie levitates them both to the castle, as her powers are getting much stronger. They are capable, and as long as they have each other, I think they will be fine," Khelek reassured, his voice softening with confidence.

We need all the information we can get before we run headfirst into this and miss something. Let's try to get cleaned up, some sleep, prepare ourselves, and start fresh in the morning," Will motioned.

She turned to him, ready to argue the point that they needed to leave immediately, then realized he might have a point. The thought of rushing blindly into the dark, potentially towards more Media forces, with her mother's fate uncertain and her children's whereabouts unknown, suddenly seemed reckless.

A collective sigh seemed to ripple through the group, a shared acknowledgment of the wisdom in his words.

Malin met Will's gaze, Her's burning with impatience, but she offered a tight nod, knowing he was right. Nar and Khelek looked relieved to have a direction, however delayed.

Her heart urged her to run, but her doctor's mind, and now her warrior's mind, demanded strategy.

Before Malin could respond further, a soft knock came from the sitting area door. Four more tall men in robes and a young Elven serving boy, looking slightly flustered, peered in. The tall men went straight to the bedroom without addressing them with more than a nod.

The young servant said, "My lords, Lady Anariel sends word for all of you. She requests your presence for dinner, after you have had a chance to clean yourselves."

As the others went into the room, Aldrik came out with expectant eyes, which turned quizzical when he looked at her. "I had hoped to see them before they left. Where are the children?"

A wall of emotions hit her as she voiced the words aloud, "The kids are missing. Our best guess is Media attacked, and they got away, but Mom didn't. They are out in the forests alone." Her words got heavier as they came out. By the end, tears were rolling down her cheeks, prompting him to pull her into his arms. He caressed her hair.

Aldrik held her, a pillar of unyielding strength. His jaw was tight, his gaze distant, fixed on something Malin couldn't see. The woman he loved was lying in the next room, motionless, and his grandbabies, his newfound family, had vanished into the wilderness. The weight of it had to be immense, enough to shatter a lesser man, yet he remained composed. Malin could only guess at the silent torment raging beneath his stoic façade and what he had gone through in the past that made him learn to hold things in. She needed to know.

His grip on her was firm, almost desperate, and she realized he was holding onto her like a lifeline, a tangible connection to the family he was fighting so hard to protect. And, after everything he had done for her in such a short time, she, in turn, was grateful she could simply *be there* for him, a silent anchor in his storm.

Will took a moment, his gaze sweeping over Nar and Khelek. The gravity in their faces, the visible weariness, mirrored his own deeper fears. Despite the grim circumstances and Malin's silent anguish, a flicker of his familiar affection sparked. He pulled both brothers in for quick, tight hugs of greeting, a desperate need for the comfort of old friends overriding the somber mood.

Nar pulled back first, his brow furrowed. "It's good to see you, Hawk. Lady Elowen was keeping up with reports of Malin and Lord Aldrik's journey to find you. I guess you ran into some trouble?"

Will clapped him on the shoulder, a barely-there hint of his usual smirk touching his lips. "Trouble would be an understatement. Psychopathic Ex-girlfriends… Didn't I tell you she was going to be trouble?" He grimaced, the attempt at levity falling flat, his eyes briefly darkening with an unspoken shadow before he quickly composed himself. "Seriously, though, it's damn good to see you both."

Khelek's gaze was sharp, lingering on Will's face. "We kept the kids' spirits high. Zee has been learning some new skills. He is such an impressive kid. I should have done more…"

Will cut him off with a firm shake of his head. "None of that. You did what you could. We all did. Now, let's talk about what we *can* do."

"Wait. Why couldn't Anariel come here?" Malin asked.

Nar and Khelek both groaned in unison. Nar rubbed his temple with his good hand. "Ah, yes. The *other* bit of chaos to add to the mix."

Khelek sighed, running a hand over his bruised face. "Ana is to be crowned queen soon. Malin. She's… not handling this change well. She could really use you."

Malin frowned. "Queen? What happened? Wasn't she next in line for the crown, after her brother?"

Khelek's gaze hardened, losing some of its earlier dejection. "There was a poisoning, Malin. All but Anariel are gone. She's the last of the direct line. She must be crowned quickly, or the crown will pass to the House Roths, and they are almost certainly behind the poisonings, but we can find no link." His voice was laced with a grim certainty.

The weight of this new revelation settled heavily in the air, another twist in the complex web of their arrival.

"We can't leave without seeing her," Malin stated, her voice firm, a new resolve hardening her features. "She might know something, or have resources we don't. Can you arrange for me to see her before we leave in the morning?"

Nar and Khelek exchanged a quick, meaningful look. "We will make the arrangements," Nar said, a renewed purpose in his voice. "She will want to see you."

Malin watched as Aldrik lowered his face, his lips brushing Elowen's forehead with a tenderness that made Malin's heart ache. He looked up, his gaze holding Malin's with a profound gratitude.

"She's in the best hands they have," he said, his voice low and firm. "I am not leaving her side. I will get word to you when she wakes up. As for you and Will…" he turned to them both, a flicker of his ancient battle-hardened resolve in his eyes. "You have traveled far and endured much. Rest. You have a long day ahead of you." He paused, a ghost of a smile touching his lips. "And bring my grandchildren home. Safely."

Malin felt the weight of his words settled over her, not as a burden of duty, but as a shared purpose. Aldrik wasn't asking her to perform for a court; he was a fellow parent, trusting her with the lives of his family. The castle, which had briefly seemed like an overwhelming place, now felt like a true sanctuary. A place where her mother was safe, where she and Will could finally take a breath.

As Aldrik turned back to her mother, Malin reached for Will's hand. He squeezed her fingers, his thumb brushing her skin in a reassuring gesture.

They had a night to themselves, a quiet, peaceful night to reconnect and prepare. The thought of it was a tonic to her soul. She was no longer a pawn in a political game; she was a mother, a partner, a warrior. And in the morning, she and Will would leave this gilded cage to find their children and finally be a whole family again.

CHAPTER 29 – MALIN

Malin felt the familiar rumbling of morning sickness stirring in her stomach, with a low churn, as the first sliver of dawn bled through the arched window. But even as the queasiness threatened to overwhelm, her magic, like a gentle, steady current, kicked in, flowing through her system to counter it, taming the wave of nausea down to a mild, manageable hum. She hadn't left the bedroom area yet, but the tantalizing scent of something warm and savory wafted in from the sitting area. Given her stomach, she wasn't sure if she should partake or not, but she would need the energy for the day ahead.

After so many quick showers and bathing in streams, she appreciated the magically heated shower, and she knew she stood far too long under its embrace. She was awake, dressed, and acutely aware of the tiny, growing life within her.

She walked out of the bedroom to find Will already at the small table, a piece of golden-brown bread halfway to his mouth. He was staring at his map as he ate.

"They dropped off our bags from the ship a few minutes ago. I was so worried this would get lost or worse. I don't have a lot of information about the Draco mountains on there, but I think it will be handy."

Will, ever practical, had already poured them each a cup of something that smelled like rich, roasted grains. On the small table by the window, beside the steaming breakfast, lay a neatly packed camping rucksack. Its contents looked expertly arranged: compact supplies, high-energy rations, a pouch that clinked with the unfamiliar weight of Elven coins, and a set of sleek, unfamiliar communication devices that inserted into the ear. A small, elegantly penned note lay on top.

Malin picked up the note. It was from Aldrik. His precise, angular script read: *Please see me before you depart. -Aeladar.*

A knot of anticipation tightened in Malin's stomach. She exchanged a glance with Will, who merely raised an eyebrow.

They ate quickly, the food tasting even better than it smelled, fueling their bodies for the day ahead. The mild queasiness was forgotten for a moment as the delicious flavors filled her.

Soon, they were making their way to Aeladar's suite. The grandeur of the castle still felt foreign, but navigating it with Will by her side, the subtle scent of him comforting her, felt less daunting. When they arrived, the heavy door was already ajar.

Aldrik stood by a large, ornate window, staring out at the rising sun. The morning light softened his usually stern features, but the lines of exhaustion around his eyes were stark. He looked like he had hardly slept at all. Seeing him, the raw vulnerability in his posture, her heightened emotions washed over her.

She walked straight to him, pulling him close in a spontaneous hug. His arms came up to hold her, gentle and welcoming. "Aeladar," she murmured, pulling back just enough to look into his tired eyes.

"Your mother will love to hear your news. I do not know if she can hear me or not, so I have been very careful around her. I do not want to spoil your news. I feel she may be fighting whatever they did to her, and can hear us, as she twitched her finger in response to something I said last night." he took a deep breath, his composure slowly returning, though the joy lingered in his eyes.

"If she wakes up before we get back, I would really like you to tell her for me," she said. In truth, it hurt too much to see her in that condition and worry about the children. She was having enough issues keeping her emotions in check.

"Of course," he said, then he cleared his throat to compose his thoughts.

"I asked you to come because I had an idea to help your Mother. We brought the Media computer with us from the ambush site. It contains all their internal data, their plans, and their research. My concern is turning it on inside Mellyrn. If Media could sense where it is, it would be an act of war, and Media would blame *us*." He paused, his gaze earnest. "But if we could activate it *outside* the Mellryn perimeter, in neutral territory... There might be information on it. Something that could help us understand what they did to her and how to reverse it. It's a risk, but it could be the key to waking her."

Malin understood immediately. It was a calculated risk. It was dangerous, yes, but for her mother... "I'll do it," she said, without hesitation. "I'll turn it on."

"But no undue risk. I will not risk you or my Del'wyn. Will. I know you will do everything you can to keep her safe," he said, looking at her stomach.

"Yes, sir. There is no stopping her from doing what she wants, but I will do everything in my power to make sure she is safe when doing it," Will assured.

A profound relief washed over Aldrik's face. "Thank you. I knew I could count on you both." He reached down and touched her stomach, "Bring my Del'wyns home to me." A slight tear escaped his eye, and he turned away quickly, with his hand moving to his face.

"Please get some sleep, Aeladar. She will need you when she gets up," she said, grabbing his hand.

They parted ways with the traditional Elven goodbye, and they walked out, closing the door behind them. Malin was concerned for him. He was not the man of energy he had been when they met.

As they stepped out of Aldrik's suite and into the gleaming, quiet hall, Anariel, Nar, and Khelek were already there, waiting.

Anariel's expression was a mixture of regal poise and regret, a subtle tension in her jaw. She was dressed in a deep purple silk robe; the soft fabric was a stark contrast to the travel attire she had last seen her in. Her long blonde and silver hair hung down past her waist like a waterfall around her shoulders. Even early in the morning, having just woken, her Elven beauty required no artifice. She was breathtakingly gorgeous.

Malin knew she was battling with the fact that she was a queen who couldn't leave her duty to help her friends. It was a silent testament to the bond that had formed so quickly between them, a bond forged in shared fear and unexpected kinship.

Nar and Khelek, however, looked ready for action, their earlier weariness replaced by the familiar anticipation of impending movement.

Malin didn't waste time and pulled Anariel into a hug first, then the Elven greeting. She knew they were eager to depart, and this news was too important to hold.

"Kin'ael, I have something to tell you," she announced, looking between the three of them, a small, proud smile touching her lips. "Will and I are having a baby."

A ripple of surprise, then delight, spread across their faces. Anariel's eyes widened, then filled with genuine warmth as she stepped forward to embrace Malin. Nar and Khelek exchanged quick, heartfelt glances, their grins widening.

"We are expecting, also," she beamed.

Malin stared, her jaw dropping. Then, a radiant smile broke across her face. "You're... you're pregnant too?" she asked. The realization of what she said took a moment to sink in.

She pulled Anariel into another tight embrace. "Oh, Anariel, that's incredible! And Nar and Khelek..." She looked over at the two elves, who were now beaming, their earlier solemnity completely forgotten. "They'll be such amazing fathers," Malin murmured, a warmth spreading through her chest. "They're already so good with Ellie and Zee. This is... this is truly wonderful news. It makes everything feel a little less impossible."

Malin pulled back, her eyes still sparkling with tears of joy. "I wish we had more time," she said, a hint of genuine frustration in her voice. "I want to talk with you about all of this... about being a Queen and what that means for you."

Anariel's smile dimmed slightly, a familiar weariness returning to her eyes. "There will be plenty of time for that, Malin," she said, her voice a low murmur. "Once the children are safely back with us, we will have almost a month-long coronation celebration. It will be the perfect opportunity." She rolled her eyes playfully at the thought of it. "And you will be a main part of the festivities. With our shared news, you may be considered more of an important member of the family than you were before."

They embraced again and performed the traditional departure, pausing slightly longer as they smiled at the shared news, a new, joyful bond forming between the expectant mothers.

Anariel then turned to Nar and Khelek, her gaze lingering on each of them. With a tender, almost possessive gesture, she gave each man a deep, lingering kiss goodbye. It was a kiss that spoke of a shared history, fierce love, and the unspoken dangers that lay ahead.

"Be well, my loves," she murmured, her voice soft but firm, a queen's blessing and a lover's plea. "Return to me safely."

The gravity of their departure settled over them all, but the excitement of the mission and the new life Malin carried propelled them forward.

Malin, Will, Nar, and Khelek walked together through the ornate archway of the inner castle gates. She couldn't express the hopefulness she had in words. They would find the children. She knew it.

The early morning air outside was crisp, carrying the scent of damp earth and distant evergreens.

Nar, already fiddling with one of the new communication devices, mumbled, "I wish we had portalers here. It would make this so much faster."

"What are those?" Malin asked.

"They are a form of instant transport that can cross immense distances. Ana is a portaler, but she has limited range in comparison to someone with that as their main power," Khelek responded.

"Are they not available?" she asked.

"No. It is a rare power, and the few that Mellyrn have are devoted to moving troops and supplies to and from Lumara or Aloria," Nar confirmed.

"It should take us about three hours to get to where the trackers are at the foothills of the Draco mountains," Will said, tapping the screen of a device, a small light on it blinking steadily. "Seems our earpieces are working. We'll be able to stay in touch with them, in case anything changes."

As they passed through the last arch of the inner gates, stepping onto the winding path that led away from the castle, a figure detached itself from the shadows near a large, ancient oak tree.

She had to do a double take. It was Caelum. He looked disheveled, his clothes wrinkled and slept in, but his eyes were wide and focused.

"Malin! Will!" he called out, his voice a strained mix of relief and urgency. He hurried towards them, his gaze sweeping over their faces. "Aldrik isn't with you... Is he?" Upon not seeing him, Caelum continued, "I couldn't get back into the castle last night. I... I slept on the streets outside, hoping that I would see you."

His expression crumpled as he looked at Malin with a look of confusion. "Where is Ellie?"

Malin felt a pang of sympathy. Despite his past, his genuine distress was undeniable. The fact that he had slept on the streets for the sheer hope of seeing his daughter meant something to her.

"She's missing, Caelum," Malin said softly, the truth a heavy weight. "We found a trail leading towards the Draco Mountains. We are heading there now." She watched his face fall, his shoulders slumping.

"I…" he whispered, then looked up, his jaw tightening with a new resolve. "I want to come with you. To find them." He looked directly at Malin, his gaze pleading. "I know I might not be the bravest man out there. I'm no warrior like Will, or these two..." He gestured vaguely at the imposing Elves. "But Ellie… she's the only family I have left. I want to meet her at least. To try to be the father she deserves. Please, Malin. Give me this chance."

"Caelum, this will be dangerous, and we can't babysit you. There will be life-or-death situations. Are you sure you want to risk this?"

"I did what you asked before. I did my part… but I can be of help. I know I can… Please." The look of desperation on his face reminded her of college. He had made up his mind. He really would follow through.

She pulled Will aside. "I don't think he will be much help in a fight, but I do think he means well, and his knowledge of tracking, animals, and being a decoy may come in handy."

As soon as she said "decoy," she saw Will's eyes light up. "I'm rubbing off on you, and it turns me on so much," he teased. "But seriously, this is your ex we are talking about. We all saw how lousy a choice it was to have my ex with us. I'm staying out of this decision, but I'm leaning toward offering him a nice suite in the castle and letting him wait here for us... Then again, if something happens to him while he's out there... he would make a good decoy." She smiled back at him, then walked back over to the others.

"Alright, Caelum," Malin said, a decision solidifying in her mind. "You can come., but we can't promise your safety."

Malin felt the words leave her lips, and a cold wave of something akin to dread, yet undeniably practical, washed over her. She had just given him a choice, yes, but was it truly a choice if one option was survival and the other was... unknown peril? The healer in her recoiled from the thought of knowingly putting someone in harm's way, but the pragmatist, the protector she was becoming, justified it.

He's volunteered. He wants to help.

But beneath that logic, a chilling question lingered: Had she just condemned Caelum to death, trading his life for a chance at theirs?

CHAPTER 30 – MALIN

The sharp crack of a twig underfoot echoed through the ancient silence of the forest. They had been hiking for a couple of hours, the steady rhythm of their boots on the damp earth a stark contrast to the pampered luxury of the castle they had just left.

Each step was a step closer to the Draco Mountains, a place of myth and danger, but more importantly, a place where her children might be.

The deep woods surrounding Mellyrn were ancient, the trees towering, their canopies so thick that only dappled light reached the ground. It was beautiful, serene even, but Malin barely registered it. Her mind was a relentless churn of *what if?*

Were they hurt? Were they scared? She was in awe of Ellie's bravery, but surrounded by so many unknowns and without a parent nearby... Would her bravery turn?

The thought of Zee, so quick and curious, facing unknown dangers in dragon territory, made her stomach clench harder than any lingering morning sickness. Khelek proudly detailed Zee's advances in his magic with animals, how he could summon large groups of animals. He also started being able to absorb some of their animalistic traits, such as agility like a cat, and heightened strength. He was still working on it, but he was making progress.

Knowing that Zee's powers were growing like that helped to ease Malin's worries. Then she wondered... Dragons were sentient beings... would his powers work on them?

Her magic still worked tirelessly to keep the physical nausea at bay, taming it to a faint, persistent awareness of the life growing inside her, a gentle hum in her core. But it couldn't quell the churning anxiety for her missing children. That was a different kind of sickness, one that settled deep in her bones and drove her forward with a fierce, almost desperate resolve. She needed to find them. She *had* to.

Will walked beside her, his presence a comforting anchor. Nar and Khelek, tireless as ever, scouted ahead and behind, their Elven senses attuned to the subtle shifts of the wilderness. Caelum, surprisingly, kept pace, though his breath was heavier, and his face was already smudged with dirt. He carried his share of the gear, his determination a quiet surprise.

"We've left Mellyrn boundaries," Nar announced, his voice carrying clearly from a short distance ahead.

He had paused, pointing to a gnarled, ancient oak whose bark bore faint, almost invisible carvings. This was it… The end of Mellyrn territory.

Will nodded, looking around. "Good. Let's take a break here." He dropped his pack, pulling out a waterskin.

The others followed suit, settling down among the roots of the massive trees. The air was cool and smelled of pine and damp earth.

They knew there was a chance that when they opened the computer, it might send a signal to Media. Could they be walking into a trap?

Malin's gaze went to the computer, carefully wrapped in Will's pack. She needed those answers for her mother. A flicker of anxiety stirred, not for the danger of the computer, but for what it might reveal… or not reveal. Could this be the key?

Trap or key to answers they needed… She would never be sure until she tried. She pulled the device out, and the sleek, dark casing felt cold and alien in her hands. The design was all Media: sharp angles, minimalist, and utterly devoid of the organic warmth of Elven craftsmanship.

Nar and Khelek watched, their expressions unreadable, while Will knelt beside her, his hand resting reassuringly on her arm. Caelum shifted closer, his eyes wide with curiosity.

"Alright," Malin murmured, taking a deep breath. "Here goes nothing."

The Media computer lay on a mossy root, its black surface reflecting the dappled sunlight. Malin knew the general process, the step-by-step instructions the captured guard had reluctantly provided, but she was a doctor, not a tech specialist.

Her fingers, accustomed to the delicate precision of healing, felt clumsy on its smooth, unmarked casing. She pressed the activation sequence that the guard they kept alive from the past battle had shown her, but nothing happened. A small, almost invisible port glowed faintly, demanding something more.

"That's right. I forgot about that device the guard used," Will said, searching his pockets. He reached into a hidden pouch on his belt, pulling out a small, metallic device that looked like an oversized metal stick. "The guard used this to open it the last time."

Malin took the dongle and inserted it into the glowing port. With a soft click, the black surface flickered, then an eerie blue light pulsed, humming softly to life. A holographic interface projected into the air above the device, its complex symbols and menus suddenly navigable. A faint, almost imperceptible tremor ran through the ground beneath them.

"What was that?" Nar asked, looking around, expecting danger.

"I don't know, but let's stay on watch," Will cautioned.

Most of what she saw made sense. She had seen her Dad working with these computers for years, and even the medical clinic had had some she had to interface with. Her fingers flew across the holographic interface, guided by the guard's explicit instructions and her own desperate need.

Her heart hammered against her ribs, a drumbeat of urgency. As she typed, more and more came back to her. She didn't understand everything, but when they started getting into medical testing, she began to recognize the work.

Find something. Anything.

She searched for anything that might refer to nanotechnology, magic, or defense. Then, a file marked "Project Overtone" flashed. Her breath hitched. She accessed it, and the screen was filled with schematics and detailed reports.

Her eyes scanned rapidly. The tech used on her mother wasn't just some crude magic-suppressor. It was a sophisticated system of nanoparticles; a microscopic network designed to infiltrate the body and suppress magical abilities upon command.

Years ago, she had worked on a biomechanical program for her Dad at Masoncore, as an intern, which had used similar terminology.

If she read it right, they produced a frequency that magic cannot stand, but not the same frequency that the current microchips use. This variant, however, merely stuns the magic within the host; the frequency halts, allowing the magic to awaken from its slumber when the signal is removed.

Her stomach twisted as she read on, recognizing disturbing parallels. This tech acted precisely like the controller that had once been used on Will, the one embedded in his neck. The one that Nemilos had said came from the Fellspire Citadel prisons.

 Only this was more insidious, a system not just to control, but to *contain* and *control* magical energy.

But then, a word leaped out at her: "Controller." This nanotechnology had a central controller, similar to a master switch. The reports detailed its location: within Media's central servers, deep inside Masoncore.

"I found it," Malin whispered, her voice tight with a mix of dread and furious hope. "It's going to be almost impossible to get to without going back to Media and breaking into my Dad's building."

Will's jaw tightened. "That place is a fortress, not to mention that just getting close to the city will be risky. Does the device or nano things have any vulnerabilities?"

"I agree. It's a suicide mission. We couldn't exactly blend in there with you, so you'd be alone. I like the idea of finding a way around going back there," Khelek rumbled from across from them, his brow furrowed. "Media City is a death sentence."

"Suicide missions seem to be our specialty lately," she joked, though in reality… she would likely risk everything if it meant she could solve this for her mother and Aeladar.

Nar nodded, his gaze distant. "He's not wrong. It would be a direct assault on the heart of Media's power."

Malin's fingers kept moving, a desperate energy propelling her. *There has to be another way. A weakness.*

She scrolled through more documents, her search parameters broadening to "countermeasures," "vulnerabilities," and "disruptive technology."

And then, she found it.

A highly classified section detailing "defensive measures against disruptive technologies." The city was clearly paranoid about anything that could undo its technological dominance. Among the listed threats, one stood out: an EMP, like they used in No Man's Land in Media."

At Nar and Khelek's quizzical faces, she expanded, "An Electromagnetic Pulse, designed to render specific technologies useless. It is why Media has that pile of rubble in No Man's Land. Aloria had attacked the city with both a series of long-lasting

EMPs and a flight of dragons. An EMP would render the nanotechnology inert. Basically dead."

Her heart leaped.

"This is it!" she exclaimed, spinning the screen towards them. "An EMP. It would shut down the nanoparticles. They would be floating through her bloodstream or body, but they couldn't turn on."

"Where would we get something like that?" Caelum questioned, his brow furrowed.

Malin scrolled further, her eyes darting across the text. "It doesn't say where to find one. It does mention that Fellspire Citadel is where they are at highest risk of this type of attack."

A collective groan rippled through the group. "Fellspire?" Nar muttered, shaking his head. "Another impossible place to break into."

"But at least we have two options now," Malin countered, trying to inject some optimism she didn't entirely feel.

Masoncore or Fellspire. Both sounded like death traps, but they were *options*. A sliver of hope started to weave its way through her fear.

She began to search for more information, anything that could give them an edge on either path. Her fingers danced across the interface, pulling up blueprints, security schematics, troop deployments, none of which she understood, but as each person reviewed, they provided some input…

Suddenly, the air around them crackled. A low, rhythmic hum vibrated through the forest, growing louder, more menacing.

Malin's head snapped up.

The blue glow of the computer screen reflected dozens of small, red lights appearing through the trees. They were surrounded.

The hum intensified, a mechanical buzzing.

Out of the dense foliage emerged the sleek, menacing forms of Media guards, their weapons already raised. Above them, like predatory birds, several drones whirred, their optical sensors fixed on the group, glowing with an ominous, infernal light.

"Damn it!" Will growled, already pulling his blade beside her. "They did track the computer!"

Malin felt the cold dread spread through her, quickly followed by a surge of fiery determination. They had found answers, yes, but now they had to fight their way out.

Before she shut the computer screen, she saw a message flash on the screen. It was a communication between Media and the Order of Tamris... They sent Will's location within the Kingdom of Mellyrn. It looks like the City of Media is trying to start a war, without firing a shot. If his concerns about the Order of Tamris are right, anyone in that castle is in danger.

In front of her, Nar and Khelek, with Elven speed and agility, moved like blurs, dropping low. Nar's hands began to glow with fiery energy, his blades drawn, a stark contrast to Khelek, whose breath misted in the suddenly colder air around him, with his solitary long sword. They were menacing and ready for the onslaught.

In the corner of her eyes, she saw a flicker. Caelum activated his invisibility, vanishing from sight.

It figures. She knew she couldn't count on him. Aeladar was right after all.

Media's opening barrage was swift and brutal. Energy blasts sizzled through the air, shearing off branches and impacting trees with dull thuds.

She knew that this was a risk, but being in the moment, she realized the danger to her unborn child. *What was she thinking?*

Drones descended, their weapon ports glowing, unleashing concentrated fire and attempting to deploy capture nets.

Malin dove behind a wide oak, the blasts crackling just inches from her head.

Too close. She pushed her fear out of her head. They have had three battles with Media, and three times, she demolished them. This was a slightly larger group, energy weapons instead of bullets, and they brought drones this time, but she still had confidence they would prevail in the end

It means it will take longer. That's all. She tried to calm herself, placing her hand on her stomach as she focused her breath. She was slightly closer to the guards than she had been to the pirate ship. She could do this.

She stood and pushed out a wave of flames, aiming for the guards blocking their path. The fire washed over them, but instead of hearing screams, she saw only steam rising from their dark uniforms. They had upgraded their equipment. Their fire-retardant suits held, smoking but not incinerating, sent a jolt of alarm through her.

Will, a whirlwind of motion, aggressively engaged the closest guards, his blade a silver blur, deflecting energy shots and forcing them back, trying to create an opening.

Nar let out a furious roar, unleashing focused jets of scorching flame at the guards' visors and joints, pushing his firepower, desperate to break through their defenses.

Khelek moved like ice, creating sudden bursts of freezing air that glazed the ground, making guards slip and shatter their weapon's energy cells with precise ice shards. He even created temporary, shimmering ice shields that deflected the incoming fire.

Malin strained, her usual torrent of fire proving inefficient against the specialized armor. Without her flames, she needed another way to help. She couldn't just hide behind things and let them do all the work.

She had been working on some of her other powers to expand her skill set. Levitation was her best bet. A fallen guard's weapon was lying on the ground. If she could get to it, she could fire back. Malin focused her power on the energy rifle; she could see it waver, then fly through the air to her, into her arms. The levitation was subtle, but it got the job done.

She had never fired a weapon before, but she had played shooting games with Ellie at home, and she knew the basics. Hopefully, this was not a mistake. She raised it to her shoulder and aimed. She had played shooting games with Ellie in Media, and she knew the basics.

When the first blast left the gun, she flew back, not prepared for the kick. After that, she felt she knew how to compensate, and she tried again. This one hit the guard's head, but she was aiming for his chest.

A win?

Will looked over, "Flames, martial arts... now guns? Can you get any hotter, Sparks?"

She continued firing, her aim still imperfect, but the sheer volume of blasts forced the guards to scatter, making a dent in their formation. Where she could get close enough, she used her flame powers at the highest heat level to get past their fire-retardant suits.

The drones, however, continued to pose a critical threat. Their constant hum filled the air, and their targeting lasers painted red dots on them, though she noticed they avoided her.

Media guards focused their lethal fire on the Elves while attempting to subdue Malin and Will with non-lethal (but still painful) blasts. The distinction in their aim was chillingly clear. They are trying to capture her and Will.

Nar yelled as an energy blast grazed his side, making him stagger.

The trap was tightening.

Malin's magic was thinning. Even healing herself as she went didn't sustain her enough. Her exhaustion grew with every sustained burst of flame.

There was no clear escape.

She rushed to Nar's side, gun blasting. If they avoided lethal strikes on her, then it would help them if she were near Nar and Khelek. She attempted to heal their wounds, though with frequent movements to avoid being a target, the effort was unsuccessful.

Just as the pressure became unbearable, and a drone hovered dangerously close to Nar's wounded side, her eyes flicked to an elevated position nearby. She caught a fleeting, almost imperceptible shimmer in the air near two Media guards, who seemed to be controlling the drones from a slightly more secure vantage point. She squinted, disbelieving.

Then, with shocking speed and silence, a figure materialized behind the two drone operators.

Caelum. It was quick, but it was him.

His arm flashed, a glint of metal catching the dappled light. He made swift, brutal cuts to each of their throats. Just as quickly as he was there, he disappeared.

The guards collapsed.

Distracted by him, she almost missed the guard with an injector device running toward her. Luckily, he was distracted by the remaining drones sputtering and falling from the sky with heavy thuds, crashing into the trees and undergrowth.

The oppressive hum of their engines ceased, leaving an eerie silence that was broken only by the sounds of ground combat and the gasps of the remaining Media guards.

Empowered by this reprieve and the shocking knowledge of Caelum's grim intervention, Malin decided to push her limits. She unleashed a devastating, focused firestorm, burning bright white. Focused and oppressive, it finally began melting a section of armor from three guards in front of her, sending them screaming to the ground.

Emanating from Khelek was a dense, swirling fog that blossomed, shrouding the clearing in a thick mist. It swirled around the trees, obscuring Media's line of sight and disorienting the remaining guards. There were still too many of them. Her flame power was draining her faster than she could heal herself. She was just too tired.

"Go! Now!" Will roared, calling for her to join him, deeper into the forest.

Just then, a guard grabbed her arm. She tried her martial arts maneuvers, and his grasp was like a vice, but she twisted his hand enough that his glove came off, and he grabbed her arm with his bare hand… a better, tighter hold. She kicked, but the armor was too thick.

The only option she could think of was sickening to her… Should she? She thought of her baby and Ellie. For them, she could….

Her healing power, twisted and reversed, sucking the life essence from the guard. His eyes, wide with confusion, slowly began to sink into their sockets. A horrifying pallor spread across his face, his skin rapidly turning a mottled, ashen gray, as if all color and vitality were leached from him. His hand fell away.

The surge. The energy. It was intoxicating. The rush of power that hit her was intense. She meant to stop when he let go, but the pull. The pull of that energy made her grab him and hold on, draining everything from him.

The veins beneath his skin seemed to flatten, hollowing, leaving behind a shell of a man. His body, once solid and muscled, began to shrivel, collapsing in on itself, bone and sinew shrinking as the essence within him was devoured. A choked gasp escaped his lips, thin and bloodless, before his form finally crumpled to the ground, a husk of a man, barely recognizable.

When she finally let go and witnessed the horror frozen on the shell that was this man, she felt sick of what she had just done.

Will's yell brought her back to the events at hand. Guards were locking onto her position. She shot a wall of fire, making them step back, and ran to Will, before they both took off deep into the forest, away from the battle.

They ran, as fast as they could, deeper into the mountains, where Media dared not follow.

"This is Draco territory. There is something about tech that drives the dragons nuts, and they immediately attack it. We're safe, for now. With the risk of Dragons, Media would not be able to chase them, as technology was a beacon for dragon attacks," Nar explained.

Looking back, she scanned for the signs of movement. It seems they were not being followed. She was shocked by how much harder this battle was; her warning to Media through the guard was obviously ignored. What did that mean for them? Would Media be back? The assassins were heading to Mellryn. When they get back with the kids, will they just go back to more problems? When would this end for them?

CHAPTER 31 – WILL

Will's boots pounded against the forest floor, every breath a rasp, every stride a fresh ache. He didn't think that anyone was behind them any longer. The chase pounded through him, not from the sound of active pursuit now, but from the lingering adrenaline in his veins.

They'd lost. Not utterly, not a wipeout, but a tactical retreat.

Will ground his teeth, the bitter taste of defeat coating his tongue. He wasn't used to this. He was the one who always found the impossible path. To be outmaneuvered, pushed back by sheer numbers and relentless tracking, chafed at him like a fresh wound. It was a failure, plain and simple, and it festered.

Sensing that they were out of danger, but still wanting to get farther away, the group changed to a hurried hiking pace, attempting to cover as much ground as possible at a sustainable pace.

Nar slammed a fist against a tree trunk nearby, the muffled thud echoing the frustration building in Will's chest. "Damn them!" he growled, his voice raw. "They just... kept coming. Like a tide."

"Relentless," Khelek added from behind them, his breath still ragged. "And too organized. They learn fast, these Media operatives."

Media had come prepared, and they'd been pushed back hard. He scanned the tree line behind them, a familiar habit, but saw no glint of red light and heard no telltale hum. For now, they were clear.

Malin hiked beside him, her face set, focused, a fierce fire still burning in her eyes. She hadn't looked back, hadn't questioned, just moved. Nar and Khelek, tireless as always, kept pace, their Elven grace barely disturbed by the sprint.

His left leg screamed with a dull burn, and his right shoulder felt heavy, a radiating throb. Two energy blasts had grazed him, one on the calf, the other on the shoulder. He'd seen worse, much worse, but the sting was a constant reminder of how close they'd come. He wasn't about to bother Malin with it yet. She had enough on her plate, especially after…

The image flashed unbidden in his mind: Malin, her hand on that guard, and the man just… *shriveling*. It had been instantaneous, horrifying, and undeniably effective. He didn't really know what she did, not exactly, but it had to be her. It was like she'd sucked the very life out of him, leaving nothing but a husk.

Flames, martial arts, pulling a rifle out of thin air, and now *that*. He was proud of her, awed even, but a prickle of unease ran down his spine. She was getting stronger, yes, but also… deadlier. Each new layer of power she unearthed was more formidable than the last, pushing the boundaries of what he understood, what he thought possible.

Good thing my ego can handle a woman who could probably turn me into dust with a touch, he thought, a familiar roguish smirk ghosting his lips despite the grim circumstances.

He glanced over at her, by his side… Perfectly dangerous. *He'd better make sure not to piss her off.*

He glanced back, a quick assessment of their situation. And then he saw him. Caelum, their quiet shadow, was there, behind them, keeping up. He hadn't seen him since the initial ambush, hadn't expected to. A quick, almost imperceptible nod passed between them; he lived. *Impressive.*

"Little Kobold," Will muttered, almost to himself, a grim respect stirring beneath the surface.

Malin, still running hard beside him, turned her head slightly. "Kobold? What are you talking about?"

Will managed a short, breathless chuckle. "Kobolds are these small, tricky spirits. You rarely see 'em, but they're incredibly tough and persistent. Once they latch onto a place or a person, they're damn near impossible to get rid of." He nodded back toward Caelum, who, despite his lack of a discernible aura, was still effortlessly shadowing their pace. "Just like our friend there. Keeps up, stays invisible, and pops up when you least expect him."

She gave an exhausted chuckle.

Will's mind raced, pulling up the mental map he'd meticulously memorized. The terrain was changing; the trees were thicker and older. They were pushing deeper into uncharted territory, away from Media's easy reach.

There should be a small lake ahead. He remembered the contour lines, the slight dip in the elevation. It was a good place, secluded, with fresh water. It was a place they could regroup, assess, and hopefully… breathe.

He spoke in a low, raspy whisper into the comms unit that linked them. "If I'm remembering right, there's a lake ahead, maybe fifteen minutes out. We're stopping there."

Khelek gave a terse nod. They pushed on, the promise of a halt, of even a temporary respite, a powerful motivator.

They burst from the final thicket of trees, staggering slightly as their momentum carried them into a small, open clearing. The ground sloped gently down to the edge of a mountain lake.

Will's breath hitched.

It was a sight that silenced the roar in his ears, momentarily eclipsing the ache in his muscles.

On the far side, rising sharply into the distant sky, stood the Draco Mountains themselves. Their craggy peaks, dusted with what looked like perpetual snow even from this distance, loomed majestically, framing the vast expanse of water. If he looked close enough, he wondered if he could see a dragon flying.

The water itself was impossibly still and clear, reflecting the inverted image of the sky and the towering mountains with perfect, glass-like precision. Not a ripple disturbed its surface, save for the faint, concentric rings spreading from where a bird had just dipped its beak. The only sounds were the gentle lapping of the water against the shore and the soft, melodious calls of birds hidden deep within the surrounding trees. It was a place of profound peace, a tranquility so absolute it felt almost otherworldly, a stark contrast to the chaos they had just escaped.

Malin came to him then, stepping into his space. She took his arm and wrapped it around her waist, leaning into his side with a hopeful look on her face.

Will felt the tension begin to drain from his shoulders, and the drum of adrenaline slowly subsided, replaced by the sheer, overwhelming presence of natural beauty. This was an excellent place to regroup, a place to confront the unspoken.

Will returned Malin's hug, drawing strength from her familiar warmth, even as his mind circled back to the unsettling memory of the guard.

As she pulled back, her eyes still scanning the distant mountains, he decided this was the moment. No delay. He pulled her down to the moss-covered ground to rest.

"Malin," he began, his voice dropping low, serious. He gestured towards the thick forest they'd just exited, then back towards the way they'd come. "What… what was that, back there? With that guard."

He didn't accuse, didn't judge, just sought understanding. His gaze fixed on her face, searching for answers, trying to gauge her reaction to what she had done.

Malin's hopeful expression faltered, a shadow passing over her features. She looked away, towards the still, clear lake. "I... I don't know, exactly. I used my healing power, but... reversed it. I just wanted him to let go, to stop. My flames were on fumes... But then... the energy, it was like a pull. I couldn't... I didn't mean to drain him." Her voice was a strained whisper, a mix of horror and bewilderment. She shuddered, pressing her hands to her stomach as if to physically push the memory away. "It was sickening, Will. I felt sick of what I had done."

Will reached out, gently taking her hands, feeling the faint tremor in them. "I saw it. It was... effective. Downright deadly and exactly what was needed at that moment. Malin, you're getting stronger every day, but this was... different. Are you okay? Are you sure you're in control?" He squeezed her hands, his concern genuine.

She met his gaze, a profound weariness in her eyes. "I don't know. It was exhilarating, in a way, but terrifying. I don't want to do that again." She leaned her head against his shoulder, her breath ragged. "We just have to find the kids, Will. Then maybe... then I can figure this out."

Will held her close, a silent promise.

He looked up, catching Nar and Khelek's eyes. Nar offered a steady, understanding nod, while Khelek's gaze was unreadable, perhaps resigned.

He saw the movement out of the corner of his eyes as Caelum materialized near the water.

"Alright, Kobold," Will called out, his voice carrying across the quiet clearing. "Quit skulking in the shadows and join the discussion. We've been hiking for hours without a break."

Nar and Khelek exchanged quick, amused glances, and Will caught the subtle snicker that escaped Nar.

Caelum's expression was unreadable as he walked towards them. "Kobolds are known for their cleverness and loyalty. I take that as a compliment," Caelum stated, his voice quiet but firm, a hint of dry wit in his eyes as he met Will's gaze.

"It was meant as a compliment," Will chuckled, a genuine smile spreading across his face. "Aldrik still might want to kill you, but you have proven yourself to me, so far… Kobold. Especially, the loyalty part. We have been hiking at quite a pace since the pirate encampment, and you stayed up. You didn't leave us high and dry back there, even when things got ugly."

"He did more than that," Malin interjected, her voice suddenly sharper, catching their attention. Her eyes flashed with a newfound appreciation for Caelum. "I saw him. When the drones were still active, he went invisible and took out their operators. Those drones were wreaking havoc, and I'm not sure we would have gotten away if they had still been up there. He saved us."

Nar and Khelek exchanged surprised looks, their previous amusement fading into a fresh wave of respect.

"Is that right, Caelum?" Nar asked, his voice low, his expression serious now, as he pulled a horn filled with liquid from his pack, took a drink, and passed it to Khelek. "That was you?"

Caelum gave a slight, almost imperceptible nod.

"Impressive, Kobold," Khelek rumbled, a rare note of approval in his deep voice, passing the horn to Will after taking a drink. "Very impressive."

"You certainly pulled your weight, little man," Will added, his tone devoid of any teasing, only genuine gratitude. He smelled the liquid inside, wrinkled his nose, but took a drink. It didn't smell very pleasant, but it was bursting with flavors. "Thank you. What is that?" he asked Nar.

"You haven't had Nambrose before? It is a complete meal in liquid form, magically infused in bubbles. Elves don't have the same nourishment needs you humans do. This should be good to keep us going for a while," Khelek said.

"Do you see that in the distance?" Khelek asked, pointing in the direction of the base of one of the distant mountains.

"No. What?" his eyes searched the distant peaks. He couldn't see anything.

"I see it, Elven eyes for the win," Nar joked. "There are faint smoke lines that look like they could be a village."

"It's as good a place to check as any," Will said. "I think I can see it… But how far do you think it is?"

"With this rocky terrain, a full-day hike at least. We could be there by morning if we don't run into any issues," Khelek provided.

"Sounds like no time for delays. Let's go. We have kids to find and that is the best sign we have had so far," Will declared, helping Malin up from the mossy patch they were relaxing on.

Their silent hike in the mountainous hillside was broken by Malin asking, "So, you said we were in Draco mountains. What does that mean? I'm guessing it means dragons, but doesn't that mean we need to be worried? What do we even know about them? Are they friendly? Dangerous? Knowing what we are up against might help me feel less worried about being here."

"Dragons are few and far between. We may see them, but they tend to avoid people. If that is a village in the distance, it's deep in Draconian lands, most likely Dracnors or Dragnaughts, depending on which type of dragon they have ancestry from. Let's hope they are not Dragnaughts, from black dragons. They are not the friendliest," Khelek stated.

Will looked at Nar and Khelek. "This is more your knowledge base. I stuck to the coastline of the Draco's most of the time. Nar, Khelek, give Malin the rundown."

Nar, ever the historian, began. "The Draco Mountains are home to three distinct inhabitants, all descended from the ancient dragons themselves, who live in deep caves, usually in small clutches, though some prefer a solitary existence. Each type of dragon has different preferences. Some are drawn to the highest, coldest peaks, while others are drawn to volcanic heat. Others stay in normal climate areas. The Mellyrn have never had issues with them, but with others, they're territorial, fierce, and interact violently. We leave them alone and they leave us alone."

Khelek picked up the thread, his voice rumbled low. "Dracnors and Dragnaughts can pass as human in many ways, but if you look closely, their skin has a subtle, almost imperceptible scaly pattern, sometimes even iridescence. They live all over these lands, blending into villages and communities, often where you'd least expect them."

"The Dracos are the most unknown group. They are very distrustful of other groups, but that is because they've been hunted relentlessly by many magical groups throughout history. Taken as slaves, and worse, for their blood, which is said to have powerful healing properties," Nar explained. They resemble humans physically, but their skin resembles that of lizards, often featuring subtle scales or rough textures. They tend to live in the drier, more arid regions, at least that is what we were told… Not much is known about them. They're known for their resilience in harsh environments."

Malin was silent for a bit in thought, hiking with the others. "Do we know which group lives in this area? How would they treat children?" she asked, her concerns not abated with the history lesson.

"We don't know what we will find. I don't know what they would do with children. I know they are not a fan of outsiders, but I think a lot of the concerns were that they were slavers or potions hunters. I can't imagine that children would be a concern. No, but we will find them. The few interactions I have had with Dracnors were that they were honorable," Will assured as he helped her over a steep incline by taking her hand in his and helping her up. They were hiking toward the smoke and the possible village. They were hiking to get their children.

About an hour into their hike from their resting spot, Malin tensed. Her eyes unfocused for a moment, her gaze was distant, fixed on something Will couldn't see. He reached out instinctively, with concern etched on his face.

Malin gasped, her hand flying to her ear, then pressing against her temple. A radiant, fragile hope bloomed on her face, chasing away the shadows of fear and exhaustion. "Ellie," she breathed, tears welling in her eyes. "She's… she's safe! She said… she said we're going to find them soon." Malin's voice was choked with emotion. "They're… they're in a nearby mountain village. I bet it is that one."

Her eyes snapped back to Will, blazing with an almost frantic energy. "They have to be there. In that village,"

Hope still bright in her eyes, but mixed now with a desperate urgency, Malin.

"It was more images than words, though I did hear a few words. She cut out," Malin whispered, a tremor in her voice. "But they are safe. Zee is with her. They're staying with a nice family, and there are kids their age."

Will felt a surge of adrenaline, distinct from the rush of battle. This was pure, unadulterated hope.

He grasped Malin's shoulders, his grin wide. "Alright, alright, that's huge. Let's see the maps. We need to see if there are other closer villages than that one in this area."

They immediately spread out their maps. Nar pulled out an old, meticulously drawn leather scroll, while Will checked his map.

Malin hovered over Will, her finger tracing lines, her gaze intense. Based on the smoke's distance and the terrain, they quickly identified a handful of potential locations, each marked as small settlements or clusters of dwellings.

Their search began. They spent the rest of that day until the sky would not provide enough light to walk, navigating the winding mountain trails. They set a large fire and slept on the ground.

They got moving before dawn.

Malin received another message, her eyes distant, her hand pressed to her temple. The kids were missing them. Will wished he could hear her. He could not get to them fast enough. She seemed to feel that the signal was getting stronger, as if they might be closer. Will lead the way with a renewed sense of purpose.

They found a path that seemed to have regular foot traffic. That was a good sign.

When they rounded a bend, Malin paused and got excited. "This… These rocks," she said, pointing to a large outcropping of balanced stones. "They match one of the images Ellie sent. We are on the right path!"

They hiked as fast as they could given the precarious terrain. It was, obviously, not a path for wagons.

The path led to a clearing at the top of a small mountain. Tucked into a sheltered valley below, nestled beside a roaring stream and protected by ancient, gnarled trees, was a small, bustling village. The smoke from hearths curled lazily into the sky, just as they had seen from the lake.

They approached cautiously, their weapons ready, but the scene was one of peaceful domesticity. Children played in the dirt, their laughter echoing. Elders sat on carved wooden benches, whispering, probably about the newcomers.

And there, near a small, welcoming house on the edge of town, were Ellie and Zee.

Will stopped dead, every muscle in his body locking. For a split second, his mind refused to process what his eyes were seeing. Their blond human hair was unmistakable even from a distance, playing near a sun-dappled stoop.

Then, a wave of unbearable relief crashed over him, so potent it stole the air from his lungs. It wasn't a gentle tide; it was a tidal wave, ripping through the lingering fear, the pain of his torture, the gnawing anxiety that had been his constant companion.

A choked, raw sound tore from his throat, somewhere between a sob and a desperate, thankful gasp.

They were real. They were safe. They were *there*.

His legs, which had carried him through so much, suddenly felt weak, threatening to give out beneath him. He wanted to run, to shout, to drop to his knees and weep.

He glanced at Malin beside him. Her breath had hitched, a sharp, audible gasp that mirrored the sudden, agonizing release in his chest. Her hands flew to her mouth, shaking, and her eyes, usually so composed, were wide, brimming with a mix of disbelief and overwhelming, fragile joy.

He saw the immediate, powerful urge to run to them, but she, too, seemed rooted to the spot, almost as if moving would shatter the perfect image. A single tear traced a path down her cheek, quickly followed by another, but her gaze never left the children.

It was a raw, beautiful, and utterly devastating display of a mother's love, and at that moment, he loved her more fiercely than he thought possible. She had been through hell for them, just like him.

Now, seeing her break in that vulnerable, joyous way made every sacrifice worth it.

Sitting on the front steps of a small farmhouse, a woman with unusual copper-colored hair was braiding Ellie's hair, while a man with short brown hair shoveled food into the feeders with Zee by his side, both of them roaring with delight.

Who were these people who had taken care of their children, and how could he ever repay them?

Ellie saw her mother first, as she stood and ran into Malin's waiting arms. Zee, followed, and they both crashed into her, nearly knocking her over.

He hung back for a moment, letting her have the reunion. Then, he felt a familiar shift beside him. Caelum stood beside him, watching the reunion with an unreadable expression.

Will clapped him gently on the shoulder, as he walked toward the gathering. "Come on, Kobold," he said, a genuine smile replacing his usual smirk. "Time to meet the family." He steered Caelum forward, towards the joyful, tearful embrace.

Ellie, still with her arms wrapped around Malin, looked up as Will approached, then ran to him, jumping into his arms, followed by Zee. He held both of his children as tightly as he could, legs dangling, feeling all was right in the world.

After a few moments, he noticed Ellie's gaze land on Nar and Khelek, standing stoically off to the side. She asked to be set down and ran to them, jumping into both of their arms at the same time. They laughed together as Zee joined shortly after.

After a few moments, Ellie asked, "Who's he?" as she noticed Caelum standing off to the side.

"Ellie," Will said, his voice soft. "This is Caelum. He helped us."

Ellie's wide, curious eyes took in Caelum's unassuming form, then a small smile touched her lips. "Hi, Caelum," she said, no fear, only innocent curiosity.

Caelum, to Will's surprise, offered another, slightly less imperceptible nod in return. "We were worried about you. I've heard a lot of good things about you. Nice to finally meet you," he said, walking closer.

Maybe there was hope for the little Kobold. As Malin, Nar, Khelek, and the children reminisced, Will pulled Caelum aside.

"So, how do you want to play this? I can see in your eyes that you are itching to tell her… to blurt it out even. I was just in your same boat. I literally found out Zee was my son a few weeks ago," he admitted, causing Caelum's eyes to widen. "In my case, Zee's mother left before I found out about him, and I only found out when she died. I know what you are going through, in some ways, but I waited… waited until he got to know me before telling him. I gave Zee a week or two. She's a smart one. Telling her now might backfire. You really want to give her a chance to see who you are and believe in you, as I'm starting to… She told me that she always wanted a Dad, so I've filled in. I don't plan on going anywhere in her life. I will fight you tooth and nail… and I would win… if you take her from me, but I know there is room for both of us."

He was trying to be logical, as Malin would want him to be, but also wanted to make sure Caelum knew that he wasn't going anywhere.

"Wow. I had no idea," he said. "Waiting until she knows who I am is probably a good idea, unless she won't like who I am." Will could hear the concern in his tone.

"Look. I'm no angel. I have done more things that would make people run in fear, if they knew… but those kids. They don't see that. I can't explain it. I can't understand it, but… They trust that I will always do what it takes to love them and to earn their love… even if it means getting dirty every once in a while. They know I'm there for them." He'd thought it, felt it, but hearing the words out loud, raw and honest… it anchored something deep inside him.

The initial chaos of the reunion gradually gave way to a quieter, profound relief. A tangible warmth, like sunshine after a storm, settled over the clearing. After introductions, Malin, Will, Nar, and Khelek, with Caelum still quietly at their side, gathered around the Volkov family, the Dracnors who had taken their children in and cared for them as though they were their own. The air, crisp and carrying the scent of pine and damp earth, now seemed to hum with unspoken gratitude.

"Your children are truly a blessing and so brave," Ruslan, the father's deep voice rumbled in his broad chest. He was slightly taller than Malin.

He stood tall. Will had to look closely to realize that his skin was not flesh, but small scales in a deep, rich brown that blended with the bark of the ancient trees. The slits and double lids of his eyes were jarring.

"Ellie has been super helpful, showing the children some very interesting physical moves. Are these moves common among your people?" His wife, Varya, asked, her gentle smile warming her features.

Her copper-colored hair, which she wore in a practical braid, shimmered with an unusual, almost metallic sheen in the fading light. The light color of her skin was slightly iridescent with a smooth, pebbled texture.

"No, those moves are not common," Malin replied, placing a hand over her heart in a gesture of sincere gratitude. "She is quite skilled at them, though. I'm glad she was sharing. I hope they weren't any trouble."

Their children, Misha, Lila, and the youngest, Kael, watched the newcomers shyly. The younger sat next to their mother, their skin showing faint, iridescent patterns when the light caught them just right.

"They have been so helpful," Ruslan added with honest appreciation. His voice was warm and filled with genuine gratitude. "Zee has been able to double the production of the fowl, and the oxen are providing more milk than they usually do. Ellie has been able to help, too. Her levitation is amazing. She was able to help me move more bales of hay than I could have moved by hand in a week. I've never seen someone so young with her level of powers."

"We... we can't thank you enough," Malin said, her voice still thick with emotion, looking from Ellie and Zee to the Dracnor family. "You saved them."

Ruslan waved a dismissive hand, a quiet strength in his voice. "They were lost, and we found them. The Medny Rod Dracnors value honor above all else, and to do anything other than the honorable thing would have been unheard of." He paused, his gaze resting on Ellie and Zee, a faint, almost imperceptible shift in his expression. "Though, truth be told, they did more for us than we for them."

Will's brow furrowed slightly. "What do you mean?"

Varya stepped forward, a soft, knowing look in her eyes as she glanced at her children. "This land... it can be harsh. If it hadn't been for their help, we would have lost our farm, everything, just a few days ago. It was because of these two that the dragon left without any damage." Her voice dropped to a near whisper, laden with a past fear that was slowly being replaced by gratitude. "It is their tale to tell you, but your children... they showed remarkable courage. After some of the tales they told of you both, I can see where they learned it. They helped us. It was because they were here, because of what they did, that our home stands now."

He couldn't help but realize that he had only just come into these children's lives. Their courage, their kindness, their selflessness... that wasn't from him. With Ellie, it was all Malin, a result of the love and strength she had poured into her for years. This was her win, her legacy. And with Zee, he had Felicity, who, much like Malin, had raised her son into this amazing kid.

He hadn't participated in their lives until weeks ago. But that ends now. He was here, he was present, and he would be an active part of their lives... all of them, including the new little one on the way. These kids were his new purpose in life... from this day forward.

She didn't elaborate, simply letting the words hang in the air, weighted with unspoken details of close calls and unexpected bravery. Nar and Khelek exchanged curious glances, while Malin looked from Varya to her children, a mix of pride and profound wonder blooming on her face.

Will felt a shiver run down his spine, a testament to the unwritten saga his kids had lived. He already knew his children were special, but the idea of them somehow playing a pivotal role in saving a Dracnor family's farm from a dragon... that was a story he would definitely be pressing for later.

"We are forever in your debt, nonetheless. For their safety, and for... everything else," Malin chimed in, her voice earnest.

"Do you mind if we rest here tonight, as it is late? Media will likely be after us once we leave the mountains till, we get to Mellryn border," Will asked, the fatigue finally seeping into his bones.

"Actually, we had already been in discussions about how to help get the children back to Mellyrn. We will know more in the morning," Varya said, a comforting assurance in her tone. She gestured towards a small, sturdy hut. "Ellie informed us yesterday that you would be here soon. We've prepared a room for you," she explained, leading them towards the room where their children and Misha had been staying.

Nar and Khelek, ever preferring the open air or simpler accommodation, felt more comfortable staying in the stables. Still, Malin and he would be sharing a room with Ellie and Zee, and Misha would be staying in the bedroom of the younger two for the evening. Caelum decided to stay out in the barn with Nar and Khelek.

The room, though simple, was large enough for a double bed, a sturdy dresser, and a woven rug that felt soft beneath Will's aching feet. Everything was remarkably clean and well cared for, smelling faintly of dried herbs and fresh wood. A deep sense of peace permeated the small space, a stark contrast to the danger and uncertainty of the outside world. If it meant his family was together, he would sleep outside in the yard, if needed. The thought of them all safe under one roof, even a borrowed one, brought a powerful wave of emotional exhaustion and profound gratitude.

Following a satisfying meal filled with rich, flavorful dishes and engaging conversation, Will felt thoroughly exhausted. The aromas of spices and herbs still lingered in the air as he pushed back from the table, feeling the weight of the delicious fare settle in his stomach. The warmth of the room and the laughter shared around the table left him with a sense of contentment, yet the day's events weighed heavily on him, urging him toward a well-deserved rest.

Later that evening, nestled close together on the shared bed, blankets pulled up to their chins, Will and Malin exchanged a knowing glance. This was it.

"Kids," Malin began, her voice soft, her fingers gently stroking Ellie's hair. "We have something really special to tell you."

Ellie, her eyes wide and curious, propped herself up on an elbow. "What is it, Mom?"

Malin and Will locked eyes, a shared smile passing between them.

Then Malin blurted out, "We are going to have a baby."

Ellie's eyes, usually so observant, widened further, filling with pure awe. "A baby? Like, a real baby? With tiny fingers and tiny toes?" She leaned forward, a gasp escaping her lips.

Turning to Zee, she got a huge grin on her face and pulled him in for a quick hug. "We're going to be big sisters and big brothers?"

"That's exactly right," Malin beamed, pulling both kids into a tight hug. "We are going to get to safety, and we are going to be a real family."

Zee, who had been listening intently from his spot beside Will, suddenly pushed himself up, his brow furrowed in a surprisingly mature, almost pre-teen angst. "I hope I'm not going to have to change a diaper," he grumbled, though a faint smile played at the corners of his lips. "But I do like the idea of having a little brother or sister. I always wanted one. Now I'll have two. Ellie and this one." He gestured vaguely at Malin's stomach, a hint of genuine excitement breaking through his shell.

Ellie bounced on the bed, her earlier exhaustion completely forgotten, already planning games and lullabies for the new arrival. The small room filled with their excited whispers and happy giggles, a precious, fragile moment of pure family bliss.

"Since everything is set here, I'm going to check in on Comms with Aldrik. I tried earlier to reach him, and he was not available. I wanted to be the one to tell him we found the kids," Will said, standing and preparing to walk out of the room.

Malin nodded, her eyes soft with understanding. "Be careful."

He squeezed her hand and walked outside, the low murmur of the Volkov family's voices drifting from the main house. The crisp mountain air bit at his cheeks, carrying the faint scent of pine and distant woodsmoke. Above, the sea of stars were like pinpricks of light in the inky black sky, stretching out like a vast, glittering blanket.

He found a secluded spot near the stables, the comforting presence of Nar and Khelek nearby, their quiet Elven conversation barely audible.

Will activated his encrypted communication system; the hum that had become familiar over the last few days was a low thrum in his ear.

"Are they truly safe? All of them?" Aldrik's voice, usually so steady, was tight with barely contained hope; relief was palpable, even with the digital connection.

Will grinned, a genuine, unburdened smile. "Safe as can be. Just found them. They were with a good family here. And they saved some people from dragons or something like that. Can you believe our kids? I know they'll be happy to provide you with the details. I'm looking forward to hearing the details myself." He paused, his expression growing serious. "What's the status on Malin's mother? Any change?"

Aldrik's expression sobered. "That does sound like our little ones. The Ministers have tried every healing spell, every magical intervention, but they can't find a way to wake her. She's stable, vital signs strong, but… unresponsive. They've put a powerful protective shield around her, just in case Media could activate something virtually, given their tech, or try something else."

"Good," Will murmured, a knot of worry easing slightly in his gut. "Look, we have more news, big news. I want to tell you so that you can prepare, but you have to promise me you won't go out on your own. You have to wait for us to get back to Mellryn." Will's voice was cautious. Aldrik was too much like him, and he desperately hoped the man's desire to see his grandchildren again would temper his recklessness.

"Holding information that might save my love hostage is a good way to get yourself killed," Aldrik said, his voice becoming harsh and calculated.

"Oh, I realize I'm walking a line," Will assured. "To be fair, your daughter suggested I not tell you anything until we got back. But I've been where you are, and if I knew there was hope… I would want to know."

"Very well. I promise I will not act on the news until you get back, though that had better be expeditious," Aldrik said. Will thought he heard a hint of a sly smile, but he could have been imagining it.

Will went on to detail the two options and provided information he had on how to get into Fellspire Citadel and the need to get the artifact from their vault for the Order of Tamris. The two men discussed strategies for a short time.

"Look, I do want to continue this discussion, but I want to get back to the family," Will said. "There are options. I'm not sure how long a walk it will be back to Mellryn. Avoiding the Eastern border to dodge Media would mean a longer walk, but we'd be safer. Either way, you'd better be there when we arrive, or Malin will have my head. I'm already going to be in trouble for telling you," he teased.

"Ael'kin. You have brought me hope. Having you by my side when we gather what we need to save Ael'an will be my honor… You… and your brothers," Aldrik proclaimed.

"Anariel told you," Will laughed.

"Yes. She loves the idea," Aldrik said with a bit of life in his voice.

The next morning, the aroma of sizzling fat and freshly brewed herbal tea filled the hut, a comforting contrast to the crisp mountain air outside.

As they finished a hearty breakfast, warming their hands around steaming mugs, Varya cleared her throat, a twinkle in her eye. "We have good news," she announced, her voice brimming with quiet triumph. "We were able to get in touch with a family of Dracos, who knew where to find them, and they, in turn, reached out to the Copper Dragon of this territory. The one that Zee and Ellie helped save the wyrmling of."

Will, Malin, Nar, and Khelek exchanged astonished glances. A real dragon. And their kids had *saved* the offspring of a dragon? The sheer improbability of it hit Will with a wave of disbelieving awe.

"The Dragon… Mednik is his name… has agreed to provide transportation for the seven of you to the edge of the Mellyrn border, if not all the way. We had not expected him to agree, but it seemed reasonable to ask," Varya continued, watching their reactions with a satisfied smile. "This will save you days of grueling hiking through treacherous terrain and ensure that Media is not able to get to the children once you leave the safety of these mountains."

Before anyone could fully process the news, a low, resonant hum vibrated through the very ground outside the hut. It began as a distant drumbeat, growing swiftly into a mighty rush of air that stirred the leaves on the trees and rattled the hut's simple windows. The group hurried outside, their jaws dropping at the spectacle unfolding in the sky.

Two magnificent adult Copper Dragons and a smaller one descended from the heavens.

The largest, a colossal beast, larger than two houses, covered in burnished scales that caught the morning light like a thousand gleaming pennies, landed first. Its immense weight shook the earth, a deep tremor that radiated through Will's boots. Its wings, vast and leathery, folded back with a sound like sails being furled in a strong gale.

The second, slightly smaller but no less majestic, landed gracefully beside it, its scales shimmering with an inner warmth.

The third, clearly still young but larger than any non-Draconic creature Will had ever seen, settled nearby, its movements lithe and more eager. The air itself crackled with ozone and the ancient scent of rock and fire, a powerful, primeval aroma that filled Will's lungs and sent a thrill of fear and wonder down his spine. This wasn't a sight of fantasy; it was a living, breathing force of nature, and for the first time in his life, Will felt profoundly, terrifyingly small.

He'd faced countless mystical beasts in his travels. Goblins, trolls, Basat, even a few angry Fae… but nothing had prepared him for this. This was a different class of power, an existence so old and vast that it made every one of his carefully honed survival skills feel utterly useless. The thought of entrusting his family to these colossal, primeval beings was paralyzing. He fought the urge to pull Malin behind him, to shield her, but he knew it would be a futile, meaningless gesture.

He glanced at the others. Malin's expression was a mixture of awe and trepidation, her face a canvas of wonder that mirrored his own, but without the underlying panic. But it was the children who truly caught his eye. Ellie was pointing, her face alight with pure, uninhibited joy. Zee, usually so quiet and reserved, was watching the dragons with a look of intense, calm focus, his hands balled into tight fists of concentration. He did not seem scared, more as if he were using his magic and communicating.

Will felt a surge of protectiveness, followed by a jolt of pure wonder. He stepped away from Malin, moving toward Zee, his voice low. "Zee. Hey. Are you... Are you okay?"

Zee's focus didn't break. "The little one and I are friends," he whispered, his eyes still fixed on the dragons. "He is sad we are leaving." He turned to look at Will, a knowing seriousness on his young face. "I told him we will come back. We will, right?"

"If my son wants to go hang out with dragons, I am not going to stop him," he said proudly. Zee smiled at him, then ran over to the smallest one and threw his arms around its neck.

Will stood speechless for a moment, watching his son hug a creature that could turn him to ash. The terror he had felt only moments ago gave way to a new kind of joy. The boy was so much more than Will himself could ever be. This was his son, a boy with power so immense and unique he could speak to dragons, and with it came a breathtakingly beautiful fearlessness.

Will no longer saw these magnificent creatures as a terrifying, but as something his son loved, a new kind of friend. If he could face Malin with the truth, dragons were easy.

This was an adventure, a wild, exhilarating adventure, and he was ready to embrace it.

The largest dragon, Mednik, lowered his massive head, his huge, intelligent eyes, like pools of molten gold, fixing on them. His voice, a deep resonance that vibrated through their very bones more than it struck their ears, filled the clearing.

"You have the rope as I ordered?" Mednik growled.

Ruslan Volkov stepped forward, holding three large lines of rope. "Will, would you and the others be able to help me secure these on the dragons? They would not usually have them, but as you are new to riding, they said that it would be for your benefit.

Ruslan showed them how to secure the lines so that they wrapped around the neck and under the arms of the dragons, giving some security.

Once that was complete, in a slow, deliberate movement, the two adult dragons and the smaller one lowered themselves, their immense bodies settling with a grace that defied their size. The air stirred with the scent of ozone and the ancient aroma of sun-warmed stone. The little one, Ryzhik, chirped excitedly, but stayed still near Caelum.

Will blinked, then looked at Caelum. Caelum, usually so composed, looked utterly flummoxed at the prospect of riding a dragon. His calm, almost detached demeanor cracked, revealing a flicker of genuine apprehension.

"I… I am fine walking," Caelum offered, his voice unusually hesitant, his gaze fixed on the powerful beast, a clear note of discomfort in his tone.

Will couldn't help but grin, the sheer absurdity of the situation almost making him laugh despite the gravity. "Nonsense, Kobold," he said, clapping Caelum firmly on the shoulder. "You've faced drone operators and Media agents. You can handle a dragon. That dragon is Zee's friend. You'll be safe." He gave Caelum a gentle but firm push towards Ryzhik. "Besides, it'll be faster. And you've earned a front-row seat for the express ride home."

If Caelum could have summoned a weapon with his mind, Will was sure he would have… Mind you, it wouldn't have helped him much, but… Instead, the man shot him a glare so cold it could have frozen lava, a silent promise of future retribution.

The look said, *I will enjoy watching you burn, and I hope they roast you.*

"You will be fine. If you fall, I will give you a free punch," Will offered, his grin wide.

"I'll be dead. What will that help?" Caelum bit back.

"Fair enough," Will conceded with a theatrical shrug. "Tell you what… I'll let you have one punch right now. No questions. To help you release that tension so that you can enjoy your trip."

Caelum considered, his eyes narrowing.

Malin pulled Will aside, her whisper sharp, "You aren't serious, are you? This is embarrassing. What kind of people will they think we are?"

"Awe. Come on. It's Caelum. How bad can it be?" Will's eyes danced as he chuckled.

"So… I get one punch and you can't fight back, but I have to get on that…" Caelum's voice trailed off as Ryzhik snorted a plume of flames from its nose. "…magnificently scary creature."

"That's right," Will affirmed, then noticed Nar and Khelek exchanging a conspiratorial glance.

"That's a deal I can't pass up," Caelum said, squaring up to Will, his stance coiled and ready.

Will stood solid, his hands at his sides, then paused. "Just not the face… too pretty," he quipped with a wink.

Caelum didn't hesitate. He pulled back and punched Will squarely in the gut. The blow landed with a solid thud, forcing a grunt from Will's lungs as he dropped to one knee.

"That was a good one, Kobold," Will groaned, hunched over but still grinning. "Good one indeed."

Just then, he noticed Nar and Khelek. Khelek was shaking Nar's hand, coins passing between them.

"What was that? You bet on me?" Will accused, pushing himself back to his feet.

"Nar said you would not drop. I saw Caelum in action. I figured he could do it," Khelek smiled.

"Ellie… Remember when I said boys don't grow up… This is your example to remember," Malin said, a wry smile on her face. Ellie just smiled.

Mednik tipped his massive head, his ancient eyes locking onto the group. "Is there an issue?" he rumbled, the sound vibrating through the air like distant thunder.

Malin stepped forward, her voice cautious. "We apologize. We had an internal dispute, but it is resolved, now," she said, and then, after an encouraging glance from Will, she added, "and very grateful."

To Will, she whispered, "I'm not healing that."

"This one pleases me," Miedzian rumbled, a delicate curl of smoke drifting from her nostrils. "There is a reason our kind has always favored female riders."

This earned him an elbow from Malin.

Zee climbed up on the large dragon like it was nothing but a hill. Will was awed by his courage. He wasn't sure where to step, as he imagined that his weight would cause injury.

"Come on, Dad. Even as big as you are, he will barely be able to tell you are there," Zee called out, his voice filled with an easy confidence.

Will's heart seized in his chest, a profound wave of emotion washing over him. The word, "Dad," slipped from Zee's lips so naturally, so casually, as if it were a title he'd always held.

As he climbed onto the mountain of a beast, the brilliant, iridescent bronze scales didn't indent when he stepped. They felt warm and smooth under his touch. The thick, scaled hide was surprisingly comfortable, but the sheer size of the beast, with its raw, primal power radiating from it, was humbling.

The climb alone was challenging in spots, as it was like a rock wall in one area, using the large scales as hand and footholds. Climbing up to the only place he could envision sitting. The sharp, bony spines that ran down the entire length of his neck to a large bony frill the size of a person at the base of the spine. Then, there was a gap between the series of flattened, leathery spines that ran down the rest of the back, starting just before the wings. This gap was a perfect location to sit, holding the bony frill, which he imagined would provide some protection from the winds. Zee was already in place, as Malin and Will carefully climbed onto the dragon's back.

Will wasted no time once they all got seated. He reached forward under each of their arms, pulling them both securely against him as he gripped the bony frill of the dragon's spine.

In front, Zee's hands were already wrapped around a section of the frill, and Malin's arms were braced under his, her grip firm. Will's stronger hands covered both of theirs, creating a secure, layered hold. His family was safe. The ropes were used to secure their legs.

As the three of them got situated, he looked around to see Ellie in the front, then Nar and Khelek on the back of the dragon, Miedzian. Ellie was all smiles and excitement. Nar looked cautious, but steady. Will met his eye with a nod.

The youngest dragon, Ryzhik, was still on the ground waiting for Caelum to get on.

"Caelum. We had a deal," Will said.

He reluctantly climbed on, stating clearly, "If I die, I'm coming back to haunt you," making everyone laugh.

With everyone boarded, they waved goodbye to the Volkov family waiting below. They were above the tree line, and the view of the valley was amazing. He could only imagine what it would look like when they were in the air.

"With all the excitement of the dragons, we forgot to say goodbye," Malin worried.

"I think they understand, besides, Zee here says he wants to come back," Will said, ruffling his hair.

Just then, the world around them tilted, and they had to hold on tightly. "Apologies. It has been a while since I have had to deal with riders," Mednick rumbled, his deep voice carrying a note of humor.

Will was in awe of the power and strength of Mednik. He was not a fan of horse riding, but this was so much more than that.

"Hold on tight!" Mednik yelled over the rising wind, though the immense, building power swallowed his voice.

A profound mix of excitement and terror surged through him. He could hear Ellie's excited squeals from Miedzian's back.

Mednik gathered his colossal strength. With a mighty roar that shook the entire valley and echoed off the distant peaks, followed by a single, earth-shaking beat of his colossal wings, the dragon launched himself into the sky.

Will felt a violent lurch in his stomach, a dizzying mix of exhilaration and stark terror as the ground plummeted beneath them. The wind tore at their clothes, whipping their hair and bringing tears to Will's eyes, the sheer speed was breathtaking.

He pressed Malin and Zee tighter against him. The thick rope Mednik had allowed was a reassuring yet straightforward measure of protection that had been much appreciated.

He noticed Malin was quiet and frozen like a statue. Her knuckles were bright white.

Heights.

"I forgot you don't like heights," he said in her ear. "Last time, I listed all the things more terrifying than this. I've got to say… probably not many that you are going to believe are worse than this…" He squeezed his arms tighter with his elbows.

He gently squeezed her hand, his voice dropping to a low, soothing murmur that was for her alone.

"Hey, Sparks. It's just a little flyin'. You've faced down an army and melted guards and pirates to ash, but a little altitude is where you draw the line?" he teased softly, the hint of a grin in his voice. "Open your eyes, love. I promise you're not going anywhere." He tightened his arms around her, a firm, unwavering presence against the immense power of the dragon. "I've got you. All of you. Now and always. Besides," he continued, a playful note returning to his voice, "it's going to be a long trip."

He saw her shake her head, realizing her eyes were closed tightly, "Don't you want to see this? It's a view worth seeing."

Realizing that she was still not moving he was about to switch tactics to his more disarming charm when Zee spoke up, "Zee's head turned, his eyes wide with a mix of wonder and concern. "Mom," he said, his voice a bright, innocent whisper. "You have to open your eyes! The sun is making all the mountains look like gold, and there's a river that looks like a little tiny snake."

Malin's body, which had been rigid, seemed to soften just a fraction.

"Listen to the kid, love," Will whispered into her hair. "He's not lying. It's beautiful. And I want you to see it with me."

He felt her gasp against him.

He murmured, a hint of a smile in his voice. "Which is it, Sparks?"

"Terrifying, but good," she said, her voice muffled against his chest. "Do not let me go!"

"Never," he promised. He let one of the hands holding the bone frill go so that he could tighten it around her. He could feel her loosen the moment his arm was around her.

The world stretched out beneath them, a vast tapestry of mountains and forests, bathed in the brilliant morning sun. It was breathtaking.

"Mednik," Will yelled.

Then he felt a presence in his mind respond, "Yes."

"You said there were riders? How long ago was that? I've never heard of anyone riding dragons," Will yelled.

"I have the ability to allow the four of us to mentally hold a conversation together. They will hear you also, you do not need to yell," Mednik stated. "Dragons do not allow just anyone on our backs. It is a place of honor," His voice rumbled within his head.

"Millenia ago, we had riders. I assure you. You are in no danger of falling off."

"You don't have riders any longer?" Malin probed.

"There was a time when the other races would actively petition us to bond, but that time ended over a thousand years ago, though the way Zee is with Ryzhik, it may begin again. Your offspring are remarkable young ones. We honor our debts to the young ones by this offering," Mednik rumbled, his words echoing in their minds. "Dragon eggs take hundreds of years to hatch, and we have so few clutches. Miedzian and I only have four offspring. Ryzhik is my oldest and the only one to survive his clutch. When these young ones saved my youngest wyrmling from traders, there are no words to explain how much it meant to us. This is how we pay, and even this does not seem enough."

"We can understand what you mean. My children mean the world to me. I'm looking forward to getting them home," Will said.

This was it. The fastest, most improbable way home.

CHAPTER 32 – MALIN

The roar of Mednik's launch, a sound that resonated deep in Malin's bones, still echoed in her ears, and they had been in the air for a good while. Will had convinced her to open her eyes. It was beautiful, she had to admit, but still terrifying.

A dizzying mix of elation and sheer terror surged through her. Her stomach clenched, and she pressed herself tighter against Will's back, her arms wrapped around Zee, whose heart was beating like a bird.

The air grew thinner with every powerful beat of Mednik's colossal wings. It wasn't just cold; it was an icy bite that seemed to steal the breath right from her lungs. The crisp, earthy scents of the forest floor were replaced by something vast and clean, a faint, metallic tang of ozone mixed with the sharp, almost sterile smell of high-altitude ice. It was the scent of the untouched sky, raw and exhilarating, a profound contrast to the chaos they had just endured.

"This is amazing Mednick! What a blessing to be able to see this whenever you want?" she proclaimed to the giant in their mental connection.

"I wasn't sure you were enjoying it at first. I am grateful to hear such words from the likes of the Feniks Talavo," the great one proclaimed.

"The what?" she asked.

"You will know in time. That is assured," he spoke back, in a tone that was not up for discussion.

That did not sound like an answer, but she did not want to anger the one who carried her this high above the ground.

"Do you think that we would be able to fly all the way to Mellyrn? Would you mind?"

"If we can be assured that the city will not react poorly to us, we will take you that far," Mednick confirmed.

Will responded, "I can check, but I'm going to have to let you go so that I can trigger the communication earpiece. Nod if I can."

She nodded.

When his arm withdrew from around her, the action felt precarious at this height, the sheer drop below them a constant, dizzying reminder of their vulnerability. She did not like the feeling of leaving the protection of his arms for even a moment. It was only a moment, then his arm returned.

After a tense few moments, Will shouted into the comms, relaying their astonishing method of travel. She felt Will tense against her, then heard his triumphant shout into the comms, confirming the new plan with Aldrik. He pulled his arm away again, then returned it. She hoped he didn't have to do that too often.

"Confirmed Mednick. The large flat area outside the castle is called the fairgrounds. They will have it ready for you to have plenty of room. My father-in-law is feeling very appreciative. I hope it is acceptable. He will have several oxen available for you, along with fresh water if needed, so that you will be better able to make the journey home without issue," Will thought into the combined mental connection.

"Maybe you humans are not all bad. The gesture is appreciated. We should be there within thirty minutes."

This was so much better than the multiple-day journey through dangerous circumstances, worrying about assassins, Media, Orcs, and creatures. She would feel so much better when she had her children in the safety of the castle… even if they still needed to worry about assassins and court politics.

She worried about Ellie.

As Malin stole a glance over her shoulder, she saw Miedzian, carrying Nar, Khelek, and Ellie, keeping a steady pace beside them. Ellie's arms were out wide, feeling the wind, with both Nar and Khelek holding her tightly by the bone frill. *The girl had no fear.* That had definitely been earned from her mother. She worried for her mother's progress, but she knew Aeladar was looking out for her.

As she looked back, she also noticed the Draco Mountains, which had loomed so impressively just moments ago, now stretched out like wrinkled giants, their snow-capped peaks glistening in the morning sun. The patchwork of villages and forests blurred into an indistinct tapestry. Far in the distance, she could make out the glint of the lake they had rested by, now no more than a tiny, shimmering coin. The world unfolded beneath them, a breathtaking panorama that made every earthly concern seem distant and insignificant.

Ellie's face, though wind-whipped, was alight with an ecstatic, open-mouthed awe. She was utterly enthralled, pointing down at the miniature world below.

Behind them, Ryzhik, the youngest copper dragon, flew with a powerful grace that belied his size, Caelum an unmoving silhouette on his back. She could only imagine what he was thinking. Once she learned what a Kobold was, she agreed… so far… he is living up to the nickname.

As they ascended higher, the ground gave way to a curving horizon, the faint blue haze of the atmosphere painting the distant plains. The wind roared past her ears, a deafening gale that made conversation impossible without shouting directly into Will's ear.

A wave of profound relief washed over Malin, replacing the residual fear with a giddy excitement. Mellyrn. Home… or at least the closest thing to home they had.

Below, the world continued to unfurl, growing from a distant map into something more recognizable. Houses began to resolve into shapes, roads into lines, then the unmistakable sprawling magnificence of Mellyrn City, crowned by the towering spires of its castle.

As they drew closer, descending with a breathtaking speed that had Malin's stomach lurching again, she saw it. Not just the castle, but the city. People. Thousands of them.

Word must have spread like wildfire that dragons were coming.

People surrounded the fairgrounds, thousands of them. A sea of faces, upturned, tiny dots of awe and wonder, as three copper dragons. She imagined that the sight must have been overwhelming to the people below.

The descent was a blur of wind and the growing roar of the crowd. Mednik's massive talons touched down on the fairgrounds with a ground-shaking thud, causing a wave of cheers, deafening and overwhelming, to wash over Malin. The scent of ozone from the dragons mingled with the familiar, exciting aroma of a large crowd: dust, anticipation, and a thousand different human smells.

Before Mednik had fully settled, Will was already helping her and Zee dismount, his grip firm and reassuring. The moment Zee's feet touched the ground, he was off, a blur of motion towards a figure standing at the edge of the roaring crowd.

"Aldrik!" Will yelled, his voice thick with emotion as he watched his son bolt to him.

Malin's heart swelled as she saw him, too.

Aeladar stood there, his usually composed features broken by a wide, tearful smile, with Zee already in his arms.

Ellie, a moment later, was racing from Miedzian's back, a streak of pale blonde hair, straight into his waiting arms. With both children in his arms, it was a tangle of limbs and joyous cries. He simply knelt, enveloping them in a fierce, protective hug, his face buried in their hair. It was a reunion Malin knew would bring him immense, unburdened relief.

The cheers of the crowd intensified, shifting from general excitement to a focused roar of approval. Malin realized why: the dragons were already moving.

Three enormous oxen, pre-arranged as a payment or an offering, were laid out on the far side of the fairgrounds. With powerful, swift movements, Mednik, Miedzian, and Ryzhik began to devour them, their massive forms dwarfing the offerings. The sight was primal, awe-inspiring, and yet strangely fitting for their glorious arrival. The audience loved watching them devour their meals.

Before Mednik lifted his head from his meal, his huge, intelligent eyes, like molten gold, found Malin in the throng. His voice, a deep resonance that vibrated only in her mind, spoke one last, enigmatic message.

"It was a pleasure to meet the Feniks Talavo. It was a great honor."

Then, with a final, powerful beat of their colossal wings, all three copper dragons launched themselves skyward, disappearing into the vast blue before Malin could even fully process the words.

Feniks Talavo? What did that even mean?

The phrase lingered in her mind, a strange, beautiful echo, leaving her with more questions than answers. She would have to ask her mother, or perhaps the Minsters in the Castle, for details. The mystery would undoubtedly gnaw at her until she found an explanation.

With the dragons gone and the immediate chaos settling, Malin's thoughts turned to her mother. She needed to see her, to confirm her safety, to touch her hand.

She excused herself from the excited crowd, a new wave of urgency propelling her towards the castle.

After assuring herself that her mother was indeed stable, though still unresponsive in her shielded chamber, a heavy exhaustion settled over Malin. All she wanted was to wash away the dirt, the fear, and the lingering scent of adventure.

Later that day, Malin luxuriated under a long, hot shower in the castle's opulent bathing chambers. The steaming water washed away the grime of their journey, carrying away the lingering dust of the Draconian mountains, the subtle scent of pine and ozone, and the pervasive tension she hadn't realized she was still holding.

She scrubbed her skin until it tingled, the warmth seeping into her muscles, easing every ache.

Will eventually joined her; his familiar presence was a comforting anchor. They shared a quiet, intimate moment, the silence broken only by the rush of water, a shared breath of peace before the next storm.

The shower had done wonders. The grit of travel, the grime of the city, the lingering scent of fear—all of it washed down the drain, leaving them feeling clean for the first time in what felt like weeks. They emerged to find not their tattered travel gear, but two sets of unfamiliar, elegant clothing laid out on the bed.

Will whistled softly, a low note of surprise. He held up a shirt of fine, dark linen, a pair of trousers that fit like a second skin, and a soft, supple leather vest that seemed more for show than for protection.

"Looks like someone's trying to make a proper gentleman out of me," he murmured, a half-grin on his face. "I could get used to Elven finery." He ran a thumb over the intricate stitching. "At least they got the color right."

Malin, meanwhile, was holding a gown of deep blues and verdant greens. The fabric shimmered with an inner light, catching the soft glow of the room's lamps. It was fitted and elegant, with long, flowing sleeves that hinted at a grace she hadn't felt in a long time.

"It's beautiful," she whispered, a sense of wonder in her voice. "But... a dress? We are literally just hanging around with the kids. Attire does not need to be so fancy, and it is atrocious for fighting in."

Will chuckled, stepping behind her and wrapping his arms around her waist, his chin resting on her shoulder. "Good," he murmured against her skin. "For tonight, you don't have to. You've done enough fighting for one day." He paused, then pressed a kiss to her temple. "Besides, I'll be there to take care of anyone who tries anything. Don't you worry, Sparks. I'll make sure you don't have to lift a finger."

She smiled, leaning back into his embrace. "A gentleman and a bodyguard? You really are a man of many talents, Will Hawkson."

"Only for you," he said, his voice deep and sincere, before planting another kiss on her lips.

"Come on. Let's check on the kids. How do you think Kobold is handling his first job at childcare?" Will grinned, nudging her with his elbow as he started toward the door.

442

JOURNEY TO ALORIA

CHAPTER 33 – WILL

The feel of the formal jacket and vest, paired with the matching black shirt buttoned to his neck, felt impossibly constricting. Will hated dressing like this; the stiff fabric and tailored lines were a stark contrast to his usual practical gear. But he was all too familiar with Elven court politics.

Malin had tried to get out of going, to spend time with the kids, but Aldrik had explained that Elven politics required someone from his line to attend or it would reflect on Anariel.

Caelum had been more than happy to volunteer to watch the kids for the event in their new quarters, which Malin and he would move into tomorrow. Tonight, they were still in their original suite.

These mini events, these seemingly innocuous dinners, were like intricate chess moves, and performing poorly could be costly. The last thing he wanted was to cause his friends issues, especially not with the weight of Elowen's condition hanging over them.

He resolved to behave at his best in the crowded room, filled with Mellryn's highest-level busybodies, as well as people from around the kingdom, including a small contingents from Lumara and Aloria.

The walk down to the grand dining area of the castle was not far, but it felt like an eternity. Out of the corner of his eye, he noticed a pair of blonde heads peeking through the servants' curtains, his two rascals, no doubt. They were told to stay in the room with Caelum, but he knew them better than that. Sure enough, he saw Caelum's face behind them before they disappeared.

He would enjoy teasing Kobold about the joys of parenting in the morning.

He glanced at Malin beside him, and the low hum of anxiety in his chest momentarily faded, replaced by something akin to awe. "I thought you looked gorgeous that night at the bar, but you look utterly amazing right now," he admired, his voice a low rumble.

Her dress was made of Elven silk, in deep reds that shimmered with an almost liquid quality, making it appear as if living flames flickered across her form. It was perfectly fitted, hugging every curve, and seemed to move with her, rather than on her. Paired with strappy black heels, and offset by white stone earrings, a delicate necklace, and a simple tiara nestled in her pale blonde hair, she didn't just look elegant. She radiated power that transcended the silk and jewels. She might be human, but she was also part Elf, and from the looks of the gossips' faces, she was the talk of the town at the moment.

A hint of a smile played on her lips. "Not too bad yourself. You clean up pretty well. I'd almost think you were civilized," she teased, a playful glint in her eyes.

The easy banter was a welcome anchor in the swirling anxiety he knew she must be feeling.

Moments later, they stood at the threshold of the grand dining hall. A court herald, an Elf with a booming, melodic voice, stepped forward. "Presenting… Duchess Malin Rauno of House Trillium and her spouse!"

Will felt a jolt. *Duchess? House Trillium?*

He had somehow forgotten about the royalty part.

The thought was almost comical amidst the formal absurdity of it all. He knew General Rauno was a Lord and cousin to Lady Anariel, who was future queen of the throne… but this was a different level of recognition entirely. His eyes tracked her, catching her expression as she took in the lavish hall.

With all the opulence and grandeur, he couldn't stop staring at her. She captured his attention. Her initial playful composure had given way to genuine astonishment.

"Are all Elven events like this? This is amazing," Malin whispered, her voice filled with a hushed wonder.

Will followed her gaze, taking it all in through her reaction. He watched her eyes widen, captivated by the spectacle of the hall, and found himself almost seeing it anew through her awe. Towering, living trees formed the very pillars, their branches heavy with glowing orbs that cast a soft, ethereal light across the chamber. The walls, seamlessly carved from glittering, iridescent stone, seemed to hum with ancient, raw power that Will could feel a subtle pull from, even if he didn't fully understand it. Elaborate carvings adorned every surface, depicting scenes of Elven history and nature, spiraling upwards towards the impossibly high ceilings. He had been to the castle several times before. Seeing it through her eyes was like seeing it for the first time.

Below them, a single, impossibly long table stretched down the center of the hall, easily capable of seating almost a hundred people. It was set in a formal style that bespoke centuries of tradition, a stark contrast to the rough-and-tumble inns and hidden camps Will was used to.

Crystal goblets shimmered, reflecting the soft light from the glowing orbs, and the table itself was laden with an array of vibrant, plant-based dishes that looked more like works of art than actual food.

Another Elven eccentricity, he mused, a flicker of his usual cynicism stirring. The court itself was a dazzling display of Elven finery, hushed conversations weaving through the chamber like delicate music, a world away from the chaos they'd just escaped.

He watched Malin's face, seeing the sheer wonder that painted her features, but also the subtle tension around her eyes, the faint tremor in her hand as she unknowingly gripped his arm. This grand display was a gilded cage for her right now, he knew. She was there, playing the part, her mother lay comatose, and she was not a fan of eyes watching her. Every forced smile, every polite nod she'd have to make, would cost her. And watching her endure it, for the sake of these political niceties, only solidified his resolve to tear through every obstacle and bring their family back together, so she'd never have to pretend again.

Malin, even as the center of attention, appeared utterly captivated, a warrior of fire dropped into a world of polished, ancient elegance. Will almost chuckled. She looked like she belonged, even if she didn't realize it yet.

"This is incredible," Malin murmured, her eyes still wide. "So... where's Lady Anariel?"

As if on cue, a sudden, clear blast of horns echoed through the hall, reverberating off the stone and wood. All conversation ceased. The herald from before, joined by two others, stepped to the center of the central archway.

"Hear ye! Hear ye!" one of them boomed, his voice carrying effortlessly. "Presenting Lady Anariel, First in Line to the Sun Throne, Protector of Mellyrn, and Heir Apparent of the Elven Kingdoms with her consorts Sir Nar Warden and Sir Khelek Warden!"

The grand archway shimmered with subtle magic and glowed brighter. Through it, Lady Anariel entered, a figure of regal grace, yet with a noticeable tremor in her composure that Will's sharp eyes caught. She was flanked on either arm by Nar and Khelek. He could tell neither of them was a fan of this; they, like he and Aldrik, were men of action. These political games were almost as challenging as waging an outmatched battle.

Anariel herself was stunning in a gown of deep emerald, her silver hair braided with glittering strands that resembled moonlight. Her violet eyes, the shade of spring blooms, swept across the assembled court, then lit up as they landed on Malin. A genuine, radiant smile touched her lips, transforming her regal bearing into something warm and almost human.

She began a graceful descent into the hall, not rushing, but moving with a purpose that drew all eyes. Her path seemed to be an unerring line towards Malin.

As she drew near, the court held its breath, curious about the unexpected arrivals.

When Anariel reached them, her smile widened for Malin. She released Nar and Khelek, extending both hands towards Malin. Malin, understanding instinctively, met her grasp. Anariel then drew Malin closer, gently pressing her forehead against Malin's in the traditional Elven greeting. The gesture was brief, yet profound, an intimate moment shared amidst the watchful eyes of the court.

Will, meanwhile, moved instinctively towards Nar and Khelek. He didn't offer a handshake; instead, with a wry, understanding grin, he locked elbows with both men in a silent, warrior's greeting that bypassed the formal niceties.

Nar's strained smile returned a flicker of its old humor, and Khelek managed to make a nod of weary camaraderie.

Anariel then gestured towards the long, glittering table. "Please, join us."

She led the way to the head of the table. She indicated the seating with a subtle motion of her hand.

Malin found herself gently guided to a seat between Nar and Will, with Khelek directly across from them, taking his place on Anariel's other side, with her at the head of the table. Will held her chair for Malin, as Khelek did for Anariel, then took their seats.

The soft clinking of cutlery and the resumption of hushed conversation around them felt almost deafening after the quiet intimacy of their greetings.

The moment they settled, Anariel leaned forward, her earlier regal composure giving way to a more urgent, concerned expression; her voice dropped to a low, focused tone, audible only to their small group. "You found the children?" Her gaze flickered to Malin, a silent question in her eyes. "Nar and Khelek said they have some exciting stories to tell. I'm excited to hear them. I was very disappointed when they informed me that I had to miss your arrival."

Will saw the look of genuine concern and affection Anariel had for Malin, and a soft smile touched his lips. He squeezed Malin's hand under the table before speaking.

"We found them," he said, his voice brimming with a palpable relief that still hadn't fully left him. He gave Anariel a knowing glance. "And those 'exciting stories' are an understatement. Apparently, our kids have a knack for making friends in high places." He chuckled softly, the memory of Zee hugging a dragon still fresh in his mind. "I think you'll find their adventures a bit more… unbelievable than your average Elven tale. They started telling us this afternoon. They seem almost unbelievable that they could pack that much excitement into only a week."

Anariel responded with a weary smile, a flicker of genuine sadness in her eyes. "I'm looking forward to hearing them myself… if my captors, I mean the Ministers, will allow." She sighed, a deep, heavy sound that seemed to carry the weight of a thousand years. "There is so much to be done for the coronation. I feel like I have so little of my own time."

"Once you officially are crowned… can't you do something to improve some of those rules and expectations?" Will interjected, gesturing vaguely around the opulent hall with a slight tilt of his head. "Seems like a lot of fancy clothes and strict traditions, not much actual power to… do what you want." He couldn't help but voice the observation, the entire elaborate display feeling like a gilded cage.

He glanced at Malin beside him. She was still taking it all in, her expression a mix of wide-eyed wonder and a faint, almost imperceptible tension. He knew she felt the absurdity of it, the way this dazzling world could also feel suffocating, like a beautifully crafted trap. He luckily had avoided it most of his life, but he had to learn it at some point in his work with the Resistance.

Anariel let out a short, humorless laugh. "You speak more truth than you know, Will Hawkson. It feels like a punishment." Her gaze swept over the glimmering hall, a weariness settling over her features that the light couldn't quite hide. "I was so grateful to my brother. He wanted this. He lived for this. I live for the adventure, with my loves by my side. You would think that with all the power that comes with the position, there would be some point where you can say what you want to do, and it is done. Apparently, not within the Elven courts."

Khelek, from across the table, sighed. "For the people, it must be, Anariel. The balance of the realm depends on it."

Will watched Anariel, picking up on the subtle tension in her jaw.

He leaned slightly forward. "Maybe," he suggested, his voice thoughtful, "maybe the right ruler hasn't been in place to correct Elven politics and improve some of those distasteful rules."

Malin, who had been listening intently, her gaze flitting between Will and Anariel, leaned forward slightly as well. "Or maybe," she interjected, her voice carrying a quiet force that cut through the elegant hum of the hall, "the Elven courts have simply forgotten what it means to have a Queen who actually leads instead of just presides. True leadership isn't about rigid tradition; it's about making things better for the people, even if it means breaking a few rules." Her eyes, bright with conviction, met Anariel's.

Anariel's eyes danced between Will and Malin, a genuinely amused, crooked smile touching her lips. "Ah, Will Hawkson," she said, her voice a low murmur, "you always were one to question authority. And it seems you've found a partner who is even better at it."

The meal was served. The food was art itself, each course a testament to Elven culinary skill. Will took a bite of a shimmering, deep purple fruit, and his mouth exploded with flavors, almost magical in their intensity.

"Anariel," he declared, his voice carrying clearly but not disrupting the elegant hum of conversation, "Your chefs need a raise. This is beyond amazing."

Malin, her eyes wide with a genuine, almost childlike wonder, murmured, "Amazing doesn't even begin to cover it. I... I've never tasted anything like this. It's like every flavor is an experience, a masterpiece. This isn't just food; it's... magic on a plate." Her gaze swept the array of dishes, a profound appreciation on her face that transcended mere hunger.

"There are some perks of the position. This food is one of them," Nar acknowledged, his mouth full, a slight grimace of effort as he chewed.

The sight of it elicited a soft giggle from Malin beside Will. He loved to hear her laugh; the sound was a rare, precious thing in their lives lately.

The rest of the meal was equally impressive, with four other courses, each more exquisite than the last.

Between glances at Malin, who seemed to be genuinely enjoying the food and company despite the underlying tension, Will's mind was occupied with the children, and he could tell by the look on Malin's face that she could use some time without as many people around.

Elowen was still unconscious. Aldrik had wanted to leave that day. He had convinced him to wait until they had a more solid plan... and until he could convince Malin not to go on the mission.

Their soul-bond had gotten stronger, and he could feel the tension and concern within her. He wasn't sure how it would feel when their bond fully connected, and their mental connections were so in-tune.

Thinking of their connection made him realize how little time they had, of late, alone. He could use some time with her… without that dress. This last thought was enough to prompt him to say something.

"As much as I'm loving this time," Will began, leaning slightly towards Anariel, his voice low, "I would like to end early. I know it's a huge issue if I get up before you… Any chance I can convince you to move on sooner?" Will asked Anariel.

Anariel's eyes twinkled with a hint of amusement. "Of course, but you will need to go out on the dance floor for at least a couple of dances, or risk more of those issues you are hoping to avoid." A small smile played on her lips.

"Dancing? I don't know any of these dances. Do we have to?" Malin's eyes widened with apprehension.

"No worries, Sparks. I got you," he said, taking her hand and squeezing it reassuringly. "I had to learn them for a mission once. I won't let you down."

The memory of that particular mission, involving an overly enthusiastic ambassador and a surprisingly demanding waltz, made him suppress a grin.

Anariel nodded, satisfied. "I will try to see you after the coronation. I'm looking forward to getting that part of the transition out of the way," She paused, her gaze resting on Nar and Khelek.

She reached out and touched each of their hands. At that, Anariel stood gracefully, causing the rest of the huge table to fall silent for a moment. All eyes were on her.

"I welcome you all to an evening of dance," she announced, her voice clear and resonant.

Then, she turned, taking an arm each from Nar and Khelek, and moved with a dignified yet purposeful stride towards the gleaming dance floor that had materialized from the center of the hall, as if the very stone parted for her. The rest of the table began moving and talking amongst themselves again, the spell broken.

Will stood and held his hand out to Malin, "Shall we, Duchess…" He broke out laughing at the snort she let out upon hearing the title. "What about? Hey Sparks, wanna dance?" He pulled her chair out and helped her to her feet.

Taking her hand, he walked her to the dance floor, then twirled her, pulling her tight into his arms. Flushed and taken aback by his sudden move, she caught her breath.

He leaned in, his voice a low growl in his best rough tone, "I told you I have this covered."

He then began leading her into a sensual dance with twirls and dips, matching the intricate, flowing movements of the other Elves on the dance floor. The way her face flushed and how their bodies moved in sync naturally made her one of the most beautiful women in the room. All eyes seemed to be on her as he coaxed the enjoyment out of her, a genuine smile replacing her earlier apprehension.

As the song was ending, Will maneuvered them to dance close to the trio and said to them, "Good choice in song selection." They just smiled knowingly in response.

"The latest trend in Elven courts," Anariel cooed, a sly glint in her eyes. "Magically infused Aphrodisiac music."

The next song began, slow and soulful, featuring a haunting Elven singer. The focus was on the music itself, not the dancing, so no choreographed moves were needed for this one. Will could focus solely on her. He pulled her close, their bodies touching, and they swayed together, lost in the melody.

"It's like your kitchen in Media," he murmured, his lips brushing her ear. "I knew from that dance… maybe even before that… that you had me under a spell. You are my weakness… and I wouldn't have it any other way." Her face lit up at his words, and the sheer beauty of it made him catch his breath.

"I don't think you realize how completely stunning you are," he said, the honesty just pouring out, unfiltered. She blushed, a deep crimson spreading across her cheeks.

"As much as I would love to hold you in my arms on this dance floor and see how many times, I can make you giggle with each turn or dip," he growled in her ear, his voice dropping to a husky whisper, "I can think of better ways to spend our evening. Maybe with less layers between us, I can see how many times I can make you scream my name instead." She flushed even deeper, and he noticed her nipples strain visibly against the thin fabric of her dress.

Feeling her desire from him through their bond made him want her that much more.

"I do love the way you think sometimes," she purred back at him, her voice equally low and suggestive, as she gyrated against him to the music.

This woman was going to be the death of him.

He instantly looked for Anariel. Their dance was hypnotic and in pure synchronization, speaking of sex and pleasure. He caught the eye of Nar, who nodded back, a knowing smirk on his face. Nar whispered something to Anariel and Khelek, and they turned to look at Will, a shared expression of amusement and understanding crossing their faces. They paused from their dance to walk over, all equally flushed, though perhaps for different reasons.

Anariel immediately pulled Malin into a warm hug, then finished with the traditional good-bye, pressing her forehead to Malin's.

Meanwhile, Nar and Khelek both reached for Will, shaking elbows and pulling him close, touching foreheads in a gesture of profound acceptance. "Bran'ael," they said to him as they parted, their voices gruff with emotion.

Brother.

When the word truly dawned on him, its full weight and meaning, a genuine, unrestrained joy lit up his face. "Bran'ael," he said back, his voice thick with a sudden, unexpected emotion.

He truly appreciated this family, that, though not in blood, they were all connected in spirit.

On the walk to their chambers, the intoxicating scent of Malin's perfume, mingled with the lingering hint of the "aphrodisiac music," was a potent torment. Will's mind replayed her flushed face, the way her body had moved against his, the subtle strain of her nipples against the thin fabric of her dress.

He couldn't stop thinking of how good it would be to touch her skin, to taste her, to quench this burning need for her finally. His hands, resting at her waist, instinctively roamed, his thumbs brushing upwards, teasing her taut nipples every so often. The urge to simply scoop her up and carry her into their room, to bypass every shred of courtly pretense, became almost unbearable.

A servant waited outside their door, holding it open with a polite, expectant air.

"Thank you, but your services are no longer needed for the night," Will growled, his voice rougher than he intended, the words clipped with impatience.

Before the servant could even register his dismissal, Will lifted Malin into his arms, carrying her easily over the threshold. With a decisive swing of his foot, he kicked the door shut, leaving the open-mouthed servant to whatever impropriety they might gossip about. He didn't care. This was his wife. He would suffer whatever consequences of formal breach he had to. He wanted his wife, and he wanted her urgently.

He walked quickly through the small sitting area and into the bedroom, kicking that inner door shut with a solid thud. Setting Malin gently on her feet next to the bed, he let his gaze roam over her, a silent appreciation of the Elven silk now clinging to her curves. With a slow, deliberate motion, he ran his hands up and down her silk-covered body, savoring the whisper of the fabric beneath his palms. He could see the goosebumps rising on her skin and felt her shiver under his touch.

He plucked each thin strap off her shoulders, then inched the shimmering red gown down her form. The fabric caught briefly on her erect nipples before sliding down to expose her breasts completely, before sliding to the floor, forming a pool at her feet like discarded flames.

He watched as her breath hitched, her chest rising and falling more rapidly. He gasped at the final reveal, feeling the pulse of his need hammering through his much too tight pants as she stood in only jewels, panties, and heels.

He shouldered off his jacket and vest, dropping them unceremoniously to the floor. The cufflinks flew off, in his haste, and after removing the tie and seeing how difficult unbuttoning the top button was, he proceeded to rip the rest of the shirt buttons open, hearing the clink of them hit the floor.

"Trouble," she toyed, as she stroked his trapped length.

Her touch felt like electricity under his skin, and his only response was a deep growl as he threw the shirt to the ground.

She reached for his pants and began unbuttoning them, revealing to Malin exactly how much he needed this. She grabbed his length and stroked. The sensation was electric, forcing him to close his eyes and catch his breath. He was able to free his feet from his shoes and pull off his pants.

Standing there, both almost naked, his hands roamed her body, realizing that her underwear still blocked his desired access with the barely-there fabric. His hands coaxed them down her hips, letting them drop to her heels, where she stepped out of them. His hands reached her ass, and the curves in his hands felt so right. Everything about her body felt so right as she undulated into him, pulsing her tongue lightly against his lips with each press.

He lifted her, moving her body to the middle of the bed. Pressing their bodies close, he plunged his tongue deep, thinking of how good it would feel when he could plunge deep in her, allowing his fingers to trace down her curves. She tried to sit up, but he held her down lightly.

"Tonight is not your turn to be Bossy. Tonight, you will do what I need you to do," although it came out as a raspy order, he looked to her to make sure she agreed. He would take his power back from them. He would find his joy again with the woman he loves. He could feel the magic within him crying out for her, to make them whole.

She lay back and waited, circling her hips against his hands.

His fingers entered her as she spread her hips for him. She was already wet for him. He had missed this. He was going to savor this feeling. This was not him being used, but of mutual pleasure... and he was in control. He wanted to taste her to confirm it was her.

When she closed her eyes, he corrected, "I want you to keep those eyes open for me, so I know it is you."

He stopped her feeble attempts at helping, his hands sliding down her smooth, trembling leg with deliberate slowness. His fingers lingered on the delicate curve of her ankle, unstrapping one heel, then the other, letting them drop to the ground with a thud that echoed through the room like a drumbeat. The sound was nothing compared to the pounding of her heart, racing in anticipation of what was to come. He placed a pillow beneath her waist, elevating her hips just enough to give him the perfect angle. His eyes darkened with hunger as he traced down each leg, spreading them wide, exposing the slick, glistening folds. The sight was enough to make his cock throb.

He didn't waste another second. His mouth descended, his tongue flicking out to taste her sweetness, circling her swollen clit with expert precision.

She gasped, her body arching off the bed as pleasure shot through her like a lightning bolt. He devoured her, his tongue plunging deep inside her, fucking her with relentless strokes that had her moaning his name over and over.

Her hands fisted in his hair, pulling him closer, demanding more. He gave it to her, stopping only to tease her with whispered promises of what was to come, making her beg for release. Her body convulsed, her orgasm ripped through her. But he wasn't done with her yet.

Her legs trembled as he moved up her body, his length pressing against her soaked entrance. He hesitated for a moment, savoring the feel of her heat of her entrance against his tip, then plunged in, burying himself to the hilt in one smooth stroke. She gasped, her nails digging into his back as he stretched her open, filling her completely.

He paused, "I'm not going to hurt the baby? Am I?"

She chuckled. "No. Let that baby know Daddy's knocking," she teased, still locking her eyes with his.

He moved with slow, deliberate thrusts. Staring deep into her eyes, looking for any sign of illusions, his mind and magic both clinging to her and needing to have that confirmation that it was Malin. He knew when each thrust hit that sweet spot deep inside her. When she let out that sweet moan, he loved hearing it.

His hips rocked against hers. As much as she said going deep wasn't a problem, he was still concerned about being gentle with her. She wrapped her legs around him, pulling him closer, begging him to go harder, faster. Finally, pleasure outweighed concern, and he obliged, his thrusts becoming rougher, more desperate, as they chased their pleasure together.

The sound of flesh slapping against flesh filled the room, mingling with her desperate moans and his guttural groans. He knew he was close, but he didn't want this to end.

"Fuck me harder," she begged, her voice shaking with need.

He loved that she only used that filthy mouth with him. That was his undoing. He couldn't wait anymore.

He growled, slamming into her with a force that had her screaming his name, her body convulsing with another earth-shattering orgasm. He followed right behind her, pulsing as he came deep inside her, filling her with his seed, staring straight into her eyes.

They didn't have power over him anymore; his witch did. They collapsed together, their bodies slick with sweat, their chests heaving as they tried to catch their breath. He pressed a kiss to her trembling lips, his eyes watering at the thought that she was his answer, that they were dead, and she was all he would ever need.

"Are you okay?" she asked, brushing her hand across his jaw.

"That is something that no illusion could ever come close to. I'm more than okay, because of you. You… You are my soul. I don't think I can ever get enough of you. I love you so much," he rasped in a whisper in her ear.

The soul-bond tattoo on her arm glowed, and he could feel the one on his shoulder tingling. It was electric energy, a million voices speaking all at once. As his fingers touched her, he could feel the sensation through her. Their connection was growing.

If he could figure out how to get it solidified immediately, he would. This woman was all he would ever need in his life.

He brushed the hair away from her face, she smiled and said, "I love you too. I fought the feeling within myself, worrying that we were rushing things, that the magic was the only thing bringing us together, but the second I thought you were in trouble… I knew. I knew that you were the only one who ever wanted to touch me like that. The only one I ever want to have by my side and the only one that I want to raise our family with."

"At first, I didn't want to go tonight. We just got the kids back… surely that should mean something to the courts. It seemed silly, but I think we needed this too. The music might have helped… Our bond has been growing, but tonight… If it would let me… I would bond to you forever. You are all I ever want and all I will ever need," he vowed.

He drew her back to him and pulled her close, not wanting to let her go. His hand wrapped over her, naturally cupping her breast. She fit perfectly beside him.

He fell asleep with her in his arms, knowing that they would leave early as planned to find the kids safe and healthy. Then, regardless of whether they went to Aloria or stayed here in Mellyrn, they would be family.

CHAPTER 34 – MALIN

Malin couldn't take her eyes off her family. They were in awe of the grandeur, standing beside Caelum, who looked out of place. The kids had complained about getting dressed up, but Ellie looked like a princess in gossamer whites and frills, while Zee looked like a miniature version of Will in his formal attire.

Aldrik, who could not remove the cross look from his face, no matter the occasion, had been forced to attend the ceremony. As the Lord of the House of Trillium, his not attending, even with his consort's health in question, would not have been accepted by the courts. He looked quite formidable and dashing with his silver hair against his all-black formal attire.

As the sun began to dip below the horizon, it painted the sky in hues of orange and purple. The air in the grand hall thrummed with the solemn weight of tradition, mingling with the scent of polished wood and fresh flowers. Malin stood beside Will, whose mostly black formal attire was accented by silk touches that matched her light blue, silken ensemble. Caelum and the children stood silent sentinels a few steps behind them, their place of honor within the assembly of nobility and dignitaries feeling both earned and surreal.

"I knew your rooms were well placed, but I didn't realize you were royalty?" Caelum asked wide-eyed.

"Well…" she sputtered, uncomfortable with the thought.

"Yes. She is royalty," Will confirmed.

Her gaze, however, kept drifting from the ceremonial procession to her children, standing a little distance away with Nar and Khelek, their faces scrubbed clean and bright, eyes wide with the spectacle. Ellie fidgeted slightly, nudging Zee, who seemed more interested in the intricate carvings on a nearby pillar.

Malin's mind, despite the grandeur surrounding her, felt like a turbulent sea. Her mother, still trapped in that unresponsive state, was a constant, aching worry. She would have loved this... all the pageantry and politics were right up her alley.

Twice, she had found the men planning their next steps without her. She found herself idly wondering which impossible mission, which *suicide mission* would be the most effective. Whichever one they selected, they had better include her in the plans. They had also not spoken of the plans to deal with the potential assassin attack of Mellryn. There was no place safe.

She had spent the last few hours speaking with the historians. She didn't even have a clue what Mednik meant by Feniks Talavo. The Minsters translated it to be Phoenix Rising, but they couldn't find any information about it. They had suggested that the libraries of Aloria were well known to have prophesies from around the world.

Anariel had also suggested that she would need to travel as the Mellryn Queen to Aloria to continue that alliance formally. She asked if they could travel with her, and they unanimously agreed, though the plan was to leave after they had woken her mother up. She was looking forward to

Her healing abilities had a terrifying flip side, a darkness she barely understood, and a part of her feared that to save her mother, she might have to delve even deeper into that terrifying power.

Then, a different thought, sharp and clear, cut through her anxieties. The Tomes. The Tomes of Moreth from the Fellspire Citadel. They were Will's bargaining chip with the assassins. The Order needed them. They needed them to stop the relentless pursuit that still shadowed Will's life, that could, even now, reach out and snatch their newfound peace. The Overlords who once ran Media had retreated to Fellspire, masters of ritualistic and rune magic. It was a place teeming with danger, but perhaps one that held answers. They needed an EMP, and that was the only place they could think of where they could find one. The Resistance had been trying to get one for years.

She subtly leaned closer to Will, her voice a low murmur, barely audible over the swelling anticipation in the hall. "Will," she whispered, her eyes still on Lady Anariel, who was now approaching the High Throne. "She looks amazing up there. I know she doesn't want it, but she was born for this." Malin's hand found his, and she squeezed it, a silent testament to her admiration.

But as Malin looked from the shimmering crown that was about to be placed on Lady Anariel's head, to Will's steady, strong profile, and then to her children, laughing softly at something Caelum whispered, a profound warmth spread through her chest. The fear for her mother, the daunting mission to Fellspire, the threat of assassins… so much of the unknown that surrounded her, but these seemed small in comparison to what she had.

It wasn't forced on her.

This was a family she had chosen, ragtag as they were. They were everything she needed.

She felt like the luckiest woman alive. Despite the trials and looming threats, they were together. The bond with Will, forged in fire and deepened by shared parenthood, felt unbreakable. Ellie and Zee, safe beside them, their laughter echoing like pure music in the grand hall, represented a future. A future that would include a new life.

She couldn't imagine what it would bring, but for the first time in a long time, the uncertainty didn't paralyze her. It galvanized her.

The coming months would be challenging, as they find the solution for her mother, find a way to appease the Order of Tamris, avoid the Media guards, and finally get to Aloria, even if it was for Mellryn business and to visit their libraries.

Either way, she would have her family with her, and that was all she cared about.

Be On The Look Out For...

Welcome to Aloria is Book 3 in the Series, where…

The saga of Will and Malin continues with their found family always in their minds.

To steal items, an artifact and a bomb, from the Overlords in Fellspire Citadel, a near-impenetrable fortress. Once they steal the artifact, they must try to convince the Order of Tamris to trade it in exchange for not killing Will, but what will happen if they get their hands on it.

It turns out that Malin may be the prophecy Feniks Talavo, or Phoenix Rising, according to the dragons. She will have to travel to Aloria, to visit the libraries to discover the truth.

Caelum has decided he wants to get to know his daughter, but is he more than he seems? Where do his loyalties lie?

With both Malin and Anariel expecting babies, how will this affect life?

BONUS CHAPTERS & CONTENT

Following this, there is a bonus chapter from Caelum's perspective. It shows his point of view when he first sees Malin again.

My website will have additional short stories and Novellas that are now being developed, including the Prequel novella of Will and Lydia stealing the Tomes of Moreth from Will's point of view.

If I have time, I have a YA Fantasy Novel of Will's first kiss and his first kill, set when Will is in high school, when Malin and Will meet each other for the first time, though it is a brief meeting, and they don't realize it.

As I just found out that I am going to be a grandmother, I'm going to write the stories of Ellie and Zee into a series of Fantasy novels in the Draco mountains.

The website, www.brandystoker.com will have the additional Bonus Chapters and Content, as well as other bonus items developed for Resistance members.

Bonus Content will include:

- Additionally, a collection of larger full-color map
- Links to Merchandise
- Character Art and illustrations
- Book Club Discussion Guides for each of my books.
- As well as any fan-submitted art, I would like all my fans' abilities to be highlighted if possible.

Caelum sees Malin

Caelum had gotten word that the Marid had found a human barely alive on their shores; surely, there was some reward money from someone if he was able to bring them back safely. He recalled there were several rare herbs in that area that he had a buyer in Gosual for. It never hurt to see Clorsha again. She was one of the best parts of going to the Marid village, even if the village elders didn't approve.

He had the message from Khun MorBaan, the village elder and healer, a few days ago, so his arrival at the village didn't take him as much time as he thought. If the human was in as bad a condition as the note said, they were weeks away from being able to leave, but it would give him more time with Clorsha.

He found Khun standing outside her hut when he arrived, her expression placid and her gaze ancient. The two exchanged pleasantries, and Khun gestured to the hut, her voice low.

Caelum's interest was only partial, though it peaked slightly when he found out it was a woman. He might convince her to give him some reward of a more physical nature from her if he couldn't collect financially.

Caelum stepped to the doorway and peered inside.

Then he saw her.

Malin.

The sight of Malin, bruised and pale but unmistakably her, hit him like a physical blow. His breath hitched, a memory of her laughter and her smile in his mind. It had been eight years since he had seen her from a distance and almost twelve since he had spoken with her. He was going to marry her. He had proposed and everything, then his whole world changed. He had loved the freedom from Media rules and the security of being part of the Resistance, but she was the one thing he missed from his old life.

To this day, he had never felt that way for another woman, and the sight of her, a ghost from his past… it shattered his carefully constructed detachment. He had to know if she was okay, not just for the reward, but for the selfish need to have her back in his life.

"Will she be okay?" he asked Kuhn.

He saw movement, then heard her as she barely breathed out, "Caelum." Her eyes fluttered open, the same ice blue eyes he had fallen in love with at the beginning of college.

She looked at him, then her breath hitched. "You… You can't be here? You're dead," she spat as she sat up quickly. She shook her head a few times and blinked. She slowly and tentatively reached out, her hand trembling. Her fingers brushed his cheek. "Is it really you?" she whispered.

"Malin. I never thought I'd see you again." He pulled her to a stand, then into a deep embrace. He pulled back, holding her at arm's length, his gaze searching hers.

Tears welled in her eyes. "You're alive! How? What happened?"

Caelum's smile was bittersweet. "It's a long story, Doc. We have plenty of time to catch up."

She wouldn't want to hear the real truth right now, he didn't even know how much she knew about the world she thought she knew back in Media. He needed to wait to find out what she knew first, so he changed the subject and stated, "Khun said you were healing quickly. When they reached out to me, they told me the human was injured so badly they expected you to be in recovery for months." He looked at her in awe. "You have powers?"

She pulled her hand from his, letting it hover between them. "I… I was chipped. And I got my chip out not long ago. I have powers now. I can heal, but I also have this," she said, her voice firm with conviction. She created a small, crimson fireball ignited in her palm, then quickly extinguished it.

He stepped back, his eyes wide. "Malin," he breathed, a genuine shock in his voice. "That is… incredible." Scary actually. He had never seen a human with powers that were so strong. Sounds like Malin. She couldn't help but excel in everything she did.

Malin pulled away. "Why didn't you come back?" she questioned, the words sharp. "Why did they think you were dead? Why didn't you try to even get word to me, to anyone?"

The silence that followed was heavy, broken only by the distant, rhythmic pounding of the waves against the shores nearby.

Caelum shifted in discomfort. He needed to explain the uncomfortable truth of his sacrifice. "Malin, it's… complicated. After I left for that last supply run, things went wrong. Very wrong. I was captured, held in places I couldn't escape, couldn't send word to you. I barely survived. They made sure I couldn't communicate, and I had no way to know if anyone would even look for me, or if it would put you in more danger. I had found out that Media had orders to kill me on sight, so I knew I couldn't come back. I didn't want to risk your safety by sending you a message." His voice was low, carefully modulated, and guarded.

 He hoped she believed it. It was the truth, though adjusted a bit for the audience.

"And you?" he asked. "What happened? After I left... what happened that made you leave Media? Was it the powers?"

Malin met his gaze. "My powers made it too dangerous, eventually. My mother left with us."

"Your Mom left Media?" His eyes widened. He never expected the mighty Resistance leader to leave. He had only found out much later that was the role she played. He wondered if Malin knew.

"She told me you were in the Resistance," Malin stated.

She knew. He wondered for how long.

"Can I take you somewhere? I travel extensively and would be able to get you anywhere you needed, even Aloria." He could help her and be her hero again.

"I have someone on their way here. He will be able to help with that, but…" she said.

He knew it. It's probably her husband, he thought as he pressed his lips into a grimace and rubbed the back of his neck.

"…having another person would be great. First, we must go find someone."

"So, you have a plan?" he asked, hoping to find an opportunity to spend more time with her.

Before she could say anything, he noticed the color draining from her face. He didn't want to press her.

Kuhn suggested that he give her space to let her rest and see her the next day, then ushered him out the door of the hut.

He wanted to spend time with her, but… tomorrow would be fine. His mind flew with all the things he wanted to ask her as he walked to Clorsha's hut.

When he arrived, Clorsha was in the middle of speaking with two other Madrid. She stopped mid-sentence and walked away from them, greeting him with a warm, genuine smile on her face, then walked them into her hut and closed the door. He loved seeing how her gills flared with excitement when she saw him. It was like he was the best person on the planet.

"Caelum, you're back!" she said, her voice a melodic hum translated by the humm worm. "When I heard they called you for the human, I knew you would come for me." She was the only person on this whole crazy planet that got excited to see him, without having to pay them. It took a while to get used to the gills and scales, but she adored taking care of him and she did so, so well. He had a good imagination and it was a dark room, he usually pictured a host of women he had seen or had in her place.

He took her into his arms, a sense of relief washing over him. It was likely the pheromones the Madrid gave off when they were spawning, but he felt so confident and assured when she was in his arms.

"I'm here now," he murmured, his gaze sweeping over her face.

In all his travels and all his other women, Clorsha was the best, due largely because she was an empath; she knew exactly what he needed. She looked at him with an intensity that made him feel powerful and needed, and for a moment, the chaotic day with Malin was gone.

"You look tired," she said, her hands gently touching his face. "Let me help you."

"I could use a distraction," he admitted, a small, weary smile on his face. She poured him a cup of ceremonial aphrodisiac wine, which he downed quickly.

He knew she would see this as a sign of their deepening connection, a sign that their relationship was more serious than he let on. For him, it was a comfort that kept him coming back because of how she made him feel.

She disrobed him, then bid him to lie face down on the raised bed for his massage. He loved the Madrid sexual customs. She rubbed and washed his body down with her scrubs and salts, until every ounce of his travel filth was off of his body, rinsing it away as she went. The way she was so thorough and worked every muscle to relax, it felt amazing. After hiking for three weeks straight and sleeping in the dirt, Malin or not… he was not going to miss this… besides, there is nothing between Malin and him. Clorsha interrupted his thoughts of Malin enough to motion that she had finished his back and was ready for him to flip over.

When his cleaning was complete, as per Madrid custom, she proceeded to lick and kiss every inch of him, and she knew exactly where to touch to bring him to his erection. When he was ready, he stopped her and she bent over, asking him to enter her from behind.

Madrid didn't require long stimulation to climax, so he focused on his own enjoyment. She would cum. She did it every time. For now, he would close his eyes and imagine this was Malin he was fucking. He pounded into her over and over. Remembering her icy blue eyes and how he had been her first. He had taught her so many things to please him. The more he remembered about Malin, the more he wanted to keep going. Finally, he couldn't stop the waves as they overcame him, and he fell onto the narrow bed still connected to Clorsha.

That had been one of the most intense climaxes he had in a long time. It was Malin who had caused it. It was Malin that he wanted. They slept next to each other for a few hours, until thoughts of Malin got him hot again and he had to have Clorsha again.

As he had every morning since she got there, he spent his days calmly reminiscing with Malin and his nights wearing out his longing with Clorsha. Every morning, he carefully slipped out of Clorsha's hut and into his visitor hut. That morning was no different. He cleaned himself up and left her lying in the bed after he had once again had her.

As she was healing so quickly, he worried his timeline may be reduced. He had arranged to take Malin on a hike to learn about the local medicinal herbs. He was starting to get desperate. He knew she had someone coming soon and once they got there, he wouldn't have a chance. Up to then, she had shown no interest in rekindling their relationship. He felt confident that if she just felt that spark again… he would have a chance.

When he saw her walking around, she looked much healthier, and his heart skipped a beat. She looked almost the same as she did all those years ago. "Ready for your next lesson in medicinal herbs of this area?" he called out, his voice carrying easily over the lazy burble of the village.

She joined him with a nod, and together they followed the moss-lined path that wound through the tall fungal spires and down toward the narrow ribbon of beach where the jungle met the endless, green-tinted sea. The tide was low, exposing shelves of pinkish rock slick with brine and dotted with strange, spiky anemones.

He had spent all morning thinking about how he would convince her to be with him. In their first year of college, he had decided to win her over… it took him two years to break her down, but… it worked. He just needed to get her to remember how good they were together.

She had helped him get through college and his medicinal herbs classes. Back then, he only had books, but now he had a whole jungle, and he could impress her with how much he had learned since then. As they walked, he kept looking for opportunities to remind her. A few times, he felt his fingers brush hers, and he could feel the sparks from their touch; surely, she was just as moved.

When she had noticed the Solaferra root, he had hope. It was studying about that root where they had shared their first kiss.

When they turned a corner, there, half-buried in shadow, grew a single, enormous flower. Its petals were bright red, stalk thick as a child's arm, and stamens curling like gold wires.

"That's a bloodshade blossom," he said, with reverence. "Never seen one this close to the coast before."

She may hate him if she ever found out, but his impatience to feel that electric feeling of her touch was so intense that he made a rash decision. Bloodshade had several properties and was in demand, but the highest demand was at the Alorian courts, as it had extremely high concentrations of an aphrodisiac within it. The locals put it in their ceremonial wines, but he always assumed they traded with other tribes.

He just needed her to breathe in the fumes. He produced a small knife, flicked the blade open with practiced ease, and cut a sliver from the petal. "Watch," he said, holding the piece in his palm.

Malin leaned in, and he moved his hand close to her face. As planned, the cut edge began to ooze a silvery fluid, which bubbled and hissed in contact with the air. He could see her eyes dilate, showing him that it was taking effect.

She stepped back, shaking her head.

"I'm married, Caelum," she said, keeping her voice level.

The fact stung, but he wasn't here. "So, you've said. I'm just sharing botany." He had known chaste purists who jumped him shortly after the right dose of bloodshade. It only heightened their sexuality and loosened their inhibitions. She still wouldn't do anything she didn't want to do, and he wouldn't force her, but he hoped it would be enough to let her see how amazing they were together.

He waited, setting the petals aside, and stood, stretching the muscles in his back. He flexed and hoped she was watching. "I didn't mean to make you uncomfortable. I hope it didn't cause a reaction."

"Good. I'm feeling a bit unwell now. Maybe I should go back to the hut," she said. It had started to kick in.

"I'll look out for you. Let's head back just in case there is a reaction," he offered.

As they walked, he noticed that her balance was precarious, and he used that opportunity to reach out, putting his hands on her waist, that small, little waist and hips that were perfect handholds for him as he plowed into her. Her wobbling gave him extra reason to be there to touch her smooth skin.

He was getting turned on, and that would not work for his plan. He was starting to think this was not one of his most thought-through plans. He decided to focus their conversation on other topics, such as the failures of Media's educational system, the best way to treat a gut wound in the field, and the languages he spoke, since he knew Marid well. But he would steal glances whenever he thought she wasn't looking.

He began to kick himself for being so dumb. Of course, this wasn't going to work like this. She was smarter than that, and she had fireballs bigger than his fist.

They were almost back to the village, and she hadn't jumped him. He must not have given her the right dose, or she just wasn't interested. Maybe he could convince her to have a drink with him. The ceremonial liquor the council elders drank included bloodshade, as it affected Madrid differently. That was his last chance.

"It isn't any of my business, and you are welcome to see who you like... I saw you this morning," she said. "Leaving Clorsha's hut."

He hadn't expected that. He had been careful and had checked to ensure no one had seen him.

"That wasn't me," Caelum said, knowing that he couldn't have been seen... but... she must have. "Must have been someone else."

She stared at him. "You're the only tall human male in the area. And you were wearing that shirt." She gestured to the tan tunic, still half-unbuttoned.

He bristled, jaw tightening. "Maybe you saw wrong." He was caught. *Why was he so bothered by her knowing he was with Clorsha? Maybe she was jealous, which is a good sign. It was a sign that she might really have feelings for him.*

She said, "I didn't realize Clorsha had company. She told me she preferred to be alone."

"She does," Caelum snapped, a little too quickly. Then, softer: "I was just helping her with something." Years passed, of course, there would be other people.

The rest of the hike was quiet. When they got back to the camp, he was in a foul mood, but a quick fuck with Clorsha fixed it.

The person she was waiting for would be here soon. Tonight was his chance. He made his plan. It would happen at the fire tonight. He would show her how capable and how well he could protect her, and he would be his again.

The wood in the fire pit didn't agree with his plan, though, and everything he did was not making it light. His plans felt like they were crashing down when she lit the fire with her flame powers. It made him feel useless. What good was he too her with his limited powers?

With the fire started, he calmed himself down and focused on his plan. He found the ceremonial drink and poured some of it for both of them. He would need to be cautious, as he was already in the mood, and he wouldn't want to screw things up by crossing any of her lines.

After hours of reminiscing and enjoying each other's company, sitting with her next to the fire felt so right. They seemed to gravitate to each other, till their legs were touching. He wanted to believe she could feel it too.

"You are pretty special. You don't even realize how amazing you are. I just knew," he blushed with a soft laugh, as he stared at her lips. "I think that was always meant to be. We just got there slower than most. I didn't care how long it took as long as you would have me. I've never forgotten about you and often wished things had been different. I even considered facing the wrath of your father and heading back to Media to steal you away."

He realized he had said too much, and he wondered if she had noticed. He needed her to think about memories again.

The talk turned to other memories. To old classmates and teachers, the endless cycle of exams and failed experiments.

"Malin," he said, voice low. "I know things are different now. But I don't think I ever stopped…" She had to know how he felt.

She held his gaze. "Please. Don't say it."

He nodded, silent. The only sound was the pop of sap in the fire and the distant hiss of the tide. He heard the slur in her voice. His best chance of sparking her memories was through a kiss. Surely, she could feel the energy flowing between them. He had drunk the same drink she had, but she couldn't deny the connection they shared.

He turned to face her, eyes soft in the gloom, and leaned in before she could stop him.

She was motionless, but she hadn't pulled away or made him stop. She must want this too. He fought the urge to rush things. He made sure the kiss was slow and hesitant at first; her lips felt amazing against him. His hand tightened on hers as if anchoring himself to something irreplaceable. That vibrant electric feeling exploded within him; it was as if she were asking for more.

When she stopped him, it was abrupt. His world came crashing down. Caelum recoiled, and his hand slipped free. "I know. I'm sorry. I just…"

He lost his chance. She broke the spell. If that didn't get her, nothing would.

He wasn't really mentally participating in the conversation. He lost. He took a deep breath and added, his voice harder, "You know, we would be married by now. If things had gone differently."

She shrugged. She didn't understand what he had gone through. Maybe if he could show that he had some useful powers like her flames…

Caelum reached down and picked up a pebble from the ground. He held it between his thumb and forefinger, then, with a flick of concentration, let it float into the air, spinning slowly in the space between them. The gesture was casual but deliberate, a subtle flex of power.

Malin didn't seem impressed.

He looked up, shadows deepening the hollows of his eyes. "Your father found out about my powers… about my role in the Resistance. He was my manager at Masoncore. He made it clear I wasn't welcome back. Not just at the company, but in your life."

Malin stared at him, eyes widening. "You told me you were captured and couldn't get word back. Which is it?"

"I didn't want to immediately tell you that the fake death and your loss of me was all your father's doing until I knew where things stood."

"We have been together for days. You had time. Why now? I didn't know he was involved. Given how he is currently trying to kill my family and capture us, it is believable." Her chin trembled for a moment. He wanted so badly to pull her into his arms and make her feel better.

He nodded. "He sent a team to meet me on one of my medicine-gathering trips. He granted me my life but said if I ever set foot in Media again or contacted you, he'd have me killed. Said you deserved better."

She sat in silence.

Caelum ran his hands through his hair. He tried to explain, but she didn't understand or appreciate how difficult a choice it had been at the time. After realizing that it wouldn't change things, he decided to go. One thing he remembered about Malin was that it was possible to change her mind, but she wouldn't react well to being pushed.

Standing, he brushed the dust from his pants. "I should go," he said. "Before I say anything else stupid."

Before she could take more than a few steps, she stopped. A tall, black-clad man with silver hair stood at the entrance to the village. The two covered the distance between them in an awkward, desperate sprint, ending in a hug.

Caelum jumped in, voice brittle. "I can't even touch your hand, but this guy, you run straight into his arms. Isn't he a bit old to be your husband?"

Malin snorted. "Caelum... this... is Aldrik. He's my birth father."

Aldrik offered a hand, polite but guarded.

Caelum hesitated, then took it. He was huge and quite intimidating. His handshake left him wincing. It felt like her father had eyes that looked into his soul... and if that was the case, he was screwed.

"Your father?"

"Yes... We will be leaving in the morning to get my husband. If you still want to go. Until then, Aldrik and I have some talking to do. Good night." Her dismissal was straightforward and left no room for discussion.

Damn it.

He left for Clorsha's hut. He would not bother hiding where he was going tonight.

When he got there, he didn't even wait for her to speak. He ripped her dress off and released his aphrodisiac-infused tensions on her. She was eager to please. He might not have Malin, but he had Clorsha.

The drink wore off within hours, and he spent the evening deciding what to do. Maybe if something happened to her husband, he would still have a chance. He had a lot to think about.

The next morning, he was staring out at the water in thought, trying to decide whether to go with them.

Malin's voice drew him out of his thoughts.

"Caelum," she began, her voice low, the words carefully chosen. "First, I know you tried to drug me. It was reprehensible, and if it hadn't been for this next part, you might not have made it out of this village alive today," she said menacingly.

"I see now that was clearly a mistake… I was excited… and wanted to take the easy route to make things work with us…" he stammered, slowly stepping away, as he saw her father staring chillingly back at him with those violet eyes. He was terrifying.

"Don't worry. I'm not going to kill you, though I have to admit the thought did cross my mind," she explained through tight lips.

"You might not, but… What about him?" he asked.

"There's something you need to know… Something important." She looked directly into his blue eyes and revealed, "I have an eleven-year-old daughter. She's… she's yours. You have a daughter."

He must have heard her wrong. She couldn't have said that. He kept replaying the words in his head, as the enormity of her words settled over him.

Malin continued, but he didn't truly hear what she said. *A daughter. I have a daughter,* he thought. He thought back to his lack of family, the many times he felt alone, and realized that was no longer the case. Malin and he shared a child. He would have so many more reasons to keep trying with her. If her husband were out of the way… Those dreams he had in college of the perfect life with Malin waiting at home for him might still be possible.

Then the realization occurred to him that if anything happened to her husband, she would want to raise their daughter together. He might still have a chance.

"So," he asked, "if something should happen to this husband of yours, we could raise our daughter together."

"No," she stated flatly, "Absolutely not. That's not the case at all."

All these years, he thought he was alone in the world, with no family and no one who really needed him. Even Clorsha didn't need him. He wouldn't work hard at saving the husband, but he would go, if only for the chance to see his daughter and build that need.

NOTE – My website has more Bonus Content.

I'm working on building enough Bonus Content to make it worth buying access on the website. Until then, you will be able to download each item through a Newsletter request, but don't worry… Your name is only entered once.

ABOUT THE AUTHOR

Brandy Stoker is a storyteller whose tales of love, resilience, and self-discovery captivate readers long after the final page. Growing up in Maryland, she draws inspiration from the charming landscapes and communities of her hometown to create relatable characters and vivid settings.

Brandy has been writing since middle school and is a proud mother of three adult children. Life challenges, including health scares and a difficult divorce, led her to embrace independence and inspire others to do the same. Her books reflect her passion for personal growth and the beauty of real-life connections, offering readers examples of resilience and self-discovery.

When she's not writing, Brandy enjoys coffee, watching koi, and playing games with friends. By day, she works in statistics and finance, balancing her analytical work with her creative side. Recently, she's embraced new hobbies like painting and caring for her koi pond.

Brandy invites you to explore her heartfelt stories and encourages you to leave a review. She loves hearing from readers and values their feedback.

Facebook, Instagram, YouTube, Lemon - brandystoker.author

TikTok – brandystoker.auth

Pinterest - brandystokerauthor

Her website is https://www.brandystoker.com

Check it out, to find some hidden treasures related to these stories.

ACKNOWLEDGEMENTS

The author would like to thank her family and friends for their encouragement over the years to follow her dreams and persevere in her pursuit of happiness. Without their gracious feedback and support, I would not have been able to complete this novel.

I would like to thank my editor, Jennifer Windrow for her efforts in helping me get this ready for publication. Her honest and experienced feedback enabled me to create this quality work.

I would like to thank Angelee Van Allman for the Cover/Cover Art and character illustrations.

A big thank you to Laura Holowitz and Walker Williams for their amazing talents in the Audiobook,

Escape from Media is expected in December 2025

Journey to Aloria will be in June 2026

JOURNEY TO ALORIA

THANK YOU FOR READING!

I hope you enjoyed your time in the world of Aloria.

YOUR OPINION MATTERS.

Leaving a review on Goodreads or Amazon is one of the most powerful ways you can support an author like me. It helps new readers discover the series and allows me to keep writing the stories you love.

It only takes a minute, and it means the world to me.

WHERE CAN YOU SHARE YOUR THOUGHTS?
GOODREADS

https://www.goodreads.com/author/show/4381996.Brandy_Stoker

AMAZON

https://www.amazon.com/stores/Brandy-Stoker/author/B0DQK22GZJ

You can also find me on social media to share your thoughts and join the conversation about the series!

Soul-Bond Rune